MURDER
WORTH THE WEIGHT

D.M. BARR

DEDICATION

To Josh, for a lifetime of backrubs, back scratches, and the occasional kick in the butt or talk off the ledge when needed. Your support has made all this possible and you have my everlasting love and thanks.

THEY SAY YOUR first novel is your favorite because it's your first. But the second one is important because it proves that the first one wasn't just a fluke. And for that reason, this book will always have a special place in my heart.

Thanks to NaNoWriMo, National Novel Writing Month, and the NJRWA *Put Your Heart into a Book* conference for giving me the incentive to polish off *Murder Worth the Weight* in a month. I'd sat with the first 9,000+ words for over a year, but those two events combined got me off the fence and onto the computer for a one-month marathon session.

And thanks to Calum T. (I won't put you through the embarrassment of stating your full name) who, many years back, told me that if I gained weight, it would be like slashing the *Mona Lisa*. That comment constituted a great break-up rationale, and in the end, provided me with a kick-ass book plot.

As always, thanks to the long-suffering Mr. Barr, the little Barrs, and my one remaining hairy, four-legged, rescue Barr, all of whom tolerated my abject neglect so I could concentrate on something so important to me. To my father, and to my brother, who never fails to make me laugh, even (especially?) at myself. To everyone who purchased *Expired Listings*, reviewed it online, and told me I had a sick sense of humor, and was a naughty girl, I thank you all…and no comment.

To Pamela Tyner of Beachwalk Press, the publisher of the original e-book edition of this book, thanks for believing in me and making my work the best it can be. And to my pre-submission team: John Paine, developmental editor extraordinaire, working with you was one of the highlights of my writing life and I look forward to doing so again. Thank you for being a sounding board as well as a great visionary. To Ginny Glass of Book Helpline, thank you for your line edit and proofreading efforts. To the dulcet-toned Stephanie Murphy, thanks for your kick-ass job narrating my audio book! To Syneca Featherstone and Joshua Jedwab, thanks for the art, as well as to Victory Editing for the formatting! Finally, to Michael Lujan Bevacqua, professor at the University of Guam, thank you so much for verifying my Chamorro and to Kenneth Gofigan Kuper for perfecting the pronunciation for the audio book.

To some very, very special people in my life who are part of the Hudson Valley Romance Writers of America (especially those in my critique group, all amazing writers, including Elf Ahearn, Gianna Simone, Elizabeth Shore, Liz Matis, Janet Lane Walters, Debbi Cracovia, Kelly Janicello, Yolanda Kozuha, and Tara Andrews plus private critiquer Jamie Sterling) as well as fellow members of the New York and Guppy chapters of Sisters in Crime, thank you for your ongoing support and friendship. You are the best!

To my favorite dueling pianists in the entire world, ultra-talented all: James Byrom (and Annie Ster!), Rhonda Hughes, James Sakal, Whitney Maxwell, Rob Steidel and the ever-generous Orin Sands, thank you for welcoming Josh and I into your world. I can't tell you how much your friendship has meant to us but I'm delighted to have had a chance to commemorate it here.

Finally, to Colin Randolph Purser, who in my late teens introduced me to the wonders of Cockney rhyming slang, along with "Dying Flies" and the moors of England: here is proof that I was paying attention and I will always remember those days fondly.

PROLOGUE

LETICIA REGAN, THE shapely and dark-haired owner of Illinois' original Blubber Be Gone weight loss clinic, hugged the last of her clients and wished them a pleasant and 'on target' week as they wandered back onto the caloric-laden, Chicago streets. The enemies all beckoned: deep dish pizza, Garrett Mix popcorn, Maxwell Street Polish kielbasa, not to mention the béchamel-heavy pastitsio in Greek Town. The majority of her minions didn't stand a chance against the city's delicacies, she acknowledged with a twinge of regret, but that was the secret sauce that kept her coffers filled.

As she straightened the cartons of BBG boxed meals that lined the shelves and picked up diet candy wrappers left behind by clients too hungry to wait until they got home, Leticia reflected upon the evening's meeting. Attendance had been light, only about thirty out of her usual fifty, but that was to be expected, what with all the commotion. She wasn't too concerned. Weight loss fads were transient and therefore not real competition. Those who had strayed tonight would likely be back next week, contrite and perhaps a few pounds heavier than before. And she would greet them as she always did, with a hug and a smile, reassuring them that if they stayed the course—her course—one day, they'd be as thin and beautiful as they'd always dreamed.

She wasn't in the weight loss business, she'd known that from the start. She marketed the world's most desirable commodity: hope. She'd quickly learned that hope had no price ceiling, a realization that had catapulted her to the top. In the last two years, her franchise had become the hallmark of the chain, winning awards for both attendance and profit. Not bad for a waitress from Honduras who'd taken her cue from the dining gluttony she'd studied daily, saved her tips, and risked them on one life-altering gamble that had paid off big time.

Just as she noticed the BBG signature pink-and-green tote bag on one of the chairs—Mrs. Pascucci must have left her welcome materials and introductory recipes behind—she heard the doorbell's chime. Had she returned to retrieve them? Scooping up the tote, she headed into the front room. Rather than the 250-pound, curly-haired woman in the Bulls jacket she'd expected, a large figure in a black fedora and raincoat stood on the 'BBG Moment of Truth' scale, back turned toward Leticia.

Normally, she would have been concerned. While the South Side was rapidly gentrifying, gangs occasionally did roam the streets, remnants of the neighborhood's past. However, few of them took time to check their weight, so she approached less cautiously than she might have otherwise, eager to add another client to her roster.

"Hello, I'm Ms. Regan, the owner of Blubber Be Gone. I'm sorry, tonight's meeting is over, but we'd love to have you come back tomorrow morning and learn about our program. We open at nine AM."

To her surprise, the figure neither stirred nor spoke. She felt her pulse rate increase, anger at being ignored mixed with unease over a stranger in her midst. Territoriality superseded caution and she approached, putting a hand on the intruder's shoulder.

"Excuse me, perhaps you didn't hear. I said we're closed."

"Maybe it's time you were opened." The figure turned quickly, pulling a machete from underneath the raincoat, and plunging it into the diet clinic owner's stomach.

"Arghhhh—" The tote bag and its contents plummeted to the floor as Leticia staggered backward, torn between shock and searing pain, her eyes staring into the coldest expression she'd ever seen.

She fell to her knees, hand on her abdomen, unsuccessfully trying to stymie the torrents of blood pouring through her dress onto the cold, white tile floor. The stranger used a foot to push her onto her back, and she collapsed, feeling the life force slip from her body, the room growing dark. Too weak to move, through the haze she watched in horror as the interloper raised the knife again and brought it down with a vengeance, slicing off half of her right thigh.

"Thin enough now?" was the last thing she heard before unconsciousness sucked her into the abyss.

CHAPTER
0 1 2

C AMARIN TORRES PEERED down the tracks again, as if
repeated checking would cause her delayed train to
magically appear. It was a warm April afternoon, but the
unexpected heat did little to lift her spirits. She was heading
back to her apartment after yet another unsuccessful
interview. If this kept up, she'd be the only one of her NYU
friends graduating next month without a job lined up. How
ironic not to be able to afford the food she wouldn't allow
herself to eat anyway. She checked her watch a third time.
The 5:03 from White Plains to Grand Central was already
ten minutes late.

Camarin heard a voice a few feet behind her softly
exclaim, "Dammit!" Curiosity aroused, she spied a girl in her
late teens standing by the vending machine, fervently
searching through her handbag.

Camarin stared, mesmerized by what could have been a
mirror image of her late twin sister Monaeka. Long, dark hair
partially obscured her tanned, pretty face, and despite the
temperature, she'd draped her two-hundred-plus pound
body in an oversized raincoat. But as Camarin well knew,
yards of fabric didn't really fool anyone. The girl hunched

over slightly, a stance her sister Monaeka had perfected, a sign of deference to a world demanding an apology for violating their arbitrary standards.

Camarin felt a familiar tug of compassion as the girl plunked a few coins into the machine and then searched for more. Looking on, she debated the merits of acquiescing to her own desire for a late-afternoon sweet. *What's really the harm?* Cam reached into the pocket of her dress and pulled out three quarters, which she held out toward the stranger as she walked toward her.

"Want to share something?"

The girl tensed and gave her a quizzical look, but after a moment her shoulders relaxed. "That's so nice of you. Thanks."

Camarin winked and pushed the quarters into the machine. One click and clunk later, she retrieved their prize—a Kit Kat bar. One of Monaeka's favorites. As she held it out to the girl, a slim, stylish woman clad in black came out of nowhere and snatched the chocolate bar right out of her hand.

"You don't need it," she said. "You'll thank me later."

The girl's face turned bright red, but she said nothing, just watched in shock as the thief continued down the platform.

Camarin felt the blood rush to her temples. No matter how many years and miles she'd put between herself and her past, the critical voices kept seeking her out, today in the form of this interloper. Enough, she decided. She set down the briefcase containing her resume and clips and tore after the woman, grabbing her arm and pulling her around so they stood face-to-face.

"What the hell do you think you're doing?" Camarin yelled.

Heads turned. Conversations ceased.

"What's it to you?" the offender shot back.

Camarin pointed at the girl, whose eyes were wide in disbelief. "That girl happens to be a friend of mine, so I'm asking a second time… what are you doing?"

"Saving her from herself, that's what. Your friend is huge, and it's unhealthy. If she can't control herself, she needs others to do it for her."

"Well, Miss High-and-Mighty, since you know everything about everyone, did you ever consider that my friend…Sabrina's…size might have nothing to do with self-control? Could it be the result of…the lithium she takes to control her bipolar disorder? Are you a psychiatrist who has a better suggestion for more appropriate meds that don't put on weight?"

"Well, no… no," the woman stammered, as if the rush of passion suddenly drained from her, leaving her feeling exposed.

"You know what I think?"

The fat shamer glared back but remained silent, so Camarin summoned her courage and repeated herself, a few decibels louder. "I said, do you know what I think?"

"No. What?" The woman sneered.

"I think you should go over to Sabrina and apologize."

"Apologize for helping her get thin?" Her voice dripped with indignation.

"No, apologize for sticking your big nose where it doesn't belong," interjected a young, beer-bellied man in overalls a few feet away. A *Joe's Plumbing* patch was embroidered on his chest pocket.

"What exactly do we have to do to be accepted by you people? Why can't you just leave us alone?" screamed a plump, older woman with perfectly coiffed hair and a fitted suit.

"Give her back the Kit Kat bar," hollered a man clad in military garb, who then started chanting, "Kit Kat, Kit Kat, Kit Kat…" Others joined in, and the cacophony grew stronger.

"You may have grabbed a Kit Kat, but you ended up with Snickers," said Cam with a smirk. "Maybe you want to just hand over the candy, so we can forget this whole ugly incident?"

The woman spat at the ground in front of Camarin and defiantly threw the chocolate bar on the tracks, eliciting loud boos from the small but agitated crowd. Then she ran down the platform, heading for the stairs that led to the parking lot.

"Good riddance," the plumber called after her.

Camarin stood for a moment, shaking from the encounter. Then she returned to the now teary-eyed girl. "Sorry I made you bipolar," she whispered. "I needed to make a point, and it was all I could come up with on the spur of the moment. Hi, I'm Camarin."

"I'm Lexie," the girl said. "No one has ever stood up for me before. Thank you."

"Hey, I know what it's like. I used to deal with jerks like that all the time."

The plumber pushed a run of quarters into the vending machine and took out two Kit Kat bars, handing one to each of the women. Others on the platform clapped and cheered. The sound was slowly drowned out by the roar of the oncoming 5:03 PM train.

As the doors opened, Camarin noticed Lexie and the plumber now chatting animatedly. Not wishing to intrude, she entered the next car over. It was practically empty, not unusual considering most people were traveling in the opposite direction at this hour. A perfect opportunity to relax after an upsetting confrontation. *Perhaps savor that chocolate bar.* She could always purge later.

Given the plethora of unoccupied seats, she was surprised when a handsome man in an expensive-looking suit asked if the spot beside her was taken. She guessed he was in his early forties, since his face was too young for the silver in his hair and beard. He spoke with a confidence so lacking in her gawky college-boy contemporaries. She felt a shiver as the silk of his sleeve touched her bare arm as he settled in.

She wondered what clever icebreaker she could use to engage her attractive new neighbor in conversation. *Nice weather, huh?* would be too lame. Seconds passed. Other passengers shuffled by. Soon, the moment would be lost.

Then, to her delight, he leaned in covertly, as if sharing a private confidence. "Nice going. You'd never seen that girl before in your life, had you?"

She pulled back and studied his expression. Affable or accusatory? His smile assured her of his friendly intentions.

"What gave me away?"

"Nothing. Just a hunch. One you just confirmed."

Camarin twisted her mouth, irked at having been so easily played.

"Do you always go around tricking strangers into confessing their secrets?" she asked.

"Probably as often as you go around defending the underdog." The man winked. "Nothing to be ashamed of though. Quite the opposite. As I think you've already figured out, life is just a series of bluffs."

Camarin considered the comment as the train rumbled along the tracks toward Scarsdale.

"And do *you* bluff much?"

"Funny you should ask. These days, it's all I do."

Grateful for such a provocative opening, she pressed forward. "That sounds intriguing. Care to elaborate?"

"Thought you'd never ask," he said with a smile. "Up until a few years ago, I'd spent my entire career practicing law. Then my circumstances and interests changed, and I decided to become a redeemer of lost causes. I just purchased a failing magazine, which I intend to make profitable again. If that's not the bluff of the century, I don't know what is."

Elegant and he owns a magazine? Camarin's heart skipped a beat.

"That's such a coincidence. I'm just coming from an interview with a magazine."

"Some might call it a coincidence. I call it kismet," the man said as he held out his hand. "Lyle Fletcher, fledgling publisher."

CHAPTER

AS THE TRAIN rolled down the tracks toward Manhattan, Camarin sensed her future suddenly lurching ahead as well. "Camarin Torres, journalism and prelaw major. Pleased to make your acquaintance."

She reached out to shake his hand, eager to see if his grip would be as firm as she imagined, but the conductor interrupted, asking to punch their tickets. There was no way to try again without looking awkward, so she swallowed her disappointment and returned her hand to her side.

Fletcher broke the pregnant pause. "So, there must be many professions out there for someone as bold and beautiful as you. Why journalism and law?"

Camarin's face grew warm. Had anyone else handed her that line, she would have regarded it as a come-on. But he seemed sincere, so she felt comfortable opening up. "All my life I've seen bullying and discrimination. As a child, I felt helpless to stop it. But as an adult, I can make a difference."

"Bullying because of your ethnicity? You're… "

"My mother's side of the family comes from Guam. But no, fortunately, I've encountered very little bias because of my roots. Maybe it's because we live just outside Los

Angeles, where I'm part of a large Chamorro community who share an intense sense of cultural pride. In fact, I think my background may have worked in my favor, that push for diversity in colleges and all."

"So, discriminated against as a woman?"

"No again," she said, reluctant to share too much of her past with a stranger, no matter how charming. "Let's just say I've seen how cruel people can be to those who don't quite fit in, no matter how hard they try. I'm going to make sure that doesn't happen to anyone else ever again."

"You're going to personally end intolerance?" Fletcher seemed both dubious and amused.

"Well, at least make a sizeable dent in it," she said with a smile. It wasn't the first time that people had appeared incredulous at her idealism. "You're speaking to the world's first female Chamorro anti-discrimination crusader. After graduation anyway. And eventually law school, when I can afford it."

"Lofty ambitions. You'll need them in a world that doesn't always cooperate with people's dreams. Again, I'm impressed."

"Thank you," she said, her face growing even hotter. A charismatic publisher thought she was impressive. A once-disappointing day was rapidly metamorphosing into something magical, like a child's giant, colorful carnival balloon.

"Have you interviewed at my magazine, *Trend?*"

Pop! Camarin did her best not to cringe with contempt. *Trend* represented everything in the world she'd come to hate: the brainwashing of women to fit into narrow, permissible roles dictated by fashion designers and greedy advertisers. And this man, appealing or not, was one of their leaders. Camarin paused, trying to formulate a polite and diplomatic response.

"You have heard of it, right?"

"Yes, of course. But no, I didn't interview there. No offense, but as you said, it's failing. As a matter of fact, I turned down an unsolicited offer from one of your competitors, *Drift*. I'm just interested in more…serious publications."

"No offense taken," he said with a grin. "I realize that up to now *Trend* has just covered style and gossip—total fluff. That's what I'm planning to change. In your words, go in a more serious direction."

She wondered if the comment was authentic or if he was just another jerk and this was an excuse that allowed him to live with himself. They remained quiet for a bit, and then curiosity got the better of her.

"I didn't realize *Trend* is based in Westchester."

Fletcher's face clouded over. "No, it's in Manhattan. I was out here today because…my late wife owned a condo in White Plains that we'd been renting out. I was just meeting with the real estate agent I might hire to sell it for me."

Cam looked down at her pumps, annoyed at herself for bringing up such a sensitive subject. "I'm so sorry for your loss."

"Of my wife or the condo?"

She glanced back, astonished. He started to laugh, and she felt the earlier harshness of her judgment soften by a smidgen. He really was quite charming—for a body shamer.

"Are you ever serious?" she asked.

"Oh, when I am, you'll definitely know it. Like now. How many years of college do you have left?"

His tone switched from whimsical to all business, and something about the way he commanded control sent a shiver up her spine. *Hot as hell. Dammit.* "About a month. Then I'm done."

The conductor announced that they would soon be arriving at Grand Central Station, their final destination, and the windows grew dark as they entered the tunnel.

He reached into his suit pocket and pulled out a business card. It read *Trend Magazine*, with a fashionable NoHo address, close to her own apartment.

She held up her hand. "That's kind of you, but I really don't think—"

"Hey, I can see you're not enamored with our current format. Nevertheless, I'd still like you to come in, show us your work. Allow us to describe the magazine's revamped editorial direction. I think it may surprise you. I can use someone with your guts and ambition to develop our investigative-reporting beat. That is, if you have any interest."

She took the card, slipping it into her jacket pocket. "If you're really serious about moving away from your current focus, I'll try to keep an open mind." After all, a job was a job, and up to now, no one else but *Drift* had made an offer.

"Call tomorrow and speak to Rachel. She'll set everything up. You're going to be a superstar. Of that, I'm already certain." He reached out to shake her hand. It felt as forceful as Camarin had imagined earlier. She didn't try to read anything into the almost imperceptible squeeze he added at the end. Until proven otherwise, he was still the enemy.

As he rose and headed for the exit, she waited a few beats longer before also joining the crowd jostling toward the platform. By the stairs a newsstand featured the latest issue of *Trend*. Hating herself, she slapped down her $3.50 for a copy. Magazines like this were part of what had driven her sister over the edge, but she needed to see if there was anything redeemable within its pages. The jury was still out until Lyle Fletcher had proven himself a reformer, and not an enabler.

CHAPTER
2 3 4

*T*REND'S CORPORATE OFFICES were located on Bond Street, about a mile's walk from Camarin's East Village apartment. Despite the gathering storm clouds on the morning of her interview, she decided to walk. She was crouched down, rummaging through the front hall closet for an umbrella, when a bleary-eyed Annalise wandered in, dressed in an oversized t-shirt that read *What doesn't kill you disappoints me.*

"A little early for all this noise, isn't it?" asked Annalise.

"I'm sorry. I've got that thing this morning."

"Wearing that?"

Camarin strode over to the one full-length mirror in the cramped, fourth-floor walk-up that they shared with a third roommate, DeAndre. Staring back was a shapely figure shrouded by a gray tweed, oversized suit, a markdown she'd found at the local consignment shop.

"What's wrong with this?"

"Didn't you say it was a fashion magazine?"

"Yeah, but they're trying to get more serious."

"Are they planning to reopen as *Morgue Monthly*?"

"Oh, please. Is it that bad?"

"Worse."

"Why can't this interview just be about the way I write? Why does it have to be an indictment of my appearance?"

Annalise ignored her plea. "People may talk a big game about skills, but when it's between you and some other bitch? It's gonna all come down to looks. And if you'll join me in my closet, I think I've got something that would be perfect."

"It'll be too short on me," Camarin moaned. At five-eight, she was three inches taller than her roommate.

"Showing a little thigh never hurt anyone, especially when there's—ahem—someone you want to get to know better."

Not a surprising comment, thought Cam, especially from someone who interpreted an innocuous "Hello" from a stranger as an invitation to a weekend in Acapulco. "I knew I shouldn't have mentioned anything to you, that you'd bend it all out of shape. What I said was that he was attractive. I also said he's on the front lines of objectification. This is about paying my third of the rent and saving for law school. Nothing more."

"Words, words, words." Annalise waved Cam off. "You say one thing, but that blushing face of yours just let the pussy out of the bag. Hopefully, it will soon be bagging something of its own. So, let's dress accordingly, shall we?"

Outrageousness, in both word and deed, was what had initially attracted Cam to move in with Annalise after responding to her 'Roommates Wanted' ad on Craigslist. Older by a few years and far more daring, the native New Yorker perpetually yanked Camarin from her more sedate and sheltered lifestyle, thrusting her into all the possibilities life in Manhattan had to offer. Most days Cam enjoyed the journey, but today, with the anxiety of the interview hanging over her head, she wasn't so sure.

Annalise dragged her roommate back into their shared bedroom. She pulled out a tight-fitting fuchsia number that she sometimes wore while waitressing at Benji's. The dueling-piano bar was where all three of them spent their nights, with DeAndre working the keyboards and Camarin mixing drinks to earn the rent money her scholarship didn't cover.

"Ugh. *Trend* may not be *Morgue Monthly*, but it isn't *Skank World* either. But that might work," she said, pointing to a more subdued black Chanel knockoff.

Annalise snatched the stylish suit off its hanger. "Sure, why not? Anything's better than that Salvation Army tent you've currently got on."

Cam reluctantly disrobed. "Let's hope it fits, because if not, the tweed's going to have to do. I have to get there by nine."

Annalise glanced at the clock. "And it's only eight. You've got plenty of time. Meanwhile, I do believe I hear caffeine calling my name."

Annalise ambled off toward the kitchen. She was stirring in artificial sweetener when Camarin reemerged in the black suit, pulling at the skirt, which fell four inches shy of corporate.

"Stop fidgeting and relax," said Annalise, setting down her spoon. "Now you're ready to—ahem—interview."

"You can 'ahem' all day long, but assuming that *Trend* really is on a different trajectory, all I expect to get today is a fair shake. That would be a nice departure from every other publication I've met with." She reached out and grabbed Annalise's coffee cup before her roommate could take her first sip.

"Almost every one. Are we going to talk about the elephant in the room?"

"You mean DeAndre?"

"Uh, yeah. After his parents offered you the *Drift* gig, how are you going to explain snagging a job with their archrival?"

"I know. Carl and Diana have been so good to me. But they know better than anyone where my priorities lie. I want to publish serious stories at a magazine where I didn't get the job because my best friend's parents were the owners. I'll…I'll worry about breaking the news to them if and when I actually get an offer. And who knows? Maybe they wouldn't even care. A little journalistic competition never hurt anyone."

"Journalistic? That's being overly generous, don't you think? I've thumbed through both magazines at the check-out counter. Nothing but a collection of ads with some gossip thrown in for good measure."

Cam recalled a health club ad from her recently purchased copy of *Trend* featuring a topless model riding atop a giraffe. The legend read *Achieve a level of fitness that's easy to spot!* It certainly proved Annalise's point.

"Lyle says he wants to change all that. If it's true, I'm going to help him." She blew away the steam drifting up from the mug, as if wafting away her own apprehensions.

"Lyle, is it now?" said Annalise with a chuckle. "What is it with you and older men anyway?"

She reflected for a minute. "Well, I suppose the *Psychology Today* explanation is that whenever my dad came home on leave, which was rare, he always accepted Monaeka and me for who we were. No demands to look different, act different. There was something very comforting about that. And then…"

"Ooh, here comes the juicy part."

"I'm not sure it's all that juicy, especially since at this point it's all speculation," she scoffed, "but I've always imagined that—unlike Brad—when you're with an older man, he'll know what to do when he takes you in his arms."

"Maybe Brad's learned something since sophomore year, and that's why he keeps calling, trying to get back together."

"Ever google Peter Pan Complex? Up pops a photo of Brad, smoking weed and drinking beer directly from the keg. He has no interest in transitioning into adulthood, and I have no interest in repeating bad mistakes." *And he told me I'd look better with a few more pounds on my body. Who am I, Monaeka? Jerk.*

"Right. Well, when you're at your interview, *not* concentrating on the sexy, older man across the desk, try not to do that thing you always do with your handbag."

Camarin set down the mug. "What thing?"

"You know, when you keep the bag on your lap."

Camarin squinted and thought back. "It's to hide my tummy bulge," she admitted.

"What tummy bulge? You're flat as a board, probably because you never eat. Promise you'll keep the damn thing on the floor."

Camarin held up two fingers. "Scout's honor."

"I'd take that more seriously if you'd ever been a scout. But fine," she said, snatching back her coffee cup. "Just come back employed, 'kay? It would be nice to not have to move."

"I'm going to do my best," she said. "But just in case, hold off buying anything too expensive."

"You mean those dream purchases I've been saving for, like brand-name cereal and toilet paper?"

"Exactly."

Camarin ventured over to the window and peeked through the blinds. The sun was asserting itself through some breaks in the clouds, negating her need for an umbrella after all. She grabbed her black-leather briefcase, containing copies of articles she hoped would dazzle Lyle, called out her goodbyes, and headed out to seize the day.

Despite the humidity, she didn't mind the longish, muggy walk from Avenue C to Bond Street, her satchel occasionally banging against her calf. She loved the area's vibe, especially where the East Village blended into NoHo, short for 'North of Houston Street.' It was a stylistic jumble, where chic cafes coexisted next to former warehouses, and decaying brownstones cowered in the shadow of nineteenth-century Greek revival–style lofts. Today, most of the tenements were under renovation, swathed in scaffolding as investors sought to cash in on the area's growing popularity.

Against her best judgment, as she hit Lafayette Street, she trembled with excitement over the prospect of again verbally sparring with the handsome Lyle Fletcher. Then she caught herself and banished the memory of his sparkling blue eyes and wicked sense of humor from her thoughts. Whatever happened today could have serious repercussions, she reminded herself. *Trend* could end up as the first major, full-time entry on her resume. If she didn't reverse the magazine's focus and raise the body-acceptance consciousness of millions of its propagandized readers, she'd not only have failed her own expectations, but the memory of her sister as well.

Yes, you owe me at least that much, Camarin, especially after what you did.

The offices were three flights up in a nondescript building of indeterminate age and style, serviced by a tiny elevator barely large enough for three adults. Thinking optimistically, she decided it was more cozy than rickety. On the third floor, she was greeted by two massive oak doors bearing the gold-engraved legend *Trend Magazine*. She fought to pull open the oversized portal, wondering if its purpose was to intimidate visitors or just to test the strength of aspiring journalists before their actual interview commenced. Either way, the plan succeeded.

A Godzilla of a desk dwarfed the reception area, filling almost every inch. Behind it sat a slip of a girl in her twenties, sporting a red, boyish haircut circa 1960s Twiggy, reading a copy of the *New York Post*. The headline blared *Blubber Be Goner: Weight Loss Clinic Owner Reduced to Shreds*. She lifted her eyes as Camarin entered.

"Bloody well about time," she said, in a clipped British accent.

Camarin balked. "I-I'm sorry. I thought I was early."

"Hello, Early. I'm Rachel," she said, her stern face brightening. "Sorry to sound like such a tosser. It's so bleeding dull around here, I thought it would be fun to *take the mick* out of you."

"The what?"

"Take the mick. It means to have some fun with you. I mean, I'm so bloody bored, I'm actually reading the paper." She pointed to the cover photo. "What do you think about this chav in Chicago, the one who owned the fatty rehab center?"

This woman is bonkers.

"I think Mr. Fletcher is expecting me?" she said through a forced smile.

"You didn't hear? It's all over the internet. Butchered right in her office, her butt and thighs made...err...smaller. My guess is that someone woke up that morning, seriously missing their French fries and Flake bars. Anyway, imagine what those women were thinking when they showed up for their morning weigh-in. Quite the shock, eh?" ·

Camarin blinked. *What does she want from me? How do I get past her?*

"Sorry to change the subject, but is Mr. Fletcher available? I have a nine AM. appointment with him this morning."

"As opposed to nine AM this afternoon?"

Camarin sighed. "I'm sorry. I don't know what I've done to offend you. I'm just a little nervous today. Could you please take it easy on me?"

"Nothing to be nervous about, love." Rachel giggled. "I was just having some fun. You're already hired. Mr. Fletcher left a contract for you to read and sign." She handed Camarin a thin manila envelope and pointed to two chairs on either side of a water cooler wedged into the corner of the room.

"You mean he isn't here? And he's offering me a job without reading any of my clips?" Camarin was torn between disappointment and suspicion.

"He said something about having read them online. He must have liked them, eh? And now, he's off somewhere, as per usual, no doubt trying to raise funds to keep this place open." She lowered her voice a decibel. "I'm afraid you'll have to use your knees to lean on. There are desks in the back, but I'm not allowed to let anyone past the entrance area."

Camarin immediately switched modes from crestfallen to curious. "Why not?" she whispered back.

"Can you keep a secret?"

"Secret-keeper is my middle name."

"Really? Your parents must have been a right pair of sadists. Anyway, it's because you, prospective employee, are supposed to think there is a massive office complex behind me. Rows upon rows of desks filled with writers and copyeditors and layout people and what-not."

"And there aren't?"

"You might as well know before you sign that contract. There are four rooms behind that door," she said, signaling to her right with a tilt of her head. "First, there's Fletcher's office. Then one glorified cubby where the accountant usually spends his monthly visits looking through the books, stifling his tears. All the meetings are held in a cramped conference space they call the war room. And last, and certainly least, a run-down little piece of heaven they call the bullpen, where all the writers and editors work. Though I picture them spending most of their time quaking, waiting for the ax to fall. Once you sign on the dotted line, you'll get to join them. Unless I've totally dissuaded you with these shocking truths."

The reasons why Fletcher might have hired Camarin in absentia were suddenly coming into sharp focus. No need to defend *Trend*'s financial health, for one. "Sounds like you need someone to turn this place around."

"A miracle worker. Might you be she? I do hope so. It would be nice to have someone else around here who isn't a total prat."

Camarin relaxed slightly, her nerves slowing from a boil to a simmer. Despite her earlier misgivings, she couldn't help but like this blunt, flippant receptionist. "Let me check out the contract, and I'll let you know."

Deep down, she knew she would sign, no matter what it said. She needed the paycheck.

She sat in the corner—handbag by her feet, thank you very much—and gave the document a perfunctory read through. There was no real job description, other than the title Investigative Reporter/Editorial Assistant, and no restrictive, noncompete clause that would prevent her from working elsewhere if this job didn't pan out. The hours seemed reasonable. The start date was open; she imagined that was to accommodate her finals and graduation.

The salary, at a thousand dollars a week, was much higher than she'd expected, especially surprising considering Rachel's depressing appraisal of the magazine's bottom line. It was even more than *Drift* would have paid. At least that alone gave her enough ammunition to explain to DeAndre why she'd chosen *Trend* over the job his parents had offered. Plus, the unexpected income would go a long way toward saving for law school.

She laid the contract on her lap, reached down and rummaged through her handbag for a pen, and added her name to the bottom with a flourish.

"You're one of us now," Rachel said as Camarin handed her the signed agreement. "And as the greeters said on the *Titanic*, glad to have you aboard."

CHAPTER
3 4 5

L YLE FLETCHER ANXIOUSLY sat at the dining table of his Manhattan apartment as his real estate agent gave the grand tour to a prospective buyer, some millennial from Long Island. He hoped Remy could negotiate a better deal for him than his Westchester agent had procured for the White Plains property, a measly $450,000. He could eat through that amount in three months, especially considering *Trend*'s hefty payroll and overinflated NoHo rents.

For this sale, a two-bedroom, high-rise duplex on the Upper West Side that he'd once shared with his late wife, Margaret, he needed at least $3.5 million. It was a giveaway price, maybe half of its true value, but desperate times called for desperate measures. With that sum, even if his plans hit a snag, he could still keep operations going for what...two, three years? Long enough, he suspected, to accomplish his goal of avenging Margaret's untimely demise.

He stared out the window at the southern exposure that Remy guaranteed would pad his bottom line by an additional ten percent. Under his breath, he cursed the buyer who had demanded a rush showing this morning—the one day he had warned his Realtor was sacrosanct. Then he had the audacity to show up thirty minutes late. After all that, if this joker didn't make an offer...

Fletcher strummed his fingers anxiously on his thigh, a tic that betrayed his normally confident demeanor. What if Camarin turned down the contract? He had impulsively offered double what he normally might have paid a junior reporter, but perhaps a better job had come along? If she didn't agree to work for *Trend*, it would definitely be a setback. He'd done his research, read some of the articles she'd posted on her website. They were impressive. Cam could add the cover he needed to turn some of his more elaborate plans into reality.

As much as he hated to admit it, her activism and audacity reminded him of Margaret. Not to mention her allure—that long, lustrous hair, her smooth cappuccino skin, that unwavering optimism. He wanted to have her in his orbit, even if he had no intention of acting on his attraction. While he was at a loss to decipher the dating scene—one he hadn't navigated in nearly two decades, not even during the three years since his wife's passing—he was not clueless enough to risk being accused of sexual harassment in the workplace. And anyway, she'd probably laugh at him, a foolish widower almost twice her age, making overtures.

He heard someone turn on the shower upstairs—*the water pressure is perfect, you supercilious hedge funder*—and felt his fingers strum even faster. He glanced over at the Louis XIV sideboard where their wedding portrait sat encased in an eight-by-ten-inch Baccarat crystal frame, flanked by a pair of antique candlestick holders that he and Margaret had picked up at a flea market one carefree day early in their courtship. Though they were brass, and therefore conspicuously out of place, he displayed them prominently—a statement of substance over style. Guilt stabbed at his gut as he realized he'd been daydreaming about Camarin while staring into his wife's wise and trusting eyes.

"I'll never stop loving you, Maggie," he whispered. "Everything I'm doing is to fulfill my promise to you. They're already starting to pay for what they did."

Two sets of footsteps barreled down the stairs. The buyer remained out in the foyer while Remy joined Fletcher at the dining room table. She leaned in close, like a conspirator sharing classified government secrets.

"He's offering $3.25 million," she said in hushed tones. "I know it's lower than what you were hoping for. But it's all cash, and he's willing to close as soon as his lawyers can pull title, so probably less than three weeks from now. No inspection, no contingencies."

He stopped strumming and instead dug his nails against his Brioni suit pants.

"Do you think you can find me a cheap place to move into that quickly?"

"You were thinking Putnam, right?"

"Whatever. Just something with an easy Manhattan commute that will run me under two grand a month."

"Yes, I can absolutely do that. No problem."

Fletcher eased the attack on his thighs. "Fine, but $3.25 million is too low. Tell him $3.4 million, with half at contract. Nonrefundable. I don't want anyone playing games. Think that will fly?"

"Whatever you say," Remy said with a wink.

Was she flirting? he wondered, and then decided it didn't matter. Romance was a distraction he didn't need right now. Once the appointment ended, he could call Rachel and see if Camarin had agreed to work by his side. For credibility. Nothing more. If he repeated the mantra often enough, maybe even he might start to believe it.

CHAPTER
4 5 6

CAMARIN STOOD IN front of Carl and Diana Robinson's prewar town house on Riverside Drive, ten minutes late, willing herself to ring the doorbell. She'd been invited to Friday dinner at least once a month since she'd befriended DeAndre in Journalism 101. The Robinsons were like her adopted family, in many ways kinder and more accepting than her own. But ever since she'd affixed her signature to the bottom of *Trend*'s contract, she had been dreading this moment when she'd have to share the news with them.

Courage. She pressed the buzzer and heard footsteps rumbling down the stairs. Xavier, their butler, opened the door with his usual smile and beckoned her inside. "Good evening, Ms. Camarin. Mr. DeAndre was speculating that you might not show, but his parents assured him you'd never skip dinner without calling."

"It's nice to know that at least they had faith in me. Thanks, X-Man."

She followed him up the stairs, past the dining parlor with its carved mahogany and antique mirrors, and into the kitchen, which, as always, was a madhouse. Trying to ignore the room's seductive aromas—and the hungry voice at the back of her head, begging to be fed—Cam concentrated instead on Carter, Jamal, and Kit, her roommate's three younger brothers. The carousing trio paused from chasing each other around the granite-topped island long enough to hug her en masse before returning to their gameplay.

Dee was in the corner, absentmindedly pulling on his dreadlocks and yelling into his cellphone to be heard over the din. Carl was sitting at the island, attempting to ignore the hubbub and concentrate on his newspaper. Diana, still clad in an elegant Dolce & Gabbana blue pinstripe suit, blew Cam a kiss and then continued to ladle tomato bisque into individual tureens. Though they could have easily afforded a cook, Diana wouldn't hear of it. She said that preparing dinner was her only way to reconnect with family after a busy day at work.

"I'm so sorry to be late, Diana, especially on soup night," Camarin said. "If tomatoes had free will, yours would be the only soup delicious enough for them to willingly sacrifice themselves."

"No apologies necessary. You can do no wrong," Carl said as he rose, walked over, and embraced her. "You are, after all, our favorite daughter."

"She's our only daughter," corrected his wife. "And even then, only on loan until they call her back home."

In a fleeting memory, Camarin pictured her actual father, one of the few things she hadn't blocked out from her early childhood. Looking debonair in his Navy uniform, he'd hug her tightly upon returning home between stints in the South Pacific. His embrace was always loving and unconditional, with no mention of size or looks. Even back then, she could appreciate the value of true acceptance, a rare commodity in the Torres household. She'd found it again years later with Carl and Diana. She only hoped that tonight's revelations wouldn't destroy the bond they'd forged together.

"I have no plans to head back to California. I'll stay your daughter...no matter what happens," she said weakly.

"Hmm, what could possibly happen?" DeAndre said, slipping his phone back into his pocket.

She shot him a dirty look. Breaking the news to him back at the apartment had been had hard enough. He didn't need to twist the knife deeper.

Diana peered into the oven. "Okay, everybody, take a bowl by its handles and carefully carry them to the table. Prime rib in about fifteen. Let's go."

Feed me! Feed me! Camarin gave her head a quick shake, attempting to silence the intrusive voice that plagued her whenever food was near. Then she picked up her tureen and joined the others.

Soon everyone was busily slurping their soup. The Robinsons launched into their usual monthly litany of questions: How were her parents? Was Benji, her boss at the piano bar, still as demanding as ever? How was the job search progressing?

DeAndre jumped on that as his cue to bring up the issue she'd been carefully dodging. "Mom, Dad, I think Camarin has something she wants to share with you. Don't you, Cam?"

She was certain her face was redder than her bisque. "Dee, really, it can wait until after dinner."

"No, it cannot. When my roomie gets her first big job, everyone has to hear about it before the main course."

Traitor! And after all she'd done for him—poor, easily duped, heart-on-his-sleeve Dee. All the nights she'd consoled him over this girl or that one. The cupcake baker who needed a backer. There was five hundred dollars he'd never see again. The botanist searching for a safe place to hide her pot. The rebellious daughter of the Saudi Arabian diplomat who used their apartment as a haven to trade in her burqa for a minidress before she and Dee went out clubbing. Cam had been his counsel and confidante through every ugly breakup.

She got it though. He'd been hurt by her decision. Just like her sister had been by one of her decisions a few years before. Hopefully, Dee's voice wouldn't continually play in her head the way Monaeka's did, accusing her of selfishness and abandonment.

"Yes, tell us, Cam. We're so happy for you. Where will you be working?" asked Diana.

She looked down at her bowl, having suddenly lost her appetite. "I took a job at *Trend*. I didn't expect to get it. It was sort of an accident," she said sheepishly.

"*Trend*? Why would you do that?" asked Carl. "We offered you the junior editor's job at *Drift*. Why would you want to work for strangers?"

Carl had a valid point. It would have been fun working every day alongside Dee. She'd watched him push himself hard all semester, taking publishing classes in the mornings, then apprenticing at the magazine every afternoon, all before hitting the keyboards at Benji's at night. But even if she had been interested in writing about fashion and gossip, where would the challenge have been in working for friends?

She shrugged. "I met this man on a train. He just took over the magazine, and they're going to steer it in a different, newsier direction. It's an opportunity for me to write stories about prejudice and hate, just like I've always told you I wanted to do."

Diana, who'd remained silent up to this point, pushed back from the table and started collecting empty soup tureens to carry into the kitchen. "Carl, didn't you say something a few months back about some guy named

Fletcher buying *Trend* and bringing in some hotshot from *Business Day* to run their editorial?"

"Yeah, and their ad pages have been climbing steadily ever since. They must be rolling in cash these days, certainly enough to pay our girl more than we can afford."

That's odd, Camarin thought. Didn't Rachel say the magazine was floundering, that the accountant cried every time he looked at the books? How exactly were they able to afford to pay her the high salary they'd offered?

"The thing is, Cam, we understand," Carl continued. "If this is what you want, we're with you. No matter how uncomfortable our lousy son is trying to make you feel. He's just sorry to lose the talent. Aren't you, Dee?"

Now it was DeAndre's turn to look sheepish.

"Maybe you can be a spy," suggested Kit, bouncing up and down with the level of enthusiasm only a six-year-old could muster. "You tell us what they're writing about, and we'll beat them to the newsstands. Right, Dad?"

Carl shook his head. "Son, calm down. You know that's not how we do things. We don't snoop on our competitors. Anyway, in another year, those decisions will all be up to your big brother. After he graduates, we'll be retiring, and he'll be running the place."

Kit settled back down in his seat. "You should let me run it. He'll just put girls on the cover, but I want pictures of more important things, like Transformers and the Guardians of the Galaxy."

While Kit rattled on, Camarin stood up and joined Diana in the kitchen, seeking any excuse to duck the awkward conversation. Together, they prepared and carried out dinner plates stacked high with rare prime rib, mashed potatoes, and broccoli.

"My new position won't be an issue, I assure you," Camarin said while she served Carter and Jamal. "If anything, *Trend* will soon be less of a competitor to *Drift* because of its new focus." She stuck out her tongue at her roommate before heading back to help Diana bring out the remainder of the meals.

Diana set down Carl's dinner plate, and then finally her own, before sitting back down at the table. "Whatever makes you happy, Cam. Just know, if you ever change your mind, there will always be a place for you at *Drift*."

Cam set down her own plate, piled high with broccoli over a thimbleful of beef, and walked over to Diana and Carl. She bent down to give them each a hug. "Thank you for your understanding. And your professionalism. I love you both. I would hate for this to come between us in the future."

"Nah," said DeAndre, throwing a rolled-up napkin in her direction. "It's all good. Maybe now she'll stop getting on my case about changing *our* content. But Ma, next time she comes to dinner, instead of prime rib, she gets gruel."

CHAPTER
5 6 7

I N THE PREDAWN hours of a Monday morning three weeks later, Camarin tossed and turned on sweat-drenched sheets, her fevered dreams the result of her refusal to consciously admit to first-day-of-work jitters.

Age eleven. She, along with Monaeka, were sleeping over at their Aunt Sirena's house, a necessity on nights when her mother Ana worked a second job as a hospice nurse. But her slumber was infiltrated by the disturbing sound of incantations emanating from down the hall, yanking her into an unwelcome state of semi-consciousness.

"Ya este siha manma'pos para i taihinekkok na mina'sa'pet, lao i manunas para i taihinekkok na lina'la'…"

Camarin sat up, dizzily trying to make out Monaeka's silhouette in the dark of the dining room, which had been outfitted with two portable cots. "Mon? Mon?" she whispered, but her voice was drowned out by the growing volume of the unexpected nighttime tribal concerto. Rubbing her eyes, she slipped on her bathrobe and slippers and wandered, still drowsy, toward the chants, now in English.

"And these shall go away into everlasting punishment, but the righteous into life eternal..."

Even half-asleep, Camarin recognized the biblical passage from Matthew 25:46. Suddenly, she flashed back to the last time she'd heard chanting like this—the night two years ago when her aunt had tried to exorcise the seizure demons from Monaeka's body. *Oh God, not again!* She snapped to full consciousness and sprinted down the hall toward the commotion.

Her aunt's room was filled with the sickening scent of burning basil. Just as last time, Monaeka lay tied to the four posters of the bed frame, clad only in her pajamas. Feathers were stuck between the toes of her right foot. She struggled, trying to break free, wide-eyed and clearly terrified by the spectacle. From just outside the room, Camarin watched in horror, sympathetically experiencing her twin's dilemma—the tightness of the bindings, the panic of the predicament.

A ring made of salt ran along the periphery of the bedroom, Inside the ring stood Aunt Sirena and several of their neighbors—all immigrants from their native Guam. Arm-in-arm, they swayed back and forth. Leading their chanting was Husto, their community's *suruhånu*, or traditional healer. He was joined by a priest Camarin had never seen before, dressed in black robes with a large crucifix hanging from his neck. It matched the one he held high above her sister's head.

Camarin silently stepped inside, her entrance unnoticed by all but Monaeka, who gave her the look she knew all too well: a silent, imploring *help me; get me out of here.* Camarin nodded, trying to figure out how to calm her frantic sister while conjuring up some way to stop the ceremony.

"Be gone, Demon of Gluttony," intoned the priest, taking over from the healer. "For as we learn from Corinthians 6:20, your body is the temple of the Holy Spirit, who lives in you and was given to you by God. You do not belong to yourself, for God bought you with a high price. So, you must honor God with your body." He started to walk away and then turned around, pulled a sharp knife to Monaeka's throat, and added, "And put a knife to your throat if you are given to appetite. Proverbs 23:2."

A terrified Monaeka started to scream, and Camarin knew there was no more time to contemplate potential strategies. She pushed her way through the circle and jumped onto the bed, stunning the priest, who retracted his knife.

"She's not a glutton. It's the pills the doctors gave her. The ones for the seizures." She looked straight into the priest's eyes and then back at her aunt. "*They* made her gain weight. That's what my mother says. And she's a nurse, so she should know!"

Camarin's words fell on deaf ears. Aunt Sirena tried to pull her from the bed, but Camarin dodged her, carefully trying not to step on Monaeka in the process. The priest again took up the cross and held it high above the bound girl's head.

Desperate, Camarin did the only thing she knew would grab the crowd's attention. She stuck her pointer finger down her throat and regurgitated every ounce of the delicious beef tinaktak they'd enjoyed for dinner. The spew hit the priest right in the face, and he backed off, cursing and spluttering as he wiped the vomit from his eyes.

Camarin caught Husto trying unsuccessfully to stifle a chuckle. That broke the mood. The rest of the chanters joined in, laughing at the spectacle. The priest violently shook his head, mumbled something about Camarin's own demonic possession, and stomped out of the room, Aunt Sirena running after him.

Camarin wasted no time untying the scarves that held her twin's wrists and ankles to the bedposts. The two clung together, sharing a long, uninterrupted hug as the crowd dispersed.

"Don't worry, Mon," Camarin whispered, trying to calm Monaeka's whimpers. "I'm here to protect you. You can always count on me."

Camarin sprang awake, shaken by the memory and overcome with the same nausea she'd felt that night and every instance over the past decade since that night when she'd repeated that authentic, heartfelt promise to her sister. It was one she'd grown to resent as time went on.

Monaeka had been a pure, sweet spirit of light. She didn't deserve what life had dealt her—the epilepsy, the struggle with weight. Camarin, on the other hand, had been blessed with dark Chamorro beauty and good fortune, along with the ingenuity to adopt surreptitious ways to remain thin and in her family's good graces. The disparity had ultimately been the wedge permanently dividing the two.

The acid churning in Cam's stomach was evidence that her body still wouldn't stomach what her mind refused to acknowledge. How she'd tried to break free of her familial obligations after arriving at college, grab a life for herself. And how her sister had despised her for it, finally cutting off communications. Her fall from defender to pariah. But even the expanse of the country hadn't distanced her from the guilt surrounding her betrayal and abandonment of Monaeka just when her twin needed her the most.

Brrrrrrrr! Her cellphone alarm screamed out 7:00, sparing her from further introspection. She had to get up and embrace life's next big adventure. Camarin Torres, investigative reporter.

CHAPTER 7

A T 9:00, CAMARIN found herself challenged by something greater than the nervous excitement of starting a new job—the unyielding behemoth of an entranceway that fortressed *Trend* magazine from the outside world. Unlike the morning of her interview, today she was simultaneously attempting to open the door while steadying a tray of Starbucks coffee—one caramel macchiato, one café Americano, and one iced vanilla latte. She had thought it would be a nice gesture to treat Fletcher and Rachel to coffee on her first day of work, and prayed she'd guessed right at what they might enjoy. But she'd forgotten about the heft of the doors and hadn't counted on having to perform caffeine acrobatics to gain access to the office.

"Oh, thank goodness you're back. I thought you might have come to your senses," chirped Rachel as Camarin moved her balancing act into the foyer.

"No such luck," Camarin volleyed back, resting the tray on Rachel's enormous desk. "I'm just moonlighting as a barista until Mr. Fletcher hands me my first assignment. So, take a coffee, before I magically transform myself into the miracle worker you wished for a few weeks back."

"Well, thank you kindly. But you'd better get busy channeling your best Annie Sullivan. Fletcher's got two visitors in the war room, and he told me that when you arrived I should send you right in."

"There's three of them in there? Ugh. I don't have enough for everyone. Do you mind…"

"Yeah, yeah, no worries. You can treat me some other time."

"Thanks, I owe you. Hold all my calls, okay?" she joked.

"Uh-huh. Sure. Who knows, you might get one this decade."

Feeling comfortable in their budding friendship, Cam winked and stuck out her tongue. Rachel reciprocated and then, out of an apparent pang of mercy for Camarin's lack of a free hand, she squeezed out from behind her desk and opened the door that led to the inner offices.

"Second door to the right, though there's not really much of an opportunity to get lost," she whispered to the recruit.

Outside the war room, Camarin sucked in a deep, calming breath, determined to make a good first impression. Balancing the coffee tray in one hand, she pulled at the handle with the other, attempting to open yet another door heavy enough to ward off the invasion of Normandy.

As she entered, she tripped on a loose fold of carpet and stumbled forward, causing the café Americano to go flying over one of the visitor's heads and onto the papers spread out in the middle of the boardroom table. Camarin lurched over, attempting to catch the errant container, and in the process, dropped the tray holding the other two drinks, which tumbled to the floor. Covers dislodged and coffee of differing hues merged to form a large taupe puddle on the office's prized imitation beige Berber rug.

Mortified, her body frozen in place, she silently berated herself for what she had already nicknamed the Caffeine Cataclysm of 2018. Before uttering a single word, much less revamping the magazine's editorial calendar, she'd managed to embarrass her boss in front of two potential advertisers and put her job at risk. She bit her lower lip, torn between terror and laughing out loud at the slapstick of it all. She searched the room for any sight of napkins—there were none—and watched helplessly as the stain continued to rapidly increase in diameter.

Fletcher pressed the intercom, breaking the awkward silence. "Ms. Thorsen? Could you please come into the conference room with paper towels and carpet cleaner? There's been a…slight incident we need attending to."

"Certainly, Mr. Fletcher. I'll be there in a moment."

He walked over to Camarin and put his hand on her arm. She felt every nerve ending spring to attention, waiting to be chewed out for her inelegant entrance.

"Ms. Torres, why don't you sit down and join our discussion? This may be something we'd like you to be involved in." He led her to the far end of the table and, like a true gentleman, pulled out a chair for her. His compassion warmed her, reassuring her that perhaps joining *Trend* wasn't such an unwise decision after all. As she watched him return to his own seat, directly opposite, she silently vowed to repay his mercy and make him proud.

"I'm so sorry about that," she said with a shake of her head. "I guess it's clear why I opted for journalism over hospitality."

"No need to cry over spilled Starbucks," said one of the visitors, inordinately pleased at his own cleverness. His colleague joined him and together they began to howl with laughter, humiliating her even further.

She forced a polite laugh, unwilling to concede to her disgrace.

As the uproar died down, Camarin attempted to ignore the last few drops of coffee still dripping from the boardroom table and instead concentrate on the others at the meeting. First, Lyle, looking dapper in a charcoal-striped suit accented by a periwinkle shirt. To his left, a disheveled-looking gentleman whose arched eyebrows reminded Camarin of a barnyard owl. And across from Hoots, the second visitor: a hard-looking, middle-aged woman whose brunette bun made her face appear even more unforgiving.

"Camarin," started Fletcher, "I'd like you to meet Declan McManus and Emma Galan. They represent Live Happier Liposuction, with twenty-three offices throughout the tristate area. They've run a few small campaigns with us in the past and are now considering an increase in their advertising spend."

Camarin noted that both clients' expressions were now devoid of emotion. Though they represented everything Camarin hoped to spend her entire career eradicating, she sucked back her disdain. "That's wonderful," she said, forcing herself to brim with enthusiasm. "How can I help?"

Fletcher lifted an eyebrow at her Pollyanna tone. "I was telling them about our proposed, more serious editorial direction. Perhaps you could share a few examples of the types of stories you're planning?"

Talk about being put on the spot. Camarin grappled for something to say as Emma gave her the once-over, breaking into an incredulous sneer. "She's a bit young, no?"

"You want someone young," Fletcher countered, championing his newest hire. "You want someone who can interview people without making them feel threatened or overwhelmed."

"Young works for me," said McManus, winking at Camarin the way that old drunks leered as she walked past them on the subway platform. She tried to squelch her growing revulsion toward the duo.

The door opened, and in walked Rachel, armed with carpet cleaner, a sponge, and towels. She threw a teasing glance in Camarin's direction as she sopped up the spilled coffee from the boardroom table before attacking the stain on the carpet before it could set.

The interruption bought Camarin time to rack her brain for article topics. She nervously scratched at the handbag set on her lap, trying to ignore her galloping pulse and Galan's foot, impatiently tap-tap-tapping against the oak of the table's leg. Coming up short, she was about to admit defeat when Rachel's unexpected groan triggered a memory.

"I do have a few ideas," she improvised. "There's been a murder of a Blubber Be Gone owner in Chicago. Whoever carved up the woman made it clear he or she was none too happy about being judged as fat. Maybe that's a line of thought we could examine."

She could feel Rachel's glare but refused to look over at the receptionist as she departed the boardroom. McManus and Galan fidgeted uncomfortably in their seats.

"You do realize that we're in the same business, correct?" said Galan. "We use liposuction, not to judge anyone, of course, but to make people feel better about themselves."

Fletcher intervened. "It's important to understand that we're not going to pursue that particular story. But we do plan to target more sobering topics in the future, focus on the issues that keep our readers up at night."

Camarin looked over at her boss, shocked at how quickly he had thrown her under the bus. But rather than meet her gaze, he stared down at the unsigned advertising contract on the table. She knew that if she allowed her ideas to be fluffed off on day one, she'd never be taken seriously by him or anyone else at the magazine. She dug deep, eager to save face while still preserving the company's crucial revenue sources.

"I don't see you as being in the same business," she countered, feigning a degree of confidence that even surprised her. "Blubber Be Gone is frequented by people who are pressured to work hard to lose their excess pounds. Weekly weigh-ins, limited diet, daily exercise. Your product is the exact opposite, isn't it? Walk in heavy, walk out thinner, no effort involved. The Blubber Be Gone Butcher, so to speak, is really an advocate, shining a spotlight on your better solution. And I believe that the people I choose to interview for the story are all going to agree."

She felt queasy promoting her point. She hadn't fought her way through *Trend*'s enormous doors to campaign a cause in direct contrast to her own personal beliefs. Plus, she'd directly contradicted her boss to argue her case. But glancing at Fletcher, who was now aglow with pride and hope, she knew she had found the right approach.

McManus leaned over and whispered into Galan's ear. She listened intently and shook her head. Then she turned back and addressed Fletcher.

"If you are telling us that your intended direction could benefit us in this way, we'll sign the contract. But if anything changes, we reserve the right to pull out before the year is over."

Now it was Fletcher's turn to clear his throat. "This entire line of editorial can absolutely be expanded, but it will take some time. Bearing that in mind, I'd like to extend this agreement to a full twenty-four months. Of course, as you say, you can always back out after we've had sufficient time to switch course. Perhaps a year."

Nice counter, thought Camarin. Before Fletcher could spring any other unexpected requests, she rose from her chair. "If you all would excuse me, I have an interviewee waiting in my office." She summoned up every ounce of bravado she had left and firmly shook each client's hand before taking her leave. If *fake it 'til you make it* was the firm's motto, based on its mammoth doors and reception desk, she could certainly adopt it as hers as well.

She headed out to the cooler in the reception area, trying not to dwell upon how she was going to write articles premised on viewpoints she found highly objectionable. She poured and quickly downed a cup of icy water, trying to drown her trepidations.

"Well, you were quite the *tea* in there," quipped the receptionist.

"I'm sorry?"

"Cockney rhyming slang. Let me translate. Tea leaf. Rhymes with thief. You stole my idea."

"I know. I apologize. He took me by total surprise, and I had nothing. I'll make it up to you, I promise."

"Glass of wine one night after work?"

"You got it. Thank you."

"Eh, we millennials got to stick together. When you meet the old Nazi that Fletcher just hired as second-in-command, you'll understand. Hope you're up for the occasional *read*."

"Read?"

"Read and write. Fight. The guy can be downright nasty."

"Indeed. Well, I'll do my best to slug it out," answered Camarin, a concept slowly forming. Why stop at a story that suggested a mere undercurrent of dissatisfaction? Why not uncover the actual BBG murderer and find out the real motivation behind the crime? Then Fletcher wouldn't be so quick to override her editorial suggestions or backtrack on his promise to overhaul the magazine's format.

"Can you show me to my desk?" she asked Rachel. "I need to get started researching. I may have just figured out how to set this whole situation straight."

CHAPTER
7 8 9

RACHEL PILOTED CAMARIN into the writer's/editor's bullpen and pointed out her cubicle, where she was practically tackled by the alleged Nazi, who introduced himself as Hans Wynan, the executive editor. He was a tall, eccentric-looking thirty-something with a Dutch accent, dark-rimmed glasses, and blond hair that seemed to have a mind of its own. He pulled her into *Trend*'s only unoccupied private office, desk piled high with accounting ledgers, and asked her to have a seat. He remained standing, pacing, a commander addressing his troops.

"I'm not sure why, but for some reason, we didn't meet during the interviewing process. Nothing goes into the magazine without my approval. Did you bring your resume and clips so I can review them?" He picked up a pencil and tapped it repeatedly against the side of the desk.

"I-I'm sorry, since I was already hired, I didn't know I'd need them," she said, a bit dazed. Interviewing process? There hadn't been one. And Fletcher had never mentioned that she would have to answer to anyone else. Of course, she'd been too naïve to consider the logistics behind running a magazine or the chain of command.

"It's not your fault. Lyle—Mr. Fletcher—should have really considered having you meet with me before extending an offer of employment. I suppose we'll just have to make do. How are your copyediting skills?"

"They're fine. But Mr. Fletcher led me to believe I'd been hired as an investigative report—"

"I don't know what he told you," he said, cutting her short. "What I do know is that my lead copyeditor just left for Des Moines because her daughter is in labor, and she's going to be out for the next month. I'm shorthanded, and I need you to fill in."

Camarin sat silent, her mouth slightly agape.

"That's not a problem, is it?" asked Wynan. "I mean, we're all team players here."

"No, no…of course not. I'll do whatever it takes to make *Trend* the best it can be."

Well, at least the last part of her statement was true. She was going to do whatever it took. As soon as she could pull Fletcher aside, she'd get him to sort out this misunderstanding before the Blubber Be Gone buzz grew cold.

Wynan briefly introduced her to the others in the office. Every person was overly polite but eyed her with suspicion, no doubt possessive of jobs they feared they could lose. Then the two returned to her cubicle, where he gave her a computer password and told her to check her Outlook folder. "There are fourteen freelancer columns that need to be edited, which in this place usually means rewritten. I need them back by four o'clock so I have time to re-edit them, if need be, before forwarding them to layout. Got it?"

"No problem, Mr. Wynan. I'll get right to it," she said, trying to hide her disappointment behind a cheery facade.

She spent the afternoon fending off a stupor as she sifted through the drivel that the magazine passed off as content. Some pieces were superficial, others inane, but all had one thing in common: the subliminal message that no matter who you were or what you'd accomplished in life, you were always one step shy of acceptable. Article after article designed to make the typical reader question her fashion sense, her recipe knowledge, her parenting skills, and most of all, her size and how to make or keep it as small as possible.

That was the one message that irked Cam most, one she hated herself for having bought into since childhood, thanks to her mother's constant harping. "Camarin, please, no—fill in the blank: cookies, seconds, snacks, etcetera—you don't want to end up heavy and alone…" followed by two words left unsaid as her voice trailed off…*like Monaeka*. Depression set in as Cam realized that *Trend*'s 'new' direction was either just an extension of her mother's oppressive voice, and therefore diametrically opposed to what Fletcher had described, or had not yet been implemented.

Wynan's assignment left Camarin with little time to research the BBG murder. She needed to talk to Fletcher, get her role sorted out. She kept an occasional eye on the windowed wall that overlooked the entrance to the war room, waiting for him to emerge. Instead, she witnessed a constant flow of visitors streaming in and out, no doubt advertisers like Live Happier Liposuction, being wooed by Fletcher to place or keep their ad dollars with *Trend*. She wished Fletcher would rescue her from this brain-numbing busy work so she could again pitch the BBG idea, perhaps this time to a more receptive audience. But how likely was that, especially after she'd contradicted him her first time out?

At 4:20, after she had sent Wynan the last of her edits, Camarin saw Fletcher emerge and head back to his office. A few minutes later he summoned her via intercom, asking her to join him. Grabbing a pad and pen, she dashed across the hall. He'd left his door ajar, and she peeked in, but he was too engrossed in a phone call to do more than motion to her to take a seat. The office was surprisingly tiny for someone of his stature, with barely an inch of uncluttered space on his desk where she could set down her pad and pen. Yet he'd found room for knickknacks here and there, various awards and plaques from a former life but, oddly, no photos.

As she waited, Camarin realized her hands were shaking slightly. She wondered if she was more nervous about confronting her boss over Wynan, being chewed out over disputing his authority earlier, or merely the fact they were finally alone together. He looked so powerful, reclining in his overstuffed mahogany chair, absentmindedly tapping his fingers against the upholstered arm, his ever-friendly expression uncharacteristically solemn.

She pictured herself sitting on his lap, rubbing her finger against the creases in his brow until they unfurrowed. Then moving it down to his chin, which she'd lift so his lips would meet hers. And then... *What the hell?* She shooed away the fantasy, and instead, mentally chanted her mantra—*Play it cool. Stay on point. Professional always.*—as Fletcher wrapped up his sales pitch.

"I understand your concerns, but we've got that aspect well under control...Yes, just the way I described...Absolutely...Okay, good to know that I can count on you, Howard. I'll send the contracts by email. Thanks again." As he hung up the phone and gave her his full attention, the twinkle returned to his eyes. "So, Ms. Torres, how have you enjoyed your first day at *Trend*?"

"May I be completely honest?"

"I absolutely insist," he said, looking a bit surprised. "By all means, please tell me everything you're thinking."

That one statement was all it took to weaken her dam of self-restraint. Mantra forgotten, a flood of emotion came gushing out. "Mr. Fletcher, I appreciate this opportunity. And I know that Mr. Wynan needs help copyediting hard-hitting stories on ideal pore size, not to mention the deodorant dilemma—spray versus powder. Don't even get me started on roll-on. But I think it's more important that I take on the Blubber Be Gone investigation. And not as an advertorial, like I suggested during the meeting, but as part of something bigger. I think it could be indicative of a real growing sentiment in this country. The murderer might have quite a story to tell, if we were able to help the police pinpoint his or her whereabouts."

"The *murderer* might have a story to tell?" he spluttered.

Camarin disregarded Fletcher's skepticism, her voice growing louder as she got caught up in her own excitement. "Yes. I think if you want to make a big splash with our new direction, we should go all-out. Help the police find this person, then ask what's behind his or her wrath. Can you imagine all the people who would want to read that exclusive?" She gestured expansively, including the entire world in their future audience.

Fletcher held up a palm, as if stopping traffic. "Camarin, I appreciate your enthusiasm. I truly do. And I do want *Trend* to start running more serious pieces. But you've only been out of school for a week. I'm not prepared to send you out investigating murders. I was thinking you could start out slower and on a smaller scale, interview some of our readers, get inside their heads. Maybe their need for self-respect and acceptance could cause our advertisers to rethink their approach."

Camarin remained silent, trying to calm down, regroup. What Fletcher had suggested wasn't the hard-hitting story she'd been hoping for, but at least it was a reasonable compromise. And yet she could foresee a major problem.

"I agree that giving our readers a voice is certainly a step in the right direction. But I might have a conflict."

"Already? You've only been here—" He checked his watch. "—a whole seven hours."

"I know. And I don't want to be a problem child. But the copyedits aside, I also need to be true to myself. I fear that if I interview our readers, and I'm honest in my reporting—truly honest, no holding back—I might ruffle a lot of your advertisers' feathers. And…" Cam's voice trailed off as she realized what she wanted to say might be overstepping.

"Go on."

"Well, you told me when we met that the magazine was failing. As much as I want to do this, I need you to realize, it could be professional suicide for you to give me the go-ahead. And for me to follow through. I mean, what's the point of turning in Pulitzer-worthy stories if there's nowhere to publish them?"

Fletcher looked slightly taken aback. "It *was* failing, before I threw money in. What makes you think we're still in trouble?"

Camarin hesitated, unwilling to implicate Rachel as a mole. "I've heard talk. Even though I understand ad pages are up. Which is something else I wanted to ask you about. I am an investigative reporter, after all."

He smiled. "Indeed, you are. And one that's as nimble on her feet as I remembered from the railroad platform. Every one of the advertisers I courted today was intrigued that we were going to become more provocative in our reporting.

They all signed on in the hopes that our future editorial focus would sway our growing readership their way."

His praise was an injection of adrenaline, convincing her to press her argument forward, even if he had sidestepped the financial issue. "After my edits today, the one thing I am absolutely certain of is that each of your advertisers has a vested interest in making people think they're lacking in some way. That readers must buy their products to become worthy, whole. Don't you agree?"

He nodded. "Every last one of them."

"But I want to help people feel good about themselves just the way they are. So, it really would be a conflict of interest."

"Not at all. What these advertisers want is readership. If we have the numbers and enough of those people see their ads and buy, they won't care what we run in editorial. It's just that..."

"What?"

"I know how eager you are. Believe me. And if anyone can find the story behind the story, I'm betting on you. But...well, three things. First, keep both eyes open and don't try to force a story where one might not exist. In other words, don't let righteous indignation fuel your position if the facts don't support it," Fletcher said, with a tone more paternal than supervisory.

"I understand," Camarin said, her stomach sinking at the thought that her story instinct might be off-kilter.

"Second, no murder investigation. That idea dies here and now, no pun intended."

We'll see about that, she thought. "And the third thing?"

"I need you to work with Hans. You don't know what I went through to lure him over here. Try to find a way to handle any editing he throws your way, at least until we aren't so shorthanded. Maybe you can find pockets of time here and there to work on the reader interviews or any other story ideas you might come up with." The phone rang. He held up one finger. "Just let me get this and then we'll wrap up."

He picked up the receiver and started his advertising sales pitch. She tuned him out, lost in her thoughts as she lifted and studied the paperweight on his desk, a piece of the Berlin Wall encased in Lucite. It was a symbol of broken barriers. Yet Fletcher, self-proclaimed redeemer of lost causes, was ignoring another symbol: that the Blubber Be Gone murder was proof that when society is persistently cruel to a disenfranchised group like the overweight, the oppressed could rise up and rebel. Why was he suggesting that she push off a story that could spotlight this injustice, unmask a murderer and possibly save the lives of future unsuspecting victims?

She set the paperweight back down and looked at Fletcher's face, so animated as he assured the caller that this was going to be the year of *Trend*. Not my version of *Trend*, Camarin thought. As he hung up the phone, she decided to press forward.

"Mr. Fletcher, I'd be happy to help with the copyediting. But if I can safely prove to you that there's something more behind the Blubber Be Gone murder, without going out and personally putting myself in harm's way, would you consider a piece on the possible implications behind it? I'd get in at five o'clock every morning to research it."

Fletcher shook his head and laughed.

"Camarin, you strike me as a persistent young lady, and it's clear you're not easily dissuaded. Hans Wynan must approve all copy decisions. Do you honestly think you can investigate this subtly, without letting him know you're not giving him a hundred percent of your attention?"

"I do."

"Okay, let's keep this just between us for now. I'd like you to work up a preliminary outline of the story you propose. Get it to me by Friday?"

Camarin smiled her first big smile of the day. Inside, she was performing mental cartwheels. "I'd be delighted to, Mr. Fletcher."

"Camarin, I do have one problem with you."

"You do?" Her high-flying elation took a sudden nosedive.

"Yes, and I'm only going to say this once. Please call me Lyle."

She took a deep breath. "Lyle...it just doesn't feel right. You're my boss, and in the Chamorro culture, we pay profound respect to—"

"The elderly?"

She was about to apologize, to tell him that she was referring to supervisors, when she caught the evil glimmer in his eyes and realized he was just kidding with her. Emboldened by her big win of the day, she ignored Monaeka's voice telling her to play it safe, that a handsome man of stature would never be interested in a girl like her, and instead her impulsive streak took over. She decided to take a gamble.

"If I was indicating you were elderly, you'd definitely know it," she countered, echoing the line he'd used the day they'd met.

"Oh, how so?"

"You really want to know?"

Fletcher nodded.

She stood up, silently begging her knees not to buckle underneath her, and shot a look backward to ensure the door was closed. Then she walked around the desk until she was standing at Fletcher's side.

"Give me your hand."

Fletcher held out his right arm. Locking her gaze with his, Camarin grasped his palm, bowed her head slightly, lifted the back of his hand to her nose and sniffed deeply. The sweet-soapy-musky tones of Tabac romanced her olfactory glands, reminding her of summers spent at Macy's, selling men's fragrances.

"This custom is called *nginge'*," she explained. "Elders are considered *manåmko'*, and those who are considered to hold wisdom are called *mañaina*. When we sniff the back of your hand, it is our way of taking in the essence of your spirit while expressing respect and honor."

"Really? Hmmm," he said softly, the words smooth as lip gloss, his eyes never wavering from her. The heat emanating from their clasped hands hinted at secrets yet unspoken.

"Yes. And I would curtsy slightly, like this, and since you are a man—"

"I am indeed a man," he murmured.

Camarin felt herself blushing but persevered. "Since you are a man, I would say *ñot*, and you would say—" She felt him squeeze her hand as they continued their unbroken stare.

"I would say…"

She paused, lightheaded, the air suddenly as thin as atop Mt. Baldy back home. "You would say *dioste ayudi*, which means—"

At that moment, there was a loud knock on the door. Startled, Camarin pulled away just as Hans barged inside.

"Lyle, I need your approval on the *Have You Heard?* seg—oh, Camarin, I didn't realize you were in here."

"I-I was just leaving." She grabbed at her pad and pen but hit the edge of the ballpoint instead, sending it careening through the air and crash-landing in a corner by the window.

Klutz! "Thanks again, Mr....L-Lyle," she stammered and practically slammed into Wynan as she made a beeline for the door.

Once outside, she leaned against the wall, trying to ignore Monaeka's laughter at her failed attempt at flirtation, her heart pounding as loud and fast as a native drumbeat.

"*Pitch* giving you trouble, Cam?" asked Rachel as she passed, her hands filled with office supplies.

"Excuse me?" she answered, still disoriented from whatever *that* was.

"Pitch and toss. Boss."

"Oh, no, nothing like that. I was just—" Camarin's cellphone started vibrating, interrupting her thought. She pulled it from her pocket and, hand quivering, put it up to her ear. "Yes?"

"You were saying, which means... "

Her knees grew weak again. Fletcher had her private number?

Camarin turned away from Rachel and whispered into the phone, "Which means *God help you.*"

"Ah. Well, considering our upcoming plans to turn this magazine around, I'd say, He'd better help us both."

CHAPTER

W YNAN LOOKED ON with incredulity as Fletcher hung
up the phone.

"Lyle, what's your take? Do we 'elaborate' on the Phoebe
Ellington piece and 'suggest' that she had to have been coked
out of her mind to wear that *schmatta* to a premiere, or should
we leave that to the readers' imagination?"

Fletcher tried to concentrate on the blathering of his
editorial director and ignore the stiffness in his pants, a
throbbing reminder of the flirtatious moment he and his new
reporter had just shared. Yet he was grateful for the raging
hard-on straining against his fly—it felt good to have
something, someone, remind him that he was still a man. For
that someone to be a girl almost half his age sniffing the back
of his hand? That's something he could never have predicted
two months prior.

"Earth to Lyle. What do you think?"

He sighed as he forced himself back to the issues at hand,
superfluous as they might be. In the overall scheme of
things, with his investment on the line and his cock on high
alert, some pubescent model's fashion misstep seemed
somewhat immaterial. He grabbed a pencil and weaved it

absentmindedly between his fingers. "Print what you want but just be sure to stick to the facts. No innuendo. I want us to start moving in a more serious direction, and honestly, I can't afford a libel suit right now, especially over something that isn't going to significantly spike circulation. Got it?"

"This again. I know you want to make *Trend* more 'serious.' But are *you* serious? Or just infatuated?"

Fletcher stared at the blond Dutchman and tried to feign innocence. "You're crazy. She's young enough to be my—"

"First sexual harassment lawsuit? Yes, Lyle, she certainly is. Fuck, I've known you how many years?"

"Too many."

"Right. Through Cassie Manos. Through Brenda Baez. And, of course, through Margaret. So yeah, to me, your infatuation is pretty obvious."

Fletcher sighed, annoyed at how easily his close friend could see through him, especially since he'd almost convinced himself of his lack of romantic interest toward Camarin. "Think she knows?"

"She's not old enough to know that McCartney was in a band before Wings. So, no, probably not. But still, you've got a lot on your plate right now, don't you think?"

"Yeah."

"So maybe it's not the best time to start learning Snapchat and shopping at Vineyard Vines just to be able to relate."

He half-admired and half-resented Hans's unflinching clarity, the way he targeted the essence of an issue without allowing himself to be muddied by empathy or emotion. "She's not like that, she's—"

"One step past jailbait?"

"I was going to say an old soul. There's this uncanny wisdom about her. Very goal-oriented and resolute. But guided by some deep sadness I can't put my finger on yet."

"Maybe a safer bet not to put a finger on any part of her until we sort out our editorial and budget problems. If ever. In the meantime, let's keep her busy with the copyedits until Perla comes back from Iowa."

Fletcher cleared his throat as he changed the topic. "In terms of budget, everyone I spoke to yesterday is on board. We're solvent for another six months at a minimum. I need you to give Camarin some space. Leave her alone for part of each day to do some research on her own stories. It will keep her happy. Meanwhile, I'll drum up a few choice assignments to keep her busy, more on target with our plans. Who knows? Maybe she'll attract an entirely new crop of advertisers."

Hans's expression was a mixture of relief and skepticism. "That's encouraging, at least about the advertisers staying on. We're going to have trouble finding enough competent editorial to support all these ad pages. You're clearly as persuasive as ever. I'll go tell the guys to tone down the Ellington angle. And if you want to talk about this more over dinner…"

"Not tonight, but thanks, Hans. I knew I didn't make a mistake when I brought you aboard."

"Brought me aboard? You fucking begged me to help save you from yourself when you bought this rag."

"Hey, we can't all be *Business Day*."

"Uh-huh. But at least when I was over there, I didn't have to lower my voice in shame when people asked me where I worked."

"No, but you also wore less expensive suits than you can afford now, didn't you?"

Wynan stuck up his middle finger and walked out of the office as Fletcher sat back in his chair, reveling in verbal triumph. Then, turning his mind to more serious matters, he unlocked his top desk drawer and pulled out a thick booklet with *Lehming Brothers Annual Report* printed on its cover.

He flipped through the worn pages yet again, looking for the profile of Blubber Be Gone. And there it was, on page twenty-six, just one of the conglomerate's thousands of businesses promoting weight loss and personal improvement. He grabbed a magic marker and drew a giant X on the page.

CHAPTER
10

THE MAN AT the bar raised his voice to be heard over the din. "Miss, I asked for a gin and tonic five minutes ago. Did you forget about me?"

Camarin considered countering with *how could anyone forget someone wearing a suit two sizes too tight?* but then realized that kind of comment would make her as bad as the magazine she worked for. *Fuck,* Trend *is already wearing off on me.* Instead, she apologized and reached for a bottle of Tanqueray.

Benji's was midtown's only dueling-piano bar, and it was located off the lobby of the Laidlaw, one of the city's largest convention hotels. Which meant that unlike most city nightspots on a Monday night, the place was packed. The patrons were mostly out-of-town businessmen, from less exotic climes like Omaha and Pensacola, attending medical symposiums, banking conferences, insurance seminars. Annalise called them the *bridge and toll brigade*, all feigning that innate 'Manhattan cool,' as they attempted to outspend each other on filet mignon, surf-and-turf—whatever overpriced menu item might best impress their dinner companions. Camarin witnessed the same posturing at the bar. If only these poseurs tried half as hard to impress the waitstaff and bartenders with the size of their tips, the roommates could have afforded a less dingy apartment.

"Cover for me, okay?" Camarin yelled over to Viviana, her fellow bartender, as she headed to the ladies' room.

There, she bumped into Annalise, looking like a fairy dominatrix in her sparkly pink-and-silver cat suit, applying a deep crimson to her pale cheeks and ample lips.

"Bet your tips are through the roof tonight, wearing that thing." Cam shook her head in mock disbelief at the outrageous looks her roommate managed to pull off.

"Same old, same old. I could be standing there stark naked, and they'd still blow their money on the shrimp and skimp on the server. Whatever. As long as they keep tossing twenties on the piano for DeAndre, at least one of us can cover the rent."

"Yeah, as if he *wasn't* going to play *Living on a Prayer*, with or without their requests."

Both girls shared a knowing laugh.

"Anyway, girl, you'd better be on your best behavior. I know your first day at the magazine was hard—and from the sound of it, your boss was too—but tourists are three deep at the bar, and Benji keeps throwing you dirty looks. We can't afford for you to get fired for daydreaming about Mr. Publisher."

Camarin rolled her eyes and made a mental note not to confide in her roomie if she didn't want the details reshuffled and later flung back in her face.

"Oh, please. He's probably just flirty with everyone. And I still don't have any proof that he's going to switch his editorial. But point taken. I'll spend the evening focusing on martinis, not men."

Annalise squeezed Camarin's upper arm, a show of solidarity, before heading back into the fray. Camarin entered the stall and closed her eyes. What her roommate had said was true. She had been preoccupied, trying to analyze every moment of her encounter with Fletcher, or Lyle, as he'd insisted she call him. Was he interested in her? Monaeka would say no, but Cam needed to look at this clearly, rationally, unmuddied by the ghosts of the past. If she misread the cues and acted inappropriately, it could spell professional disaster.

She had a flashback to her childhood, her mother reading her a cautionary passage from a native poem, which she did whenever Cam was overeager about an upcoming event. It was called *Tåno' na Dåkkon*, which literally meant *A Deceitful World.*

"A tree behind the house looks strong and healthy. We wait, and yet it bears no fruit. The sea looks calm. But lives perish that same 'calm' day when some unseen swell tips the boat over. We swear we saw something. It turns out to be a mirage."

Someone banged on the stall door, wrenching Camarin back into the present.

"Are you done in there? There's a line waiting."

Concentrate on investigating the BBG story, she told herself as she exited the stall. The rest would unfold as it should, if there really was anything there to unfold. Only time would tell what was truth and what really *was* just a mirage.

CAMARIN SPENT MOST of her second day at *Trend* editing two thrilling features: *How the Right Breed of Dog Can Attract a Man with a Stellar Pedigree* and *The Best Wedding Dresses to Hide That Baby Bulge*. Sheesh, they couldn't even let a pregnant mother feel proud about gaining weight.

Despite an invitation from Rachel, she skipped lunch, hanging instead with her best friend, Google. In an hour, she'd clandestinely plowed through every link she could find concerning the Blubber Be Gone victim, Leticia Regan.

Whenever Wynan left the bullpen, she alternated between editing and placing phone calls to anyone interviewed in the newspaper accounts who had phone numbers she could locate online. Cam had initially feared that when she identified herself as calling from *Trend*, they'd just hang up. To her astonishment, her self-affixed title of 'senior investigative and features reporter' seemed to carry some heft.

She had prepared what she considered to be a well-thought-out series of questions for anyone who answered her call: Had Ms. Regan received any death threats that you were aware of? Had any of the franchise's clients expressed dissatisfaction with the body-shaming nature of the business? Do you have any theories about the reason behind the attacks that the police and other reporters might have overlooked? The result: nothing, nada, *seru*.

She was about to give up for the day when her last call, to a BBG client named Michael Milligan, turned up pay dirt. Milligan mentioned how attendance at the last few weekly meetings had been spotty, what with Terry Mangel coming to town.

"Terry who?" she asked, keeping a wary eye out for Wynan.

"Terry Mangel. You know, the guy who runs the revival meetings."

"Revival, like a religious gathering?" Camarin tilted her head to her shoulder to cradle the receiver while she used both hands to type *Terry Mangel* into Google.

"It may just be my opinion, ma'am, but the only thing Mangel does religiously is hoodwink folks. He goes around the country, telling people who are trying to eat right and exercise that they're wasting their time. Then he sets up his tents and invites them to come in and listen while he spends hours assuring them they're okay just the way they are."

"So, what's wrong with that?" asked Camarin, amazed to hear that someone, anyone, was out there, espousing her personal doctrine. She struggled to simultaneously interview Milligan, type notes into Word, and search the internet for details. Second day on the job and she already needed an assistant.

"To the naked eye, nothing," he responded. "His dogma is valid. The problem is Mangel charges them a ton to attend his meetings and then bilks them for even more once they get inside. Books, DVDs, Feel Good About Yourself clothing, you name it. He's taking advantage of them, worse than all the Blubber Be Gone–type places put together. I guess when it comes to hope, us fatties are easy pickings. Hustlers get us coming and going."

"I agree, this is awful. Would you happen to have the names and numbers of any of the fellow BBGers who attended? I mean, in case they can shed any information on the case?" Camarin figured she was probably grasping at straws, but even a single straw was better than sipping from an empty glass.

"Tell you what. Mangel's packing up his circus and leaving town tomorrow. Those members will be back at BBG next week, I'm guessing, as long as someone new comes in to run the place. I'll tell 'em about you and your story, and if they're interested, I'll give them your number. That fair enough?"

"More than fair, Mr. Milligan. I really appreciate the help. Do you have a pen? I'm at *Trend* magazine, 212-555-0777."

"Sure, I got it. I wish you luck with your story. Someone's gotta put a stop to folks like Mangel. We shouldn't have to decide between hating ourselves or going broke, you know?"

"I know. Better than you can imagine. I'll get to the bottom of it. Thanks again."

Camarin hung up, Milligan's words having ignited imaginary firecrackers inside her brain like it was a neurological 4th of July. Her first real lead! She quickly looked behind her. Thankfully, still no sign of Wynan.

She returned her attention to Google and the first 250,000 results from her *Terry Mangel* search. The home page of his website contained nothing but a large photo of an obese woman in a bikini with the legend *YOU HAVE NOTHING TO APOLOGIZE FOR.* She clicked on the pic, and the obligatory sales spiel popped up.

Tired of people telling you you're nothing if you are not skinny?

Weary of hating yourself for not conforming to society's 'norms'?

Stop. Because you have nothing to apologize for.

Terry Mangel sees you for the beautiful person you are, inside and out.

Buy Terry's book and 10 CD or DVD Series: Self-Esteem is a Terrible Thing to Waste—Stop Swallowing Society's View of Legitimacy.

Better yet, come renew and regenerate!

Spend a full week with Terry at his Ohio lakeside retreat.

Don't have a week? No problem! Come attend Terry's two-day traveling seminar: Feel Good About Yourself!

Camarin clicked on the price links for each purchase. The book and CD or DVD series ran $249. The week with Terry—$1,999, plus hotel and airfare. The seminar price wasn't even listed; those interested were encouraged to email or call for more information.

She grew hot with anger as she pondered how a typical overweight person could save up that kind of money, especially when her research showed they typically earned ten thousand dollars less per year than a thin person. Unless they were desperate enough to go into debt, using credit cards at nineteen percent interest, never once considering how they'd ever get past the monthly minimum payments to eventually pay off the principal.

"You finished with that editing yet, Cam?" Wynan had managed to sneak up behind her without making a sound.

"Almost," she said, unapologetically minimizing the search engine and bringing Word back up onto the screen.

"Anything I can do to help?"

"Only if you can reverse all of human behavior so that the world can actually accept people who are a little different than themselves."

Camarin realized, in horror, that she'd spoken those private thoughts aloud, snidely attacking her immediate supervisor for posing a simple question. She froze, furious at her inability to keep her big mouth shut and unsure of how to proceed.

Wynan's expression switched from surprised to bemused. "Um, I was thinking more along the lines of getting you a cup of coffee. Something to speed up the process."

"I'm sorry. Really. Just because people out there are jerks, there's no excuse for taking it out on you. Coffee would be great. I take it black."

"Like your outlook?"

She smirked and shook her head. "I'm usually pretty optimistic. You'll see. Something like this won't happen again."

"Lyle sees something in you, so I'm giving you the benefit of the doubt, Cam. But if you miss deadlines, I can't substantiate keeping you on the team. I'll be back in five." He harrumphed as he headed out the door.

Well, that was pleasant. She'd had nasty coworkers and bosses before, at summer jobs and at Benji's, but this one certainly had it out for her. She wondered why. Still, he was bringing her coffee. Maybe there was a glimmer of hope?

In any case, there was no time for speculation about her editor's likes and dislikes. She needed to focus if she wanted to uncover more information before Wynan's return.

Maximizing the Google window, Camarin typed *Terry Mangel reviews* into the search bar and was again rewarded by an extensive list of entries. She clicked on a consumer-alert link about halfway down the screen that listed *444 Reviews and Complaints About Terry Mangel.* An overall four out of five stars. Impressive. She started reading, cutting, and pasting the most interesting details into her digital notes.

> *5 Stars! The meeting changed my world,* wrote RebornandHappy3017. *Thank you, Terry, for being the one person out there who understands that I am a living, breathing, feeling person, not just a number on a scale!*

More like numbers on a check, Camarin thought. She clicked on the next review, four stars from someone named Never_apologize_again.

> *The room listened in silence as I told my story, and at the end, I saw the crowd clapping, but all I could hear was the applause in my own head. It's like I came out, when I never should have been in. Terry helped me realize that I'm a person of worth, even if the Thin Police out there don't agree.*

The words touched Camarin somewhere deep inside, and any cynicism she might have harbored started dissipating.

> FinallyWhole1959: *I'm almost sixty, and for the first time in my life, I've found a place where I fit in. I was surrounded by thousands of people who, like me, wasted their entire lives drowning in self-doubt, trying to find a place of peace and acceptance. In that crowd, we weren't constantly urged to fix ourselves, to make our bodies as pretty as our faces. I may not have much time left, but I plan to spend it listening to Terry and not the haters out there.*

Camarin felt the tears brimming in her eyes. The quote resonated. All that lost time.

She thought of her mother and aunt, Navy brides transplanted from their native Guam, unwavering in their resolve to adapt to the Los Angeles landscape. Aunt Sirena, once a follower of tribal religion, fell in with a fundamentalist Christian group and recreated her community there. Her mother Ana, less religious but equally eager to assimilate, found refuge in her nursing career but devoted every spare moment to her true calling: cautioning her family to do whatever it took to fit in, fit in, fit in.

Whereas Guam culture had been easygoing and tolerant, even of rounder bodies, Ana insisted that LA was the heartland of judgment. She pointed to its actresses and models, bone thin and anorexic, and to the restaurants and health food stores that lent the city its reputation as the epicenter of everything holistic and organic. When the pediatrician diagnosed childhood epilepsy? *"Don't tell anyone. They might not be accepting."* The weight gained because of the drugs? *"Lose it or die a virgin."* Ana's message to her family had always been very clear: don't stand out or you'll stand alone.

The sisters had reacted differently to their mother's doomsday directive. Monaeka had swallowed the warning whole, hating herself along with every morsel she consumed. But whenever weight crept on, Camarin had found an alternate way to expel her mother's disdain. After every misbegotten meal, she'd excuse herself from the table, head to the bathroom, and thrust one finger down her throat.

But there was one other constant message that Cam couldn't dismiss so easily—the one about Chamorro solidarity, how you respected your parents' wishes and you never abandoned your people. It was a conflict that caused Camarin great resentment every day of her adolescence.

As a twin, she considered herself half of a larger whole. She couldn't just turn her back on her weaker half or abide anyone's harassment of the heavier of the two sisters. So, she and Monaeka isolated themselves from the other kids at school, the ones who laughed at anyone even slightly different. No parties. No dates. For years, her honor became her albatross, because it simultaneously separated herself from whatever supposed group her mother insisted was her unequivocal duty to join. Until that fateful day when she finally took matters into her own hands and broke free…

"Cam…are you crying? Are you okay?"

Wynan stood by her side bearing espresso, the holy water of journalism.

"It's nothing," she said, angrily wiping a tear from her eyes. "A speck of dust, that's all."

"Ah, good, because if it was something more, I'd need you to set it aside and buckle down. Any progress?"

Camarin quickly reclaimed her composure and tried to ignore her boss's glaring lack of empathy. "Thank you for the coffee. I'm almost done with the preggo-in-a-bridal-gown story. I'll get it to you in a few."

As he walked away, she wished she really was the miracle worker Rachel had alluded to during her initial visit. She was going to need divine intervention to survive at *Trend* long enough to make the type of impact she intended. One that would make millions of women who hated their bodies take notice and start loving themselves, no matter what their size. And simultaneously force Wynan to realize her talents extended beyond copyediting, all while making Lyle proud? Just icing on the proverbial cake.

CHAPTER
11 12 13

FLETCHER WAS TOURING the third of four Putnam house rentals with Remy, his Realtor, when his phone began vibrating. Recognizing the caller ID, he excused himself and sought privacy in the kitchen while Remy remained in the living room, chatting up the owners.

"I told you no interruptions."

"She was on the computer, crying. I thought you should know."

"Did you yell at her? Is that why she broke down?"

"Fuck, no. I've been a veritable saint, just like you ordered, boss man. No, I think it was something she saw online."

"Well, I did tell her I wanted her to research some of her own stories wherever she could snatch a minute or two, as long as it didn't interfere with whatever she was doing for you. Thanks for giving her a little slack, Hans. I know you weren't the biggest fan of this hire but——"

"Biggest fan? I told you flat-out it was unwarranted. The last thing this magazine needed was another unnecessary expense. Especially an overinflated salary."

"I know, but you must have a little faith. I know what I'm doing."

"Do you? Or is your cock calling the shots on this one? You lured me over here, promised me absolute editorial control. Then you take a train ride, meet a girl, and suddenly you're espousing our magazine's 'new direction' when the old one was absolutely fine."

"If that direction was fine, the magazine wouldn't have been losing money hand over fist before I took over. Even now, we're barely coasting by. Look, I don't want to rehash this. It's done. You'll change your tune fast enough if her stories bring in double her salary in new ad revenues. Help her if you think she needs it and keep me apprised. I should be back in the office a little later."

There was a pause.

"Any luck with the rental search?" Wynan asked in a less combative tone.

Fletcher winced as he surveyed the 1970s high ranch, with its decades-old green appliances and black-and-white checkerboard floor. "Remy claims that for two grand a month, it's the best Carmel has to offer. Maybe I'll just bite the bullet, eat into my savings, and rent something more expensive in town. Or Jersey City. At least the commute won't kill me."

"I told you that you can always stay with Austin and me until you get situated."

"And barge in on your newly wedded bliss? No way."

"Honeymoon ended two years ago. What we need now is some conflict, something to fan the flames. It's always hotter when we're fighting."

Fletcher's attention strayed from the conversation as he remembered his own conflict with Camarin the previous day, when he'd been forced to douse her hopes concerning the Blubber Be Gone investigation. How quickly that encounter had turned scorching hot as she'd sniffed the back of his palm…

"Lyle, are you still there?" Wynan's voice quickly snuffed out the blaze that had started to sizzle in Fletcher's imagination.

"So, what I'm hearing is that I get to be a catalyst for makeup sex? That's what my life has come down to? Maybe I'll just go home and shoot myself in the head."

"Nah, I'd miss all this witty repartee. Not to mention the salary. The offer stands. Den with a sofa bed, midtown, for as long as you need it. I'll see you later."

Fletcher ended the call, slipped his phone back into his pocket, and then pulled open the sliders to the deck, yearning to be alone with his thoughts. More than his precarious living situation, or *Trend's* financial situation, Camarin's feelings of distress were what concerned him most.

He couldn't rid his mind of the fantasy that had intrigued him since the afternoon they'd met: the vulnerable editorial newbie, her tight body leaning on him for comfort, craving direction and support. He'd pull her closer, adorn her face with butterfly kisses, look deep in her eyes…and she'd cry foul, call him a perverted old man, and go running for a lawyer. He hated the way that daydream always took a turn toward litigation and assisted living.

He debated for about half a second and then pulled his phone back out and dialed the office.

"Good afternoon. How's your day *Trend*-ing?"

"Really, Rachel? We don't just say hello anymore?"

"I'm sorry, Mr. Fletcher, I was trying to make us sound a little edgier."

"I prefer the simple, old, boring greeting. Could we please go back to 'Good afternoon'?"

Silence. "Of course, sir, if that's what you want."

"It is, and could you kindly put me through to Ms. Torres?"

"One moment please."

The phone clicked, followed by one ring.

"Camarin Torres, senior investigative reporter."

He stifled a laugh.

"Senior? Did I miss that promotion somehow?" he said, hoping humor would lighten her mood.

She *tsked* his sarcasm away. "For your information, Mr. Fletcher, it lends gravitas when I request interviews from potential leads."

"Uh-huh. And have you found time today to interview any of those leads?"

"I've actually made some headway." She sounded excited. His anxiety lessened, at least about her mood. He really had to concentrate on finding her something other than BBG to research.

"I'll be back at the office in a few hours. How about dinner?" he said on a whim. Then he realized what he had just done and tried to mitigate the damage. "A business dinner. We can celebrate your second day on the job, and you can debrief me on all of your progress."

The pause that followed made him want to kick himself for rushing things. *Damn.* He had absolutely no sense about how people 'hooked up' or whatever they called it these days. He was about to apologize when she broke the silence.

"I'd love to. Really. But I'm afraid I can't—"

"That's okay," he said in a more professional tone, trying to quickly save face. "I should be back in around forty minutes. We can discuss it all then, yes?"

"Absolutely. That would be great. See you later." *Click.*

He looked at the phone, cursed his impulsivity, and wandered back into the dreary living room to give his real estate agent some unwelcome news: he was relocating to his friend's guest room. Not only would it save him money, he'd never be more than ten blocks from any desolate reporter who might need his shoulder to cry on. Namely one Camarin Torres.

CHAPTER
12 13 14

WITH WYNAN IN a meeting with the layout team, and her edits on the bridal gown exposé already complete, Cam followed up on a hunch and researched Terry Mangel's Feel Good About Yourself revival tour schedule prior to Chicago.

His year, thus far, had included stops in San Diego and Los Angeles in January—*no fool*, she thought, *scheduling warm-weather stops during the winter months*—Phoenix and Santa Fe in February, and then heading east to Dallas and then north to St. Louis in March. Effusive reviews followed each appearance, but that was no longer what held her interest. She checked the local newspapers in those cities for any Blubber Be Gone franchise disturbances during those periods but came up short. Nothing. Damn. She'd been so sure.

She strolled over to the reception area to stretch her legs. Rachel glanced up from her crossword puzzle, apparently welcoming the interruption in her day of paid leisure.

"Ah, good, something to do. Grab a *lion*, and we'll have a *bowler*."

Camarin shook her head. "I swear I'll never understand you."

"Ah, it's easy. Look, I'll teach you—I desperately need someone in this godforsaken place to talk to. What's something you might grab if you walked into a room?"

Camarin squinted and shrugged. "No idea. A drink of water?"

"Nah, that would be a *ten*. Ten furlongs is a mile and a quarter, water. Think… wouldn't you want to sit down?"

"Yeah, I guess."

"So, what would you grab?"

"A chair?"

"There you go. A chair. Lion's lair, chair," Rachel explained in triumph.

Camarin hit her head in mock epiphany. "And what was the rest?"

"A bowler. That you should get easily enough. What's a bowler?"

"A hat?"

"Yes. Of course. And if you were sitting in a chair and having something that rhymed with bowler hat…" Rachel waited in exasperation.

"A chat?"

"Finally. You're practically an honorary Cockney. Go on and sit down. Let's have a chat."

"Ah, can't. No time."

"After all that? You're shitting me." Rachel threw her crossword magazine at Camarin's head. She ducked just in time. It landed by the entry door.

"No, really. I'm trying to work something out. Remember the Blubber Be Gone murder?"

"How could I forget? I'm the one who told you about it."

"And I eternally owe you one. So, it turns out that the clinic wasn't as crowded as usual that week because a weight-loss evangelist was in town with some traveling revival show."

"And…"

"And, I thought maybe, if Terry Mangel—that's the leader—stirred up enough emotions during that Come-to-Jesus-type gathering that every riled-up overweight attendee was encouraged to strike out against their so-called oppressors, then other BBG franchise in the show's path might have experienced a similar type of attack."

"But no?"

"Unfortunately not."

"Ah, I see. Well, I'm no hotshot reporter, but why would it have to be limited to BBG franchises? Wouldn't the fatties be *mum and dad* about anyone they thought was having a laugh at their expense?"

Camarin decided not to protest the derogatory term fatty or request another translation but instead seized upon the revelation inspired by Rachel. Of course, it didn't need to be a BBG franchise! They weren't the only ones out there offering to fix something not everyone considered to be broken. Blowing the confused receptionist a kiss, she pulled open the door to the inner offices and raced back to her deck, ignoring Rachel's call behind her.

"Looks like you owe me a second drink!"

Cam started to click on the link for the *San Diego Union-Tribune* when her cellphone started vibrating. One look at the caller ID, and she grimaced. Just what she needed right now. Her mother.

"Hello, Nana."

"*Håfa ådai*, Camarita. *Håfa tatamanu hao?*"

"I'm fine, thanks for asking. Why are you calling? Is something wrong?"

"Nothing is wrong, *bonita*. Do you have some time to talk?

"*Hunggan, didide' ha'*. Only a little, I'm at work."

"Working? During the day? I thought the bartending was only at night."

Cam lowered her voice to a whisper. She didn't want anyone to know she was moonlighting, that one hundred percent of her attention wasn't focused here, on her day job.

"I told you last week. I took a second job. At *Trend* magazine. As a writer. Remember?"

Camarin felt the sensation of pins and needles on her skin, a reaction to anxiety that she'd had to contend with since childhood. Sometimes her mother could be so infuriating.

"*Ilå'å*, I remember now. Are you enjoying it?"

"It's only my second day. So far so good."

"Are you…"

"No, Nana, I know what you're going to ask, and, no, I'm not seeing anyone."

"You think you are so smart, but that is not what I was going to say. I was going to ask if you are taking care of yourself, eating right."

Camarin sighed deeply and considered banging her head on her desk until she rendered herself unconscious. Then she wouldn't have to finish the editing either. Two birds…

"Why not say what you're really thinking?" Cam asked.

There was an awkward silence on the other end of the line, followed by a cough.

"Fine, Camarita. Are you still…*dalalai*?"

It was all her mother ever worried about, her weight and her dates. She should write a country song.

"Funny you should ask. I thought I could stay *dalalai* eating Entenmann's and Ben and Jerry's all day, but the joke's on me. I'm starting to look like quite the *guäkä*," she said with a smile. She knew the idea of her daughter resembling a cow would drive her mother insane.

"Camarin Torres, that is not funny."

"I'm not trying to be funny, Nana. I'm trying to make a point. I need you to love me just the way I am. Is that so much to ask?"

"You know that I do, *kirida*. But you know that no man is going to want to marry—"

Camarin looked over toward the door and saw Fletcher entering the bullpen area, right on cue. She felt a pang of regret, remembering the dinner invitation she'd been forced to decline. Even dressed down in faded jeans and a lightweight, gray cashmere pullover, he still looked good.

"I'm sorry, Nana, but I have to run to a meeting. You can remind me some other time of my impending spinsterhood as a *chebo'*." Satisfied that the unmarried pig reference would continue to horrify her mother for the remainder of the afternoon, she disconnected the call.

Fletcher was chatting with Wynan, but as soon as she put down her phone, he called out and asked her to head over to his office, where he would soon join her.

It was the first time Camarin was in the office alone. She studied the titles in his bookcase, a combination of business hardcovers like *Swim with the Sharks Without Being Eaten Alive*, textbooks on journalism and publishing, and surprisingly, *A Prayer for Owen Meany*. She pulled out the novel and was thumbing through it when Fletcher walked in and caught her red-handed. Startled, she dropped the book and started to tremble.

"I-I'm so sorry. I shouldn't have been going through your things."

He walked past her, bent down to pick up the book, and handed it back to her before taking a seat behind his desk.

"I wouldn't worry too much. Those books are for anyone who cares to read them. And that one? You might particularly enjoy it since, like me, you enjoy rooting for the underdog."

"That's me, a cheerleader for life's runners-up," she murmured. She took a seat across the desk from him, scrunching her toes inside her shoes to ease her nerves.

Fletcher also seemed edgy, fumbling with the pencils on his desk. She waited, unwilling to disturb the silence. Finally, he cleared his throat.

"First off, Ms. Torres, I owe you an apology."

She was confused. Was he trying to make amends for demoting her from investigative reporter to Wynan's lackey?

"The dinner invitation was out of line and—"

"Oh, that. Don't be sorry. I really wanted to go. It's just that—" She glanced at the clock on his desk. 5:15. Dammit. If she didn't leave now, she was going to be late for work, something they didn't tolerate at Benji's. She stood up abruptly. "It's me who should apologize. I didn't notice the time. I'm afraid I have to run. Can we meet and discuss this tomorrow?"

"Sure, of course. Sorry to keep you after work hours," she heard him call as she ran back to her desk. She grabbed her purse and raced out the door.

CHAPTER
13 14 15

F LETCHER WAS STILL sitting in his office, staring blankly at the seat Camarin had just vacated, when Wynan stuck his head through the door.

"Did you find out what upset her?"

"I think she has a boyfriend."

"He's the one who made her cry?"

"No…I don't know. I think she has a date tonight. A date with him."

Wynan shrugged. "Wanna talk about it over dinner?"

M OST NEW YORKERS had to wait weeks to get a table at Le Bernardin. Wynan's husband, Austin, could arrange it with a half hour's notice, but only because his brother Dallas was the maître d'. Hence Austin's motto: *It's never about what you do; it's all about who you know.*

"Get that guy to smile," Fletcher overheard Dallas whisper to his brother after they'd been seated at a prized corner table. "We are an exclusive restaurant, not a wake."

"Austin, tell your brother to fuck himself." Fletcher was already feeling no pain, thanks to the three jiggers of Glenlivet they'd each downed at the bar.

"I'd prefer to relay that information after it's too late for the waiter to spit in our entrees," Austin shot back. "Order the baked lobster, by the way. They serve it with a white corn polenta and a red-wine gumbo sauce. It's amazing."

"Hans, you didn't tell me you were married to fucking Chef Ramsay. Tell us, Gordon, do the scallops have a nice sear on them?" Fletcher was so proud of his *Hell's Kitchen* reference, delivered in his best mock British accent, he broke into an unstoppable laughing jag.

Dallas threw them an annoyed look.

Fletcher held up his middle finger in response. "Happy, sad, happy, sad. Mr. Dallas can't decide what to be angrier about. And what's with your parents' obsession with Texas anyway? Are San Antonio and Galveston going to wander out from the kitchen any time soon?"

"I think we'd better keep it down, guys, before they throw us out of here," Austin said, hand-signaling to his brother to keep his distance, that all was under control. "Really, Lyle, I don't think I've ever seen you like this."

Wynan took a piece of warm bread from the basket. "You've just never seen him take a chance and not come out ahead. He's the fucking golden boy, and he just got tarnished by a gal half his age."

"Almost half," Fletcher said with mock indignation. "I'm not even forty. She's twenty-two. It's far more respectable than you're making it out to be." The absurdity of the entire situation suddenly struck, and he again collapsed into guffaws.

The waiter attempted to take their orders, clearly trying his best to mask his scorn at their inappropriate howls and chuckles. Diners at surrounding tables cringed in disapproval at the disrespectful display, which continued unabated until their food arrived.

"Seriously, Lyle," said Wynan, once their dinner started dampening the effects of the alcohol. "She's pretty and all, but what made you think that some stranger on Metro North could advocate better for the magazine than I could?"

Fletcher's mood flip-flopped from lighthearted to somber. "What the hell are you talking about?"

"Don't be offended. It could happen to anyone. Lonely widower with deep pockets and his very own fashion magazine, sitting alone on a train. Enter a sexy, little flirt who proceeds to sidle up beside him and chat him up. What do you know? She happens to be looking for a job at a magazine. Wink, wink, nudge, nudge, instant payday."

Fletcher blinked twice. "Trust me, you have absolutely no idea what you're talking about," he said, trying to keep his anger down to a simmer. "Yes, I admit I was attracted to her, but not just because she was pretty. She showed compassion and courage. I approached her. I suggested the job. At the time, she had absolutely no interest in working for something as trivial as *Trend*, so I told her about our new editorial direction, which is something I'd been contemplating anyway. Believe me, we're lucky to have her."

"It was all your idea?" Hans still seemed skeptical.

"It was the only thing I could say that would make her even consider the job. I admit I was smitten. It's ironic, huh? I hired her because, crazy or not, I wanted to get to know her better, and as it turns out, she's going to help my magazine more than my love life."

"I'm sorry. I didn't know." Wynan stared down at his plate.

"I hate when that happens," Austin interjected.

"Fuck you," responded Wynan and Fletcher in unison.

"My concern still stands," said Wynan. "We're a fashion and gossip magazine. You called me in to tweak it into a more profitable piece of fluff, not transform it into *Newsweek*. You can't succeed by pretending to be something you're not."

"There's more to it than that."

"What then?"

"Hans, I don't want to go into it right now." Drunk as he was after downing a half-bottle of expensive whiskey, he still wasn't so far gone as to launch into an explanation of his plot against Lehming Brothers.

Austin interrupted the discourse by waving his American Express card in the air, trying to attract the waiter's attention. "It's on me tonight, gentlemen. We haven't had the chance to spend so much quality time together since before Marg…well, not for a long time. And it's my way of apologizing for Hans's appalling mangling of the facts."

"I still have time to redeem myself," Wynan said, ignoring his partner's sarcastic jab. "Lyle's in no condition— physically or mentally—to go home alone. You're bunking in with us tonight, buddy."

"No rush though. The evening isn't over yet," added Austin. "I heard there's some piano bar in the hotel around the corner. Let's order another round here and then head over there for a nightcap. Get us all back into a more jovial mood."

B ENJI'S WAS PACKED—probably because some famed Florida-based dueling-piano player named Orin Sands was sitting in with the band—so Wynan had to slip the host a fifty to bypass the mob. The inebriated trio bumped and collided their way through rows of seated customers before squeezing in at a table of fourteen toward the front.

Fletcher normally hated crowds, but tonight he wanted to surround himself with as many distractions as possible. Through blurred vision, he attempted to focus on the two pianists under the spotlight—one African American with undeniable stage presence, and the other, an intense, curly-haired version of Richie Sambora in his heyday.

Fletcher closed his eyes as they pounded out Queen's *Don't Stop Me Now* on the keyboards, trying to lose himself in the frenetic beat and the crowd's fervent cheers. But a sense of loss kept nagging at him. Not one as profound as the night he found his wife's lifeless body, but a loss all the same. While not quite the lovelorn patsy of Hans's narrative, he was indeed lonely.

The song ended, and DeAndre introduced himself as the 'ebony half' of the team. "You're a great crowd. Don't forget to tip your waitresses, and keep those requests coming. The ones with the twenties are the ones that usually get played first."

Then he pointed over to Orin, his ivory counterpart, who launched into a rousing version of Billy Joel's *Only the Good Die Young*.

"You look like you could use a refill, buddy," shouted Wynan over the chorus. "You want another scotch?"

Orin's musical account of Virginia, the Catholic girl who hid behind religious dogma and watched potential passion pass her by, just depressed Fletcher even more. "The usual," he shouted back. "Make it a double."

CAMARIN DIDN'T THINK the night could get much more chaotic. They were two waitresses short, prompting impatient customers to crowd the bar, demanding their drinks. And whichever highbrow industry spawned this week's obnoxious crop of conventioneers, she was not amused. Every order came packaged with some lame pickup line.

"Hey, baby, was your mother a beaver? 'Cause damn!"

"Hi, honey. Your tits remind me of Mount Rushmore—my face should be among them."

"Your nickname must be 'appendix.' This feeling you're giving me really makes me want to take you out."

Any other shift, she'd reply with a zinger of her own, but on this particular night her patience had been stretched to its limits. Dealing with Wynan all day had been bad enough. Compounded with having to turn down Lyle's offer of a night out? She gave up silent thanks as the band wrapped up Virginia's tale of woe and went on break, dropping the noise level by several decibels.

She turned her back to the clients, checking the shelves for a bottle of Captain Morgan, when behind her she heard a man's voice call out, "Three doubles, miss. Glenlivet, please." The request had been polite and respectful, but it came at the wrong time on the wrong night, and it tipped her over the edge.

"Why?" she retorted, spinning back around to face her heckler. "You want to 'whisk-ey' me away?"

"A little over dram-atic, no?" Wynan punned back with a cat's-got-the-canary smile.

Camarin took a double-take and felt her stomach fall. Fuck! What else could possibly go wrong tonight? And this, the one thing she'd been determined to avoid, her boss learning the secret about her having a second job.

"I-I-I didn't know it was you," she stammered and then fumbled for the bottle of scotch.

"I figured. Don't sweat it." He looked around the club. "So, this is where you ran off to."

Annalise, dressed as inappropriately as usual for her waitressing duties, pushed through the masses and leaned up against the bar. "Cam, I need one vodka tonic, two chardonnays, and a tequila sunrise." Then she looked at Hans. "This guy giving you trouble?"

"No, I'm good. Could you give that order to Viviana? I need to take a break." And then, fighting off an urge to run off and hide under a rock, she addressed Wynan. "Please come into the back. Give me a chance to explain."

She led him to a quieter, staff-only area where the club kept its liquor inventory and the barbacks washed the glassware.

"Why didn't you tell any of us you had another job?" he asked over the sound of running water and employee murmurs.

She steeled her trembling hands. "I didn't want you to think that I wasn't devoting all of my attention to *Trend*. I can handle both, I promise."

"What you do during your off-hours is your business. But when you're at the magazine, you need to be awake, alert, and focused. What if you find you can't?"

"I'll give this up if I have to. I'm just hoping that won't be necessary. We really need the money right now."

"We? Who's we? You married?"

She noticed a strange, almost accusatory look in his eyes. Why would he care if she was married? Was he asking for himself, or perhaps for a friend? "No. Of course not. I have two roommates. Maybe you saw one of them at the bar— that woman in the hideous tiger-print bodysuit? That's Annalise. And the guy with the dreadlocks, rocking it on stage? That's DeAndre. We share a place in the East Village, and they just hiked the rent, so we're doing what we can to get by."

"I see."

One of the barbacks dropped a tray of glasses, and they shattered in a thousand different directions as they hit the floor. The others started applauding. Camarin shushed them and beckoned Wynan to join her in a less shard-ridden section of the staging area.

"Is this going to be a problem?" she asked. It was more of a dare than a question, but she was so damn sick of apologizing to everyone for everything. Maybe she was overplaying her hand, especially since he had her at a disadvantage, but if she didn't start asserting herself now, she might not have another chance later.

"I'll make you a deal. You keep giving me your best work, and there won't be any issues. But if I sense that you're burning the candle at both ends, you're going to have to make a choice. Fair?"

She breathed a sigh of relief. "More than fair. Thank you. Can we keep this just between us?"

"I won't breathe a word. But there is one other thing."

"What's that?" she asked, trying to downplay her sense of foreboding.

"I need you to serve those three scotches to our table. Not some other waitress, you."

"Why?"

"Don't ask questions and we'll get along swimmingly. Deal?"

The request seemed suspicious, but she had no recourse but to comply. He held all the cards. "Fine. I'll swap spots with Annalise for an hour or so. Maybe no one will notice."

"Only one person needs to," she heard Wynan murmur as he returned to his seat.

Shit! Camarin slumped against the wall, willing her pulse to slow. If one day Hans Wynan arbitrarily decided he no longer wanted her at *Trend*, he now had the ammunition he needed to control, blackmail, even fire her.

According to Fletcher, they'd known each other for years. If Wynan wanted to keep her at the copy desk forever, who was Fletcher going to listen to? His old friend, or the new girl with her focus skewed between two jobs? And what did this guy have against her anyway?

Nerves rattled, she ventured out of the staging area and found Annalise.

"I'll explain later. I just have to trade duties with you for a little while and serve some drinks to one table."

"Hey, be my guest. I'm sure my tips will be better behind the bar anyway."

"Great, pour me three double scotches—Glenlivet, I think he said—and I'll take them over."

Camarin frantically scanned the audience, trying to figure out where Wynan and his party were sitting. It didn't help that the light show on stage backing up Michael Jackson's *Billie Jean* alternately bathed the audience in blues, then greens, then purples.

Annalise handed her the tray bearing three tumblers filled with amber. "End of table four, I watched him as he walked back."

"I owe you big time."

"Just remember old Anna when you're the next Katie Couric and I'm still stuck here, waiting tables."

Camarin maneuvered her way through two hundred jeering, rowdy revelers, ignoring the calls of the patrons trying to wave her down for drink orders. She finally saw the back of Wynan's head. She didn't recognize the person sitting opposite, an elegant man with jet-black hair and angular features. He reminded her of an elegantly dressed, slightly older John Cho. The silver-haired, bearded man to his left…

Fucker! Sure, Wynan wasn't going to breathe a word about her working two jobs. He was going to make sure she outed herself to Fletcher, here, tonight. She felt her blood pressure soar, and any deference she'd felt toward the editor melted away under the heat of her anger. To hell with all of them. She didn't have to answer to anyone for what she did after work hours. If Wynan wanted war, bring it on. But she had the power of seduction on her side. There was no fiercer warrior than a Chamorro, especially a flirtatious one.

A thin one, perhaps. But not you, Camarin. Not you.

"Here you go, boys," Camarin said, ignoring Monaeka's perpetually derogatory voice as she arrived at the table.

Fletcher gawked in seeming disbelief. She served Wynan first, then his friend, leaving her boss for last.

"Mr. Fletcher, it's a pleasure to see you." She crouched by the side of his chair so she could whisper directly into his ear as she set the third drink down next to him. "Yours is last because it's extra special."

"Ca-Camwin?"

Pupils glassed over, cheeks flushed, slurred speech. She had never imagined he could be so vulnerable and out of control, and she didn't like it. He didn't need a temptress— he needed a caretaker.

"That's it. No more liquor for you. Let's go get some air."

There was no pushback from his companions who, with scotch in their hands, were oblivious to anything except the show on stage. She pulled Fletcher up and, with his arm around her shoulders and hers wrapped around his waist, guided his staggering body through the aisles and out the front. He complied, as docile as an exhausted three-year-old leaving the park with his nanny. They stopped a few yards past the door to avoid the lengthy line of eager merrymakers still waiting to get inside.

She waved to get the bouncer's attention. "Gary, inebriated customer here. Can you get Annalise or one of the other waitresses to bring us something to eat? Anything to sop up the alcohol."

Gary nodded and hurried inside.

Fletcher sagged against the club's brick exterior, staring blankly ahead. A vigilant Camarin remained by his side, prepared to prop him up should he slump farther. "Take deep breaths," she counseled him. "The cool night air will help until we get some food into you."

Gary returned with a chicken wrap and a cold glass of water. Fletcher was staring off into the stars. She whistled to get her boss's attention.

"Hey, Mr. Glenlivet? Yes, you. Eat this. It will help sober you up." She held half a wrap up to his mouth, and he took one bite, then another.

She kept silent until he finished both halves and drank the entire glass of water.

"Better? Night air helping a little?"

Fletcher shook his head, clearly embarrassed. "I'm so sorry you had to see me like this, Ms. Torres."

"Oh, please. This kind of thing happens every night. One drink too many. And call me Camarin. Please. Or even Cam, if you like."

"Is that what your friends call you? Cam?" His voice was weak, but he was starting to sound more like himself again.

"Cam, Cammie. My mom calls me Camarita."

"And do you take such loving care of every customer who overdoes it…Cam?"

Maybe it was the food, or time away from the scotch, but his speech was clearer and his eyes better focused. She allowed herself to relax a little.

"Not every customer, no," she said shyly. "Do you feel well enough to go back inside, Mr. Fl—Lyle?"

"In a minute. Tell me, is this why you ran out of our meeting today? You work here at night?"

It was the topic she'd hoped to avoid, but now she had no choice but to come clean. Perhaps she could mitigate the damage? "Some nights, yes. I hope that's okay. I promise to devote every hour during the day to improving *Trend*."

"I have no doubt. I'm just relieved."

"Relieved? About what?"

"It's silly." He looked down at the ground and then up at her again with hopeful eyes.

She smiled, which he must have interpreted as encouragement, because he slowly reached out and touched her shoulder. Her skin pulsated with desire beneath his fingertips.

"I doubt anything you'd do would be silly," she purred.

He ran his hand down her arm, and she bit her lip in eagerness. Then, as if suddenly spooked, he pulled away and looked down at the cement. "I don't deserve your kind attentions," he said, shaking his head. "Maybe I'm not the person you think I am."

"Why don't you let me be the judge of that?"

He looked back up and stared into her eyes with an expression she interpreted as a cry for understanding and forgiveness that touched her heart. Setting aside her earlier misgivings, she inched closer, her hunger for him growing. He lifted his hand and ran it slowly through her hair, studying each strand like it was something he'd never seen before. She moaned softly and ran a finger along his cheek to where it brushed against the bristles of his beard. The air between them grew electric with anticipation.

"Camarita…"

"There you are! The waitress said you came out here. What the hell is going on?"

They sprang apart as Wynan and his partner bolted over. These interruptions were becoming an annoying habit.

"He's fine…now. Not so much under your watch. I brought him out here to get some air and get some food into him."

"That was very thoughtful of you, Cam," Wynan said, striking a more amicable tone than she'd heard from him before. "Frankly, I'm ashamed I didn't pick up on it myself. Oh, I'm sorry. I never introduced you to my husband, Austin."

"A pleasure," said Austin.

Cam attempted a handshake but he surprised her by lifting the back of her hand to his lips for a kiss. Why couldn't her editor be half as charming as his mate? She mock-curtsied and then returned her attention to Wynan.

"Don't blame yourself. As I was telling Mr. Fletcher, it happens here every night. People get so wrapped up in the music, they overindulge without realizing it. Maybe you should get him home and into bed so he can sleep it off."

Wynan nodded. "Thank you, Camarin, for both your compassion and, I trust, your discretion. I'll see you tomorrow."

"We'll continue our discussion at the office," added Fletcher, sending a frisson of excitement coursing through her body. "Enjoy the rest of your evening."

She winked and headed back to face the pandemonium inside.

CHAPTER
14 15 16

CAMARIN ARRIVED AT the office early the next morning, bearing two espresso macchiatos, one for her and one as an overdue gift for Rachel. She hoped the caffeine would revive her after a sleepless night analyzing another flirtatious encounter with Fletcher. Had she overstepped? Would he even remember now that he was sober? This has to stop, here and now, she decided. He was off-limits from this minute onward. She had more important things on her agenda, such as the research she planned to delve into before Wynan shut her down with some other lame-ass story to edit.

"You're a bit *Liz*, aren't you?

"Don't tell me," she said, setting one of the coffees down for the receptionist. "Liz…Liz…Liz Hurley…early?"

Rachel gave her a little clap. "I knew you'd catch on and, look, it's only Wednesday. You'll be moving to East End of London before the end of the week! And thanks for the *sticky*. Sticky toffee, coffee. But I'm sure you'd already figured that out. What's the occasion?"

"It's thanks for the brainstorm you gave me yesterday," she said as she wrenched open the door to the inner offices. "I'm going to suss it all out now and see where it leads me."

"Well, take these with you." She pulled out a box of business cards from her top drawer. "They arrived yesterday, just after you left. Makes you oh, so official. Should I bow in your presence?"

One raspberry later, *Trend*'s newest—and only, she mused—card-carrying investigative reporter sat down at her desk and signed into her computer, skin tingling with anticipation. She immediately googled the *San Diego Union-Tribune* and then the news for the week of January seventh, the date when Mangel's traveling body-acceptance circus rolled into town. Not until Thursday's issue did she uncover anything even slightly nefarious: the disappearance of Morgan McGee, owner of a local lingerie store. Not really what she was looking for. She was about to change course, but on gut instinct, she further researched the owner's name and uncovered a line of advertisements announcing McGee as San Diego's 'girdle queen.' *Huh, I didn't know they still made girdles.*

Intrigued, she kept reading through the week's issues. She was rewarded when she reached Saturday's edition. Splashed on the front page was a gruesome picture of McGee's squashed and nearly unrecognizable body. Spurred by a combination of horror, anticipation, and triumph, she read the accompanying story.

Murder's a Cinch: Girdle Queen Found Squashed on Vista Porno Set
by Dora Lewis, special to the Times Union

January 12: The owner of ten San Diego-area lingerie stores was found dead Friday afternoon on a soundstage in Vista. Morgan McGee, 47, of

Chula Vista, was reported missing by her husband on Thursday. She was discovered by the production crew of Sunshine Studios, crushed underneath a steamroller being used as a prop on the adult film, "Hardhats and Hardbodies 3." McGee was pronounced dead at the scene.

An autopsy is scheduled, but Mordechai Weiss, the death investigator, told this reporter that the probable cause of death was a combination of suffocation, drowning due to ribs piercing the lungs, and trauma due to broken bones. With McGee's crushed skull making identification through dental records impossible, authorities said Gill McGee, the deceased's husband, identified the self-proclaimed Girdle Queen by the color of her hair and the dress and underlying signature girdle they peeled off the corpse. "It was gold lamé with tiny diamonds," said McGee. "I'd know it anywhere...and would like it back, if at all possible."

"We needed to move the vehicle to film an orgy scene but boy, were we surprised with what popped up," said Dick Pierce, male lead on the film. "She was flatter than a pancake. You couldn't even make out her face. I guess she found that to become really thin, heavy machinery beats out Spandex any day of the week."

Funeral services are scheduled for Tuesday at St. Thomas More Catholic Church.

A fitting end for someone who spent her life forcing women into stifling garments.

Though it seemed patently immoral to revel over something as tragic as a lingerie store owner's death—or any death, for that matter—Camarin wouldn't allow Monaeka's cynical voice to squash her excitement over this new discovery. Could this be the beginning of a pattern?

Pursuing her theory, she virtually tracked Mangel's trail, and sure enough, death followed the caravan wherever they set up their tents. Two weeks after the McGee story ran, Camarin found the *Los Angeles Times'* account of another tragedy befalling someone in the weight loss or self-improvement industry.

Police Move Ahead in Disappearance of Fat Boys' Camp Owner

By Zoe Miller

January 21: James Masterson, owner of the Twenty Pounds Off Camp for Boys, was found decapitated yesterday on the grounds of his thirty-acre facility in Thousand Oaks. His head, found about thirty feet from his body, had been partially eaten by local wildlife. Authorities made a positive identification using dental records.

Masterson's wife, Amy, told the Times that she had no idea of the killer's identity since her husband had been well-liked throughout his fourteen-year tenure as the camp's owner. "We've helped more than 1,600 chunky boys change their lives for the better since we opened. That's more than fifteen tons of unwanted pounds. Maybe someone was angry that they gained the weight back, but we're very clear in our contract, in life there are no guarantees."

Want to lose ten pounds of ugly fat? Chop off your head.

Camarin ignored Monaeka's irreverent comments and continued her research.

In Phoenix, the victim was the proprietor of a store that specialized in weight-loss supplements. She was discovered collapsed at her desk, having overdosed on a bottle of her own stimulants. Camarin wasn't sure if she fit the modus operandi since it could have been your standard drug overdose, but her heart continued to pound with the thrill of the digital chase.

The *Santa Fe New Mexican* reported the untimely demise of a high school principal in Pojoaque. He had made recent headlines by denying special services, like a wheelchair, to a student who ultimately dropped out because she was too obese to hike up the hill from the bus drop-off point to the school's entrance. The principal was found bound, gagged, and half-eaten by maggots in a six-foot ditch on campus— the beginnings of the school's future outdoor swimming pool. Definitely hard to climb out of that one, thought Cam.

She started searching the *Dallas Morning News* when Wynan finally wandered in around nine-thirty AM, holding a venti-sized coffee from Starbucks. She attributed his pallor to one hell of a hangover. He invited her into the war room, and she followed, fearing the worst. Had Fletcher confided in him about their near-kiss? Was he going to fire her for fraternizing with the boss? She sucked in a deep breath and braced herself for whatever tongue-lashing awaited.

"How are you feeling this morning?" he began, sounding upbeat.

"I'm good, thanks. You?"

"Camarin, I won't beat around the bush," he said, dispensing with formalities. "I was way out of line the last few days, and I'm not above apologizing. Lyle and I had a long talk last night after we left the club, and he filled me in on a few details I was unaware of…that encounter on the railroad platform with the Kit Kat girl for one. I had no idea."

Camarin felt herself blush but said nothing.

"That showed a lot of character. It showed…a level of compassion for the disenfranchised that's frankly missing from most people's playbooks. Kudos for that. There's something you must know. About me…" He took a gulp of his coffee. A long pause followed.

"What's that?" Her curiosity piqued, she didn't want him to change his mind about opening up to her.

He set down his cup and looked her straight in the eye. "When I was younger…in boarding school in Connecticut…I came out early. I knew who I was and what I was around the time I turned fourteen. What I didn't realize was how other boys would react, how threatened they'd be by that. I…I never dated. I never spoke about being gay to other students. I kept to myself. But still…"

Wynan paused again and took another sip of his Starbucks. Camarin noticed his hands were shaking. "It's okay. You don't have to tell me," she said, but he waved her off.

"One Saturday night, a pack of drunken, rowdy seniors broke into my dorm room, looking for a fight. They beat the living shit out of me. After they'd had their fun, they warned me to pack my bags and drag my faggot ass off campus by morning, or they'd finish the job."

"Oh my God, how awful." Her heart went out to Wynan, whom she started to see in a totally different light.

"I sat in my room, shivering and bloody, trying to figure out if I had enough money to buy a plane ticket back to Amsterdam, when this skinny kid from down the hall peeked in. I'd never spoken to him before. He asked if I was okay. I said I didn't really know. Then he came in and sat on the bed beside me. We just stayed like that for about twenty minutes, silent, thinking. Finally, he looked over at me and asked, 'Do you know the names of the kids who did this to you?' I nodded, and he told me to write them down on a piece of paper."

"And then what happened?" Camarin's could barely hear herself over the throbbing in her temples. It was as if she was in the dorm room alongside them.

"I don't really know. I never saw those ruffians again. I assume they were expelled. That boy—as you might have already gathered—was Lyle. He and I roomed together until graduation, and he guarded over me like a Doberman Pinscher. No one even threw another sexual epithet my way, much less laid a finger on me."

Camarin nodded, wiping a tear from her eye. She was torn between her sympathy for Wynan and admiration for Fletcher.

"I tell you this for two reasons, especially since Lyle is far too modest to tell you the story himself. One is that, like you, I have a deep appreciation for those who deviate from the mainstream, primarily because I count myself among their ranks. As well as a soft spot for anyone who grasps the extent of the challenges we go through each day. And second, I wanted you to understand why I'm so overprotective of Lyle. Why I gave up a senior position at *Business Day* to help him run this piece of dreck. He stuck his neck way out for a kid he'd never met. I will always be there to pay back the favor."

"I do understand, better than you know. Mr. Fletcher also extended himself for a stranger when he offered me this job, and I don't take kindness like that for granted. I have no intention of letting him—or you—down. I just need you to trust that my intentions are good and what I don't know, I'll learn. Or die trying."

"Well, work ethic is all well and good, but please, no dying," Wynan said with a laugh. "I'm hoping we can start over. Lyle says you want to research stories dealing with body acceptance. I have an assignment that might interest you. Have you heard of Perri Evans?"

Her heart jumped. "The country singer? The one who won *American Dynamo*?"

"The very one. Ridiculed for competing at over three hundred pounds and still beat the odds. She's got a new album coming out next month, and she's starting a publicity tour. I'd like you to go to DC and interview her Saturday afternoon. Take the Acela down early in the morning, return home in the late afternoon. I know it's over the weekend, and I can't pay you overtime, but I'll try to make it up to you some other way. Sound good?"

"It...it sounds great," she stammered.

"I'll leave the background material on your desk later. And I'd be open to hearing any other story ideas you might have. Speaking of which, Lyle mentioned you're also pursuing some research concerning the Blubber Be Gone murder. Have you come up with anything so far?"

"Not really," she hedged, not wanting to divulge anything until she was sure—sure that Wynan was on the level with this generous offer, and positive that the pattern of destruction continued through Mangel's tour stops to Dallas and St. Louis.

"Well, let's leave that investigation to the police, shall we? There are plenty of more interesting—and safer—stories out there to keep you busy. In the meantime, I do have some more pieces that need your editing assistance."

"No problem," she lied. She knew it had all sounded too good to be true.

While she appreciated Wynan handing her more editorial freedom, she wasn't about to just set aside what she'd learned up to now. She'd find a way to continue to research the connection between Mangel and all these murders without the editorial director becoming any the wiser.

"Just one other thing..." he said.

What now? Camarin bit the inside of her lip and waited.

"If you come up with a story idea that I feel diverges too far from our focus and would be better suited to a more serious magazine than *Trend*, say one of the wire services or *Business Day*, I reserve the right to help you get it placed over there instead. Under your byline, of course. Sound good to you?"

Her heart skipped a beat. This almost made up for them passing on the BBG story. Her name on a story for Reuters? Or the AP? Or *Business Day*? What a coup that would be! But more importantly, she would have a larger audience to crusade for the rights of the oppressed. People who had been ignored and overlooked. People like Monaeka.

"Absolutely!"

"Great. Let's get to work," said Wynan. "We have a magazine to turn around."

CHAPTER

15 16 17

B ACK AT HER desk, Camarin tried to put off her fact-finding mission surrounding Terry Mangel's recent tour long enough to edit an article on the wonders of CoolSculpting. But as soon as Wynan headed off to the printers, she took advantage of the opportunity to research without reproach.

Sure enough, his last two stops before Chicago did not disappoint. About a week after the caravan pulled out of Dallas, a Realtor stumbled upon the lifeless body of Ramona Bernstein, the manufacturer of a line of low-calorie, low-carb frozen meals in nearby Trophy Club. Alleged cause of death: starvation and dehydration. She'd been tied to a chair in the pantry of an overpriced, and therefore rarely toured, home listed for sale, surrounded by packages of foods she couldn't reach.

And in Creve Coeur, just outside St. Louis, the victim was Claude Chapelle. He was the owner of Rez-de-Chaussée, a French restaurant that had been repeatedly sued for firing waitresses because of weight gain. Since weight was not a protected class, none of the plaintiffs won their suits, but the murderer got the last laugh. Chapelle turned up at a local rifle range, tied to a target, his limp, bloodied body riddled with bullets. *Guess you were fired too.* Whoever this killer was, he or she had an ironic and macabre sense of humor.

Cam leaned back in her seat, closed her eyes, and contemplated what she had stumbled onto. Her first story— a serial killing spree. All one-off local killings in small suburbs of big cities, which was probably why no one had recognized the connection on a national level. Or if anyone had, they had yet to go public with the information.

What next? She couldn't go to Fletcher or Wynan, not after they'd made her promise to lay off the story. Who could she call? The police? The FBI? Were they really going to pay attention to a cub reporter from *Trend* magazine? Probably not. More likely they would advise her to restrict her concerns to how Björk and Whoopi Goldberg were murdering fashion on a daily basis.

Maybe she could share her suspicions anonymously on the internet. But she had no street cred. She'd just add one more conspiracy theory to the millions already out there in the blogosphere.

And if she leaked her suspicions to CNN or one of the wire services, what would that get her? Nary a thank-you, much less any credit for uncovering the crime. And certainly no one would report the deaths in context, drawing attention to the real motivation behind them—the plight of those who wasted every precious minute of their lives hating themselves because of their weight.

No, she had to investigate this herself, figure out which of Mangel's followers had been so incensed by his rhetoric, he or she was singlehandedly eliminating the entities he railed against in his 'sermons.'

She mused at the irony. Here was someone garnering national attention for doing exactly what she yearned to do—pointing out the injustices waged daily against people like her sister. His propaganda espoused her personal cause to thousands each week, albeit for his own financial gain. His convictions made Mangel her comrade in arms, but his greed, her enemy. Alas, in the pursuit of justice, she was going to have to besmirch their shared cause by exposing the calamity his words had inspired. Sort of like cutting off your foes to spite your case.

"I don't pay you to doze off on the job, Ms. Torres."

Startled, she opened her eyes. A long night's sleep seemed to have done wonders for Fletcher. The twinkle in his eyes matched his facetious tone.

"You don't pay me to fetch you chicken wraps after-hours either, but I do what needs to be done. That is what you pay me for."

"Touché. Thank you for last night. You were a lifesaver. Would you care to join me in my office so we can continue our discussion?"

"Of course, sir. I'll be right in."

Cam decided by his officious tone that he'd written off their momentary flirtation as a drunken hallucination, and for the moment, she was in the clear. She strolled over slowly, determined to retain her cool, all the while silently repeating her vow to keep things one hundred percent professional.

A few moments later, she knocked twice, then pushed through the door he'd left ajar. Before her, overwhelming the room with a burst of color and sweet fragrance, was a vase filled with about two dozen wild rainbow roses, a mélange of purples and pinks, blues, reds, and oranges. Entranced by their beauty, she approached the desk, leaned over, and sniffed deeply.

"They're lovely, aren't they? Something to brighten up the office," Fletcher said, emerging from behind the door she'd just opened.

"They're so beautiful. I've never seen anything like them."

"Ditto," he said, joining her by the flowers.

She could feel his breath caressing her hair, his cologne as sweet as the floral tones of the bouquet. Her breath grew shallow, and her chin quivered.

"You can consider them a thank-you gift, if you like," he whispered into her ear.

She turned by a quarter, so she could stare directly into those soulful blue eyes, daring her to let down her guard, forget the magazine he owned and what causes it supported, and indulge in their mutual yearning. While she wanted to stand firm in her resolve against discrimination, her impulsive streak beckoned her to explore the one thing she realized she wanted even more.

She smiled and held up a finger. "Just one second."

She took two steps back and pressed the door shut, checking to make sure it was locked.

"I just don't want your executive editor interrupting us again."

"You want this to be strictly Hans off?"

She grinned and slinked closer. "I'm just grateful for the thumbs-up," she murmured, sliding her arms around his neck.

He ran his fingers down the sides of her dress, lingering at her hips. So close, so warm; he felt as good as she'd dreamt he would.

He's going to feel those rolls of fat. She tried to ignore the voices, and instead focused on his lips, slightly apart, plump and tempting. She leaned in, unable to resist their lusciousness any longer.

To her dismay, he suddenly froze in place like a statue and then took a step backward, extricating himself from her embrace.

See, he was never really interested. He knows you could blow up like a balloon after your next meal.

"You know you don't have to," he said, almost teary-eyed, his voice tinged with desire and dread. "This has nothing to do with your job. And if you choose to leave right now, walk back to your desk...I'd never hold it against you."

"Pity," she whispered, stepping forward and placing her arms back around his neck, her face resting on his shoulder so her lips were at his ear. Their bodies were even closer than before, and she pressed her hips tight enough against his to feel his excitement, long and hard, rubbing against her. "I like having you hold it against me. Please don't stop."

"You're sure?"

"Positive."

Before he could speak again, she moved her head and pressed her mouth against his, enjoying the tickle of his beard. His tongue darted out to tango with hers. She luxuriated in his touch, her hands straying from his neck to press against the front of his shirt, which hinted at the muscular chest underneath. She unbuttoned his top button and then the next as his hands lifted her dress and palmed each of her ass cheeks, forcing her closer still to his throbbing member.

And then the phone rang.

"Ignore it," she whispered, drunk in the moment.

They continued their heated grasping and groping through four rings, relieved when the noise ended. But when Fletcher's cellphone started vibrating immediately afterward, the mood was broken. They reluctantly relaxed their heated embrace.

"I'm sorry. It might be important. I have to take it."

"I understand," she lied.

She smoothed her dress and regained her composure. Maybe it was for the best anyway. He obviously thought work was more important than any potential romance, and of course, he was right. She had no business flirting with her boss, especially when she was on the verge of making a major breakthrough on the BBG case.

"Dinner tonight?" he asked Cam as his cell buzzed a third time.

"Thanks, but I can't. I have work." For once she was grateful for the excuse. Time to cool down, reflect.

She turned and walked out as he answered his goddamned phone.

CHAPTER

16 17 18

CAMARIN STUMBLED BACK to her desk, trying to steady both her breath and her pulse. What the hell was she thinking? Sure, he was hotter than Hades itself, but she had to shelve those desires, at least for now. This was her first job, and he was the publisher of a major publication, whether or not she agreed with its content. If this blew up in her face, it could ruin her reputation in journalism circles forever. Her writing—and the Mangel murders in particular—had to remain foremost on her agenda, and right now, she needed to decide on her next move.

Rachel sauntered by, sporting a Cheshire cat grin. "I couldn't help but notice, that was kind of a long *central* you and Fletcher had, eh?"

Camarin was too dazed to attempt to decipher on her own. "Huh?"

"Oh, please, I thought you'd gotten this. Central heating. Meeting."

"Go *Peking* yourself," Camarin said, apparently coherent enough for verbal sparring. "That's Cam rhyming slang, and I'm willing to bet you can figure it out."

"Ah, suit yourself, but you still owe me a drink, young lady. How about after work tonight? We can have a chin wag then."

"You like piano music?" *Why not? The cat's out of the bag about Job #2 anyway.*

"Well enough, I suppose."

"I work at Benji's nights, bartending. It's over by Times Square, inside the Laidlaw Hotel. Stop by early, around six, before the crowd floods in. First one's on me."

"Sounds like a *Manfred*. Manfred Mann, plan. I should come around your desk more often. By the way, your lipstick's all smudged. You might want to fix that before anyone else sees you."

"Got it, thanks."

"Apparently, you did. At least someone's getting some. See you anon."

Camarin pulled out her phone and reversed the camera app to turn it into a makeshift mirror. What a mess! Thankfully, no one except Rachel had seen her. Could she count on the receptionist keeping the secret to herself? Only time would tell; time and perhaps more than one drink tonight.

She spent a few minutes primping, erasing all evidence of her earlier indiscretion. Then she returned to researching all things Mangel before Wynan could drop off another inane editing assignment or thoughts of Lyle could again destroy her concentration.

Thinking proactively, she checked the upcoming schedule of the Feel Good About Yourself revival. Philadelphia, this Friday. Only about a ninety-minute train ride away. She could attend over the weekend and no one at work would be the wiser—no need to incur any embarrassment if her hunch was off. It was a perfect opportunity to see what's going on firsthand. Talk to some of the attendees. Figure out possible suspects. And, if she played her cards right, maybe solve the case before the next issue's deadline. Surely if she fingered the killer, *Trend* would have to print the story.

She felt the pins and needles again in her fingers and toes. No doubt jitters over the possibility of tackling her first major case. Then she glanced down at the admission price: a steep five hundred dollars. Apparently, whoever said self-esteem was priceless hadn't met Terry Mangel. It took two weeks' worth of tips at Benji's to earn that much money, which normally covered a hefty slice of her share of the rent. Wasn't going to happen.

Time to think this through. She could ask Annalise or DeAndre for a loan, but no, they were as strapped as she was. Her mother? Ack, Cam didn't want to deal with the aftermath of *that* request—the questions, the arguments, the debates—especially when her mother realized the revival was a gathering of people promoting self-acceptance at any size, the antithesis of everything she stood for. Cam could already hear her mother's objections ringing in her ears: *"You don't want to be part of a group of outcasts, do you? The 'right' people might shun you, and then how will you ever find a man?"*

She banged her fist on her desk, trying to summon a solution to reveal itself. And in her signature slapstick style, the side of her palm grazed the side of her box of business cards, which toppled to the floor. She stared down at them, a tiny smile spreading across her lips. *Si Yu'os Ma'åse!* God is merciful, she thought as she scooped up the mess.

Thinking back on her Journalism 243 course, Research and Resourcefulness, she phoned the *Philadelphia Inquirer*'s advertising department and asked how she could reach the Mangel administrative team. Since they'd advertised in the paper, the *Inquirer* had to have some type of contact information. They hemmed and hawed until she told them that it was the revival ad in their newspaper that inspired her idea to interview Mangel for *Trend*. Wouldn't it be a nice plug for the *Inquirer* if she mentioned that fact to the powers that be? Perhaps they'd consider an entire campaign? The *Inquirer* concurred. Ah, the power of self-interest.

She called the number they'd provided, identified herself as the senior reporter for the magazine, and reached April Lowery, the lead public relations director for Mangel Enterprises. *Could Terry Mangel spare an hour for an interview on Sunday morning?* Camarin asked, reminding Lowery that *Trend*'s more elite, high-income readers would surely clamor to learn how to lift their self-image, no matter what the cost. Lowery put Camarin on hold for five minutes and then confirmed the interview for eleven AM Sunday.

Oh, and by the way, Cam asked as an aside, *would it be possible for her to arrive Friday and experience two nights of the revival for herself? Background for the article and all.* Lowery agreed it was a terrific idea, and said that a press pass would be waiting at the ticket window. All she needed to do was show her business card. The publicist did advise that Mangel Enterprises would require final copy approval of all manuscripts, but Camarin saw no problem, since she had no plan to actually write the article. That's that, I am on my way! she thought, bopping up and down gently in her chair.

She spent the rest of the day alternating between editing a hard-hitting news story on *Choosing the Right Toenail Color to Reflect Your Mood* and preparing for her upcoming trip to Philly. She located a cheap Airbnb, brainstormed some sample questions for Mangel, and even considered some ways to approach her fellow revival attendees.

When she looked up from her monitor, it was past five, and most of the other staff had already left. She realized that she had almost completely blocked any lascivious fantasies about her boss from interfering with her day. She rewarded her singlemindedness with a virtual pat on the back, lifted her bag from her lap, and ran out the door to meet Rachel.

Benji's really didn't get hopping until after seven-thirty PM. Only a few diehards stopped by for happy hour, and DeAndre would occasionally entertain them by playing requests while warming up for that evening's show. When Cam arrived just past six, he was chatting enthusiastically with Rachel, who had taken introductions into her own hands by draping herself face-up across the top of his Steinway.

"Well, there's our girl," he announced. "Better late than never."

Camarin gave her roommate a peck on the cheek and then mock-pushed Rachel off the piano. "No tantalizing the talent. He has a show tonight, and you're going to get him too razzed to concentrate."

"Well, if anyone would know anything about giving someone in the workplace the *Kournikova*, I guess it would be you," Rachel teased back.

"Don't even ask," Camarin warned her roommate. "You don't know what you'll start if you do."

"Once-over," a defiant Rachel said under her breath, loud enough for both Cam and DeAndre to hear.

"You never told me you had such a sexy coworker, roomie."

Rachel beamed at the compliment.

"Oh, please, Dee, careful what you say. She's like a stray cocker spaniel puppy. Give her something to nosh on, and she'll follow you around forever."

Rachel rolled from her back to her stomach and stared at the piano player, elbows bent and chin on palms, flirting unabashedly. "Mmm, you remind me of Taye Diggs and Shemar Moore, all rolled into one. I'd love to see who you look like when you're unrolled."

Camarin stuck her head between them. "Unrolled, he's a layer of tarmac—black, smooth, but easy to walk all over. As his exes have regrettably demonstrated on a regular basis, and which is why I'm intervening now. Hands off, young lady. I don't have time to pick up the pieces when this accident-in-the-making explodes in both of your faces. Clear?"

She reached out and palmed the tops of both of their heads and forced them to nod in agreement. Rachel rolled her eyes.

"Great. Glad that's all cleared up." Cam headed over to the bar. "In the meantime, what can I get you?"

"I'll have a fireball," said DeAndre. "So there's more than one thing up here that's red-hot and spicy."

"And I'll have a Blow Job. It's Bailey's Irish Cream—"

"Yeah, yeah, I know how to make it." Camarin frowned, reaching for the Kahlua and then the Amaretto. "We're low on whipped cream. Are you sure you wouldn't rather have a 'Fuck Me Behind the Piano During Your Break'?"

"Funny, funny girl." Unperturbed by her coworker's sarcasm, Rachel gingerly lowered herself from atop the instrument and squeezed in next to her newfound admirer on his piano bench.

Then, as if daring Camarin to intervene, Rachel ran one finger up DeAndre's arm while he played and sang Elton John's *Sacrifice*. Her caress caused him to miss a note or two, but he pressed on.

"I give up," Camarin said as she set both drinks on the Steinway. "Go at it like rabbits. Just don't say I didn't warn you."

She headed into the back room to grab a few extra bottles of Grey Goose. They'd need it tonight, with a mortgage bankers' convention in town. As she rummaged, she overheard a familiar voice out front that made her heart jump.

"Why, Ms. Thorsen, what a surprise seeing you here. Have you switched from super-receptionist to star entertainer?"

"No need to switch, Mr. Fletcher. I'm able to handle both. And I take requests. What can we play for you?"

"Do you know *The Most Beautiful Girl* by Charlie Rich?"

"That's an oldie, for sure, but I believe I remember it," said DeAndre.

He started singing, and Camarin strode out, right on cue.

"Mr. Fletcher, this is an unexpected treat. What can I get you?" She hoped her attempts to modulate her voice masked her delight. It was the first time she'd seen him since their memorable, heart-stopping kiss, followed by his unfortunate choice to answer his cellphone. Maybe his appearance meant he had decided to choose romance over work.

Play it cool. Play it cool. Play it cool.

"I thought we agreed you'd call me Lyle. And water, please. I've learned my lesson." He held up a large, brown paper bag. "Since you brought me dinner last night, I thought I would return the favor. Perhaps we might share it here at the bar."

Despite her earlier resolve, she couldn't help but admire his chivalrous gesture. "It's usually slow for another twenty minutes or so. I'd love to join you, though I may have to excuse myself to serve the occasional customer." She glanced over at Rachel, busily nuzzling DeAndre, who had given up rehearsing to practice his less orchestral maneuvers. "Or to gag from overexposure to the PDAs over there."

She ambled over to his side of the bar. He set the bag on a barstool and gave her his full attention, running his hand through her wavy, black locks and then winding a few strands around his fingers and pulling gently, just forcefully enough to show his desire for ownership.

She let out a gasp and tilted her head in the direction of his tug, a tiny display of submission. She was tempted, so tempted, to embrace him, but couldn't chance it. Benji kept his workers on a tight leash, looking for the slightest provocation to fire old-timers like Camarin so he could provide his regulars with 'fresh meat.'

"I can't," she said with a sigh, gently pushing his hand from her hair. "Not here, during work hours. I'm sorry."

"I am as well. But I understand." He donned a half smile, grudgingly lowered his hand, and reached into the bag to pull out dinner. "I hope you like lobster Newburg. Delmonico's usually doesn't do takeout, but I promised them a great review in *Trend*. Put that on your to-do list for tomorrow. I hope it's still warm."

"I've never tried any type of lobster," she admitted.

It must be two thousand calories. Really the last thing you need.

"Well, then you're in for a treat," he said.

He pulled a set of forks and a Limoges porcelain dinner plate and then spooned out some rice, topping it with the delicacy for her to enjoy. Then he dipped a fork into a succulent piece and brought it to her lips. Heaven. And the food was good too.

"Shit. First DeAndre slacking off and now you!" Benji's indignant voice crackled with displeasure from across the room. "Are we eating, or are we serving? Because any minute now, I'll have a room full of thirsty customers, who will be that much thirstier and pissed off because I'll have one less bartender to serve them."

"Cool it, Benji. I'm sorry. It won't happen again."

"Damn right, it won't. I'm watching you." He made a V with his fingers, pointing first to his eyes and then to hers.

"Hey, Benji, 2010 called and they want their hand gesture back." DeAndre interrupted his make out session long enough to crack wise.

"Shut up, piano man. You too can be replaced."

Fletcher turned in Benji's direction, and Camarin could see the outraged look burning in his eyes. She stopped him before he could utter a word. "Please, I appreciate the effort, but I really need this job. Thank you for all this. It was so kind of you. How does it taste reheated?"

"Anything can be delicious when heated up again. Didn't you know that?"

"I certainly hope so," she said, playing into his innuendo.

"Take it in the back and enjoy it during your break," he said with a smile. "Just bring the plate back into the office tomorrow. It belongs to Hans. I just wanted to come by, make sure your stomach was full, and wish you a good evening." He gave her a squeeze, kissed her on the cheek, and took off.

Pouting, she retreated into the back room to hide her care package until her seven-thirty break. To her surprise, Rachel wandered in right behind her.

"What are you doing here? No customers allowed. I'm already skating on thin ice as it is."

"You're no fun. How am I supposed to tease you about snogging the boss?"

"I didn't realize you noticed. Weren't you busy at the piano with your tongue halfway down my roommate's throat?"

"And I will be again, I assure you. But right now, he's off resting before his performance."

"Seriously, Rachel. You're my friend, and no one wants you to have *Oedipus* more than me…" She waited until her friend acknowledged her correct use of the one slang term she'd looked up in a Cockney Rhyming Slang dictionary online. "But I gotta tell you, he's been through a lot. His ex-girlfriends have put him through the ringer. If you're only looking for a one-nighter, look somewhere else. What he needs now is space and stability."

"Ah, ye of little faith. Trust me. I might flirt a good game, but I'm not looking to break anyone's heart. I really like him."

"Fair enough. Who am I to stand in the path of true…acquaintance? But take it slow. DeAndre is the closest thing I've ever had to a brother, and I'm going to rip apart the next person who hurts him."

"Hear you loud and clear. How about another Blow Job 'til the music comes back on?"

CHAPTER 18

L ESS THAN TWELVE hours later, Camarin found Rachel sitting across the kitchen table from Annalise, clad only in DeAndre's Foo Fighters t-shirt. So much for restraint. She didn't know why she was the least bit surprised.

"Good morning. I see you're chatting with the one roommate you didn't spend all night screwing silly."

"Well, look who's finally up," answered Rachel, mouth full of their generic version of Cap'n Crunch. "Smashing. We can walk to work together."

"Don't you have to stop home and change? Can't go into work wearing what you had on yesterday."

"No need," Annalise interjected. "She's my size. She can borrow whatever and send it back with you on Friday."

"Oh, lucky me. Today reporter, tomorrow messenger girl. Afraid you'll have to come up with a change of plans though. I'm not planning on coming home after work tomorrow." She grabbed a spoon and a dirty bowl from the sink, gave each a quick wash, and carried them to the table.

"Ah, do tell. Planning on spending a cozy little weekend with—"

"Mr. Wonderful?" Annalise finished Rachel's sentence.

Just what I need, two nosey parkers instead of one, Cam thought.

"If you must know," she said, carefully meting out a 110-calorie ounce of cereal and dousing it with the remaining drizzle of skim milk, "I'm taking the train down to Philadelphia. There's a weight-loss revival coming to town, and it might be the perfect place to catch the person responsible for the murder I'm writing about."

Rachel fidgeted uneasily. "Does the aforementioned Mr. Wonderful know what you're up to?"

"No, and I prefer that it stay that way. If I'm wrong, I really don't want to end my first week on the job with egg on my face."

"Of course not," said Annalise. "I'm sure Lyle could think of some other viscous protein that he'd prefer there instead."

Both girls broke into giggles, prompting Camarin to stick out her tongue. "Eww. That's just gross."

"Seriously, though, Cam, this can't be Wynan's idea of a first assignment. Have you ever investigated a murder before?" Rachel asked.

"Not a one," she said, oozing false confidence.

"Do you really think you should go alone? I mean, it could be dangerous," added Annalise.

Tag team nagging. Happy Thursday!

"It's a fucking Feel Good About Yourself celebration. The worst thing that's likely to happen is that they convince me I'm okay the way I am, and then, supremely secure in my 'okayness,' I dive into a box of Godiva chocolates on the train ride home."

Both ladies stared at her open-jawed, apparently unconvinced.

"It's your funeral," said Annalise, "but I am not going in black, I'll tell you that. Not when I have a chartreuse minidress I have been jonesing for any excuse to wear." She stood up, dumped her dishes in the sink, and squeezed Rachel's shoulder. "Come on, future roomie. Let's leave Nancy Drew here to figure out *The Secret of the Unwanted Weight*. I've got a lavender pantsuit with your name on it."

Rachel followed along and then looked back at Cam. "How are you going to do it?"

"What do you mean?"

"I mean, go to Philly when you have to be in Washington on Saturday? Wynan told me to ask you about your preferred schedule and then book the train tickets."

Camarin flinched from a bolt of shock as the memory of the Perri Evans interview resurfaced.

"Oh my God, I completely forgot. Fuck. Well, I bet I can do them both. Do you mind if I handle my own train tickets and you just give me the credit card to charge them to?"

"Hey, no problem. You can take over any chores of mine you like. I'll bring over the card when we're at the office. But really, you should think twice about going to Philadelphia at all. It's not safe. You're a recent college grad, not Wonder Woman."

Camarin's head started to pound as she watched Rachel leave the room, and her nerves began to tingle with anticipation, or was it dread? Did her travel plans reveal more bravado than brains? What was really the worst thing that could happen? Chat up some rich but depressed overweight people desperate for hope? Meet Mangel? Jot down some notes and come home perhaps better prepared to write the story than before?

She did acknowledge there was the tiniest chance she could incense the killer with her presence. After all, a writer for a fashion magazine probably represented the objectification he or she hated most. She'd have to be very clear that she was on their side, that she understood their issues and was slanting the story their way.

The most she had to lose was the cost of the train ride between Philly and Washington and two nights' stay at an Airbnb. And, of course, her pride if she was wrong about it all. One big excuse for Rachel and Annalise to taunt her from now until December. Oh well. She sighed. *Felis Påsguan Nochebuena!* Merry Christmas! Maybe Santa Claus could join in the joke as well.

CHAPTER
18 19 20

CaMARIN SLIPPED OUT the door early, leaving an unsuspecting Rachel tittering and gossiping with Annalise. She had no desire to eavesdrop on a detailed account of anyone else's sexual exploits, especially when Benji had cut her own prospects short the night before.

If she hurts DeAndre, I'll kill her. And if I don't get any soon, I'll kill myself.

Apparently, she wasn't the only one who had been left wanting. As soon as she entered the bullpen, she noticed the note on her keyboard. Without stopping to hang up her jacket, she unfolded the missive, fingers trembling.

Camarita,

I must head out of town to meet with some investors, whom I plan to lure to Trend with your bold plans for our new direction. I greatly anticipate reading your interview with Perri Evans. I'm sure it will be spectacular.

I am sorry last night didn't work out, but I look forward to dining with you again in the near future.

Lyle

In spite of herself and her better judgment, she felt the warmth spread from her face, past her heart, right down to her *bebe'*, which throbbed with desire. How she craved this witty, smart, supportive man who looked past spilt coffee and airborne pens, and nevertheless accepted her, encouraged her to explore her true self.

Perhaps she could take off an evening from Benji's next week and, instead, spend it sitting on his lap in some private space. Between their hungry kisses, he could spoon-feed her tiny dollops of caviar, and she could regale him with tales of her adventure with Mangel, assuming she made some progress this weekend and could justify having defied his order not to investigate in person.

She turned on her computer and typed *Amtrak* into the search bar. Despite her initial excitement, this Evans assignment certainly presented a major kink in her plans to cover the revival. She searched through train schedules and prices, crazed as a college senior studying for midterms. Her main concern: making it from Philly to DC and back Saturday without missing any of the second evening's revival meeting.

It turned out she'd worried for nothing. The cost of a roundtrip Acela ticket between New York to DC more than covered the cost of the cheaper, slower Northeast Regional local she was planning to take to Philly and back, plus the side trip between Philly and Washington. The surplus was even enough to cover her two nights at the Airbnb. Score! Even the schedules worked in her favor, with trains between DC and Philadelphia departing frequently enough to ensure she'd make the revival's seven PM start, even if her interview with the singer ran overtime.

She relaxed into editing the newest feature Wynan had sent to her in-box, a thought piece analyzing how the growth speed of the average female's fingernails equated to her life span. All hail the mystical powers of alpha-keratin. Almost as a joke, she shot off a sarcastic email to Wynan.

Any chance of including a sidebar on the dangers of biting your nails? Not only will it prevent you from predicting how long you'll live, it can lead to several illnesses, according to Google.

A few minutes later, she received a return message.

Not a bad thought. Put something together with a few original quotes, and I'll see if we have room to include it. Way to go. That kind of thinking is exactly how you transition a fluff magazine into something with a little more weight!

Apparently, nothing was too inconsequential for *Trend* to cover. No matter. Camarin sat back and grinned. Fletcher's unannounced departure aside, this flurry of love notes, new assignments, and unexpected pocket change had transformed what had started as a questionable morning into a terrific afternoon.

CHAPTER
19 20 21

THE NEXT DAY, over lunch at ToFusion, Camarin tried to concentrate on Rachel's blathering on about DeAndre this and DeAndre that, but she could think of little else aside from her own upcoming adventure.

"So, has he said anything? Do you think he's appropriately besotten?" Rachel asked.

"I really haven't spoken to him about you. I've been preparing for this trip." Camarin pushed her chunks of Tofu a la King back and forth on her plate. Rearranging them seemed preferable to eating them. Why had she let Rachel talk her into a vegan restaurant?

"You're holding back. You are, I can tell. You do that little thing with your mouth whenever you're lying."

Camarin flinched. "What thing with my mouth?"

"You open it."

"That's ridiculous. Take that back!" She skewered a piece of tofu and then started mashing it to pieces with her fork.

"You know I'm only joking, luv. But you can be a bit of a *holy friar* at times. Take this trip. You're saying you're not nervous?"

"I'm excited. I'll admit that. Especially now, with meeting Perri Evans. She's the closest thing I've ever had to an idol."

"I'm not concerned about the warbler, worst she'll do is sit on you, all three hundred pounds of her. No, I'm worried about the bloke with the knife, carving fat off your thighs and *Khyber*."

Camarin blinked. "I'm sorry, I can usually follow your Cockney rhyming whatever, and I know what you're saying, but *Khyber*?"

Rachel bowed her head, feigning disapproval. "I really thought you were catching on. I'll take pity on you, just this one time. Khyber Pass, ass. Should have said *Aris*, short for Aristotle. Aristotle rhymes with bottle. Bottle and glass equals ass. Therefore, *Aris* is also slang for ass."

"Ah, fascinating. Well, I promise if I sense any trouble, I'll hike both my Khyber and my Aris right out of there. Happy?"

AT FIVE PM, Camarin stuffed her research notes into her backpack, ran out of the office, and would have made the 6:25 PM to Philadelphia an hour early had the subways been running. Turned out the entire system was in disarray, thanks to a noon derailment outside Canal Street. She ended up half-walking, half-jogging the entire three miles to Penn Station.

Sweaty and out of breath, with no time to even grab a diet soda, she found her track with a minute to spare. The car was packed, but she collapsed into an empty seat close to the restroom, closed her eyes, and willed herself to use the eighty-seven-minute train ride to calm her nerves.

Normally, the gentle rocking of the train would have lulled her to sleep, but her racing thoughts quickly put an end to any hopes on that score. Besides her concerns over tonight's mini-revival—the prelude to Saturday's spectacular—she wondered how she was going to get through tomorrow's interview with Perri Evans without fawning all over her like some star-struck idiot.

She reached into her backpack and pulled out her research notes, including a three-year-old story from *Bible Belter* magazine, the self-proclaimed official journal of the Christian-country music scene. It was the most in-depth portrait of Evans to date. It detailed the singer's dire adolescence, including a string of foster homes and a heroin addiction she overcame by substituting Jesus and food as her drugs of choice. Over the course of a year, she got clean but corpulent. She joined the church chorus, where everyone urged her to take her singing to the next level. However, because of her weight, she was laughed off the stage at most auditions. Nevertheless, she auditioned for, and subsequently won *American Dynamo*.

With that triumph. Evans had metaphorically stuck up her middle finger at every naysayer and fat hater out there who'd peppered their compliments about her singing with one or two obligatory digs about her size. Afterward, she disappeared from public view—and scrutiny—and no one had seen her on stage since. But why? That was the question on every fan's mind. This assignment from Wynan was quite the coup. Camarin hoped to return to *Trend* with the answers to not just one mystery but two.

She arrived exhausted in Philadelphia, eager to find a cab and begin her quest. Her Airbnb was only a few blocks from Fairmount Park, the site of the revival, and during the short trip, they drove past the enormous tents Mangel's roadies must have mounted only hours earlier. She awed at the hordes already storming the grounds, a full hour prior to the start of the event. A line at least four-deep extended from the tent's main entrance through the park and several blocks down the sidewalk.

She tried to do the math: thousands of ticketholders at five hundred dollars a pop. The calculations made her heart ache. What people would endure for even a soupçon of hope and acknowledgment. Everyone deserved acceptance, and it was her mission to make that widely understood. What wasn't necessary: people paying a fortune for it.

Just like you accepted me, Cam? Ditching me as soon as you could fly out east to college?

The cab pulled up outside a large, purple Victorian about two blocks from the Mangel masses. Mrs. Hawkins, one of the owners, led her to a clean room with two twin beds on the second floor. "You were lucky we had a cancellation. Every room in town is occupied by Feel Gooders. I bet the McDonald's in town is going to have a field day."

Camarin knew it was meant as an innocent comment, just a host trying to strike up rapport with a customer. But it took some self-restraint not to tear into this woman and remind her that everyone needed to eat, no matter what their size.

She changed out of her work clothes into a pair of comfortable jeans and a t-shirt, topped by a hoodie in case the late May evening turned chilly. Casual and a little baggy. Nothing form-fitting that might attract the attention or ire of other, heavier attendees.

Once she reached the park, she made her way past the hundreds of overflow spectators seated outside the main tent. Jumbotrons, accompanied by huge auxiliary speakers, were scattered throughout this secondary audience, lest even one person miss the ubiquitous commercials for Mangel-related products. Meanwhile, the line leading into the main arena slowly snaked forward. To its left, a unit of five employees manned a smaller pop-up canopy labeled *CUSTOMER SERVICE*. Cam headed their way.

She introduced herself to a chubby, raven-haired woman wearing a *Terry's Tubbies* t-shirt and pulled out her business card to exchange for a press pass. The worker, whose nametag identified her as Grace, asked her to wait and ran into the main tent. She reemerged with an attractive but anorexic, thirty-something brunette in a herringbone suit, carrying a clipboard.

"Ms. Torres? I'm April Lowery. We spoke on the phone." April held out her hand and gave Camarin's a firm shake. "Mr. Mangel asked me to personally escort you to your seat and to make myself available should you have any questions we can answer any time before or after your interview on Sunday. I trust your trip down was enjoyable?"

"So nice to meet you. My trip was fine, thanks for asking, but I made the train by the skin of my teeth, and the snack car was closed. Is there anywhere here where I can buy a salad or something? Perhaps some place where I might meet some of the other staff members and speakers?"

"I'm not sure that anyone will want to speak with you right now, while they're prepping for the event," said April after a momentary hesitation. "But we do have a whole spread laid out in the back for the staff. Come on, let's get you something before the action starts."

April walked Camarin down the main aisle of the tent, its eighty-odd rows already abuzz with activity. Several of the attendees held up signs like *In Terry's World, We Count!* and *Mangia with Mangel!* Others bounced beach balls around the arena, like at a rock concert. Each ball portrayed a picture of a happy face, cheeks filled with food.

When the two women reached the front, April led Cam through a flap in the canvas, back outdoors, and then into an ancillary tent that housed what appeared to be the heart and brains of the operation. In every direction, people were in motion—from those carrying mounds of t-shirts to the kiosks outside, to others testing the audio-visual controls or counting the evening's proceeds.

"The food's over here," April said, waving from ten steps ahead.

As Cam sped up to join the public relations exec, something in the corner of the room caught her eye. Two bodies, a man and a woman, half-hidden by a curtain, deep in spirited conversation. The woman's cheeks were stained with tears. Camarin watched, mesmerized, as the man, very average-looking apart from his savior-like white robes—similar in style to those of the exorcist that still plagued her nightmares—reached for the woman and pulled her to him. She pushed back at first and then yielded to his embrace and finally, to a kiss.

Must find her afterward. Figure out what that crying—not to mention that kiss—was all about. Exactly what kind of help did this revival profess to dole out anyway?

April tugged at her arm, like a retriever pawing its gun-toting master. "Ms. Torres, please. Have something to eat so you'll be able to concentrate on Mr. Mangel's oration. I don't want you—or your readers—to miss a second of his message or his followers' reactions."

She linked her arm with Camarin's and dragged her to the buffet at the back of the tent. It was an ostentatious display, better suited to an expensive wedding than a revival meeting. She bypassed the salmon cakes and pasta primavera, instead opting for fresh vegetables and salad. She didn't even stop at the dessert table with its elaborate selection of cheesecakes.

"The night begins with Terry welcoming his followers," April explained as they wolfed down their dinner in the ten minutes that remained before the lights dimmed. "It's always extremely inspirational. People get unbelievably emotional. Then he brings up one person to tell their story. Others also quickly volunteer to share, but he tells them to write down their thoughts and come back tomorrow night. Saturday's event is made up almost entirely of whoever wants to come up to the podium and relate their experiences. Or ask Terry for his blessing. You'll see—it makes for two quite memorable evenings."

"Are the crowds always this large?"

"This is about average. In LA, we had twice this number. In Santa Fe, about half. In general, the bigger the city, the bigger the crowds. But Terry was born in Philadelphia, so we usually draw a fairly sizeable and enthusiastic group here."

Grace, the woman from the customer service table, came up behind them and tapped April on the shoulder. "Lights at half, Ms. Lowery. You and Ms. Torres may want to take your seats."

April thanked her and escorted Camarin to a front-row seat, directly in front of the raised podium. The room grew dark, and the audience hushed.

Camarin pulled out her smartphone and turned on the camera.

"I'm sorry, Ms. Torres. No videotaping or photography is permitted. We will be happy to provide you with stock digital pictures of the audience for your story. Terry never permits himself to be photographed. He insists his message remain the star of the show."

"I assume that means no sound recordings either?"

"I'm afraid not. But feel free to use your phone to take notes."

A spectator from the row behind tapped her on the shoulder. "I'm sorry. Do you mind? I can't hear."

Camarin turned around to see a man whose heft took up two seats. "I'm a magazine reporter," she whispered. "If you're free later, I'd love to ask you your impression of—"

"Oh, I'm sorry, Ms. Torres," interrupted April. "We'll be happy to provide you with appropriate people to interview after the show."

Camarin scrunched her brow. "Appropriate? What do you mean?"

"You know, ones that have been vetted by Mr. Mangel." She lowered her voice so only Camarin could hear. "Sometimes, haters infiltrate our events. I wouldn't want your article to be tainted by people harboring an ill-meaning agenda."

"Of course not. I completely understand," she said, already plotting how to approach random Mangelites without her overprotective chaperone.

What exactly was his staff hiding? Perhaps those who'd realized that five hundred dollars was an absurd price for admittance. The real question was, would they feel ripped off enough to take out their frustration in some murderous fashion?

And the others—those who were the most electrified by Mangel's words—would they head off after the event to scour the streets of Philadelphia, searching for some diet-related merchant to sacrifice to the cause? She prayed that Saturday's headlines wouldn't fill her with the guilt of realizing that more persistence tonight might have paid off in spared lives tomorrow.

CHAPTER
20 21 22

SPRINGSTEEN WAS RIGHT, fifty-seven channels and nothing on. But this was more like 108. Fletcher stretched out on the hotel's king-sized bed, wearing a thick, terrycloth robe, head propped up on an assortment of feather pillows. He clicked mindlessly through the lineup, bypassing the news, the weather, sports, the endless array of juvenile comedies. The empty dinner dishes sat on a tray on the desk to the right, waiting to be taken outside the door for room service to retrieve.

He wondered how Camarin had reacted to his note. Would she be upset that he'd left town without a mention? Was the invitation to dinner too much, too soon? Why did this dating stuff have to be so complicated? Why couldn't you just say how you felt and then live happily ever after?

The ring of his cellphone startled him out of contemplation. A call after nine o'clock was normally not a good sign. He didn't recognize the number, but since it was past legal telemarketing hours, he figured it was legit.

"Fletcher."

"Mr. Fletcher, it's Rachel. From the office." Her voice competed with peals of laughter and piano music.

"Of course, I know which Rachel. What's up?"

"Mr. Fletcher…I wasn't going to call. I was going to butt out, but I can't stop thinking about it."

"Go on."

"I'm not one to tell tales out of school, but I'm concerned about Camarin."

Fletcher's heart took a somersault and ended up lodged in his throat. "What's happened to Cam? Is she all right?"

"She started reading up on that Blubber Be Gone killing and found other similar murders…she thinks it's connected to some weight-loss evangelist. I'm not sure of all the details, but she's in Philadelphia right now playing Mata Hari, and I don't feel good about it. I thought you should know."

He clutched his iPhone so tightly that his hand started to ache. "Philadelphia? We sent her to Washington to do an interview."

"I know…some singer…I believe she's planning to do that too. I just think she could get herself into a lot of trouble snooping around without a clue."

Fletcher could barely breathe. What was Camarin thinking, heading off without a word? When he'd specifically forbidden her from getting involved in investigating the murder anywhere but online. And stumbling onto something he'd sworn he'd never let her discover.

"Rachel, you were right to call me. I'll take care of it. Bonus in your paycheck next week for looking out for a coworker. Excellent job."

He disconnected the call, gave up a silent prayer, and reached for his laptop. Time to readdress the Feel Good About Yourself program, perhaps move up his plans. He needed to make sure there was nothing on the revival's website or sales materials that tied Mangel to Lehming Brothers. He couldn't risk any leads that might tip Camarin off to the connection. And then he would purchase himself a revival ticket online, under some anonymous name. Too late for tonight but he could make it Saturday. Hopefully in enough time to save both Camarin and the secrecy of his well-laid plans.

CHAPTER
21 22 23

T HE MUSIC WAS so loud it was practically deafening. Camarin covered her ears as *Fanfare for the Common Man* blared from the speakers only twenty feet to the right of her seat. The audience leaped to its feet, cheering and applauding, waving banners, creating a discord that could have woken Benjamin Franklin from his nearby grave. She shook her head. How did mere men grow to such power and reverence?

A spotlight split the darkness, and a short, thin milquetoast of a man, dressed in long, white robes emerged from the back of the tent and took his place at the podium. About forty, with a receding hairline and a small, black mustache, he resembled a shoe salesman who used to wait on her as a child back in LA. But she instantly recognized him from the *tête-à-tête* she'd witnessed only minutes earlier, where he had kissed his crying companion out of her despair. No surprise there.

The crowd grew even louder. Two enormous women screaming, "Terry, Terry!" stormed the stage, but security tackled them and led them out the side entrance.

He stood an extended period, reveling in the crowd's veneration, before he held his hands out, willing the assembly to settle down and retake their seats. The room grew silent for a long moment, waiting for their idol to address them.

"You're fat!" he yelled out at the crowd.

"Thank you. We're big, and we're proud of it!"

Camarin sat open-jawed, stunned first by his opening greeting and then by the hordes who screamed back in unison. She looked behind her and saw each person standing back up, fists held high in the air. Reading about Mangel from the safety of her office had been one thing. She could remain detached, like a researcher. But seeing the audience rise in solidarity, screaming for acceptance, for their—and for Monaeka's—deserved place in the world, set her nerve ends tingling. She fought back tears.

"You're pigs. You make me sick," he called out.

"Oink, oink," they yelled back.

"You need to lose fifty pounds!"

"You need to lose the fucking attitude!"

"Society is thin, so they're better than you!"

"Society is filled with fat haters. Shamers. Bigots. They're better than no one!"

The crowd erupted into applause and high-fived each other. Camarin was left shaking from the revelation that the surrounding audience spoke her language. It was as if the voices had left her head and taken residence behind and around her, that each cheering person was the embodiment of Monaeka. The flush of revelation overwhelmed her with its power.

Then she wondered, what if April Lowery noticed her reaction? Fighting to return to some semblance of an impartial reporter, she forced herself to type notes furiously into her phone's notepad.

"It's on the tapes that Terry sells!" April shouted into her ear, trying to be heard over the clamor. "He prepares them for lots of insults and feeds them tons of comebacks, forgive the pun. I'll get you a set of the recordings before you head back to New York, if you like."

"That would be great, thank you," she yelled back.

"I need to tell you a story," Mangel announced through his microphone.

The crowd instantly hushed, hanging on his every syllable.

"Who wants to hear a story?"

"We do!" they exclaimed as one.

She felt herself as captivated as the rest of the audience. Despite his commonplace appearance, his stage presence was magnetic, his charisma undeniable.

"It's a story about a young girl named Christina Corrigan. I never knew Christina, and I'm sure most of you didn't know her either. According to a lawyer named Sondra Solovay, who wrote a book called *Tipping the Scales of Justice*, Christina was a smart girl, a pretty girl, a girl with hopes and dreams like so many of your daughters. She had big ambitions, like working as a marine biologist and visiting Australia and its Great Barrier Reef. Instead, she died at thirteen, alone in her living room."

A collective gasp arose.

"The papers didn't seem to care about anything except her weight, which at the time of her death was 680 pounds. It was that weight that made her a pariah among other girls in the neighborhood, and a high school dropout. Why, you ask? Because her school wouldn't accommodate her inability to climb the hill to their entrance or install an elevator to help her—or any of the other students with mobility issues—attend classes on the second and third floors."

Camarin's ears pricked up, and she halted her typing, suddenly remembering her original reason for attending. No way to get to the school's entrance? She remembered the murder of the school principal outside Santa Fe, left to die in a ditch for the same reason. She had definitely stumbled onto something here. The question was, did Mangel inspire violence in each city he visited, or did he have homicidal groupies who followed him from state to state?

"Marlene Corrigan, her mom, did everything in her power to help her daughter. Everything the so-called experts told her to do. The doctors advised her not to feed Christina whole milk as a baby. That probably threw off her metabolism. She gained weight, more weight than the society around her felt comfortable with. Who here has felt the scorn of society?"

"We have, Terry!"

"Well, Christina felt it too. Her mother dragged her from doctor to doctor, who prescribed diet upon diet, but nothing worked. Sound familiar?"

"Too familiar!"

"Do diets work, my friends?"

"No! Diets don't work! Diets are the punishment society levels on those who dare to be different!"

Not to mention that diets are the tool that our mother—the one person we trusted to provide protection and support—used to manipulate us and impose her will. A constant reminder that we're nothing to any man except a face and a body, a present to keep tied up with a pretty bow for him to unwrap when the time is right.

"Another of Terry's mottos," April explained in Camarin's ear.

"So I gathered."

"She exercised. She tried Deal-a-Meal and diet pills. She did what she was asked to do," Terry continued. "And at seven years of age, that poor, beleaguered girl weighed 180 pounds. And do you think people offered her any sympathy?"

"No, Terry!"

"Did they show her compassion?"

"No, Terry!"

"Did they teach her to hate herself?"

"Yes, Terry, they did!"

"Well, life went on like that—with Christina alone at home, shunned by her classmates, hating every moment of her life. She was clearly suffering from a glandular condition that caused her to gain weight at an alarming rate, no matter what she ate. But did the doctors ever send her to an endocrinologist? No. To them, fat meant laziness, lack of self-control. Hand her a diet and send her home. Who were the lazy people there, my friends? Christina or the doctors who believed if you starved someone, it would solve everything?"

"The doctors, the doctors!"

She's lucky they didn't try to exorcise the devil from her.

"Meanwhile, Marlene, Christina's harried mother, who was recovering from the death of both of her parents, spent her days shuttling between homeschooling her daughter and working two jobs to make ends meet. She came home from running an errand one day to find lonely, overweight Christina lying stone-cold dead on the living room floor!"

The audience exploded into chaos. Through the pandemonium, Camarin pictured her own version of the Corrigan tragedy on the morning her mother and aunt discovered Monaeka's lifeless body, the blood-splattered room heavy with the scent of sulfur.

It took another five minutes before Mangel could continue his rabble-rousing.

"That's not the worst part, my friends." He banged his fist on the podium for effect. Camarin braced herself, waiting for what could possibly be worse.

"No?"

"No. The police accused poor Marlene of felony child endangerment, of being responsible for her own daughter's death. The newspapers convicted that poor, grieving mother in the court of public opinion before she could even get a fair trial. Six years! If convicted, that's how long they wanted Marlene to rot away in prison for doing nothing more than trying to help her daughter gain acceptance from the fat-hating world."

Again, the agitation of the crowd forced Mangel to pause before continuing. Cam herself was shaking with upset over Christina, Marlene, and the closemindedness of the people in their world. For the moment, she was Monaeka, overcome by a need for justice. It was comforting that the entire room felt the same.

As she looked around to watch others commiserating, she noticed April looking at her strangely. She realized how her response to the revival could give her away. She forced Monaeka back into the narrow constraints of her memory, straightened up, and willed herself to remain still.

April, misinterpreting her reaction, smiled and gave her a sympathetic squeeze on the forearm. "It's okay. He has that effect on everyone."

"There's more," Mangel continued. "We will never know what killed poor, sweet, young Christina Corrigan. Marlene begged for a full autopsy, because she suspected heart issues. But what did the medical examiner do?"

"What, Terry?"

"A visual autopsy. Do you want to know why?"

"Why?"

"Because she was heavy. And because of those extra pounds, the investigation might have run overtime, and the examiner might have missed lunch. Or his golf game. So, they just gave Christina's cold, dead body a quick glance and forgot about her. Think that was fair?"

"It was not fair!"

"Think people are ever fair to fat people?"

"Everyone hates us! No one understands us!" the crowd yelled. Mangel again waited as the audience chanted, "Fairness for the fat! Equality for the enormous! Objectivity for the obese!"

Fairness for me. Camarin heard her sister begging for help from the depths of her consciousness and felt the familiar pain jab at her heart. I killed off my own sister, she admitted to herself. Whatever terrible things might befall her in the future, she deserved them all.

Her eyes started tearing, but she couldn't let April see. Instead, she stood again, did a 360-degree turn, and marveled at the froth that practically oozed from people's mouths. Mangel had clearly hit a collective nerve with these forgotten masses. And at five hundred dollars a pop, he was being well-rewarded for his efforts. But to these people, could you put any price tag on the value of finally having their raised voices be heard? Their psychic pain acknowledged? She sat back down as the oration continued.

"In the end, my friends, I'm happy to say that fairness did prevail. Marlene was convicted, but only of a misdemeanor. She was put on probation and ordered to undergo counseling and perform community service."

"She was put on fucking probation for trying to help her daughter?" yelled one particularly outraged man in the third row.

"How about a conviction and community service for the people who turned their backs on Christina Corrigan?" a distraught woman screamed from the depths of the tent.

"I know you're angry," consoled the evangelist.

Of course they're angry. You've riled them up into a rabid mob. Camarin made a note to read up on the newspaper accounts of the Corrigan case. Despite Mangel's fire-and-brimstone condemnation, she was sure the truth lay somewhere between innocence and hyperbole.

"I can feel your fury. I join you in your outrage. They hate us!"

Us? All 140 pounds of you? You're part of 'us'? I think not.

"And do you know how we deal with their hatred, my friends? Do you know what they deserve, all those people out there who live to mock those of us who have the nerve to weigh more than their capricious charts allow?"

Here it comes. Camarin's heart pounded wildly. *He's going to incite them to go out and kill. This is what I've been waiting for.*

"We repay them with love. The more they hate us, the more we forgive them. The more they mock us, the more we embrace them. Because only with love can we get them to know us, to understand us, to realize that weight is about size, not character. Make them see that fat is not a pejorative. Fat is not a state of mind. It's an excess of intake over output, nothing more and nothing less. Only by inviting the haters into our world, urging them to spend time with us, allowing them to witness our daily struggles, will we neutralize their bias against us. Because what are we?"

Shocked, Camarin listened to the repartee between Mangel and his Mangelites. They seemed utterly, totally sincere in their outpouring of affection.

"We are more than just our bodies!"

"And how will we silence our enemies?"

"Through love!"

"I didn't hear you. How?"

"Through love!"

Mangel paused yet again until the racket his words inspired faded to a low hum. With the crowd simmering and the evangelist fanning down his inflammatory rhetoric, Camarin felt herself returning to her old, impartial self.

"That's right, my friends," he said, reaching for a cup of water. "I want to thank you for your faith. I want to thank you for your allegiance. And most of all, I want to thank you for your struggle. Every one of you inspires me every day. And that's why I want to invite someone up here to inspire everyone else with her story and her success. Is Maria here?"

"I'm here, Terry! I'm coming!"

As the roly-poly woman lumbered her way to the stage, April tapped Camarin on the shoulder. "Are you okay? You look a little out of it."

"I'm fine. I'm just a little surprised. That whole speech about love—it's not what I thought he was going to say."

"You're not the first to admit that. It's easy to get swept up in the message. That was me, once upon a time," she said, pointing out at the crowd. "Terry turned it all around for me. Once I lost the chip on my shoulder, I was able to shed the weight from my body. He's amazing. I owe him everything!"

Her words made Camarin realize there was an entire category of suspects she'd previously overlooked. His staff!

"That's fascinating. Tell me, would you consider allowing me to interview you for my story? I think the reasons that you and others like you work for Terry and follow him from city to city could make for a great sidebar."

April's entire face became bright and animated. "No one has ever asked for my story before. I'd...I'd be honored. Terry has been so wonderful to me, so much more than just a boss."

There was excitement in April's eyes, but also something more. Gratitude? Pride? Camarin couldn't put her finger on it, but given time...

"And the others? Are there others in Mangel's circle who might be willing to speak to me?"

"I'm not sure, but I can't see why not. We give our hearts and souls to this cause. When would you want to do this?"

She did some quick schedule calculations. "Maybe tomorrow, about five PM? That would still give people plenty of time to prepare for the evening's event."

"That sounds good. I'll put some thoughts down and see who else might be free."

Maria cleared her throat, ready to address the crowd, and Mangel faded back into the shadows. She looked so familiar, and it took a few minutes before Camarin realized where she had seen her before—the woman whose tears Mangel had wiped away prior to the event's commencement. Had they been merely an expression of fear over addressing the audience? And hadn't Mangel's kiss been a bit of an exaggerated way to calm a speaker's nerves?

"Hey, y'all. My name is Maria Whalen. I'd been out of work for over a year when I came to Terry." Maria's Southern drawl quaked slightly, as if the sound of her words over the loudspeaker unnerved her. "I had been working as a programmer for a cosmetics company, not even a position where I was seen very often by clients. But after talking to some of my thinner coworkers, I realized that I was being paid a much smaller salary than they were. There was absolutely no difference between my skills and theirs. If anything, I had even more experience and worked longer hours."

The room remained silent, eating up Maria's every word.

"I went to my boss and asked for an explanation. Why were they earning more than I was for doing less of a job? He didn't deny the fact that I had been discriminated against. He said if I didn't like it, I could quit. I told him I imagined several overweight employees in other departments might be curious how their salaries stacked up against those of their thinner counterparts. He fired me on the spot."

Camarin could see Maria's eyes tearing up. A familiar pang of nausea reminded her that it could have easily been her sister up there. How often had Monaeka complained about the inequities in life, like how it was hard to get hired when you're overweight? How tiresome it was to have every bite at every meal judged?

By choosing a college across the country, Cam had put some distance between herself and all that noise. She'd used her heavy coursework as another excuse to ignore her sister's ramblings. She felt her own tears well up as she recalled how the calls had come less and less frequently until one day they'd stopped entirely.

"I went to see a lawyer about suing the company to get my job back, but of course, he explained that I had no recourse," Maria continued. "He told me that anyone can discriminate against fat people in any way they choose. Which is ridiculous. I mean, no offense to anyone here, but I worked with smokers and their clothes reeked of tobacco. It made me sick, but as long as they smoked off-premises, they couldn't get fired for it. I worked with another guy, again no offense, who suffered from Tourette's. His work was top-notch, but every so often, he'd scream out a string of swear words, and frankly, it was disruptive as hell. But again, his job was protected. Me? My weight didn't disturb my coworkers or break anyone's concentration. But I was the one let go."

She stopped to wipe a tear from her cheek.

"I went to the papers, figuring it would make a mighty good story, one that might interest other people my size, get them to boycott the company. But the reporter said my story had no merit, wouldn't even speak to me. Turns out they got major cosmetics advertising dollars from my former employer. I was despondent. No job, no justice. But the day Terry's caravan rolled into Atlanta, everything changed."

Seated in the front row, Camarin could still see Mangel, standing several feet behind the podium, far from the glare of the spotlight. He seemed to be in deep conversation with yet another woman, this one quite shapely. He whispered into her ear, and she tilted her head back, laughing. Cozy. To the uninitiated, it looked as if Terry Mangel wasn't just staging a revival tour—he was auditioning his own personal harem.

"I listened to his insights, just like you're doing now. He was the first person who really understood what an overweight person like me goes through every day."

"You're not overweight! You're your weight!" cried out several persons from the audience. Others joined in, and for five minutes, the chant reverberated throughout the tent. Maria stood at the podium, basking in the group's support.

"Thank you, friends. You are right. Anyway, it was Terry who listened to my plight, Terry who offered me his shoulder to cry on."

I bet it wasn't the only body part he offered you.

"And it was Terry who offered me a job. For the last two years, I've worked with the Feel Good About Yourself revival, and I've never been happier!"

Terry retook his place along Maria at the lectern, kissing her paternally on the cheek and holding up her hand high above her head, joining in her triumph as the crowds went wild. For a minute or two, Camarin allowed herself to get caught up in the excitement, and then cynicism took hold again. *Check deaths in Atlanta two years ago*, she typed into her smartphone.

Mangel again addressed his devotees over the din as an army of hawkers entered the tent, peddling CDs, DVDs, books, t-shirt and mugs. "Thank you, Maria. Your story has moved us all. The important lesson is to remember that, in the end, what helped this lovely lady?"

"Love!" screamed the spectators in unison.

"Correct. Love cures prejudice. Love cures hate. Love cures all!"

He paused for another rabid ovation.

"My friends, your turn is coming. We want to hear your stories. We want to help you where it hurts. Come back tomorrow night for our Saturday night Feel Good About Yourself finale, where you'll do the speaking, and we'll do the healing!"

Mangel wallowed in the admiration of his fans until their attention was diverted by the peddlers. Then he and Maria disappeared from the dais, no doubt to count the evening's take.

April stood up and smoothed her skirt. "If you'll come with me back to the other tent, I'll introduce you around and get you some background material and a set of DVDs."

"That would be terrific."

But would it? In one sense, she was a bit in awe of the great, mighty Terry Mangel, especially up close. If he was anything in person like he was on stage, perhaps he'd see right through her to her core. But on the other hand, like *Trend*, he represented everything that she railed against, taking advantage of people's low self-image for his own financial gain. Would she be able to mask her scorn?

The two women walked out of the tent and into the cool evening air. Camarin breathed deeply. She hadn't realized how stuffy it had become inside, with all that outpouring of righteousness and angst. They made their way past a second outdoor legion of salespeople flogging their Mangel wares and back into the administration tent where they had dined earlier.

A celebratory vibe permeated the atmosphere inside. Corks popping, champagne flowing, the slap of high fives everywhere. Mangel was standing in the corner, with Maria lingering by his side. Camarin noted how many of the female admins in the tent were scowling and throwing an evil eye in the couple's direction. *Where's the love there?* thought Camarin. *I bet they have a story to tell.*

"Just help yourself to something to eat," said April, pointing at the buffet table and a newly added carving station where a waiter was serving up copious portions of turkey and roast beef. "I'll let him know you're here."

She started over toward the food but then, as if drawn by an invisible magnet, veered over to a group of women who appeared to be engaged in an impassioned discussion. They grew suddenly silent as Camarin infiltrated their ranks.

"Ladies, good evening. I'm Camarin Torres, and I'm a features editor with *Trend* magazine. I was wondering if I could—"

A heavyset African American woman shot her an acidic glare. "*Trend?* The magazine with all the skinny models and the articles that constantly remind us of how imperfect and damaged we are?"

"Unless, of course, we buy the products you advertise," added a little person, standing by her side. "Then we'll all be magically saved." She spat in disgust at the ground in front of Camarin's feet.

Stunned by their revulsion, Camarin realized that these spontaneous interviews were not going to be as easy as she'd previously thought. In this audience, she was the enemy, and no one was going to give a rat's ass about her magazine's proposed change of focus. She took two steps back, reeling from the vitriolic assault, and naturally, in true Camarin style, backed right into the person behind her.

"Oh, I'm so sorry. Excuse me," she said, spinning around and finding herself standing face-to-face with Terry Mangel himself. Up close, the facial lines looked more prominent, perhaps the price he paid for months spent on the road, galvanizing his followers.

"Ms. Torres, what a pleasure," he said, firmly shaking her outstretched hand. She heard a snort from the women she'd just turned away from. "Ladies, have we forgotten our manners and our motto? We treat everyone with love. Especially those who have taken time out of their busy schedules to cover us in national magazines."

The ladies blushed, murmured apologies, and backed away.

Much to her surprise, Camarin felt a jolt of electricity flow from his arm through hers. There was something undeniably mesmeric about this man, something that prompted people to want to follow his lead. She stood transfixed as his gaze danced playfully with hers, and she felt herself drawn to him.

This is ridiculous. He's a con man, a huckster, a false prophet. Walk away. Walk away now.

"Can I offer you a drink, Ms. Torres? Or some dinner? It was a long event. Surely you're hungry?"

"No, I'm good," she sputtered, aware of the heat blazing in her cheeks. "But if you have a moment, I'd love to ask you some questions."

"I know our meeting is set for..." He looked over at April. "Eleven AM on Sunday, is it?"

April nodded affirmatively.

"But for someone as lovely as you, I always have time for a chat."

He led her to a quieter corner of the venue, away from April, Maria, and the cackling trio of women who'd nearly attacked her earlier.

"You have my full attention, Ms. Torres. What do you think your readers would be most interested in knowing about our small—but growing—movement?" He flashed her his warmest smile, and while Camarin searched for even a smidgen of smarminess, she came up short. He seemed authentically interested, as if she were the only person in this congested, bustling space.

"I'd hardly consider this small. It's quite impressive. I wish something like this had been around when my sister was alive. I think she wouldn't have felt so...alone."

Where did that come from? She'd had no intention of sharing anything so personal with this charlatan. And yet, he made you feel so comfortable. Maybe she'd leaped to conclusions too early. Maybe he was legit, and all these women felt what she felt—a longing to remain in his circle. Maybe there was no hanky-panky involved. Maybe.

"It sounds like losing her...it must have been devastating."

"It was...I...well, listening to you, to Maria earlier, it all came flooding back."

"She was heavy, your sister?"

"Yes. She was on meds as a kid, and they messed up her metabolism. She struggled to lose the weight, but she'd go up and down. She never really felt comfortable in her own skin. If she could have only known someone like you...or like Maria..."

"Did I just hear my name being bandied about?" Maria sidled up beside Mangel and insinuated herself into the conversation.

"Yes, darling. Maria, meet Camarin Torres, a reporter from *Trend* magazine. She's come to do a story about us. Camarin, meet Maria Whalen, my fiancée."

Camarin's head drew back in surprise. "Fiancée? Wow, I had no idea. Congratulations!"

"He just popped the question tonight. I accepted, of course!" She bubbled over with excitement. "We haven't formally announced it, so please, it's off the record." Maria put up her hand and showed off her ring. It was a silver ring from a pop-top soda can. "It's a placeholder until we can pick out the real thing. But it will be something equally low-key," she said in a lowered voice. "Nothing that could draw attention away from our message."

"We trust you will keep our confidence. No one else knows, and we'd like to keep it that way, for now," added Mangel.

I bet you do. Wouldn't do for any of the other girls to find out, would it? No matter how she tried to trust Mangel, that cynical, distrustful, little voice kept popping into her brain. *Well, Mr. Mangel, your 'prey-dar' is off the mark this time. I'm immune to your charms.*

"Of course I will. Thank you for trusting me."

April came over and whispered into Mangel's ear.

"Ms. Torres, I'm afraid you'll have to excuse me. Pressing business. But I do so look forward to our chat on Sunday." He reached out to shake her hand again, but this time, he squeezed it tightly, and for a moment longer than necessary.

Then April led him away, leaving her with Maria. *Perfect.*

"Maria, I'm so happy for your engagement! How wonderful, and how romantic, traveling together from city to city." If she was the one killing off fat shamers around the country, it would be good to know now.

"I wish. That would be wonderful. But I have a sick mother back in Atlanta on dialysis. I fly in occasionally to address the crowds, but it depends on whenever I can arrange for my sister to take over for me at home."

"So…I'm confused. I thought you worked for Terry."

"Oh, I do. I work on the website. I can do that remotely. I expect that once we get married, I'll join the caravan. Though what I really hope is that he'll settle down, give up the tour. I've been trying to convince him that he can reach more people with webinars. I don't know why he's so opposed to preaching on YouTube. He'd reach so many more people."

And sell far less merchandise.

"How often do you join the tour and address the audience?"

"Oh, only occasionally. Though—" She lowered her voice again and pointed to her stomach. "I'm incubating a little Mangel, if you know what I mean. I don't think I'll be doing any more flying after another few months."

Ah, so Terry had to say he'd marry you. Interesting. Was that what precipitated the earlier show of tears?

Disappointed that her sporadic revival attendance meant that Cam had to cross Maria off her list of potential suspects, she decided to press her luck, gain more insight into the personal side of Mangel.

"It must be very difficult for you, with Terry on the road, surrounded by all these women, throwing themselves at him."

"I know what you're thinking—men will be men. But Terry's different. They might flirt with him during the revival, but at night, I'm the one he calls and pours his heart out to. I'm the one who will be standing next to him at the chapel—Mrs. Terry Mangel." She lifted her hand and pointed around the room. "Let them all eat their hearts out. He's mine."

Camarin snuck a glance across the tent at the evangelist, charming his minions, including a portly couple, their arms laden down with 'Mangelphenalia.' April was standing by his side, about two inches too close to make a convincing case for a purely professional relationship. Exactly what magical blinders was Maria wearing?

April caught her eye and raised a finger. She walked over to the side of the tent and returned carrying a Feel Good About Yourself tote bag, teeming with lovely parting gifts. "I've got some background information about Terry in here, along with his entire inventory of our goodies, including a price list. I'm sure you'd want to include a review of these items with your story, right?"

Subtle. Camarin flashed her best attempt at a genuine smile as April led her to the tent's exit flap.

"I've set some time aside at five PM tomorrow, as we discussed, and I'm still checking around for anyone else who's interested in being interviewed for your story."

"I'll be here. I think this is going to be an article that every one of our readers will be thrilled to read." And as she walked away, she added under her breath, "Especially the officers dressed in blue."

CHAPTER
22 23 24

ON SATURDAY MORNING, Fletcher tossed back two extra-strength Excedrin as he continued to search for answers, care of Google and his Dell Inspiron. What had given Camarin cause to visit the revival? How did she uncover the connection between Mangel and the Blubber Be Gone murder? And why would she take off and investigate without consulting him first? He'd specifically told her not to research anywhere but online.

Perhaps that was the answer—she couldn't consult him without risking being dressed down by the boss. He wanted to kick himself for ever encouraging her to pursue the BBG story in any capacity, virtually or otherwise.

He was well aware of the extent of Terry's empire, as well as the conglomerate that backed his manufacturing and got a cut of all sales. He had his own plans for Mangel—but better to attack when he was fully prepared. Then he would dislodge the Lehming Brothers wall of commerce brick by brick until the whole thing toppled over, and Margaret was finally avenged. Why did Camarin have to involve herself, especially now?

He looked past the hard sell on the Feel Good About Yourself website, searching instead for the address of the evening's meeting. Instead of the fundraising dinner he'd originally planned, now he had to go down to Fairmount Park and crash the revival. Make sure Camarin was okay, hadn't gotten in over her head. What to do after that, he hadn't a clue. As long as she didn't see him. That was key. If she thought he was hovering over her, doubting her skills or her motives, that could be the end of everything between them.

If his calculations were correct, she'd be chugging down to Washington around now, off to cover the Perri Evans interview he'd pulled so many strings to procure. The comeback story of the year. It had seemed like such a promising idea at the time, something to keep her mind off the murder she was so hot to investigate. Why couldn't that have been enough for her? A reason to drop the sleuthing and still crusade for the maltreated, their common bond. One day he would make her understand that deep down they were soulmates. But only if he could keep her safe long enough to listen. And if he could recapture his own soul, the one he'd blindly lost to the gods of revenge.

CAMARIN ARRIVED AT the Hay Adams Hotel at exactly one PM. If the interview took only an hour, she could make it back to the station by two-thirty, travel the two hours back to Philly, and return to the revival in time for her late-afternoon interviews. That was if everything went like clockwork. She walked up to the concierge and asked for Perri Evans. He rang, announced her arrival, and then sent her up to the penthouse suite. Perri was living high on the proverbial hog.

Three knocks, no answer. Camarin bounced up and down on the balls of her feet, anxiously waiting for her idol to answer. After another three knocks, the door finally opened.

She gasped, unable to hide her surprise. Perri Evans, the young woman who made it to the pinnacle of success wearing a size twenty-eight dress and symbolically telling the judgmental world *Up yours!* was staring back at her, looking haggard and anorexic in a wrap-style, silk dress. She took a deep drag on her cigarette and gave Camarin the once-over.

"Sorry to keep you waiting. I was putting myself together." Her voice, famous for its hillbilly twang, now sounded coarse and raspy, as though she'd smoked one pack too many. It was hard to believe she was still in her twenties.

"No problem." She held out her hand. "Camarin Torres. So happy to meet you."

Evans ignored the offer of a handshake and waved her inside. "I won't lie to you. They're making me do this interview. Said they wouldn't release my album if I didn't promote it at least once to the press. Make no mistake—I'm doing this under duress."

"Well, it's a lovely duress, if it makes you feel any better." Camarin winced at her own bad joke. Anything to break the ice.

"Is that supposed to be funny?" She slumped down on an easy chair, dress falling slightly open, revealing half a sagging breast.

"Not from the looks of it, no." Camarin sat on the couch opposite, determined to win the singer over. "But I must tell you, I've been a fan of yours from way back. Even before *American Dynamo*. And the reason was—aside from your amazing voice—you were so secure in your own skin. You didn't conform to what people expected, and I respected you for it."

"And so, your unspoken question is, what fucking happened, right?"

"Between you and me, totally off the record, yeah."

"Twats like you happened, that's what."

Camarin opened her mouth to protest, but Evans kept right on talking.

"Not you personally, of course, but all you fucking journalists and critics. All telling me what a great voice I had, if only I'd lose the weight. Contest winner or not, the record company refused to sign me if I didn't drop two hundred pounds. So that's what I did. But what I should have done was just release the songs over the internet like everyone else. Fuck the record companies. Fuck the critics. Plenty of people do just fine selling direct on iTunes, Spotify, YouTube. But stupid me, I believed my agent. Conveniently forgetting that if I released directly, she'd get nothing. Zilch. Lesson learned."

She glared at Camarin with daggers in her eyes.

"You know what really kills me though?"

Camarin shook her head, dumbstruck by the singer's wrath. Journalist or not, she was the last person who deserved Evans's contempt. More than anyone, she understood the injustice of having to lose weight to be socially accepted.

"I beat out thousands of other singers to compete in that contest, and fuck if I didn't win. I sang my heart out on national television in front of millions of viewers. And now, all that anyone at home can talk about is the weight loss. How did I do it? Doesn't everything seem better thin? People who didn't give me the time of day before, even with the TV show, are all nice to me now, like sugar wouldn't melt in their mouths. Fuck 'em all."

Evans punched her fist in the air, causing her sleeve to slip back, revealing bare arms ravaged by track marks. There was one question answered—how the singer had lost all that weight. Heroin was a powerful appetite suppressant, at least based on what Camarin had heard. Apparently, Evans hadn't kicked the habit for good.

"You want a drink? Mini-bar's yours. My apology for being such a goddamned disappointment."

Camarin knew she had three choices here: join Evans in her despair and drink herself blotto, pick herself up and leave, or the choice she decided on—get her story. "I'm good, thanks. The thing is, no matter what your size, I want to hear about the album. I want to know what you were thinking when you wrote the songs and what you hoped to convey to the listeners who buy it."

"You for real? You listening to anything I said? The album sucks. I suck. But at least I'll be skinny when I read the one-star reviews. 'Uninspired lyrics, tone-deaf delivery, but what an ass she's got on her now.'"

Camarin remained tongue-tied, Evans's self-denigrating remarks evoking snippets from her childhood with Monaeka to flash before her. Skipping shopping trips with school friends, because they wouldn't want to be dragged to the plus section at Macy's. Turning down an invitation to go horseback riding, because the mare might not be able to handle the excess weight. Always an excuse, a refusal to meet life head-on until 'someday' when the scale read a more acceptable number.

Maybe Mangel and his followers had exerted more influence on Camarin than she previously realized, but she couldn't endure another moment of Evans's defeatism.

"That's it. I'm done." She stood up, ignoring the singer's scowl. "If you want to wallow in self-pity, that's up to you. But I'm not leaving until you hear what I have to say. The world isn't fair. We all make mistakes. Pick yourself up, dust yourself off, and try again. In your case, lay off the drugs, eat every piece of cake you want, fuck the critics, and believe in your own musical instincts."

She felt the blood surging through her veins, her heart beating a million miles a minute. She was shocked by her own audacity, telling off a woman she'd once admired. Evans just looked at her, mouth ajar. She'd gone this far, no reason to stop before completing her speech.

"I spent last night in Philadelphia covering Terry Mangel's Feel Good About Yourself revival, and I'm going back there tonight. I can't believe I'm recommending it to anyone—Terry Mangel, in my opinion, is a greedy manipulator—but listening to his followers talk about how they lifted themselves up and made something of themselves would do you a world of good. If you like, I'll bring you with me. My treat. There's even an extra bed at my Airbnb. What do you say?"

Camarin waited for Evans's response, shaking with emotion, proud to have stood her ground. Evans remained silent, drawing her knees up to her chest and embracing them, rocking back and forth. Finally, she looked up, eyes bright with resolve.

"Do you know what I think? You come in here, my first interview in years, and have the nerve to bully me, lecture me, to tell me how to live my life. How dare you. Get out. Get out now before I call security."

Evans's words hit Camarin hard, not because of the singer's indignation or the lack of a meaningful interview, but because despite her passion, logic, and determination, she couldn't break through. Nothing she said had made a dent.

Camarin hung her head, utterly defeated, and sulked her way into the foyer. "I'm sorry," she said, staring at the doorknob. "I wished I could have been there when you needed me, Monaeka. Maybe I could have saved you. But nothing can save you from yourself now."

"Who the fuck is Monaeka?"

Camarin didn't respond. Physically, she was already in the elevator, pressing the button for the ground floor. Mentally, she was visualizing a graveyard filled with tombstones which all read *Dying to be Skinny*. All people who had put off living until thin set it, only to realize—when it was too late—that they had sacrificed happiness to please an army of faceless nobodies named 'society' who really didn't give a damn about them.

And hadn't she been equally as uncaring toward her twin, her other half? Her cross-country move may have divided her from Monaeka temporarily. But the mounds of dirt the undertakers slowly shoveled onto her grave had turned that separation into forever.

CHAPTER
24
23 24 25

B Y THE TIME Camarin arrived back at Fairmount Park
later that afternoon, she had banished her ghosts, at
least temporarily, and was eager for the evening ahead. If she
couldn't rescue Perri Evans, at least she could prevent the
future deaths of countless weight-loss advocates if she asked
the right questions tonight and trusted her instincts. While it
was hard to overlook the irony, since she and the killer were
at least philosophically on the same page, there was a right
way to defeat fat prejudice, and then there was the
murderer's way. Maybe Mangel was right—maybe the
answer really was love.

It was amazing how much prep work went into making
the revival look seamless. Behind the scenes, the makeshift
arena was a madhouse, people hanging huge banners,
stocking the sales counters with t-shirts and other
tchotchkes, laying out the beginnings of another massive
post-event feast.

She spotted April Lowery by the cashier in the
administrative tent, a roll of admission tickets in her hands.
"I'll be with you in a minute," she called out, "as soon as I
finish putting out a fire or two."

Camarin strolled by the buffet table, already stocked with sustenance for the roadies and the setup crew. She was so tempted to grab a churro, just a quick, late-afternoon pick-me-up. Then she touched her fingers to her tummy and thought better of it.

"I'm so sorry to keep you waiting," said the public relations director, all smiles after wrapping up her prep work and seemingly eager to claim some of the spotlight for herself. "Let's go to my trailer where it's a bit quieter and we can hear ourselves think."

April led her out of the tent and to the parking lot, where several massive busses housed the team when offstage.

"I share this with some of the other senior staff, but they're off doing sound checks, so we should have some privacy."

"How long will we have before any of the others arrive?"

"Others? Oh...oh, no, it's just me. I asked again and the other ladies...reconsidered. Wanted to keep a low profile, you know?"

"That's okay. I completely understand," Camarin said, all the while wondering if April wanted to keep the focus on herself or was worried that some of the others might say something untoward about Mangel.

If any of his followers were naïve enough to believe that Mangel ran a non-profit organization, the inside of April's trailer would have instantly set them straight. Everything screamed luxury, from the swiveling, black-leather recliners and side tables at the front, to four oversized bunk beds, piled high with decorative pillows to the rear. They settled down opposite each other in a diner-style booth across from the one-wall kitchen.

"Would you like something to eat or drink? We've got plenty to spare," April asked.

"No, I'm good. You don't mind if I record this, do you?" she asked, pulling out her smartphone. "I like to give people my full attention, not just scribble notes onto a pad."

"No, that's fine," said April, but her body language told a different story. She squirmed uneasily in her seat as Camarin hit *record* and left the phone in the middle of the table.

"Tell me, how was it that you joined up with Terry in the first place?"

The public relations director grew a bit dreamy-eyed as she reflected. "A few years ago, I was living in Tampa, alone, just another divorcee in her mid-thirties, working at this dead-end clerical job. My ex-husband? He nicknamed me Tonsils. 'She started out small,' he'd tell his moron friends, 'but once she swelled up, I had to have her removed.' Big laughs, all at my expense."

April nervously scraped the polish from her fingernails as she recounted her past, a clue that despite putting up a brave front, the memory still tore her up inside.

"I weighed about 140 pounds when he left me," she continued. "After that, my self-esteem hit the floorboards. Before you could say 'Pass the Cracker Jack' I was up to 253. I didn't have the energy to lift my spirits, much less a set of weights. All anyone could talk to me about was diet and exercise. It was like everyone had an opinion, but the only one that didn't count was mine. At the end of the day, all I wanted to do was put on my size twenty-two swimsuit and drown myself in the Gulf of Mexico."

Camarin shuddered in commiseration. First Perri, now April, resorting to drastic measures to dampen the hatred the world had thrust upon them and they, in turn, had thrust upon themselves.

"You're so thin now. And you seem so happy. What was your moment of epiphany? What changed to get you from there to here?"

"Terry, plain and simple. Terry is why I'm alive and here with you today. The thin part? That's just gravy. I mean, now that I'm happy, I don't feel compelled to stuff myself all the time, but Terry didn't tell me to diet. He taught me to love myself."

"How did you meet him?"

"When I was at my lowest point, my friends and family hosted an intervention for me, but they didn't call it that. They called it a shower. I know, weird, right? There are baby showers and bridal showers, but this was an 'April Shower,' a party where they 'showered' me with suggestions and assistance. Not just lip service this time but real action. Everyone brought something to pull me out of my slump— a Fat Stoppers membership, a year's pass to Silver's Gym, workout clothes, a collection of exercise DVDs. But my oldest sister bought me the gift that made the difference—a plane ticket to Cleveland and a week at Terry's Haven for the Hated."

"Wow, that's one expensive gift!" Camarin recalled the price listed on Mangel's website at close to two thousand dollars, not to mention the cost of April's soul, selling out to Mangel and promoting his costly message to the masses.

"I know, but in the end, it was priceless. I could never repay her enough. I got my life back. Terry taught me everything about respecting myself for who I was, not how I looked."

"Well, for what it's worth, you look great."

April blushed.

"So how long ago did you join the organization? And how did you come to head up his public relations department?"

"I've been on the road with Terry for about a year."

Damn, that's after the murders started. Cross another name off the list, thought Camarin.

"And I've always been good with people and…wow, this is so amazing. No one ever asks about my story, and you seem so easy to talk to. Could I share something with you, off the record?"

Camarin nodded, slipping the phone off the table and into her jacket pocket.

"Don't tell anyone—this can't go anywhere beyond this room—but during that week? We fell in love. Terry said he never wanted to travel anywhere without me again…and look!"

She reached into the side pocket of her handbag and pulled out a three-carat sparkler. "We're engaged! We don't talk about it because, well, you know how tongues wag in confined spaces. Terry doesn't want to put people's noses out of joint or have them think I get preferential treatment."

Or let Maria catch on. It's no wonder he sends her back to Atlanta between speaking gigs. Can't have these two comparing notes.

"It's beautiful. When's the big day?"

"We haven't set an exact date yet. I just hope it's soon. Sometimes, I'm so scared the weight might come back on and…well, I have my heart set on a size-four wedding gown."

"Would it make a difference? Gaining the weight back? I mean, if you're happy and love yourself no matter what…"

April's face darkened, and she grew quiet and stared out the window.

"April?"

"I don't think…I don't think he'd still marry me."

"Why not?"

"It's this thing he said. We were in San Francisco, shopping for dresses. I found this gorgeous Vera Wang and modeled it for him—I couldn't believe how stunning it looked on me—and I joked to the salesgirl, 'I'd better buy it now, before I gain back any weight'—and he said…" Her voice trailed off.

"Don't leave me hanging. What did he say?" Camarin couldn't stand the suspense.

April's face contorted as if in great pain, but she forced herself to spit out the words. "He said, 'Don't do that. It would be like slashing the *Mona Lisa*.'"

That hypocritical fucker!

"Maybe he wasn't thinking when he said that. Maybe it just slipped out," Camarin suggested.

"No, I don't think so. Sometimes…I catch him staring at some of the other girls when he doesn't know I'm looking—Grace, Maria, Evelyn, the heavier ones, you know. And he's got this expression on his face. It's almost…disgust. But I must be reading into that, don't you think, Camarin? I mean, maybe it's my own jealousy and insecurity. There's no way Terry Mangel is a fat hater. Am I right?"

April's pleading expression pierced her heart. Here was yet another woman teetering on the edge of hope and self-assurance, looking to Camarin to make her whole. And all she could do was either lie to her and leave her languishing in false hope, or tell her the truth and watch her crumble, along with her dreams. She had to say something—but what? Conflicted, a sudden wave of nausea overcame her.

"Where's your ladies' room?"

April pointed with surprise to the back of the trailer, and Camarin half-ran past the bed, into the tiny bathroom, and kneeled over the commode. The distress that had been brewing since her encounter with Perri Evans assaulted her with a fury, but because she hadn't eaten since the night before, nothing was coming back up. After five minutes of dry heaving, she heard April knock at the door.

"I've poured you a glass of diet ginger ale. Drink it. It might help."

She pushed the door open and accepted the offering, chugging the sparkling elixir until the glass was empty.

April offered her a hand and helped Camarin to her feet. "Come on back to the commissary. What you need is some plain toast to sop up that upset stomach. You've got to be on your game tonight. The second night is always an amazing show."

Grateful that the moment of reckoning had past and her opinion was no longer of interest, Camarin followed along, more determined than ever to get to the bottom of this thing and, in the process, bury the mendacious Mangel along with the murderer.

CHAPTER

24 25 26

CLAD IN AN uncharacteristically informal gray cotton
hoodie, Fletcher's toned physique was the only feature
distinguishing him from the hundreds of Mangel fans
waiting in line outside the revival. Surveying the supersized
bodies around him, it was clear that Camarin was on point
concerning the magazine's prospective revamp. Surrounding
him was a small sampling of a potential audience of millions
who craved fashionable offerings beyond the tight-fitting
jeans and minidresses that inundated the advertising sections
of *Trend.*

His thoughts drifted back to Margaret. Toward the end,
she'd also rejected the accoutrements of the young and
ultrathin, the current readership of his trash publication.
Primarily because she'd no longer counted herself among
them. *Who cared about Q scores and audience opinions anyway?*
she'd rationalized. Unfortunately, she learned that one
person who did care was the owner of the network, calling
her five pounds and five years beyond her prime. All her
years of dedication were forgotten. The fact that she'd been
one of the youngest journalists ever to break stories like the
Gulf War, Jeffrey Dahmer, the Menendez Brothers?

Yesterday's news. The countless, hard-hitting interviews with headline grabbers like Amy Fisher, Heidi Fleiss, Anita Hill? All negated by an excess of ounces and hours. Once you strayed beyond those narrow constraints, what was left for you?

His heart still ached over her loss. She would always remain his queen of the airwaves. And Lehming Brothers would pay dearly for backing that clueless network exec. As well as for every message they'd sent out into the world warning people they couldn't participate unless they dressed, smelled, and ate according to their advertisers' ever-changing whims.

The ticket queue started moving, and he pulled his hood down farther to blend in with the crowd. He wasn't exactly sure what he was doing here or how he could protect Camarin with merely his presence. But the last thing he wanted, other than being recognized, was for her to get mixed up with someone like Mangel. When his empire eventually toppled, Fletcher didn't want his new princess of journalistic justice to get sullied by the debris.

E MPOWERED BY THE knowledge imparted by her new confidante, April, the 'also engaged,' Camarin calmed her stomach with toast and tea before accompanying the public relations director back to the same front-row seats they'd occupied the previous evening.

"Tonight will be very different than what you saw yesterday," said April. "Terry will come out and warm up the crowd, but he is sooo not the star of the evening. The audience is. Anyone can come up and tell their story. It's amazingly powerful. You will be blown away, I promise." She gave Cam a little hug, another reminder of the secret they now shared.

Camarin searched for any sign of Mangel loitering behind the podium, canoodling with some other unsuspecting, sycophantic employee. But if he was there, he remained out of sight.

She took a deep breath and thought about Fletcher. Once she uncovered the murderer, she was sure he'd overlook the Evans fiasco, the scoop that got away, in favor of this more explosive exclusive. No one would be able to resist the tale of someone in Mangel's inner circle spurning the evangelist's heartfelt appeals of love in favor of a bloodier, less 'Kumbaya' reality. The question was, who was that someone? Thanks to April's confession, she'd had a revelation about how to proceed.

She leaned over and whispered into her companion's ear, "Do you think I could get two words with Terry tonight after the revival?"

"I can't see why not. He was quite taken with you last night. He had the most wonderful things to say."

Camarin wondered what his opinion might be of her after they shared their little chat.

The room went pitch-black, and again, the music blaring from the nearby speakers assailed her eardrums. Tonight it was the insightful *Shut Up!* by Simple Plan, its lyrics a plea for an end to personal criticism.

The audience joined in, creating a thunderous chorus of "Shut up, shut up, shut up, don't wanna hear it…" that she was sure was loud enough to be heard as far away as Manhattan. When the song ended, a round of self-congratulatory applause filled the tent, which morphed into claps of appreciation and admiration as Mangel took the spotlight.

"My friends, you know the song. You know the message," he started as Camarin fought from cringing.

You lousy, two-faced bigamist-to-be.

"They criticize us, they try to silence us, but tonight the world will hear our collective resentment. We will douse our sorrows with each other's empathy and emerge clean, ready to show the world the love we'd like reflected our way. Who here knows how much we spend each year to make ourselves acceptable in the rigid, hypercritical eyes of society? Let me read you some figures."

He dramatically pulled out a piece of paper and slowly unfolded it, ensuring that the microphone picked up every crinkle.

"I can't estimate how much we spend on clothing, on cosmetics, on deodorant, on retouching our photographs. I can't put a dollar figure on the hours we spend alone, too ashamed to join our loved ones at family events, afraid our bulk will embarrass them."

Camarin felt a ghostly finger, invisibly poking at her shoulder.

"But what I can tell you is how much experts estimate we spend on weight loss. Sixty billion dollars. Every single year. Let me put that into perspective for you. In 2017, the gross domestic product of Luxembourg was around $59.9 billion. Think about that. We spend more on trying to get thin than the economic output of an entire European country."

One of the smallest countries in Europe, thought Camarin, but she had to concede it was still an impressive amount. The audience oohed and aahed their astonishment.

"And would they have us spend that money on curing the sick or educating the poor? I mean, with sixty billion dollars you could put the entire populations of French Polynesia and Guam— " He stared directly at Camarin, flashing his most ingratiating smile. "—through all four years of Temple University. If they could get in, that is."

The audience snickered and clapped in response to the mention of their hometown college. Mangel was no stranger to working a crowd. But the reference to her heritage sent shivers down her spine. He must have done some digging of his own.

"No. They expect us to bankrupt ourselves, so we can fit into their predefined image of how we should appear—an image that changes at the fancy of fashion designers looking to cash in on whatever latest trend they create."

Camarin wondered if the mention of her magazine was intentional.

"It's an economic issue, especially against women's pocketbooks. Expecting you to fight nature and instead squeeze into jeans designed to fit teenage boys—that's just a way to subjugate you, keep you from worrying about more important things, like advancing your career, breaking through glass ceilings. How can you concentrate on beating out the competition when you're busy focusing on the scale?"

A woman in the audience yelled, "Hallelujah," and the room suddenly pulsated with private conversations and chatter. Camarin pictured the floor of her childhood bedroom, littered with too-tight clothes thrown down in despair.

"And it isn't just the health benefits of a skinny body they're selling you. Oh, no. Who here hasn't been convinced that by losing the weight your entire world will improve? That you'd be happier, better liked, and prospective spouses would finally be able to notice the real, incredibly wonderful you? Guess what? You've been that wonderful all along. You've just been wasting your life, buying into their labels. It's time to enjoy your food, and yourself, without ever apologizing again."

The audience started chanting, "Tell 'em, Terry! Tell 'em good!"

I was wonderful too. Why did you abandon me, Camarin?

"You didn't come here tonight to hear me proselytize," he said, attempting to redirect the focus to the front of the room. "You came here to listen to each other. Some of you have written to me in advance, asking to address the audience. I'll call you up first. But everyone else, this tent... " He moved his pointing finger from left to right. "...this is your haven. Your safe place. If you feel inspired, if the spirit moves you, come up. Be heard. Be acknowledged."

Someone emerged from the shadows, and Camarin recognized her as the woman who had been snuggling backstage with Mangel during Maria's speech the evening before. She sported an hourglass figure but could never have mislabeled as overweight. The evangelist introduced her as a psychologist named Alexandra Platis, and the audience hushed as she spun a gruesome saga of her years counseling traumatized women recovering from attempts at extreme weight-loss.

"Most nearly died. My job was to bring them back from the brink, to convince them that you can't love a body that's six feet under."

Where I am, Camarin. Where you put me. As Monaeka's voice competed for attention with Alexandra's, Camarin began to tremble, enveloped by chills and a cold sweat.

"The things they went through..." Her voice cracked, and she stopped for a moment, trying to regain her composure. "I'm going to paraphrase from another Terry, this one being Terry Poulton and her book *No Fat Chicks*, because that's a book everyone here should read."

Alexandra pulled out her glasses and read from her notes.

"'Here are some of the ways we destroy ourselves to satisfy others: we wire our jaws shut, staple our stomachs, hack off our intestines, suck our fat out, inject ourselves with the urine of pregnant women, live off powdered drinks made partially from cattle hooves, starve, vomit…'"

I tried so hard to be a good sister. The word 'vomit' prompted a sudden wave of nausea that Camarin fought hard to ignore.

"We exercise ourselves into exhausted stupors. We take whatever pills they hand us to suppress our appetites, accelerate our metabolisms, drain our bodies of water—forgetting that we are ninety percent water, my friends—and most of these pills that we base our hopes on were never approved as safe. Some of us have died. But whatever they wrote on our death certificates, I assure you that it was the self-loathing, caused by society's disgust, that ultimately proved lethal."

All I needed was someone to talk to, to tell me I was okay. The tingling in Cam's limbs, the sense of almost choking made her look around in panic, wondering if anyone could save her from the voices, the guilt, the truth.

Alexandra looked up from her notes and gazed out at the audience. "This is the world of my patients. A world of beggars craving validation, of innocent adults and children criminalized for eating a few more morsels than their neighbors. But it doesn't have to be your world. And if you follow either Terry's advice, it never has to be again."

The crowd erupted into momentous applause.

That opened the floodgates of the oppressed, all stepping forward to share. One by one, members of the crowd took the stage, speaking of being bullied, ostracized, dealing with the prejudice against the plump. Unlike Mangel, every speaker was authentic, and with every tear-filled account, Camarin fell deeper and deeper into despair. Male, female, young, old, she saw their lips move, but all she heard were the veiled cries for help. The accusations of betrayal. She felt her years of guilt coming to a head, demanding to be heard and acknowledged.

"Is there anyone else present that would like to speak?" asked Mangel after the throng had cleared.

No longer thinking for herself but, rather, driven by a force beyond her control, Camarin rose and staggered to the stage. Mangel patted her on the back and guided her to the podium. She looked down and saw April, mouth agape in shock. Knees shaking, Camarin grabbed the dais with both hands and stared out into the blur of faces. One man in the fourth row almost looked like Fletcher. Now I know I'm hallucinating, she thought. Like a rock concert, several people held up lighters or cellphones with flaming candle apps and waved them rhythmically from side to side.

She breathed in deeply and leaned toward the mic. "The last thing I expected to do tonight was stand up and speak to you all. And I'm not sure I deserve one iota of the support you're sending my way. In some ways, I am you. In others…I am everything you despise."

She bit her lip, willing herself to hold back her tears.

"I have spent a lifetime hiding this, but every day I starve myself so my clothes don't get too tight, so I can look okay. And on the rare occasions when I eat too much—" She held up her pointing finger. "—this little baby makes it all come back up and go down the toilet. And it's because…I learned from an early age that if I gain weight, I won't fit in. And in our family, fitting in was all there was."

Eerily, she felt herself rise up out of her body, floating above the audience, looking down to watch herself address the crowd. It was almost comforting to finally be free of the body that had caused her unmitigated anguish for so many years. A view of the world from Monaeka's vantage point.

"My mother and her sister married US Naval officers who brought them here from Guam. They were new here, alone with no friends, their husbands usually away at sea. So, I understand why they were so desperate to belong. When my twin sister and I came along, that's the message they instilled in us. Fit in, at all costs. But Monaeka…she was the weaker of us two. She wasn't the storybook child. She had childhood epilepsy. The pills blew her metabolism apart, and she grew heavy. And my mother and my aunt…well, let's just say there was nothing they wouldn't try to transform her into their perception of what was acceptable. The problem was…"

She paused, feeling her sister's approval as she prepared to express what she had never admitted before.

"She counted on me to protect her. And while I did help, I did so with great resentment. She was the focus of the family. No matter what I did, it never registered on anyone's radar. Straight As? Great, you're so smart, help your sister lose weight. Prom coming up? How can either of you go unless you're skinny? I grew to hate my twin and everything her overweight cost me. So, the irony and the tragedy were, as much as my family went on and on about how important it was to belong, everything they told me to do pushed me further and further from hanging out with my own group of friends. And my sister…she'd look up to me. I was the skinny one, the strong one, her savior. And I grew to hate her for that too."

Camarin started to shake wildly. Mangel came up behind her and asked if she was strong enough to continue. She nodded yes and faced out at the multitudes once again.

"When my senior year came around, my mother wanted me to stay close to home, go to community college. But I knew it was my only chance to escape without hurting anyone's feelings. I secretly applied to every decent college on the East Coast, figuring that by putting three thousand miles between myself and my family duties, I could finally carve out a life of my own. But what I did…"

Another deep breath for courage. It was Monaeka talking, Monaeka who had finally invaded her body as well as her brain and forced this confession. And it was Monaeka who would laugh at the shame Camarin would endure after everyone knew the one secret she'd never spoken aloud. The day of reckoning was upon her, and there was no escape.

"My grades weren't enough. And with all the competition, I feared that being a minority wouldn't be enough either. I needed something that would blow the admissions people away. So, I took a photo of my sister, and a photo of myself, and I wrote an essay about the persistence I'd shown, losing a hundred pounds because I wanted to start my life fresh in college."

The audience gasped and booed. She grasped the dais even harder, fighting to stop the tremors and keep her knees from buckling. She wanted to run, but she knew that now that she had started, she had to complete her confession, get it all off her chest.

"Please, let me finish… I got into NYU. Full scholarship, thank God, otherwise, my family would have never let me leave. I just didn't want to hear about Monaeka's weight anymore and the opportunities she was losing because of it. I was finally meeting friends, dating, having fun. I just didn't care about Monaeka's problems anymore. Then one day I got a call."

Her voice choked with bawls waiting to escape, but she continued as best she could.

"She'd found a copy of the essay. It was hidden in my desk drawer—just in case I'd have to send it out again. She called me Benedict Arnold, a traitor, said she could never live with the memory of the betrayal. I apologized over and over again, but she wouldn't accept it. She slammed down the phone and wouldn't answer when I tried to call her back. And then a week later, my mother tried to wake her up, but she couldn't. They found the empty bottle beside the bed. Her last meal was an overdose of diet pills, downed with half a bottle of tequila. No note...but I knew what killed her. It...was...me...and no matter what I do now to fix it, I can't make it better. I can't bring her back."

From her viewpoint high above the crowd, Cam watched herself collapse in tears, her guilt compounded by the boos of the audience. One threw an empty soda can at her, another a half-eaten hot dog. Mangel and April came to her rescue, quickly escorting her off the podium to a secluded area at the rear of the tent, hidden from the staff as well as the agitated crowd. She could hear Maria over the microphone, trying to calm the melee.

"You'd better go back out there and contain the crowd, figure out some way to put a positive spin on this," Mangel told April. "I'll stay here with Camarin until she's herself again."

He stroked her back and patted her hair but said nothing until her crying jag eased. Cam slowly felt herself coming back down to reality. But Terry Mangel, comforting her? That seemed more unreal than the episode she'd just experienced. Such kindness and compassion, and it seemed so genuine.

"Feeling better now?"

"I am, thank you."

"Sounds like you've been carrying a heavy load on your conscience all these years."

"I have."

"Difficult, I'm sure. How can I help?"

He slipped his hand onto her thigh and squeezed it lightly and then leaned in to kiss her on the cheek. She recoiled in shock, the heat of anger burning off the last of the fog that had been clouding her brain. She slapped him across the face and jumped to her feet.

"Are you fucking kidding me?" Her head pounded furiously.

"I was just trying to help. You feel alone. I wanted to make sure you knew you weren't. You're young and beautiful, and there's a world of people out there who appreciate that. Me included."

"Look, you slimy, double-crossing pile of shit…"

Mangel's eyes grew wide. It was clear he wasn't used to having someone see through his carefully constructed facade.

"You're not going to include this in the interview, are you?"

"There isn't going to be an interview. I'm here because— fuck, I can't believe I'm going to tell you something that's going to help you and your money-grubbing empire. You don't fucking deserve it. I'm here because I believe there's someone in your crew, someone so dazzled by your censure of the weight-loss community, that they're ignoring your vapid pleas of 'love the fat haters' and instead are going out and knocking them off."

Mangel opened his mouth but stayed silent, clearly stunned by her tale.

"Everywhere your caravan goes—Los Angeles, Phoenix, Santa Fe, all the way to your recent stop in Chicago— somebody has died. And those somebodies have been people who have discriminated against fat people, or have sold products to help them get thin. I need copies of your employee files, so I can start investigating everyone on your team and figure out who's behind this. And if you don't cooperate, I'm going to tell your fiancée Maria about your other fiancée, April. And vice versa."

The color faded from his face. He shook his head violently. "You know! Thank God somebody knows! It's true. It's true, but it's not what you think. It's no one on my team. Stay here. I have to run back to my trailer. There's something I've got to show you. Do. Not. Move."

Mangel ran out of the tent, leaving her speechless and confused. He knew? What the hell was going on? She closed her eyes and tried to ignore the sounds next door of people buying souvenirs as well as the realization that her confession had disrupted the revival and brought shame upon herself and her family.

He returned a few minutes later, brandishing two pieces of paper. "I had to print this one out from my computer. Here, you've got to see it." He pushed both onto her lap.

She lifted the top sheet, which looked like a printout from a Facebook post, and began to read.

A Call to Arms

I pay to be touched, an hour with my masseuse every Monday. I pay to be listened to, an hour with my therapist every Wednesday. I pay to be weighed and then chastised, every Saturday at my weight-loss center where they tell me—in not so many words, of course—that if I keep eating food that tastes like cardboard and running for hours without getting anywhere, I may one day become acceptable to those around me.

I am over fifty, I am overweight, and I am overcome by the lack of respect afforded me by society. I am truly the Invisible Woman.

I am tired of those who tell people like me that we can fit in as long as we pay thousands for books, videos, camps, and foods that help us lose the weight. And I am equally tired of those who take the opposite tack, who tell us we should love ourselves as we are, as long as we pay even more to read their books and attend their therapeutic retreats, designed to guide us down the 'right' and overpriced road to self-esteem.

If you are as angry as I am of the fat jokes, the surreptitious glances, the allusions to Moby Dick, the comments about our 'pretty faces and what a shame about the rest', then join me. Together, we will employ whatever means are necessary to teach them that we won't accept this treatment, that we are a force to be reckoned with. With apologies to Shakespeare, let us demand our pound of flesh from each of our detractors. Together, we will be The Collective.

"You see? You see?" Mangel was frantic. "The part about the opposite tack, to love ourselves for what we are? The therapeutic retreats? Camarin, that's me she's talking about. And my followers. She's using my words to recruit this vigilante group to fight against me, against us. The nerve, lumping my people in with the fat shamers. The Collective must have seen our tour schedule, and they're trying to make a statement. Maybe implicate my staff in these murders so they can get away with them…I don't know. I'm just so glad someone else sees what's going on."

His voice faded as he lost himself in thought. Then, as if suddenly revived, he shoved the second piece of paper under her nose.

"And here, look at this. It was left in my trailer the other day. How they got in, I have no idea."

Camarin grabbed what looked like a lined page torn out of a spiral notepad, and squinted to read the tiny scrawl, scribbled in purple. *Enjoy the crowds in our fair city of brotherly love, Mr. Mangel. Alas, your time here will be short-lived.*

She felt the tiny hairs on her arms standing on end. "A death threat?"

"That's what it sounds like to me. I think that I may be the murder they have planned for Philadelphia."

"Did you show these papers to anyone else?"

"No one, no. I didn't want to worry them. You seem to know so much more about this than I do. Perhaps we can figure this out together?"

"Why not call the police?"

"At Mangel Enterprises, we have our own security force, so we can keep all information close to our chest. No outside influence, ever."

In other words, no bad publicity.

"But they're limited," he continued, "more like guards than detectives. Even if they do manage to protect me, there are others to consider. My staff, for example. We need to figure out the identity of the Invisible Woman and The Collective, so they won't strike out at anyone else, ever again. I implore you, please help me."

Camarin's mind was a jumble. Her carefully crafted theory of the murderer—one of Terry Mangel's legion of traveling staff, possibly an angry, jilted love interest—was destroyed, kaput. The Invisible Woman had recruited an internet army of supposed do-gooders, dedicated to body acceptance, to carry out missions on her behalf. Who knew if the perpetrators were even local to the incidents?

And ironically, here was this man who came to the aid of people like Monaeka, a healing huckster whom she alternately admired and deplored, begging *her* to save *his* life. One glimmer of a silver lining: if she did agree, wouldn't it make one hell of a first headline?

"I need to consider this. Do you have any idea who the Invisible Woman could be? Someone who attended one of your revivals perhaps? A spurned lover? Someone who got on stage and didn't get the response she'd hoped for?" She scrambled for any scrap of a lead.

"Not off the top of my head, no." They both hushed as staff members wandered into their area of the tent. "We can't stay here. The roadies are going to start breaking everything down. The caravan heads toward Charlotte tomorrow afternoon. If I'm still alive anyway. Let me go through my papers for anything that might be helpful. Could you come to my trailer tomorrow morning as planned? Maybe earlier, around nine, so April doesn't interfere? I don't want to frighten her."

She agreed to his request. Any clue he could dig up was better than none at all.

"Do you feel okay now?" he asked. "Your speech got some of the audience pretty angry. Do you need someone to accompany you back to your hotel? I have people who could drive you."

"I appreciate the offer, but no, I think I'll walk. Anyone offended by my words has likely left the area by now, and perhaps the cool evening air will help to clear my head."

FLETCHER CROUCHED IN the bushes outside the back of the tent, waiting for Camarin to appear. It had been almost an hour since they'd shepherded her backstage after her breakdown, and he wanted to be sure she got back to her hotel without any further reprisal from the incensed crowd.

How his heart had broken for her as she confessed her supposed crime against her sister. He'd ached as she had exposed her psychic pain in public, drowning in her own tears as the audience withheld their usual show of support. She really had nothing to apologize for, he reasoned. She had been entitled to live her own life, unfettered by the demands and expectations of her family. In the end, she'd taken creative, extraordinary means to extricate herself from an unfortunate situation. It was nothing to beat herself up over, even if participating in the event had been an extremely unprofessional act for a journalist.

Finally, she emerged. Her stance seemed steady as she walked from the compound into the night. He followed about a block behind, careful not to be noticed. He longed to hold her, to take her soft, supple body into his arms and protect her from the world, even from her own harsh, self-flagellating thoughts.

He trailed her to a large, purple Victorian and watched as she went inside. A few moments later, a light illuminated one of the gable windows. Her silhouette appeared, and he envisioned himself behind her, drawing her against the warmth of his body, enveloping her in his desire. He felt himself grow hard at the thought of her near him again, her full lips opening to accept his kisses, his tongue, all he had to offer.

She strayed from the window, and a few minutes later, the room went dark. He hustled back to the main road to find a cab to take him to his hotel. He had things to do before he returned tomorrow morning. He wouldn't rest easy until he saw her board that Amtrak train and head back to his offices at *Trend*, where she'd finally be safe.

CHAPTER
25 26 27

"SO HOW DID you enjoy your stay here in town? Did you go to the Mutter Museum like we suggested?"

Camarin shook her head but remained silent. Nancy and Harold Hawkins, her Airbnb hosts, were doing their best to keep her engaged, but she kept drifting off into her own private thoughts. She noshed on the breakfast they'd cooked for her—two fried eggs, no bread, please, and a fruit salad on the side—while she contemplated her next move.

If Mangel had been so perturbed over that note, why not skip the Philly event, pack up the circus, and continue on his way? Scared the murderer would follow him wherever his caravan landed? Or was the lure of all that potential income too much to resist? Even if it cost him his life?

And what about this Invisible Woman brigade? Camarin had spent the last hour searching Facebook for any glimpse of that vigilante recruiting post, or any mention of The Collective anywhere on social media. Nothing. Perhaps it was privately emailed to a select few? Or maybe she'd published it and then deleted it when her ranks grew full, less evidence to present against her in court?

She'd have to ask Mangel later where he'd found it online. People say that nothing in cyberspace ever really disappears. When she returned home, she'd have to find some internet whiz who could uncover archived or deleted files.

"What time are you checking out today, Camarin? We have another guest arriving at three, and we want to make sure his room is ready. Got to get busy Endusting and Swiffering!"

Were all Airbnb hosts as goofy and irreverent as these two? Camarin wondered. It must help to encourage repeat visits. Normally, she would have shared in their cheerful discourse, but with her meeting with Mangel only thirty minutes away, she was too distracted for levity.

"I have to run an errand, but I should be back around ten to pick up my backpack and be on my way." She stood to leave.

Nancy walked over and surprised her with an effusive hug. "Well, we loved having you, Camarin, and if there's anything we can do to make your next trip here as pleasant as this one has been, please don't hesitate to call."

It was a bright morning, and it was nice to be able to stroll back to the park without a sweater. She wished she had the time to enjoy the blue jays flittering about or sniff the blooming roses, but she had too much on her mind.

What could she really do to help Mangel? Though he was convinced his staff was not involved, she wasn't as sure. Why couldn't the Invisible Woman or her minions be among his cadre of traveling followers? She decided she would insist on examining his employee files, and then urge him to contact the local police. After all, the event in Philadelphia was complete. No need to worry that a random murder or two might stifle ticket sales.

She saw Mangel's trailer in the distance and hastened her pace, adopting a confident, capable demeanor. *Bluff your way through*, wasn't that Lyle's motto? Better get this meeting over with, while she still had her nerve.

THE PARKING LOT was deserted, other than the convoy of trailers waiting to invade the next city and fleece a fresh group of hope-starved gullibles. Hucksters and their crew must sleep late on Sunday mornings, Fletcher surmised. Unless they were all off at church. After following Camarin from the Victorian, he tucked behind a white lilac bush and watched from a distance as she knocked on the trailer door, waited a few beats, and then entered Mangel's lair.

AFTER NO ONE answered her knocks, Camarin took a chance and tested the handle. To her surprise, it opened. She pressed the door ajar and heard the whoosh of shower water. Though she knew the right thing to do would be to remain outside and wait, she couldn't resist this golden opportunity to snoop around undisturbed. She ventured inside, closing the door behind her.

The trailer's luxurious interior put April's to shame. The living room greeted guests with overstuffed couches on either side, and coffee tables set between them in the aisle. Behind that, she saw a work area—a mahogany desk covered with papers, across from a wooden lateral filing cabinet. Farther back, she could see a dining table with built-in seating for four opposite a wall of kitchen cabinets and appliances. A queen-sized bed filled the back of the trailer, across from what she assumed was the bathroom.

Shivering with prospect of potential discovery, Camarin headed directly for the desk and perused its mountain of correspondence, careful not to disturb anything. What she really sought was another glimpse of the Facebook printout from the Invisible Woman or that death threat, so she could snap them with her phone camera. But if they were there, they were buried under piles of receipts, schedules, a stack of "Dear Terry" letters proclaiming undying admiration. Not exactly the stuff of breaking headlines.

She pulled on the lateral file drawers, but to no avail. Damn. She needed to see the employee records or whatever else might be locked inside. Scanning the desk for a key, or even a paper clip to pick the lock, she spotted a letter opener with a white marbled handle. The shower water was still spritzing, so she had time. She grabbed the opener and knelt, trying to wedge the tip into the cylinder, but it was too thick to fit. She stood up, replaced the opener on the desk, and started toward the kitchen to find some thinner utensil when she heard the water shut off.

She remained glued to her spot, wondering if she should make herself comfortable or run out of the trailer and knock again. The bathroom handle turned, making the decision for her. With no time to spare, she zipped over to one of the couches and plopped down, trying to look nonchalant.

"Terry, it's Camarin," she yelled out, lest he emerge naked, a memory she preferred not to take back to Manhattan. "I let myself in. I hope that's okay."

The bathroom door opened and out walked Mangel, damp-headed and clothed in a thick, blue velour robe. "Good morning. I'm so glad you had the forethought to let yourself in. Busy day ahead, and this was the only chance I'd have to shower." He walked over to the fridge and opened it. "What can I offer you? Orange juice? Or perhaps a mimosa?" He pulled out the juice and a bottle of champagne and set them on the counter, his manner uncharacteristically calm for someone whose life had recently been threatened.

"I've already had breakfast, thanks. I'd prefer if we got right down to work." She sat forward, trying to project a confident, no-nonsense stance. "I've been thinking…there really is no downside to going to the police. Act before anything bad happens. I know how the Invisible Woman and her operatives work. They'd probably tie you to your podium with a mic stuffed down your throat."

Mangel reached for two champagne flutes and hummed as he poured them each a mimosa. Camarin watched, annoyed that he didn't seem to grasp the import of her words or the gravity of the situation. Was this the same man who had desperately begged for her help the night before?

He brought the drinks over and set them on the coffee table, then positioned himself on the couch across from hers. His robe opened slightly, and she could see Little Terry peeking out. She tried to ignore the intrusion, focusing above the chest.

"So, what precautions are you taking?" she asked, again trying to direct the conversation to the issue at hand.

"I've spoken to our security team, and they're monitoring the grounds. Other than that, I plan to stay put, have all my meetings in the trailer until we pull out later for Charlotte. Speaking of pulling out, are you on the pill?"

The world stood still for a moment as Camarin tried to determine if she'd heard him correctly. "Excuse me?"

"The pill. Are you on birth control?"

"What the fuck business is that of yours?"

He reached down and untied his robe, showing his bare body in all its questionable glory. "Well, I could get a condom, but I won't enjoy things as much. We could go bareback. You've been checked recently, I assume?"

Everything in her line of vision turned an angry shade of crimson. She was livid—both at him for making light of the situation, but even more intensely, at her own naivety, stupidly walking into a compromising situation with a serial philanderer. Without thinking, she picked up her mimosa and threw at him, but the liquid missed his face and splattered on his chest. His stunned expression slowly broke into a crooked, little smile.

"We can play rough too, if you'd like. I'd actually enjoy that more."

She stood up and started for the door, praying her knees wouldn't fail her before she made it outside. He arose to block her path. Her survival sense kicking in, she took three steps backward and reached behind her, foraging for the letter opener she'd left on the desk moments before. He took two steps forward, his erect cock leading the way. She rummaged faster, pushing papers onto the floor, certain she only had seconds to spare.

"Smart girl. A desk is hotter than a bed any day of the week."

He was almost upon her when she finally found the letter opener and wielded it menacingly. He backed off, a shocked look on his face as if no one had ever denied him before.

"One more step and you're a dead man," she said, thrusting the knife forward to shield her as she made her way around him. He held his hands out in a 'back off, we're cool' fashion and stood as still as a statue as she walked backward toward the trailer's entrance.

"Can't we still be friends?" he asked, meekly.

"I hope the Invisible Woman gets you and gets you good," Camarin hissed, drenched in sweat.

She reached for the door handle, simultaneously tossing the letter opener onto the carpet in front of the coffee table. She turned to exit and, in her haste, almost fell down the three steps between the door and the sidewalk. Then she ran from the trailer as fast as she could, grateful that no one was around to see her unceremonious exodus from Mangel World.

TWENTY MINUTES AFTER assuming guard, Fletcher watched Camarin burst out the trailer, visibly shaken and looking frenetically in all directions. He was torn: did she need his assistance? Should he reveal himself and risk her scorn? Before he could decide, she bustled away, looking back terrified, as if running from a ghost.

There was no way to catch up to her without being noticed, and there was certainly no point going into the trailer to confront Mangel without first knowing what had transpired between them.

He hurried back over to the Victorian, his only clue to her possible whereabouts. From a distance, he saw her wearing her backpack and hailing a cab. She looked in his direction and hesitated before getting inside. Then the taxi sped off, presumably toward 30th Street Station, leaving him to pray that he'd been too far away to be recognized.

Despite his concerns over her agitated state, he decided to linger a bit. Why risk an unfortunate encounter onboard and confirm any suspicions that her brief glance might have provoked? Perhaps he could stroll back to the park, have a word or two with Terry, and take the next train home.

Tomorrow at work, he'd call her into his office, they'd talk about her weekend, and surely, she would confide in him about whatever events that had transpired inside Mangel's trailer and upset her so.

CHAPTER
26 27 28

A DESPONDENT CAMARIN returned to a thankfully empty apartment and sequestered herself in her bedroom. To her surprise, she was less shaken up about the attack—most of what happened between Terry propositioning her and her running from the trailer was just an unpleasant blur—and more annoyed about how she'd handled the entire incident.

How could she have been so stupid? Perhaps she wasn't meant to be an investigative reporter after all. And what if the Invisible Woman did follow through? Had Cam been wrong to leave Philadelphia without at least telling the police something about the death threats against Mangel? Or the murders that preceded them? Could her decision result in yet another homicide?

Who could she confide in? Lyle came to mind first, perhaps because she'd kept spotting his doppelgängers all over Philadelphia. But did she really want to admit she'd defied his orders and, on top of that, was such an amateur reporter that she'd endangered herself unnecessarily? There was always Wynan. He'd seemed compassionate as of late. But he'd also warned her against the investigation. Plus, he'd go running to Lyle, what with the reputation of the magazine at stake. With DeAndre, her exploits could end up as pillow talk, and blabbermouth Rachel might feel compelled to report back to management. So, he was a no as well.

There was always her mother. Ha! Perfect if she wanted to be lectured on what the best-dressed women at the rape crisis center were wearing and how to more effectively befriend them. It looked like Annalise might be her one and only choice as confidante. Once she got back home anyway.

Cam pulled the laptop from her backpack and started scanning news portals for any mention of a Mangel assault. Nothing, which was reassuring. Still, if she'd only snuck a look at those employee files or had snapped a picture of the Invisible Woman's Facebook post and death threat. At least then, she would have some additional fodder for her story. Now, with neither evidence nor witnesses, she was no further ahead than before she'd left for Philly.

The slam of the front door signaled the arrival of the troops. The lilt of Rachel's rhyming slang accompanied DeAndre's raucous laughter. Then some muffled banter that she couldn't make out.

I can't stay locked in my bedroom forever, Cam decided, mentally juggling various explanations of the past weekend's events. She settled on the easiest—plausible deniability.

"Hey, look who's *pope!*" DeAndre sat beside Rachel on the couch, grinning sheepishly. "She's teaching me. Pope in Rome. Home."

"Terrific. Now I have the two of you spouting nonsense. Who wants a cuppa tea?" Camarin donned her best fake English accent.

"I'll have one," Rachel volunteered. "So, how did the adventure go, Miss Marple?"

Cam reached for a mug. "How about you, Dee? You want some oolong? Or maybe something herbal to soothe your throat before tonight's show? I can stir in some honey."

"Would the jury please note how the defendant is avoiding the question?"

She shot Rachel a sneer. "I can do both, you know. Discuss my disappointing weekend and serve tea. I'm talented that way. Dee? Last chance."

He briefly halted his tongue's exploration of the back of Rachel's neck. "Oolong's fine, thanks."

"Great. Hope you like Tetley's, Ms. Thorsen, because that's what you're getting."

"No need to be *bonnie*, just because I was curious."

She didn't want to ask, but her curiosity got the best of her. "Bonnie?"

Rachel took the win in stride. "Bonnie and Clyde. Snide."

"Ah, should have known."

Camarin placed two tea bags into oversized mugs and poured water into the kettle. It was old school, but sometimes the simpler ways were best. She joined them in the living room, plonking herself down on the love seat opposite her inquisitors.

"If you must know—"

"Yes, I absolutely must." Rachel batted her eyelashes annoyingly.

"It was a disaster from start to finish. The revival was so crowded and chaotic, I couldn't even reach the PR person who okayed the meeting, much less the leader himself." No point in reminding them of his name, especially if it popped up in today's papers. "And then the interview with Perri Evans…"

"You met Perri Evans?" DeAndre perked up, diverting his attention from his tongue's focus, which had graduated to the top of Rachel's shoulders. "That woman can sing."

"No doubt better than she can interview. She was downright rude, then threw me out of her hotel room."

The whistling teapot called Camarin back into the kitchen.

"I'm confused. Why would she toss you out? Are you that bad a reporter?" Rachel said with a giggle.

"Apparently so. I had the audacity to suggest that instead of shooting up heroin, perhaps there were other, less addictive means to maintain a two-hundred-pound weight loss."

"Oh, Lord, help me, I'm drowning in the sarcasm. She lost that much weight?" DeAndre asked.

Camarin couldn't remember the last time she'd seen her roommate so engaged in a conversation. Maybe Evans had been right—no matter what she'd achieved, people were more concerned with the size of her ass than her vocal range.

"She did. Even more notably, she says her new album's going to suck, and she hates her life. Trouble is, I don't know if I can use any of that stuff."

She suddenly halted her rhythmic tea bag dunking. Had Evans said any of that was off the record? Maybe she could pull off an exclusive for *Trend* after all. Something to redeem herself, get Fletcher's attention. At least it would take her mind off the Mangel debacle.

"Tea's on the counter. Help yourself to milk and sweetener. I've got an article to write."

Two hours later, her first original piece for *Trend* was ready to email to Wynan and Fletcher. It was a no-holds-barred account of her interaction with Evans—sans any coddling or pussyfooting around—meshed with background details about the album from the publicist.

UNINSPIRED LYRICS, TONE-DEAF DELIVERY:
THE SKINNY ON AMERICAN DYNAMO WINNER'S NEW ALBUM RELEASE

A Trend Exclusive by Camarin Torres

Looking languid and surprisingly anorexic in a size-four, silky wrap dress, Perri Evans sucked deeply on her Marlboro cigarette in the presidential suite of the Hay Adams Hotel, recounting the shocking details behind the recording of her sophomore effort, Carnal Collage.

Referring to this reporter as one of the gang of journalists and critics who'd ruined her career, Evans confessed that Avaricious Records wouldn't produce or release the album unless she carved off two hundred pounds from her formerly curvaceous physique. But the entire episode filled her with misgivings: "I should have...just released the songs over the internet like everyone else... Plenty of people do just fine selling direct on iTunes, Spotify andYouTube."

Evans also expressed ambivalence over the ways fans have reacted to her obligatory pound shaving.

"I sang my heart out on national television in front of millions of viewers. And now, all that anyone can talk about is the weight loss. How did I do it? Doesn't everything seem better thin? People who didn't give me the time of day before, even with the TV show, are all nice to me now."

This reporter doesn't want to speculate about the methods behind the loss, though unexplained marks on the singer's arms seemed to lend clues. What's just as disconcerting is the singer's own appraisal of her latest recording effort: "The album sucks. I suck. But at least I'll be skinny when I read the one-star reviews [saying] 'Uninspired lyrics, tone-deaf delivery, but what an ass she's got on her now.'"

Here's hoping this was all a momentary case of pre-release jitters and Evan's second album is as fabulous as her first.

Camarin congratulated herself on a solid effort. While uncompromising, she'd spared Evans some embarrassment by omitting her swear words, along with the snipe at her agent, and presented the track marks in a factual way that she hoped would provide an epiphany to the singer about her drug use. Plus, she'd incorporated a thought or two about the hypocrisy behind the appreciation for weight loss over talent. True, the article was a bit harsher than what she'd originally intended to write. But Evans had known she was speaking to the press from the moment she opened the hotel room door.

All in all, an article that would fit perfectly into *Trend*'s current sensationalistic focus, Cam rationalized, and after the Philly failure, give her reason to believe she deserved a spot on the magazine's editorial masthead. She took a deep breath and hit the *send* button.

"You almost ready to go?" DeAndre rapped loudly on her door.

"Go?"

"Work? Benji's? You gone so long you forgot where you work?"

"Yeah, yeah, where's Annalise?" Her roommate would normally have tried on and rejected about five jaw-dropping outfits by now.

"She's got the night off. Went out of town to see friends. You coming?"

So much for her confidante. "Sure, just give me five."

She ignored the audible sighs on the other side of the door as she kicked off her jeans and grabbed a simple red A-line dress. While she fumbled with the zipper, she pondered how a famous man like Mangel could get away with treating women like objects. Certainly, she hadn't been the first. Perhaps they threatened to sue, and he paid them off, or proposed to them. Anything to keep the gory details from being smeared all over the internet.

"One minute and we're leaving," Rachel called out.

"What, couldn't think of something better?" asked Camarin, yanking the door open. "Like you're *Perrying*?"

"What the fuck are you going on about?"

"Steve Perry used to be the lead singer for Journey," she explained as they hurried out of the apartment. "Journey sings *Don't Stop Believing*. Believing rhymes with leaving. Isn't that how all of this works?"

"It's not half-bad. I'll submit it for approval to the Cockney powers that be. Now let's get going before DeAndre loses his job for being late and he can't afford to take me on that cruise he promised me."

Camarin bit her lip as she locked the front door. Why warn them to take things slow and ruin all their fun? Life's too short, and the end comes too quickly. For some, it could be one unexpected trailer visit away.

CHAPTER
27 28 29
|

CAMARIN WAS GRATEFUL for the subdued atmosphere at
Benji's that evening. A convention of electronics
engineers was in town and had selected the Laidlaw as their
host hotel. She was always happy to serve geeks like these—
they were usually polite, respectful, and always over tipped.
But, boy, could they party.

Not surprisingly, Rachel had planted herself on the piano
bench by DeAndre's side. Any minute now, she expected
them to launch into a duet of *Heart and Soul*. Instead, her
roommate delivered a pounding rendition of the Violent
Femmes's *Blister in the Sun*, joined by guest pianist/songstress
Whitney Maxwell. Camarin spied Rachel clandestinely
squeezing Dee's thigh while he fought to retain his
composure. At least she was too preoccupied to ask more
questions about the Mangel trip.

Cam was mixing an order of tequila sunrises when she
glanced up and saw Lyle Fletcher ambling toward the bar.
The delight reflected by his expression mirrored her own.
Suddenly, she felt safe, as if a virtual glass dome had just
encased them both, protecting them from the outcome of
whatever had transpired over the past forty-eight hours.

"Those drinks aren't going to make themselves," shouted Benji from the back of the bar. "And there are three orders laying on the counter. Get to it, Torres, or you'll be smiling on the unemployment line next week."

"I'm on it, Benji! Give me a break!"

But even Benji's threats couldn't dampen her joy at seeing Lyle, sharply dressed in thin-welt tan cords, topped with a button-down, jet-black shirt. The blue in his eyes and the gray in his whiskers aroused her even more than usual, overriding all thoughts of Mangel.

In his hand he held a single daisy, which he set down on the bar in front of her.

"I won't keep you from your customers. What time do you get off?"

About fifteen minutes after you get me home, she thought.

"My shift ends at one, but I usually go right home and get into bed. I have this other job, you see."

"I'm sure your boss would be more than understanding if you were a few minutes late tomorrow morning. Let me buy you one drink after closing? My way of apologizing for standing you up for our meeting last Friday?"

She rested her hand gently over his and pressed softly. Now, this was how you wooed a woman, not trying to proposition her in your trailer. "How can I say no to any request accompanied by a daisy? Take a seat. Enjoy the show. Make a request or two. I'll see you later."

The next six hours dragged on longer than a semester of organic chemistry. The audience, while restrained, still drank heavily, and with one bartender short, Camarin didn't even have time to enjoy an occasional break. She did see Fletcher walk up to the piano twice during the evening, each time wrapping a song title in a twenty-dollar bill. How romantic, she thought, to be romanced by request.

The first was Eric Clapton's *Beautiful Tonight*. Before DeAndre launched the second, Boston's *Let Me Take You Home Tonight*, his attached-at-the-hip companion scrutinized the note and grabbed the mic. "This one's for you, Cam. I think he's trying to tell you something!"

Flushed with a combination of embarrassment and lust, she paused from pouring a dozen shots of whiskey to give a thumbs-up to the piano and wave at the audience, who cheered their encouragement.

Finally, Whitney announced last call and started playing her final set. Exhausted and feet aching, Camarin held up both hands in surrender and retreated to the back room for a short respite. The best thing about the evening was that she'd been too busy to check her phone for any news about Mangel. Now that she had that opportunity, she decided against it. This had the potential to be an amazing evening together. Why ruin it when there was nothing she could do about any information she might find?

Benji entered the break area, and she gritted her teeth, waiting to be called out. To her astonishment, he patted her on the back and commended her for her hard work that evening. "Why don't you take off a little early? The other girls can handle things, and I probably owe you the time anyway."

"Thanks," she said, unconvinced. Had Fletcher slipped him a twenty as well?

She hit the ladies' room to freshen up her makeup and tried to ignore the stressed-out visage she saw staring back at her in the mirror. The last few days had taken their toll, something she hoped her amorous publisher would overlook as they shared their—ahem—drink together.

The number of spectators had dwindled as she re-entered the main showroom. DeAndre was playing his last number, REM's *It's the End of the World as We Know It*, his way of telling the audience to settle their tabs and head on home. Toward the back, Fletcher was sitting alone, nursing what looked like a glass of Coca-Cola.

"You teetotaling tonight?" she asked as she pulled out the chair beside him.

"I am. Need to have my wits about me." He reached out and stroked the side of her cheek, causing her to tremble with excitement. "You must be exhausted, Ms. Torres. Are you up for having a conversation?"

"I am, Mr. Fletcher."

The last of the patrons shuffled out the door, and the lights came back on, followed by the entrance of the cleaning crew, hauling their buckets and mops. From the stage, DeAndre waved, Rachel winked and hit his shoulder, and the two disappeared behind the curtains.

"This place works, if you want to speak somewhere private," she suggested. "They won't lock up for another hour."

Her smile turned solemn as he removed his palm from her cheek and clasped both hands together, elbows on the table, as if praying. "There's actually something kind of important I'd like to discuss with you, but it's been a long night. Are you sure you're awake enough for this?"

His change of tone took her by surprise. She leaned in closer. "Of course. What's wrong?"

"It's about that article you turned in earlier this afternoon."

She felt her heart sink.

"Was it written badly?" She spoke loudly, to be heard over the sounds of the janitors moving chairs around to mop the floor.

"No, it was actually written quite well. Cover worthy, in fact. But I was under the impression you came to *Trend* expecting to write an entirely different type of editorial. Do you really want to start your career by having your byline on something this...inflammatory?"

"You think it's inflam—"

"It's the type of story that could destroy that poor woman's career. She needs help for what you made sound like a heroin addiction. She doesn't need everyone's scorn to force her into rehab. I've known some addicts, seen their struggles. Something like this could push her over the other side, out of the recording studios and into seclusion with her needles and self-pity."

His words stung and surprised like a sucker punch to the gut. "I didn't think of it that way. I felt so awful for her, and I thought that by mentioning the track marks others might wake up and help her. I had to put something down. I couldn't come back empty-handed."

And you were angry she threw you out of her hotel room. Don't forget about that.

"I knew you were too compassionate to write something like this without a good reason. Sit down with Hans tomorrow and discuss the incident with him. Between the two of you, I'm sure you can piece together something that's hard-hitting while still sympathetic. Sound fair?"

"More than fair." She was thankful for his intervention, all the while wondering if her motivation behind the article's focus had been vindictiveness over how rudely Evans had treated her and how she had refused Camarin's advice.

"How did the rest of the weekend go?" he asked in an offhand manner, interrupting her disturbing introspection.

She shrugged. "Pretty quiet. Just trying to write something you'd want to publish. And, of course, resting up for working here tonight."

An expression passed over his face that she couldn't quite identify. Then he reached over and began stroking her hair. She closed her eyes, overcome by a desperate desire for his touch.

"There's one other thing," he said in a hushed tone.

She nodded, listening but refusing to open her eyes and distract from the electricity his fingers transmitted between her hair and her core. She squeezed her thighs together as her juices dampened her thong.

"I don't want you to think that you owe me anything or that your job would be in jeopardy if you said no to me. I have enormous respect for you, and I assure you that would never, ever happen. Is that clear?"

"Yes, sir." She pressed even tighter, trying to satisfy the throbbing between her legs that was driving her insane.

"And we're clear that whatever I might say to you in private is not as a boss, but as an admirer?"

"Crystal clear."

"Excellent. Then with that understanding, I need to tell you that you are one of the most fascinating, delightful women I've met in a long, long time. I can't keep my mind off you. If you would care to join me upstairs for a drink in a more secluded setting, I'd like to show you exactly how alluring I find you."

She opened her eyes and stared into his. "That would be the prudent thing to do. In Chamorro folklore, things do not end well when lovers are kept apart."

"You will have to tell me more about that...after." His fingers wrapped around the lock of hair they'd been caressing and tugged, pulling her face closer to his. She gasped as his lips parted and he kissed her hard, passionately.

When he pulled away, she murmured only one word. "More."

The two strolled arm in arm out of the club and through the mostly deserted lobby to the elevators. He pushed her against the wall that separated two of the banks, again pulling her hair back until she faced the ceiling. As she writhed in desire, he nipped at her throat, his body pressed forcefully against hers. So primal.

Her moan gave voice to her own intense hunger. She ran her hands up from his belt to his pecs, feeling the muscles that tensed underneath his shirt. She teased slightly, gently pressing him away, only to become even more aroused when he didn't slow down or acknowledge her mock resistance.

"Wait," she whispered, and to that, he did respond, lightening the pressure, pulling away by an inch but not releasing his fistful of her hair. "Upstairs. Please. Where we can be alone."

Using his free hand, Fletcher pressed the call button. Nearby, the sound of chatter warned that other guests were approaching. He stepped away, allowing her to also turn and face forward, clinging to some semblance of decorum. When the car arrived, they entered, and he pressed twenty-nine, the floor just beneath the penthouse.

The others exited on nineteen, and she half-expected him to attack her before they reached their designated floor, but he kept his distance, and simultaneously upped the suspense. The roughness of his passion had both dazed and roused her. When would he satisfy this longing he had stirred?

The elevator opened on the penultimate floor and he put his arm around her waist, guiding her down the hall to his room. He pulled the keycard from his pocket and handed it to her.

"You want me to open it?"

"Yes. It's your unspoken consent to whatever might occur inside."

His words sent chills down her spine. "You make it sound kind of ominous. Exactly what are you planning to do?"

"Nothing you won't enjoy, I assure you," he whispered into her hair. "And certainly nothing you can't put an end to with a single word. It's a psychological thing. I'm a bit older than you, and I need to know that I haven't sweet-talked you into something you might not have interest in or be prepared for."

Flashing before her eyes stood every fumbling teenager who'd ever attempted to seduce her; every instance she'd longed for someone more mature and sophisticated who knew their way around a woman's body. Now her dream man had arrived and he was asking if she was sure? Without a second thought, she yanked the keycard away.

"I *am* a bit younger than you. Think you'll be able to keep up, old man?"

He half-laughed, half-snickered as he leaned down and smacked her hard on the ass. "Mind your manners, missy, or there will be more where that came from."

She howled in mock surprise as she pushed the door open into the suite, and he steered her inside. He slipped the *Do Not Disturb* sign onto the outside knob and then locked them inside together. At the far end of the living room were a wall of windows facing downtown, sparkling with a million points of light. She had never been so high up above the city at night, and she walked over to the door that led out to the balcony.

"What an incredible view."

"I couldn't agree more."

He came up behind her and enveloped her, his nose sniffing the back of her hair. The tighter his embrace, the further he pushed away all memory of Mangel. She could feel this hard cock pressing against her buttocks. They stood there for a time, rocking back and forth, as she basked in the cradle of his arms.

He started blowing lightly into her ear and nibbling on the lobe, and she leaned her head back, yielding to his attentions as his hands explored the front of her dress, moving from her waist to the fullness of her breasts. He cupped them and then traced his fingers around her nipples through the fabric.

"Now, what was that you said about my age?"

"Is it your hearing that's failing you or your memory?" she asked, gambling that a little ribbing couldn't fail to stir the flames.

He pinched each nipple, and a jolt of energy raced directly to her clit. She yelped in mock pain.

"Excuse me? I don't think I heard you correctly."

"I believe the last thing I said was 'Ow!'"

"Mmm, I believe you're right. I meant before that."

"I guess that settles it—it's your hearing."

She broke away and went running in the dark to what she assumed was the bedroom. Fletcher followed in hot pursuit. Inside, she stood to the right of the entrance as he ran past.

"You're in real trouble now, Camarita."

"I certainly hope so." She slammed the door behind him and waited for him to turn around.

A flicker of light streamed between the drapes, courtesy of Times Square's electronic billboards. She watched his silhouette as he took a seat on edge of the bed.

"Camarin Torres," he said in a soft voice, "what's your middle name?"

"It's Monaeka."

He paused. "I'm sorry, what?"

"I said, it's Monaeka. It means 'doll' in Chamorro."

"But…Monaeka…isn't that your…isn't that the most beautiful name ever? Well, Ms. Camarin Monaeka Torres, you come right over here."

It was a much firmer tone, and it drove her wild with craving. Him being her senior, being her boss, ordering her around—it was like every erotic fantasy she'd ever entertained come to life. She gulped and stood before him, a statue in the dark.

"Good girl. Now slowly, very slowly, pull your left arm out of your dress sleeve."

She did as she was told. She hoped that the wetness between her thighs wasn't running down her legs, staining the carpet beneath her.

"Now the other side."

His voice was stern and steady, and she knew better than to spoil the moment by disobeying, even in jest.

"Very nice. You're doing just fine. Now wriggle it over your hips and let it fall to the floor."

She complied and returned to her original pose, dressed only in a lace bra, matching thong, and heels, with her dress crumpled around her ankles. She started to step out so she could kick it away, but he cleared his throat.

"Exactly what are you doing?"

"I was just—"

"You'll do as you're told, or you'll be sent packing. I've fired employees for far less. Is that understood?"

"Yes, sir." Her heart was racing, her breath shallow. She couldn't remember ever being this turned on.

"Now you may remove it entirely."

She gingerly stepped to the side so her feet were unencumbered.

"How do you feel, Camarita?"

"Excited."

"That's a promising answer. Do you trust me?"

"Entirely."

"What do you think I should ask you to do next?"

She smiled though she wasn't sure if he could see it in the dark. *This evil, evil man.* "I think you'd ask me take off my bra."

"Why would I do that?"

"So you can see my breasts."

"Are you asking me to look at your breasts?"

You've got something better to look at? No, no, no. No smartass sarcasm now.

"I think you would enjoy it, yes."

"Show me and I'll let you know."

She lowered each strap and then reached behind and undid the clasp. She caught it before it fell and dropped it on top of her dress.

"Lovely. Please touch them as you would want me to."

She did as he commanded.

"Mmm, that's nice. And squeeze the nipples like I did before. Harder. I want to watch you wince, be sure you know how I might punish you if you disobey my orders again."

She pinched tightly and imagined it was his fingers at work. If he didn't take her soon, she would orgasm just from the sound of his voice.

"Do you want me to take off my thong?"

"No, darling. I want you to walk over here and politely ask me to do that."

"You're going to strip me of every bit of dignity and reserve, aren't you?"

"Every ounce. You are a caged, wanton tigress. And I want to be the one to tame you."

She went to him, desperate to do whatever he asked so he might relieve her longing.

"I beg you, sir. Remove the last thing that separates you from what you desire. I want to do whatever it takes to please you." She ended the request with a soft growl.

That was all it took. He reached forward and grabbed her by the hips, pulling her past him and heaving her onto the bed. He ordered her to stay still as he unbuttoned his shirt and pulled off his pants. Then he was on top of her, yanking her wrists above her head toward the pillows. He held them with one hand as he reached down and put his finger inside her thong and felt her wetness. He brought the finger back up to her mouth and pressed it to her lips.

"Open up. Taste your hunger."

She licked it clean and then took his finger into her mouth, rhythmically sucking it as she watched the yearning grow in his eyes.

"Now it's my turn," he said.

He released her wrists, pulled off her thong, and maneuvered until he was perched between her open thighs. He submerged himself in her sweetness, sucking and licking her clit in quick spurts, and then stopping until she implored him to continue. He alternated between bringing her to the brink and relaxing his attack until she begged him for release, promising to do whatever he wanted if he would only allow her to come. She wrapped her legs around his back and lost herself in pleasure. He relentlessly pursued his prize, bringing her closer and closer until she surrendered in an earth-shattering climax that made her scream.

As she came back to earth, he excused himself, walked into the bathroom, and returned wearing protection. Not sparing a second, he jumped back atop her and pounded her with an intensity that again took her breath away. She sank her nails into his back as he plunged into her again and again. Finally, he exploded inside her and then collapsed by her side with a long, satisfied groan of pleasure.

They both lay silent and sweaty, trying to catch their breath.

"What were you saying about my age, Ms. Torres?"

She rolled on her side and played with the few hairs that adorned his chest. "It's truly one of the things I like best about you. You're a man, not some gangly boy."

He propped himself up on one elbow, cupping her breast with his free hand. "You were speaking earlier about the dangers of Chamorro lovers being separated?"

"There are at least two stories warning of it in our folklore," she said, running her fingers more possessively across his chest, exploring the terrain that was now hers to claim. "One is a very Romeo-and-Juliet-type story, but here the girl is named Elena and the boy, Nicholas. Long story short, at the end, the doomed couple are to meet under a special tree with white blossoms. He believes she is dead and plunges a dagger into his chest, and his blood spurts out and covers the tree's roots.

"Elena finds him, barely alive, and they share one last meaningful glance before he succumbs to his wound. She spies a machete on the ground, and weeping uncontrollably, she plunges it into her abdomen, praying that they will be buried together. The gods look down with compassion and turn the blossoms of the tree into a burning red like the lovers' blood. From then on, that type of tree has been known as a flame tree, and when its crimson flowers burst out each year, it is a reminder that love alone should rule the world."

"Interesting. Tell me the other story, please. Don't stop, no matter what. When you stop, I stop." He pushed her onto her back and started licking her nipples while his hand explored lower.

Her breath grew shallow as she fought to remember the tale over the peals of pleasure he was inspiring. "Um…the other story…ahhh…is about a girl whose father insisted she marry a Spanish sea captain, though her heart belonged to a young warrior who…oh, oh…"

Her body was pulsing gently to the rhythm of his fingers inside her, but he paused when her storytelling did. "I'm waiting," he said patiently. "What about the warrior?"

"He was gentle…oh, yes…with a strong build and had eyes that…mmm…that searched for meaning in the stars…"

"Go on," he said, his finger again rubbing her clit but torturously slowly, drawing out the ecstasy.

Camarin fought to retain her composure and complete the tale. "She escaped to visit her lover, and her father had them pursued by soldiers…oh, yes, please don't stop… They were chased all the way to the top of a high cliff above Tumon Bay…ahhh… When they realized they were trapped, with the army on one side and the cliff on the other…oooh, yes, right there…they tied their long hair together into a single knot…kissed for one final time and leaped over the cliff to the roaring waters below…yes, oh, yes… Since that time, that couple remains a symbol of true love for the Chamorro people…uh-huh, ahhh…linked together for eternity… The point on that cliff is known as Two…Lovers…Point. That's the end of the story…please don't stop."

Torn between his one palm grazing her erect nipples and the other, finger fucking her pussy, she arched her back in rapture as he pulled another mind-bending orgasm from her yielding body. She lay in silence for a long while, luxuriating in the release.

"Sounds like falling for a Chamorro woman might be a death sentence. I'd better watch my step," he said, making a dramatic show of licking his fingers clean.

"As long as she's not denied what she wants, everything ends up okay. Speaking of which, Mr. Fletcher, I'm not sure I'll make it to work on time today."

"Ms. Torres, that's fine. You can come in late, or even work remotely if you choose, but I will need you available. In about an hour, I expect an issue may pop up that you'll need to attend to."

She giggled in delight and reached over to stroke his cock, already rock hard and pulsating. "A whole hour? Are you sure?"

"Maybe less," he said with a chuckle, rolling onto his back. "I'm sure someone as hardworking and diligent as you understands how to solve a problem when one arises."

"Indeed, I do," she said, positioning herself between his legs and licking her lips. "Though this might require some overtime."

H IS PHONE ALARM began chirping at 7:00, stirring them both from an abbreviated but much-needed sleep. She was surprised at how refreshed she was despite only getting three hours' rest. She looked over at Fletcher, who opened one eye and then closed it again.

"Coffee. My kingdom for a pot of coffee," he said.

"I'll call room service. What else would you like?"

"Maybe just two fried eggs. I can't eat much in the morning. But you order whatever you like."

I can't eat anything ever. She pulled the sheet up to her waist, suddenly aware of how the sunlight streaming through the partially opened drapes illuminated every inch of her naked body.

She reached across him to pick up the phone, making sure that her breasts pressed against his face, hoping for a morning repeat of the previous evening's festivities.

He kissed each one as she placed their order but didn't go for the bait as she'd hoped. Once she'd returned to her side of their king-sized bed, he sat up, turned from her, and stretched his arms high in the air. She admired his rippling back muscles and resisted an urge to pull him into her arms.

"I'm going to take a shower. I'd invite you with me, but I fear that we'd barricade ourselves in this hotel room and never leave. So, please know that I expect a raincheck. Agreed?"

"Agreed, sir."

"My wallet is in the pocket of my pants, wherever they are. Please hand the waiter a five when he comes. Wouldn't want to earn a reputation as a bad tipper. You never know when we may want to use this hotel again."

He wandered naked into the bathroom, an excellent opportunity for her to admire his tight ass. She listened to the whoosh of the shower water, reminiscing over the more lascivious moments of the prior evening, wondering how long it might be before he invited her out again.

Ten minutes passed, and she realized room service might arrive at any time. She walked to the front of the bed to find their discarded clothes and slipped her dress back on so she'd be presentable enough to answer the door. Catching a glance of herself in a mirror above the dresser, she playfully sucked in her cheeks and posed like a model displaying this year's most 'in' look: disheveled but well-fucked.

She heard Lyle turn off the water in the bathroom and realized she hadn't yet taken the money from his pants. It would be a tragedy to miss out on such a perfect invitation to steal a glance at his driver's license and find out how old he really was. She picked up his trousers, pulled out the black leather wallet, and sat down on his side of the bed. Knowing she only had moments to spare, she pulled out a five and then thumbed through the plastic inserts: a platinum American Express card, his license—wow, thirty-nine years old, not that much older—and then a picture that made her freeze.

It was his wedding photo with the wife he'd mentioned he'd lost. He looked so dapper in his gray morning coat and top hat, her radiant in a beaded mermaid gown. Camarin felt a twang of jealousy and silently berated herself for her stupidity. The woman was dead—what was she envious about? Yet there was something about that bride's face that was so damn familiar. Where had she seen it before?

A rap at the door signaled the arrival of room service. She carefully closed the wallet, left it on the nightstand, and then headed into the living room. After the waiter had placed the tray on the dining room table and thanked her for the generous tip, she closed the door behind him and turned to find Lyle in the bedroom doorway, bare-chested, a towel wrapped around his waist.

Unable to resist, she strolled over and reached for the one thing keeping her from the breakfast she most desired, but he caught her hand in his.

"Someone's a bit greedy this morning, isn't she?"

"Greedy or just eager to do my job?"

"Perhaps both. But this morning we must edit that article of yours. So, please, I beg you, go make yourself less desirable, if that's in any way possible, so I can concentrate on my coffee and on revamping our magazine."

She batted her eyes, slowly and seductively pulled off her dress, bulges be damned, and turned toward the bathroom. "As you wish, Mr. Fletcher. After all, you are the boss."

CHAPTER
28 29 30

FLETCHER POURED HIMSELF a cup of coffee as he watched his new lover saunter into the bathroom and wondered exactly what he'd gotten himself into. She was gorgeous, passionate, smart, and sarcastic—really everything he'd ever craved in a woman. It was a dream come true. But. There was always a but.

Why no mention of attending the revival? Of her heartfelt confession on stage? And while he regretted that she had managed to wheedle her way into Mangel's world, why not even the slightest clue about why she ran from his trailer yesterday morning?

And that middle name—Monaeka. How she must suffer, being forced to relive her guilt over her sister every time she jotted down her complete signature. What were her parents thinking, using the same moniker for both twins? So odd. Maybe it was a Chamorro thing.

But perhaps worse than the demons Camarin battled daily—a war he might soon have to help her win—was the struggle he was fighting within himself. He was at a crossroads, sacrificing everything, cautiously inching toward his goal. The last thing he needed was a woman in his life.

Hell, he didn't even have an apartment to call his own. Thank goodness she hadn't asked why they'd spent the night in a hotel room instead of his place since he currently lived chez Hans and Austin.

And yet despite all the progress he'd made, here he stood, teetering on the brink of losing himself to her, something he had experienced only once before. It was frightening to be so vulnerable, so susceptible to someone else's whims, their heartaches. He longed to again live a life spurred by joy rather than vindictiveness. Would Camarin ultimately prove to be his deliverance or his undoing?

He pictured her in the shower, the cascades of water tumbling over her firm, tan breasts, her ample hips, her shapely ass. Margaret might not approve of many of the choices he'd made lately, but this one, a woman as determined and headstrong as she? He believed she would consider Cam a worthy successor.

He set down his cup, fighting his impulse to interrupt her shower, take her a third time. Just to hear her gasp once again at the moment of release would carry him through his day. Halfway to the doorway, he heard the water turn off and froze, overwhelmed with disappointment. And then he remembered one of his favorite quotes from essayist and poet Ralph Waldo Emerson: *Never lose an opportunity for seeing anything beautiful, for beauty is God's handwriting.* He pulled the towel from around his waist, reached for the door handle, and pushed it open. It was time to write some more poetry of their own.

CHAPTER
29 30 31

"YOU LOOK LIKE absolute shit."

"Thanks, roomie. Missed you too." Camarin walked past Annalise, ignoring her jibes as well as the hall mirror, and headed right for the Keurig. One cup, maybe two of Death Wish coffee, topped by a splash of skim milk, might revitalize her sufficiently to make it through the day. She grabbed her NYU Grad mug, placed it under the spout, and waited for black liquid salvation to come pouring out.

Annalise wandered into the kitchen and moved a pile of unpaid bills from one of their mismatched chairs onto the floor so she had a place to sit. Wearing a cutoff tee that barely covered her breasts, along with low-waisted, flannel pajama bottoms, navel ring exposed, she reminded Camarin of an edgier version of *I Dream of Jeannie*.

"You want to tell me how the weekend went?"

As Cam stood hypnotized by the sight of coffee filling her mug, she realized she no longer felt the need to confide in anyone regarding the Mangel fiasco. "It went, I guess. The Perri Evans thing fell flat. I wrote something, but Lyle thought it was a little too caustic."

"Ah. So, that's where you've been all night? Editing?"

Camarin twisted her mouth to the side. "Cute. Though I do believe I managed to erase a few question marks and replace them with an exclamation point or two." She blew the rising steam from the brew as she took a seat beside her prosecutor.

"Ooh, grammar porn. I love it. The way you look this morning, you must have proofread the hell out of each other."

Cam smiled and said nothing.

"Just keep him away from your colon, baby."

"Ha, ha, ha," she said as she took a swig of coffee. "I'm not too concerned. But there was one thing…"

"Ooh, intrigue. Tell me more." Annalise leaned forward.

"I was in his wallet —"

"His wallet? I thought you were just interested in getting into his pants, but you really go the extra mile."

She set her mug down and shot her roommate a reprimanding glance. "You wanna listen, or you want to write a comedy routine? I was getting money to tip room service. And I saw this picture. It was of his wedding."

Her mouth dropped. "The fucker's married?"

"No, he's widowed. I've known that since the day I met him. It wasn't the picture that bothered me. It was his wife's face. She looked so familiar."

"What did Google say?"

Camarin blinked. Some journalist. She'd fantasized about the guy for over a month, and she'd never thought to google him. Or maybe she'd subconsciously feared what she might find.

"What's his name again? Lyle Fletcher?" Annalise typed the name into her cellphone, clicked on a link, and handed her the results.

Cam grabbed the Samsung away so quickly she even surprised herself. The headline, dating back sixteen years, read *Margaret Waldman Weds Criminal Defense Attorney Lyle Fletcher.* Of course, she thought, Margaret Waldman. No wonder the face looked so familiar. She'd watched her a thousand times on television years back.

She scanned the article quickly, picking out the key points, such as clues to Fletcher's pedigree. Wealthy New England family. Yale undergrad, Juris Doctorate from Harvard. Law Review. She studied his photo. Though younger men weren't her thing, she definitely would have done him.

Curiosity piqued, she searched under Margaret's name. Thousands of results described her firing by the Lehming Brothers, owners of WRTX, and the ensuing lawsuit over age discrimination. Newspaper editorials discussing whether five pounds and five years should disqualify a crack journalist from reporting the nightly news. *Oh my God, she and I were fighting the same fight. No wonder Fletcher reached out.*

Camarin kept reading, heart pounding, unable to look away. The ultimate ruling against Waldman. Despite rival network execs condemning the decision, the former wunderkind unable to find work elsewhere. Reports of seclusion. Deep depression. And then—

Camarin gasped.

"What, what is it?"

"His wife. She hanged herself. Right in their apartment. He found her there. Oh, that poor, poor man."

She laid down the phone, engulfed by grief for her lover as well as for a woman she'd never known. Having a loved one commit suicide was something she understood too well. How she longed to reach out to Fletcher, clasp him in her arms, make him whole again.

Annalise snatched up the phone and read the article herself. "You can't tell him you know about this."

"Why not?"

"You want to admit that first you looked through his wallet, and then you stalked him online?"

"Well, he does know I'm a journalist."

"This is like an open wound for him. I really don't think you want to go rubbing salt in it. He'll tell you when he thinks it's appropriate, I'm sure."

She hung her head. "I'm sure you're right. It makes me wonder though… why do you think he left law for journalism? I mean, after all his wife went through. He was fighting for right, defending the unjustly accused, and then he leaves that for an industry he must despise?"

"Well, maybe if you two keep 'editing' together, you'll unravel that mystery too, Nancy Drew. Speaking of which, what happened with the big revival investigation? You get what you were after?"

"I never even got to speak to him," said Camarin, determined to keep her story consistent. "I guess I'll have to find some other clues to pursue." She downed the last of her coffee.

It occurred to her that the right thing to do would be to let the police know that an active murderer was still out there, knocking people off, the latest target being Mangel, whether or not the mission had been successful. But how to let on without placing herself at the revival and risking that the information could somehow reach Fletcher and Wynan?

Annalise reached for a piece of bread and, pinching her thumb and forefinger together, proceeded to turn it into a pile of crumbs. "I'm going to sprinkle these from here to the bedroom. Give you something to follow. If you don't get changed soon, you'll never make it to work. Even if banging the boss does buy you a free pass, you don't want everyone else, AKA Rachel, to get wise and start resenting you."

Realizing that her roommate was right, Cam rose from the table. "I'm sure she already knows," she said before disappearing into the bedroom to search for alternate apparel. "Rachel was at the club last night. She may be many things, but one of them definitely isn't blind."

CHAPTER
30 31 32

RACHEL FLASHED AN enormous I-know-what-you-were-up-to-last-night smile when Camarin finally pushed open the door at *Trend* just after eleven.

"Not one word."

"I wouldn't dream of it. In case you're wondering, Mr. Fletcher hasn't arrived yet. But Wynan's been asking for you. You'd better show your face before he hands you your head."

"What, no cutesy slang innuendo?"

"Nah, I think you've got enough to work out today. But before you go in, I need your help. I'm supposed to have dinner with Dee's parents this Friday. He says you've been there tons of times before. Any advice?"

"You do know they publish *Drift*, right?"

"Yeah, he mentioned something or other about that. That's the black version of *Trend*, right?

"It's African American–owned, yes. More importantly, it was a pioneer publication. His grandparents were breaking down barriers long before *Ebony* and *Jet* came along. You want to make points? Study up on the history behind that magazine. What changes his parents have made since they took over. And be super respectful. They're like the family I never had."

"Thanks for the tip. Now get in there and dazzle the knickers off him, luv."

Cam took a deep breath, pulled open the door to the inner offices, and headed right for the bullpen and Wynan's desk.

"I'm so sorry I'm late. It won't happen again."

"You okay?" He looked concerned rather than angry.

"Yes…why? Is this about the article? I spoke to Mr. Fletcher yesterday. He expressed some concern over its tone, so we agreed that all three of us should revise it."

"Actually…I thought it was excellent. Exactly the type of snarky journalism our readers have come to expect. I told layout to run with it. It's this week's print cover story, and it's already on the website. Congratulations."

She felt her stomach drop. "No…I wrote that story in a panic because she hadn't given me the real interview. I was angry and desperate—"

"Are the facts correct? Is your account what really happened?"

"Yes, but—"

"But nothing. It's accurate. We run it."

"It's just that Lyle said…he felt my story could destroy that poor girl. That there were more compassionate ways to help, not shame her and destroy her relationship with her record company."

"That's not my problem. My problem is putting out a magazine that readers pull off the shelves. And honestly, that's now your problem too. I'll deal with Lyle. If he manages to make it in today."

Camarin's face started burning, half out of embarrassment and half out of frustration over this cover story bungle. She wondered if Wynan would even notice, much less care. She decided to take one last shot at making this right.

"One question. How is this any different than those boys beating you up at boarding school when you were friendless and vulnerable?"

"One answer. I was an innocent kid. She's an adult. She owns her own choices. She agreed to an interview, and she'll make millions from the album she's using our story to promote. Not bad for your first byline. Speaking of which, after showing me your chops with that Evans piece, I'm taking you off copyediting detail. I have a ton of articles and interviews I can assign you. You can meet any celebrity you desire."

"But once they see how I smeared Perri to hell and back   "

"They'll still kill to meet with you. Something you'll grow to understand about people in the spotlight. Any publicity is good publicity." He reached into his desk and pulled out a list of names. "Here are some ideas I came up with a few weeks ago. Controversial people who would make great interview targets. Take it to your desk and start doing some background research. Start with whomever you choose."

She picked up the paper and skulked back to her cubicle. How could Wynan be so heartless and unfeeling? She regretted ever turning in the Evans assignment. Publicly humiliating celebrities for their shortcomings was not the job she'd signed up for. It would not cleanse her soul nor garner her the redemption she craved. It would merely make her part of everything in society she despised. If this was Manhattan journalism, she wanted out now.

She closed her eyes at her desk and silently meditated. There was no problem that couldn't be solved, given enough time and thought. Of course, if one of those problems was a total absence of sleep the night before, perhaps shut-eye was not the answer. She felt herself drifting off and forced her eyelids back open. Where were a pair of toothpicks when you needed them?

Best idea, do the job. But do it her way. Study each celebrity, conduct in-depth research, find something redeemable about every name on the list. Their charitable work, how they overcame the bullies in their youth, something, anything. This she could do. A challenge worth undertaking.

Just as she was starting to feel calmer about the assignment, Rachel burst into the bullpen area and pointed the remote at the monitor hanging on the wall. "Oh my God, it's all over Twitter. You have to see this!"

Every muscle in Camarin's body tensed as she looked up at the screen and saw April Lowery. This was it, everything she had feared, the news she could have played a role in preventing. The legend said that April was speaking from Wilmington, DE. Still primped to excess, she looked a bit paler than Camarin remembered. Rachel turned up the volume, and together they watched April address the crowd from a podium covered in microphones.

"Ladies and gentlemen of the press. I'm devastated to announce that there's been…" Her voice cracked, and Cam could see she was fighting back tears. "There's been an incident. Sometime on Sunday morning, someone entered Terry Mangel's trailer. They attacked him. A man who wanted nothing more than to spread love and acceptance in the world…and someone hurt him."

"Is he alive?" yelled out one reporter.

"Where is he now?" screamed another.

Camarin braced herself, waiting for the answer.

"We cannot comment on Mr. Mangel's location or condition other than to say that he's somewhere secret and safe, being closely monitored by his organization's own team of nurses and physicians. We are doing everything possible for him, and we hope to have the Feel Good About Yourself revival continue as planned, a week from Friday in Charlotte, North Carolina, at the Metrolina Fairgrounds. We hope that everyone in the viewing audience will attend this spectacular event. Thank you for your prayers."

"I can't believe she's using the news conference to promote the business," said one editor in the bullpen. Camarin just stared at the screen, speechless, guilt engulfing her like quicksand.

The camera panned over to a reporter interviewing a policewoman. "Have you found any clues to this horrible assault?" she asked.

"Nothing to find," answered the officer, resigned. "This is Delaware. The attack was in Pennsylvania. Out of our jurisdiction. We asked to see the trailer where the crime took place, but Mangel representatives told us they're a very private organization and would investigate this internally. They said there was a surveillance camera in the trailer, but it's allegedly gone missing. So, there are no leads for us to follow up."

"Any idea why Mangel's crew might have driven their convoy from the scene of the crime?" asked the reporter.

"Not an inkling. Unless they were scared the attacker might strike again. In any case, we can't do a thing here."

"Shut it off, please. I've seen enough," Camarin called out to Rachel, who clicked the remote and hurried to her side.

"I didn't want to say anything, Cam, but isn't Mangel the bloke you went down to Philadelphia to see?" Rachel whispered.

Cam's head already felt like it was hosting a conga drum recital, and her limbs were tremoring in time to the beat. Rachel's questions intensified the clamor.

"Yes, but as I told everyone last night, it was such a madhouse, I never got close," she lied. "I feel awful. I could have helped prevent that." At least that part was true. Mangel got what was coming to him, based on the little she recalled from the trailer encounter. But that didn't make her culpability any less palpable. "I think I just need a little time alone. You understand, right, Rachel? Just please, the details about my trip to Philly—could we just keep them to ourselves?"

"You know me. I'm like a black hole of information. Nothing ever escapes." Rachel headed back to the reception area.

Camarin knew nothing of the sort, except that black holes could end up exploding, and that was the last thing she needed. She pulled a bottle of spring water from her desk drawer, downed half, and then leaned her head on her desk, trying to calm herself and alleviate her headache.

Once the pounding subsided, her curiosity returned, and she decided to see what was being reported about the incident on the internet. Maybe with her inside knowledge, she could uncover some clues the police had missed. She waited for her computer to boot up and then typed in her password. M-O-N-A-E-K-A. Her email icon was flashing as if daring her to click. A love note from Lyle perhaps, something to brighten up her morning and explain his absence? That would be nice. She could use the distraction.

Last night had been a game changer, a message cast in flames against a black sky that good men existed, and love was possible. Her future was out there, like the daisy he'd given her, waiting to be plucked. Tempted as she was to wax poetic, especially considering which words rhymed with plucked, she took another swig of water, and with a tingle of excitement, clicked on the blinking envelope.

Life truly can change in an instant, and in Camarin's case, that instant was followed by a violent coughing fit caused by a gulp of liquid swallowed the wrong way. She struggled to shut down the screen before any good Samaritan who raced to her aid could catch a glimpse.

Three well-meaning women quickly surrounded her, one pounding on her back, convinced she was a baby who needed burping, another threatening to perform the Heimlich maneuver. She held them at bay, arm extended and hand up, a wordless 'hold off.' After about a half-minute of frantically trying to catch her breath, the attack subsided, and the throng of do-gooders dispersed. Only then, when prying eyes were safely beyond viewing distance, did she attempt to steady her quivering hand long enough switch her screen back on.

The email, from someone named anon@ymouse.net, revealed a sight so hideous she tasted bile working its way up her esophagus. A digital photo, unmistakably of her, brandishing a white marble-handled letter opener at a naked Mangel. Then a second photo, showing her standing with the opener dripping in red, beside Mangel's crumpled, bloodied body. And then a third, date-stamped a minute later, documenting her exit from the trailer. There was no note, but the pictures alone sent a bolt of terror through her.

Could they be real? she wondered as she broke out in a cold sweat. She'd blocked out so much of the encounter, she couldn't be absolutely sure. But even in her wildest nightmares, she couldn't conceive of being capable of anything like this.

No, this was definitely a frame-up. Someone had taken photos from inside the trailer, altered them and was attempting to implicate her. That was the only conceivable answer. She refused to contemplate any other.

She turned her head wildly, checking to make sure no one was peering over at her screen and then, in a panic, deleted both pictures from her hard drive. Not that she believed for one minute that she'd seen the last of them. But why risk leaving them on the network for anyone else to stumble across?

She was at a loss over her next move. She'd told everyone who'd listen that she'd never met up with Mangel. How could she explain these photos away without her lies betraying her?

And then, of course, there were the people she hadn't told. Specifically, Wynan. Lyle. They'd sent her to Washington on assignment. How could she explain cashing in the tickets to cover a side trip to Philly as well?

Maybe the DC trip and the resulting article were her alibi, but it was partial at best. Especially when thousands heard her on stage, recounting her crimes against her sister. Terrific way to kill a budding relationship, being caught dead-handed before your second date. She would have appreciated her own pun more if she hadn't started shivering uncontrollably.

She closed her eyes, trying to temper her anxiety. Once she had the shakes under control, she pretended to look over Wynan's list of names, terrified to switch her screen back on lest 'Anon' decided to transmit another zinger. She practically jumped when her desk phone rang, but calmed when she saw it was from an office extension.

"Torres."

"How do you feel this morning, Camarita?" Lyle's voice was like balm soothing cramping muscles.

"A little worn out," she said, surprised that her voice didn't wobble and reveal her inner quandary. "Thanks for letting me have the morning off."

"As I recall, you turned in an extra-credit assignment that more than made up for the lost time."

Despite the Mangel trauma, she couldn't help but smile, recalling how he'd picked up her naked body and carted her back into the shower for round number three. But then this morning's discussion with the executive editor came to mind and her mood returned to somber.

"Lyle, Wynan put through the story about Perri Evans as originally written. He's making it this week's cover, and it's already on the website. Is there anything you can do to kill any of this?"

"I wish there was. He caught me as I walked through the door, filled me in on the whole dilemma. Come into my office, and we'll discuss it further."

She hung up the phone and pushed back on her chair, standing just as it rang again. She smiled as she picked up the receiver. "Forget to tell me to bring an extra bar of soap, just in case things get dirty again?"

Instead of the laughter she expected, the line was silent, other than a low crackle. Then she heard a distorted voice, not distinctly male or female, like some subway announcer or a robot from a science fiction cartoon. "Camarin Torres?"

A chill enveloped her, and her teeth began to chatter. "Y-yes?"

"Did you enjoy the pictures I sent?"

Her knees buckled, and she plopped back down. "I don't know what you want, but those pictures were faked. I had nothing to do with anything," she whispered to avoid being overheard.

"What I want will become very clear to you in time. Mangel's people chose not to elaborate on the attack or their suspicions about its perpetrator, but their reticence doesn't extend to me. I might be an Invisible Woman, but I'm not a mute one."

"Go away and leave me alone. I am not party to any of this."

"So you said earlier, but the pictures certainly tell a different story, don't they? Not to mention your fingerprints on the letter opener. Tomorrow I will call you with a task. The others have performed them voluntarily, but you, my dear, you may need a bit of extra coaxing, no? I'm sure I can make a very persuasive argument to ensure your cooperation. In the meantime, not a word to anyone, and I mean anyone. Otherwise, people very close to you are going to die. My spies are everywhere, so don't take this warning lightly. Until tomorrow then." *Click.*

Camarin stared at the dead receiver, her entire body shaking even more violently than before. She tried to focus, to think. Others? What others? The murderers in her pack of vigilantes? And people close to her…who did the caller mean? Her roommates? Lyle? Her mother?

She had to do something, extricate herself from this growing nightmare. But even if she wanted to go to the police, or even to her editor or publisher, why should they believe her? The pictures were damning, clearly putting her at the scene. Any denial would make it sound like she was making up a story to protect herself from prosecution.

"An invisible woman attacked Mangel and then threatened you?" they'd ask incredulously. *"How very convenient."* And they'd be justified in their cynicism. It's not like she had the ultimatum in print. There was no proof the Invisible Woman had ever threatened her. And she'd deleted the photos.

And what about 'the task' the Invisible Woman had alluded to? Camarin barely had any savings, certainly nothing to spare for blackmail demands, if that's what The Collective was after.

Fletcher buzzed her on the intercom. She answered without giving him time to inquire. "I'm sorry. I had a phone call. I'll be right in."

She decided on her immediate plan of attack: keep everything to herself in order to protect the innocent. Sit with Lyle, coolly discuss the Evans matter, and, when she got back to her desk, skim through every weight-loss and body-pride group on Facebook again for any mention of the Invisible Woman. Maybe she'd missed something during her earlier search. No one was that invisible. Everyone leaves a trail. And Camarin was determined to follow this one as far as necessary to catch a killer—and save herself.

CHAPTER 31 32 33

FLETCHER COULDN'T FAIL to notice Camarin's agitation as she sat down opposite him, only a desk separating them from each other's embrace. He resisted the urge, determined to maintain a professional demeanor, at least while at *Trend*. It was the only way they could make this work. While he'd made sure she'd had a good workout—not bad for an old man pushing forty—he knew that lack of sleep couldn't alone be responsible for her sallow visage and restless demeanor.

He assumed it had to do with Mangel and the breaking news that was flooding the airways and internet. Another giant X for his Lehming Brothers corporate report if it turned out the evangelist was dead and not merely injured. Cam had nothing to do with the attack—of that he was certain—but perhaps she was concerned that others had seen her flee the trailer? How he wished she would confide in him, so he could comfort her without letting on that he'd followed her to Philadelphia.

"You look exhausted. Beautiful but exhausted. I told you that you could work remotely. Would you prefer to go home, get some more sleep?"

"No, we need to discuss Perri. Everything you said last night at the club was one hundred percent on target. How am I going to earn a serious editorial reputation when I go around demolishing vulnerable women's public personas? Wynan handed me a whole list of other people he wants me to decimate. I realize I brought this on myself by turning in that article in the first place, but what do I do from here?"

Fletcher tapped his fingers against his thigh, trying to figure out what to say. He'd watched her pull out her heart and stomp it to pieces in front of thousands of strangers, and this was what was at the top of her mind? It was clear she didn't want him to know she'd been at the revival or reveal her reasons behind it. Which was especially frustrating since he was determined to find out what clues had brought her into Mangel's orbit. Maybe this conversation could be his opportunity to dig around a little and stop her before she uncovered more than he wanted her to know.

"I think you've had your finger on the answer all along, Cam. The first thing you asked to cover when you arrived was the Blubber Be Gone murder, a serious story. I know I initially put you off, but perhaps if you pursue that story in more depth now, it could counteract whatever unpleasantness the Perri Evans piece stirs up. I've been so preoccupied with nailing down advertisers, I apologize for not discussing your progress earlier. Tell me now. What have you uncovered?"

Camarin looked down at her lap in silence.

"Cam?"

"I don't have anything. I'm not used to admitting to mistakes. And I really thought I was onto something. But then new facts came into my possession that pointed me in a totally different direction. I'm sorry to disappoint you."

He was disheartened, but not at her lack of progress with the story. "I can't think of anything you could do to disappoint me, Cam, short of telling me you're married or working for a rival magazine. Either of those things true?"

Even though she still hung her head, Fletcher could see the corners of her lips edge upward.

"Cam, are they?"

She shook her head.

"So BBG aside, you think there might still be any other anti-discrimination stories out there for you to cover?"

She looked up, a hopeful glimmer in her eyes. "I'm sure there are."

"And what can I do to help?"

"There is something," she said, growing more animated. "Do you know anyone in computer forensics who can find things in cyberspace, like social media posts, that the author has since deleted?"

"Let me think."

He opened his drawer and pulled out his Rolodex, trying to buy time. What had she stumbled onto? What was she after?

"What's that thing?" she said, pointing at his antiquated filing system.

He chuckled. "This is what folks in the Stone Age used to keep track of business cards before we had smartphones that could photograph information and store it in databases. We kept them in our caves, next to our abacuses and our sundials."

He finally evoked a laugh from his lover. "I think you're screwing up your time periods a little, boss."

"You get the idea, Ms. Smartass Underling."

"Underling? Really?"

"You saying you didn't enjoy 'working' under me?"

He watched her twitch, no doubt frustrated at losing control of the conversation. Though he'd sworn he wouldn't go there, at least during work hours, he loved throwing her a little off-kilter.

He cleared his throat, giving her a pass, and pretended to shuffle through his collection of business cards, searching for anyone even slightly techie. He cared deeply for Camarin, but he had another mistress to serve, a bitterness that had been fomenting for over three years, and nothing was going to stand in his way.

"I don't see anyone offhand, but let me do some asking around. I once represented a tech firm in a lawsuit. Maybe they can offer some advice."

"I appreciate it. I'll look around too. I mean, you did hire an investigative reporter."

"I did indeed. I'm allotting you a thousand-dollar research budget for the project. You feel a little better?"

"I do, as long as you'll tell Wynan not to expect me to interview any of the people on his hit list."

"I'll let him down easy. No worries. Just go out there and find me a story that's a worthy substitute. Deal?"

"Deal. Thank you."

He decided to press his advantage. "Dinner later?"

"I'd love to. But I think I have an early evening date with my mattress. I already sent Benji a text and told him I was bailing tonight. I'm afraid any time spent with you might undermine my carefully formulated plans."

He felt his stomach fall. "Tomorrow then?"

"Sure. I'll just tell Benji I'm still feeling under the weather."

"Then it's a date." He felt grateful the desk between them prevented her from seeing his cock already growing hard in anticipation.

"Later. I've got a story to research that's going to blow your socks off."

He smiled as she exited his office. Visualizing her pulling off any of his clothing would satisfy his fantasies for a while.

CHAPTER
32 33 34

THE REST OF Camarin's Monday was a blur. She found herself free from interruptions, thanks to Wynan, who had emailed a lot of copyediting to Rachel's in-box instead of hers. Seizing on the research opportunity, she scanned through weight-loss sites and Twitter feeds, reviewing blog after blog without finding any mention of The Collective or their campaign to recruit bias-oppressed apprentices of homicide.

She wondered how it worked. Did IW, her new nickname for the Invisible Woman, just assign a random murder to someone local to Mangel's tour stop? But if she was trying to implicate Mangel in the assaults, then why attack him? Wasn't that like killing the golden scapegoat? It didn't make sense.

The digital forensics people she contacted were a bust. Not only did they charge more than a measly thousand dollars, but they estimated that any search would take them at least two weeks because of a backload of requests. She didn't see Fletcher for the remainder of the day, which meant no success on the referral front either.

She checked Philly.com every half hour, figuring that the *Inquirer*'s online portal would be the first to carry photos of a mangled Mangel, should any materialize. IW was playing on Camarin's sense of dread, figuring that given enough time to bathe her mind in frantic thoughts, she might agree to any insane request to clear her name. Bad assumption. Her foe had clearly not considered the legendary strength and fighting acumen of Chamorro warriors like Chief Gadao, who could split a coconut in his bare hands, or Chief Masala's son, who uprooted a tree at age three. Camarin's ancestors had fought their battles by tipping wooden spears with pieces of human leg bone dipped in poison. Camarin's weapons of choice, her will and her wit, were just as sharp, and guaranteed to wreak equal havoc.

She arrived home to an empty apartment and dove under her covers, praying for sleep to overtake her so she could tackle the next day clearheaded. No such luck. Photoshopped visions of the bloodied evangelist competed with mental replays of her conversation with her blackmailer, leaving her agitated and unable to relax. Around midnight, she conceded to insomnia and poured herself a shot of Hennessy. Cognac was one of her few indulgences and never failed to settle her nerves. She lay back down and was asleep within a half hour.

Tuesday morning, she felt revived yet wary. As shower sprays surged over her body, she remembered the morning before, when Fletcher's firm hands had held each side of her head and guided his cock into her willing mouth, up to its hilt and then back out again, moaning in delight at how deeply she could take him. The memory awakened her lust anew, and she reached for the shower massager, positioning its pulsating stream of water so it caressed her clit into a frenzy. The release that followed nearly caused her to lose her balance and fall onto the shower floor. Not quite a Lyle–

quality orgasm but a welcome stress reliever for the day that lay before her, something to hold her until she could see him again.

She arrived at the office just before nine. Rachel greeted her with an accusatory tone.

"Missed you last night at the club. You should have called, told me you weren't coming. I was bloody *Fredded* about you."

I'm not even going to ask. "I'm sorry. When I called Benji, I didn't realize I had to clear any absences through you as well. You absolutely must send me the updated employee manual for both of my jobs."

"Well, pardon me for being a right *Frasier*, but some of us care about you, you know," she called out, but Camarin had already pulled open the door and was halfway to her desk, where her phone was already ringing.

She squinted her eyes tight, took a deep, courage-seeking breath, and picked up the receiver. "Torres."

"You didn't even let me finish. I wanted to tell you all about last night. Rhonda Hughes was the guest dueler, and when she lay across Dee's piano and started belting out *Fever*, I thought the audience was going to bring the ceiling down."

Incredible. With all that was on Cam's mind, she was expected to listen to this?

"Brought in tons of tips, and good thing too, because Benji says the place is going to be a ghost town 'til Sunday. Some Muslim peace convention taking over the hotel, and of course, they're not into music or liquor so—"

"Gotta go, other line ringing." Pulse racing faster than Secretariat, she disconnected one line and pressed down the button for the other. "Torres."

"Good morning, Camarin," said the distorted voice. "You got home early last night. I trust you slept well?"

Oh my God, she's following me. Dislodging her heart from her throat, she decided not to give her tormentor the satisfaction of acknowledging the realization.

"What the fuck do you want? I told you I had nothing to do with anything."

"Language, young lady. Despite your denials, these photos speak volumes, and they tell quite a different story. If you don't want them hitting the internet, this is your assigned task. You know your little friend DeAndre and his family?"

What the fuck? "Yeah. I know them in passing."

"You mean like passing him in the hallway of your apartment and passing the mashed potatoes at family dinner on Fridays?"

The walls were closing in on her, and she was suffocating. She hadn't been to DeAndre's for a month. There was no way this lunatic could have known about her relationship with Dee unless she had access to her texts and email.

"What exactly is it you want?"

"*Drift* is a thorn in the side of the fat-acceptance movement. All those ads and articles featuring anorexic women wearing slinky lingerie. We are tired of it, and we want that garbage off the shelves."

"That type of content fills the pages of every fashion magazine on the market."

"Times are changing. This is our moment. Personalities like Ashley Graham, Melissa McCarthy, Aidy Bryant, Chrissy Metz—their media presence is broadening viewers' expectations of the perfect body type. We'll eventually destroy the purveyors of the idealized body image, one magazine like *Drift* at a time. But since they were industry pioneers, we're starting with them first. And since you're so well-positioned and so…beholden to the cause, as it were…this is the task at hand."

"You want me to meet with them? Tell them you demand a change in editorial direction?"

"No, dear, that's not it at all. If our records are correct—and they always are—you're due at their house for dinner this Friday. That gives you three days to prepare."

"Prepare for what exactly?"

"Don't be obtuse, my dear. Prepare for what we always do to our enemies. Neutralize them. Permanently. Nonnegotiable. Do it or your photo, standing alongside poor, pulverized Mr. Mangel, is going to be on the cover of every newspaper around the world on Saturday morning. And no doubt your smiling face behind bars by Saturday afternoon. Don't think about calling the police—I already warned you what might happen. And make no mistake, if you don't kill them, I'll make sure someone else does, someone far less compassionate than you're likely to be. This will be our last conversation until the deed is done. Be creative, but be careful. We may need you for other tasks in the future."

"But—"

The line went dead. Cam froze like a statue, grasping the receiver, unable to discern anything except the pounding in her head and the scent of garlic that filled her nostrils. A minute later, everything in her world went black.

CHAPTER
33 34 35

"CAMARIN? WAKE UP!"

She opened her eyes, a familiar aching in her limbs, and saw Wynan and Rachel kneeling by her side, a crowd of curious coworkers behind them. The editor's hand was on her shoulder, shaking her gently.

Her mind went blank as she tried to fathom where she was, and then it all came flooding back, choking her with acid reflux. She turned her head and spewed out the cereal she'd consumed earlier, grazing Rachel's silver ankle boots. The receptionist pursed her lips but said nothing, instead summoning another bystander to fetch the paper towels from the kitchen and bring a glass of water back as well.

"Camarin, you were seizing. Should we call someone?" asked Wynan as he helped her to a sitting position.

Fuck. Just what she needed right now. A recurrence. Time to renew the meds.

"Epilepsy must run in my family," she said feebly. "My sister—may she rest in peace—died from a seizure. Just give me a minute. I'll be fine."

"You gave us quite a scare," he said, taking the glass of water from a junior editor and holding it up to Cam's lips. She sipped slowly.

"Where's Lyle?" she asked weakly.

"Off fundraising, where else?" Wynan said. "As for you, Ms. Torres, I think we'd better get you into a cab and send you to a doctor. If you're up to it, that is."

"No, no…it was just a small attack. Made worse by something I ate," she lied. "The milk tasted off this morning. I don't need a doctor. But I could definitely use a day in bed to recover."

Wynan helped her as she made a woozy attempt to get back on her feet. She took another swig of water Rachel handed her, eager to rid her mouth of the sour aftertaste. Her colleagues murmured their best wishes and returned to their cubicles as she put her arm around her editor's shoulders and allowed him to help her to the door.

"I'll get you downstairs and put you in a taxi, but are you going to be all right after that? Otherwise, I can send Ms. Thorsen home with you."

"No, I can make it, thanks. I'm feeling much better." The last thing she needed was Rachel quizzing her or, even worse, making herself comfortable and waiting until DeAndre woke up.

"I don't mind, really," Rachel interjected.

"No, I insist. If you really want to help, Rachel, please bring me my purse. Thank you. And, Hans, if you get me down to the curb, I'll take it from there."

By the time she reached the elevator, she was walking without assistance, and after watching her hail a cab, Wynan seemed satisfied that she'd recovered. "Call me when you get home, so I know you're okay." He made her promise and handed a ten-dollar bill to the driver.

Thanks to the typical Manhattan morning traffic, it took her ten minutes to travel ten blocks. As she exited the cab, she looked around warily, certain that everyone on the street was part of The Collective, documenting her movements, averting their eyes when she cast her gaze in their direction. She'd never felt so violated. At least once she made it past the lobby, she'd be beyond their grasp—unless, of course, she dared to send out an email or text a friend.

Once inside, she triple-locked the apartment door and dropped down onto the living room couch. Time to start formulating her strategy. The main things she needed were the time to figure out the identity of the Invisible Woman, and the privacy to carry out her plan. She had the time: IW's deadline was three days away. Now she needed to find someone The Collective wasn't monitoring, someone who could be her feet on the ground. The question was who? She walked over to the desk and pulled out a notepad. Something unhackable.

An hour later, DeAndre emerged from his bedroom, bare-chested and clad in a pair of white boxer shorts. He stopped short when he noticed her sitting on the couch.

"You get fired or something? I still might consider hiring you, but you're going to have to ask real nice and make dinner for a month."

"Nope, I have a job. But what *we* have is a problem. A major one. Come sit down so we can talk."

She started at the beginning and recounted the whole story, from Leticia Regan's death in Chicago up until, and including, the threat made against his life a few hours ago, although she was a little sketchy about what exactly happened in Mangel's trailer. And why mention that anyway, since she was absolutely positive that she was incapable of assault? DeAndre leaned forward, elbows on knees, listening intently, nodding from time to time, but offering no emotion or commentary.

Finally, she wrapped up. "What's most important is that we keep you and your family out of danger without anyone catching on that I've let you in on the plot. She said if I didn't kill you, somebody else would. We can't risk her making her move before Friday."

"Agreed," he said, hitting his clasped hands against his chin. She could see the wheels turning. "It makes no sense. You work at *Trend*. That's where she could create the most damage with the least amount of effort. Why target *Drift*?"

"No idea. Maybe after a murder, the police would suspect insiders first, like disgruntled employees? No point in speculating. She's laid down the rules, and now we have to plan our defense."

DeAndre rocked back and forth, deep in thought for a few minutes longer, before he broke the silence. "Obviously, we can't use our own cellphones or computers if we're being hacked. What we need is a way to get a security team into the magazine without anyone catching on. That shouldn't be too hard. My parents have tons of folks walking in and out of their office all the time. And *Drift* has its own commissary, a shower, and a lot of couches. They could stay there as long as necessary. But my aunt and uncle need to get the kids out of town. These people can't have an army of spies watching my extended family all the time, can they?"

Camarin shrugged. "No idea how wide a net they are casting. She said they're everywhere. But I think we can assume that the farther removed the relative, the safer they are. Your plan has one glaring omission though—who's going to protect you?"

"Not too concerned. Martial arts black belt, remember?"

"Didn't know that a black belt could stop a bullet."

"You forget, Cam. I've got instincts like a jungle cat. If enemies are nearby, I'll sense them."

"Oh, brother," she said, rolling her eyes. "You'll sense them? Maybe if you 'common sensed' them, you'd get one of those security people to stand guard here."

He paused, considering. "I'm sure a few of those security companies have a babe or two. It could be fun, as long as Rachel doesn't find out."

"Oh God, you cannot breathe one word to her. That girl is like a human billboard. If she gets wind of any of this, we're dead."

"No problem. Lips sealed. Figure if my parents and I are safe, that just leaves you."

"Yeah, I've got to get out of here without anyone noticing. Go into hiding, do some research. Once those pictures hit, The Collective won't be the only ones after me. I bet the police will have a few questions as well."

"Do we even know if Mangel's still alive?"

"No idea."

"Hang on." He stood up, grabbed something out of the top desk drawer, and left the apartment.

She frowned, hoping that wherever he'd wandered off to, he was still in the building where no one could see. She made herself a cup of oolong and was still dunking her tea bag when he returned, smiling.

"What?" she asked.

"I went over to Hassan's place. Luckily, he was home, so I didn't have to use the spare key. I looked up the number for Mangel Enterprises on his smartphone. Then I called and asked if there were any tickets left for the Charlotte event next Friday."

"Smart move. What did they say?"

"Exactly what you'd expect. They expected a sellout crowd and remaining tickets were dwindling, so would I like to order one of the last remaining pairs right now? I politely said I had to check with the missus and hung up."

"Sounds like things are proceeding as advertised. Unless they're going to have one of his staff take over to deliver the sermon. Did you ask if Mangel himself would be speaking?"

"Of course. I said I'd seen the news reports and wanted to know Terry's condition. They said they were hopeful, but even if he wasn't there, I would get my money's worth."

"Propagating hope while fleecing the customer. Sounds about right."

"Anyway, Cam, from what you explained earlier, wouldn't a substitute speaker cause some kind of riot?"

"No doubt. So, whether Mangel is alive or dead, they're still selling tickets, and come Saturday, I'm a possible murder suspect. What next, Sherlock?"

"I used his computer and ordered a bunch of burner phones on his Amazon account so they can't be traced back to us. One for you, one for me, a couple for my parents. They'll be delivered to his apartment tomorrow. Told him I'd pay him cash when the bill came in."

She nodded as she brought her teacup to the couch. He walked over and sat beside her.

"Perfect. I doubt they're watching Hassan's cell or his Amazon account."

"Exactly. So, Cam—here's what I'm thinking. Tell me if you think this is doable."

"Shoot."

"Business as usual tomorrow and Thursday. You go to *Trend* during the day, Benji's at night. I'll follow my regular evening routine, but skip my afternoon hours at *Drift*, so anyone watching won't suspect that I've been warned and conveyed the message. Instead, I'll use my burner to call Xavier's cellphone and tell him about the danger my parents are in. He'll instruct them on what we suggest they do. I doubt their butler is on the Invisible Woman's radar."

"So far, so good. Thank God you're blessed with domestic help."

"Then Thursday...remember James Byrom, that British guy who played at the bar last year?"

"The good-looking one? Yeah, how could I forget?"

"Down, girl. Well, if you recall, the guy's such a fucking prima donna, he always travels with his own baby grand."

"Dee, when you're that hot, it's not called being a prima donna—it's called being a perfectionist. Like crazy people with money. They're not bonkers, they're eccentric."

"Whatever. You're missing the point. When Byrom imports his piano, it comes in a large case. It's big enough for—"

"A body."

"Exactly. Once unloaded, they roll the case onto the loading dock for storage. That dock, I believe, is also shared by the Laidlaw."

"So, if I'm catching your drift, so to speak, I hide in the case, they wheel me out, and if I haven't suffocated, I walk back into the hotel lobby. How is that going to help me? If someone's waiting outside, they're still going to see me."

"One sec. Wait right there."

DeAndre held up one finger and ran off to his bedroom. She could hear him rummaging through his closet.

"There's a convention in town next week," he yelled so she could hear.

"Rachel mentioned something about it," she called back. "Said the club would be deserted because of some group of Muslims."

He walked back in, holding a black burqa.

"Wow, what is that doing here?"

"Remember Ruqayya?"

"Ms. Off-with-the-Cloak-and-on-with-the-Clubwear?"

"The very one. When she dumped me, she left this behind. I figured it would come in handy one day, though I was thinking Halloween. Anyway, we'll hide this at Benji's, and you'll take it into the bathroom and put it on during a break. Then we'll load you into the piano case. When you exit the loading dock into the lobby, you'll be just another convention attendee. You'll hail yourself a cab and take off to a safe house somewhere until all the hubbub dies down."

"That's fucking brilliant." She walked over and hugged him tight. "How did you come up with all that?"

"You're not the only one who took Fiction Writing 203, you know."

"You evidently got more out of it than I did. I'm nonfiction all the way. One question though."

"And that is?"

"Where do I hide out? Whoever's trailing me probably has hacked into my Facebook account and knows everyone I've ever been friends with."

"I was thinking about that too. When I call the X-Man, I'm going to ask him if he knows of anyone who can put you up. Someone far enough removed from our usual circle of acquaintances to keep you safe until we figure out who's behind all this."

"It all sounds so doable. If we can pull this off, it would be amazing."

Her cellphone started vibrating in her pocket, causing every nerve ending to jump to attention. Was IW going to start calling her here too?

"I keep the ringer turned off at work, so I don't disturb anyone," she explained, voice quivering, as she pulled it out. The caller ID read *Trend Magazine*. She breathed a sigh of relief. "Hello?"

"Camarita, Hans called to tell me what happened. Are you all right?"

She had never heard Fletcher sound worried or unsure until now. It was endearing how his voice trembled ever so slightly, and she realized how much she wished he was there by her side, cradling her, whispering assurances into her ear. Could this be what love felt like?

"It was probably just something I ate. I'll be fine."

"Are you going to be up for dinner tonight?"

How she longed to say yes, to start at some swanky restaurant and then end up at his place, dining on each other until sunrise. There was something so satisfying about evoking that tiny groan of surrender when he came. But without knowing how closely she was being observed, she couldn't endanger his life along with hers.

"I hate to do this, but I think I have to beg off for tonight. Get a good night's undisturbed sleep. Come to work and give it my all tomorrow."

Her gung-ho response, directed more toward work than play, provoked a long silence on the other end of the phone.

"If there was something wrong, you'd tell me, right? Something I'd done or should have done?"

"Oh no, no...I mean yes. If there was anything you'd done, I'd tell you. I hate to sound like a cliché, but in this case, it's not you, it's me."

"I could come by, bring you chicken soup or whatever they say cures all ills."

"You are a darling man, and I truly appreciate your concern. Please don't misconstrue this as a brush-off, but I think I'm better off tonight on my own."

"Understood, Ms. Torres. The thing is, I'm flying out to San Francisco tomorrow. I won't be back until the weekend. Can we put Saturday night down on the calendar, preferably in indelible ink? I'll make reservations at One if by Land. Ever been there?"

She squeezed her eyes together, trying to hold back a groan. Everyone knew that One if by Land was the most romantic restaurant in New York, but by Saturday he, along with every other person in the free world, would mistakenly believe that she had attacked Mangel, left him for dead. Being seen with her, in public or otherwise, might be the last thing Fletcher would ever want. At least being in California for the next few days would keep him out of harm's way while her plan took shape. Unless the enemy was listening in on their conversation.

"No, never. I've heard it's fabulous. It's a date," she said, her voice breaking. "I'm sorry. I have to go. Until Saturday."

She disconnected the call and threw the phone onto the couch, angrily wiping a tear from her cheek. She was at risk of losing her job, her reputation, her freedom, and the man of her dreams. All because of some deranged serial murderer with a hard-on for body shamers.

Camarin knew what she had to do. Find the Invisible Woman. Unmask her. Then make sure she was the one to pay.

CHAPTER
34 35 36

FOR THE NEXT two days, Camarin and DeAndre precisely followed their plan, each carrying their new burner phones should they need to communicate privately. She went into work, kidded around with Rachel as if nothing was wrong, copyedited the articles Wynan sent to her in-box. Fletcher must have spoken to him because he hadn't uttered another word about having her interview vulnerable celebrities.

What she didn't do was try to google the Invisible Woman, The Collective, or any other clues tied to Mangel or the BBG murders, lest some hacker was monitoring her office computer and was tracking her online searches. She didn't even search CNN or Philly.com for any additional information regarding last week's attack. Instead, she researched topics like poisons, so if IW was watching, she'd believe Cam was following through on her directives.

In the evenings, she bartended as usual at Benji's, the only difference being that she arrived wearing two sets of clothes. She'd peel both off in the bathroom shortly after entering and store the bottom layer in an empty liquor box in the storeroom. Couldn't go into seclusion without several changes of clothing, after all.

Hassan came in on Wednesday night, wearing a backpack that was one burqa lighter when he departed later that evening. DeAndre said he'd hid it for her in the back of one of the food cabinets that was less frequently used. Best not to risk hiding all the getaway gear in the same spot.

When Thursday rolled around, one day prior to her murder assignment, she felt totally at the mercy of the unknown, terrified of anything that might spoil their carefully crafted plan. Everything was on target, though, starting with her iPhone. She'd transferred her important files, memos, and phone numbers onto her burner phone, and then shut the hacked one off and hid it in her dresser. It was one sure way to keep her true location safely off the grid.

Xavier had warned Carl and Diana to remain at work from Thursday night forward, accompanied by the 'IRS auditors,' who were part of a private undercover protection squad hired to provide maximum protection. Diana's sister and brother-in-law would pull Carter, Jamal, and Kit out of school after dismissal for a surprise trip to Disney World.

DeAndre had even banned Rachel from Thursday's performance, telling her Benji had threatened to fire him unless he avoided her constant distractions. It was the only way to keep her safe, while ensuring she didn't say or do anything to impede their plans. He'd held off from informing her that dinner with his folks was canceled, just so nothing would be revealed before absolutely necessary.

Camarin entered Benji's that evening at six o'clock, but five minutes in, things had already started to unravel. James Byrom was there, smiling and sexy as always, but his signature piano, and more critically, its shipping case, were nowhere to be seen.

"Too many people were calling me a prima donna. I got tired of it. Your subpar piano will have to do," he explained.

Camarin shot DeAndre an imploring look. "What do we do now?"

"I was kidding, folks," said Byrom. "I'm sure your old clunker will do just fine."

"It's not that," Dee said. "It's that...please keep it to yourself, but we need to sneak someone out of the club and into the hotel lobby, and we were hoping to use your piano case as a hiding place."

Byrom took a swig of his second fireball and set it down on the top of the Steinway. "I see. Said person can't be seen going in-between? Is that it?"

The two conspirators nodded.

"So why not just use the freight elevator? If this club is like every other hotel-based club I've ever played in, all elevators lead down to a common basement, or at worst, an underground parking area. That's where the deliveries are made, the moving vans come to transport furniture, and so forth. You know, all the activities there's no room for on the streets."

DeAndre and Camarin looked at each other in shock, a virtual slap on the forehead. What morons they were! Of course that would work.

"Thanks, James," said DeAndre, shaking the Englishman's hand and pulling Camarin behind the stage where there was more privacy. "New plan. About halfway through your shift, you go to the kitchen, grab your burqa and your changes of clothes, put everything on in the ladies' room, and then head down the freight elevator. I think it's behind the door at the back of the kitchen."

"Sounds good," she whispered back, trying to sound positive despite their previous miscalculation.

"If Benji says anything, I'll tell him you went home sick and to feel free to dock your pay. I doubt he's going to say anything anyway. It's so quiet, he might even go home early himself, like he did last night."

She pulled back the curtain and peered out into the crowd. There were about twenty people spread out in the audience, all regulars. The convention had really killed their business for the week, a strong reminder that Benji shouldn't rely so heavily on hotel guests as his sole source of revenue. The few people that were there seemed ready to party though. Annalise was already at the bar, waiting for Cam to come out and fill some orders. Time to get to work and pray this new plan went off without any further snags.

Unfortunately, for Camarin anyway, word of James Byrom's appearance attracted more horny women than they had anticipated, and by ten, the place was as packed and rollicking as normal for a Thursday night. After filling an order of seven tequila shots, she knew her window of opportunity was closing fast. She tried to catch DeAndre's eye during the pianists' rousing rendition of *Uptown Funk*, but he was too preoccupied to notice.

She asked Viviana to cover for her and then snuck into the kitchen to collect her traveling clothes. Her two outfit changes were still waiting for her in the cardboard box where she'd left them. But after pulling the burqa from its hiding place, she confronted her second disaster of the evening. There was a big tomato stain on its front, no doubt the result of its recent stay on an unwashed cabinet shelf. She grabbed it and ran to the bathroom, ensconcing herself in a stall where she could deal with the problem in secret.

Scratching at the stain dislodged the stuck-on bits, but the discoloration remained, a bull's-eye that was sure to identify her as anything but an average, modest, lobby-exiting Muslim woman. She had to think quickly, figure out how to salvage their elaborate plan, but it was almost impossible with the tomato scent romancing her olfactory glands. Memories of summer picnics kidnapped her focus—triple-decker cheeseburgers piled high with ketchup, pickles, onions, and bacon. Realizing time was fleeting, Cam forced herself to stop salivating and instead concentrate on the dilemma at hand.

She donned the two additional sets of clothes as she pondered her quandary. She needed something black. Like a magic marker. Paint. Or—wait! The answer was right there in front of her. Or at least in the general vicinity.

She needed to get something from the kitchen, and she couldn't be seen doing it. Nor could she text anyone but DeAndre, since she couldn't risk sharing evidence on any phone that might be hacked. She took a chance and sent him a message, praying he'd steal a look at his burner phone between songs. It worked. Within five minutes, Annalise was knocking on her stall.

"You needed this?" she said, slipping a jar under the door.

"Thank you."

"Dee told me not to ask any questions, but I do have one. You okay?"

"I'm fine. Everything's fine. Thanks for the help."

"Okay. See-No-Evil, out. If I only had a mic, I'd drop it."

Camarin heard the bathroom door close. She reached down and opened the jar of blackstrap molasses, the secret sauce that transformed ordinary ribs into the mainstay of Benji's menu. Hands shaking from the anxiety of plans gone awry, she dipped in two fingers, and as steadily as she could manage, rubbed the thick, sticky goo onto part of her burqa stain, watching the red slowly transform into a dark blackish-brown. It's not perfect, but it'll have to do, she decided as she spread the glob over the entire blemish. Then she pulled the sweet-smelling cloak over her ensemble, covering every inch of her other than her eyes.

The smell enveloped her as completely as the outfit, again evoking memories of guilt-ridden food orgies followed by obligatory purging. How many hours had she spent over the past fourteen years vomiting into toilets like this one? She felt a shroud of self-pity descend over her but quickly cast it off. There would be plenty of time for self-castigation once she was in hiding.

She exited the stall, disposed of the jar under some towels in the garbage, and yanked open the bathroom door, praying she could make it out of the hotel without attracting every fly in Manhattan.

Once in the corridor, instead of taking a right and heading back into the club, she took a left and walked through the kitchen, ignoring the staff's inquisitive looks, to the door at the back that Dee had assured her led to the freight elevator. To her relief, for the first time tonight, something went right. Sweating profusely—a combination of nerves and wearing four layers of clothing on a warm summer night—she hurried down the deserted hallway and pressed the elevator button. The piano music from the club drowned out the squealing of the gears.

When the door rattled opened, she entered, hit *B* and put her faith in a contraption so rickety it must have been an Otis prototype. The elevator descended at a snail's pace and stopped with a clunk that nearly made her topple over. She sprang from the death trap as soon as the doors reopened and half-walked, half-ran through the maze of massive boxes, broken tables, spare chairs, and every other discarded or not-immediately-needed item that crowded the basement level.

Spying a door at the opposite end, she pushed through the clutter toward another elevator, which she assumed led to the Laidlaw lobby. This one was even more terrifying than the last, not only because of its age but also because there was already a workman waiting inside. He gave her an odd look and took one step back as she entered and pushed the button for *Lobby*.

"I feel so stupid. I'm terribly lost," she said, in her best Arabic accent, which came out sounding more Indian than authentic.

He just nodded, giving her a wide berth. The car creaked its way up one level as they rode without further discussion.

Once the doors opened again, she turned and took a chance on the little Arabic she remembered from her brief encounter with DeAndre's girlfriend. "Which way to the hotel lobby, *Sayyed?*"

He pointed to the left, and she hurried off, smiling as she imagined him trying to fathom how the ditzy Muslim tourist in a molasses-stained burqa ever managed to drift that badly off-course.

The lobby was filled with a large contingent of conference attendees, and Cam easily blended in. The men were chatting animatedly in their native tongue, their wives standing silently nearby. When they started toward the exit, she joined them, walking about one step behind, heart racing faster every footstep closer she came to at last breaking free of her unwanted surveillance. One of the women turned to stare. Perhaps she had smelled the sickly-sweet aroma? Camarin nodded politely and said nothing.

She followed them about two blocks down Broadway and then veered off onto a side street. By that point, she figured she'd probably lost anyone attempting to trail Camarin Torres. Anyone else who spotted an unescorted woman in a burqa hailing a cab at eleven-thirty wouldn't have thought twice about it, Manhattanites being as open-minded and self-absorbed as they were.

She gave the driver the address that she had memorized from Xavier via DeAndre. It was an apartment in Harlem, owned by a friend of the butler's father, far from anywhere her enemies might have expected her to hide. Hopefully, her outfit wouldn't garner any unwelcome attention in that neighborhood, because she couldn't risk removing the garment until she was safely locked inside her safe house.

"It's pretty late for a lady like yourself to be out alone on the streets," said the driver, who continued to chat, unanswered, for the entire twenty-five-minute drive uptown.

When they arrived at 116th Street, she fished through her pockets for enough cash to pay the meter.

"This is Graham Court," he announced, apparently happy with the sizeable tip she'd given him. "It's Harlem's answer to the Dakota. You know they filmed *New Jack City* and *Jungle Fever* here?"

She nodded, eager to speed up the process, get inside, and disrobe to just one layer.

The man who answered the doorbell at 7A was an elderly gentleman leaning on his cane, his leathery face framed by white hair and a beard. There was something trustworthy and comforting about him, and she immediately felt safe in his presence.

"Come on in, miss," he said with a slight Jamaican accent. "I'm Malcolm Harvey. You call me Malcolm. I don't know what kind of trouble you're in, and I don't want to know. Xavier Edouard's father vouched for you, and that's the only visa I need. You stay here as long as you like. Cockroach nuh business inna fowl fight."

"Excuse me?"

"It means I mind my own business, stay out of yours."

First Cockney rhyming slang, now patois. She couldn't travel around New York without a translator.

"You are so kind to welcome a stranger into your home, especially one arriving at your door at midnight," said Camarin, reaching out to shake his hand. "I won't be any trouble. All I need is a mattress, a bathroom, and a computer, and I'll pay you back when I can."

"I wouldn't worry about any payment." He laughed. "Xavier sent two thousand dollars by messenger a few days ago, said I should use it to cover any food or supplies you might need. If you protested, I was told to remind you that your actions saved the lives of some people he's very fond of, so shut up and enjoy."

Camarin just shook her head and sent up thanks to God for putting her in the hands of such caring, loving people. "I won't protest a peep. But if you could show me where I could take off this damned disguise, I'd be forever in your debt. I'm burning up in here."

He pointed her to the bathroom. "I left some pajamas and a robe hanging on the back of the door. I bought them with some of that money, figured you'd need something to relax in. By the way, how do you feel about a late-night snack? I've got some jerk chicken wings I'd be happy to heat up."

Malcolm's words bathed her in calm. With the first part of their plan behind them, she was safe and in control of her circumstances. At least for tonight. "Malcolm, if your wings are as half as great as you are, this is the beginning of a wonderful friendship."

CHAPTER
35 36 37

AFTER A GLORIOUS night of uninterrupted sleep in silk pajamas on Malcolm Harvey's pullout sofa bed, Camarin awoke refreshed and less stressed than she'd felt since before her trip to Philadelphia. It seemed like a million years had passed.

Today was the day the Invisible Woman expected her to kill the family she'd grown to love. Knowing everyone was safe and her enemies were no longer privy to her whereabouts and activities, nor those of DeAndre's and his family, filled her with a sense of well-being she'd wondered if she'd ever experience again. She checked her burner phone for any urgent communiques and got out of bed.

"What'll you have?" asked Harvey, already frying up some bacon and eggs.

"I'm afraid I don't eat much in the mornings. Do you have any coffee?"

"Whole pot full, help yourself. Mugs are up there on the shelf. But if you're going to stay here, you gotta learn to eat. You barely touched your snack last night. You need food for strength, to think clearly. And don't give me that look. You pay heed to your elders. De olda de moon, de brighter it shines."

She shrugged, knowing when she'd been outranked. Maybe some real food would help her to link the puzzle pieces together. Monaeka's ever-present voice, with its constant body-shaming reprimands, had diminished substantially since the revival. Could her sister's desire for revenge have been satisfied by Cam's public humiliation? Could she finally eat without judgment?

She poured herself a mug of coffee, searched the fridge for some milk, and then sat down in front of one of the two full plates he'd set down on the table. Calorie count, at least seven hundred, and she planned to enjoy every single one. *Take that, Monaeka. Same to you, Mom.*

"What's on your schedule today, Malcolm?"

"Same as every day, miss. I give thanks that the Lord saw fit to treat me to another day. I go to church to thank him proper and then go to the soup kitchen or the hospital and help where I can. You'll have the whole place to yourself until I come home and make dinner. Fridge is full. You take whatever you need."

"You're the best. Do I need a password to get into your computer or internet?"

"Computer's on the desk in my bedroom. All signed in for you." He pointed to the fridge. "I left my phone number on that pink sheet of paper. If you need me, I won't be far."

He finished up and left his plate and silverware in the sink.

"If you wanna do something, feel free to wash the dishes. One thing I hate to do. And no leaving. Desmond—that's Xavier's dad—told me that's the one big rule. You need something, you call me, and I'll get it for you. We good?"

"We good." She saluted in jest.

"You joke, but don't forget. Chicken merry, hawk deh near."

She nodded, more somber. He was right: trouble could be waiting right outside the door.

He walked out without another word, leaving Cam with her days' worth of research. She ditched the remainder of her breakfast down the sink, at least three hundred fifty calories not destined for her hips, turned on the water, and snatched the sponge. Best do them now before she forgot.

Once she'd dried the dishes and put them in the cupboards, she entered Harvey's simple but spotless bedroom—he'd even made the bed—and sat at his computer, determined to track down some answers.

First, she checked the news sites; still no additional reports on Mangel's condition. He must be dead, she surmised. Otherwise, they'd be announcing every tiny change in his condition, looking to eke out every iota of free publicity. Then she clicked on his website, which indicated that the revival was set to open next weekend in Charlotte as planned.

A shot-in-the-dark attempt at a Google search for the Invisible Woman turned up over sixty-three million links, including movie and book titles, but nothing she was after. Something had to be here somewhere. What was she missing?

The burner rang. Heart fluttering, she ran back into the den, doubling as her makeshift bedroom. It could only be Dee.

"Hello?" she answered with trepidation.

"Looks like you made it."

"I did. A few shaky moments but everything worked out, and I'm here, safe. What's your story?"

"Benji blew a gasket when he realized you took off, but I told him you were still sick, likely a stomach virus or something, and he quieted down. You should be good on that count, at least through the weekend. I've got two new roommates, Zach and Brody, not nearly as pretty as you, but my parents insisted. I call them Tweedledee and Tweedledum, along with some other choice nicknames. They're supposed to follow me everywhere, but that's only if they can break free from Annalise."

"They're big and brawny?"

"Truth."

"Her favorites. She must be going out of her mind. How did you explain why they're there?"

"I just told her my parents received death threats from someone who was unhappy about a story. She bought it."

"And me not being there?"

"Told her you were spending the night with your boss, maybe the weekend too."

"Well, don't let her near Rachel. She knows Fletcher is out of town and will blow that story out of the water."

"I'm on it. She still believes she's banned from the club until further notice so Benji doesn't fire me. Whether she continues to listen, that's a different story."

"Do you absolutely have to go to the club tonight?" she asked. "You know it's not safe."

"James Sakal is in town. Not going to miss a chance to play opposite him."

"Just stay safe. Promise."

"Hey, with Hans and Franz here, flanking me at every turn, what choice do I have? Talk later."

She carried the phone into Malcolm's bedroom and sat back down, wondering what Wynan would think when she didn't show up this morning. She couldn't call in sick because if the phones were tapped, she couldn't risk giving her location away. And an email from Malcolm Harvey's account? Suicide. He was just going to have to figure it out on his own. Same with Rachel. No doubt one or both of them would call Fletcher, and she hated the idea of him worrying about her whereabouts, but what was the alternative? Shame to lose her job because she was off saving lives. Might make a terrific story though.

Back at the computer, she started throwing anything she could find against the proverbial wall to see what might stick. Searched the names of every speaker she could remember from the revival. Their stories all panned out. The real key to everything was Mangel. Maybe the Invisible Woman was just someone from his past who was out to get him, like an unsatisfied customer. After attempting to frame him in a series of murders didn't work, she'd gone the more direct route. Cue Camarin, stumbling onto the scene, the perfect patsy to take the fall.

The backgrounder prepared by April Lowery had been chock full of praise and platitudes but light on biographical details and absent of any pictures whatsoever. She had an idea about how she could learn more, but she needed a photo, and there were absolutely none in his bio or on his website. Frustrated, she retreated into the kitchen, turned on the radio, and made herself a pot of tea.

The '90s station was playing *Still Can't Hear You*, and as she searched for a tea bag, she sang along, remembering the time she'd stood outside the Beverly Hilton for hours, camera and jewel box in hand, waiting for the lead singer for her favorite band, Aphasiac, to come out and autograph her CD of *Paralyzed*. How times had changed. Now snake oil salesmen like Terry Mangel were the celebrities.

Wait. That was it! Would Terry's rabid fans allow a chance to photograph their idol escape them? No way. She recalled how no one had confiscated cellphones at the rally. They had just warned about prosecution for the snapping of unauthorized photos.

She set down her mug, ran back to the den, and started searching through Google Images as well as Facebook and Instagram pages of anyone who had favorably reviewed anything Mangel-related, searching for an illicitly obtained photo.

After about five minutes she found one. It was slightly blurred, shot from a distance and uncaptioned. But it was unmistakably Mangel, preaching his little heart out. She snipped and saved the photo and then downloaded a face identification app. Taking that Research for Reporters class was proving to have been worth every tuition dollar.

Once she installed the program, she entered Mangel's picture, and less than a minute later, voilà. Meet Harry Gordon Spiegel, born in Pennsylvania, raised in Possum Grape, Arkansas. Graduated from Henderson State, without honors, looking scrawny but oddly charismatic even back then.

Camarin followed the links that told of his meteoric rise to the middle of the advertising field, ending up with the burgeoning firm of Hymanson & Caliciotti outside Pittsburgh, which dissolved after some computer glitch cleared out the company's entire bank account along with those of all its major clients. No leads or indictments, no arrests. And no further mention of Spiegel anywhere on the internet.

She checked each of the affected clients, and sure enough, quite a few had to do with weight loss and fat reduction. Maybe he'd taken the money, along with all that consumer research, and studied sales and public speaking. With his newfound skills, he'd magically transformed himself into Terry Mangel, champion of the downtrodden, AKA his former advertising prey. Maybe one of the people he'd swindled was the killer? She shrugged. Theories aside, without any formal complaints or death threats against Mangel from disgruntled female consumers, all roads still led back to a photograph of Camarin standing beside a possibly slain evangelist.

Dinnertime came and went, and as she and Malcolm chomped down on spicy meat patties, she imagined the look on the Invisible Woman's face when her spies reported the lack of any dinner being enjoyed chez Robinson, not to mention the absence of Camarin from any of her usual haunts. They'd been had. She hoped the realization left them rattled. She tempered her gloating, aware that hers was only a momentary victory. IW still held the trump card. The question now was would she play it? Everyone she loved was at risk.

She laid her head down that evening, unable to relax, agonizing over what resolution the morning might bring.

CHAPTER
36 **37** 38

AROUND SEVEN, CAM awoke and peeked into Harvey's room, surprised to find it empty and the bed already made. She jumped on the computer, bracing herself for disaster. The Invisible Woman was nothing if not true to her word. Saturday's internet headlines featured the two pictures of her with Mangel, with headlines like *Body Acceptance Guru Gored, Trend Reporter Sought for Questioning*. And leave it to Buzzerbeat to print *Terry Traumatized, Camarin Connected?* She winced at the irony. She'd always wanted the headlines. She'd simply assumed she'd write them, not make them. Time for coffee. She'd need more caffeine than usual to make it through this day.

"Seems like I've got a local celebrity in my midst. I went out early and picked these up at the newsstand," said Harvey, sitting at the kitchen table. He pointed to a stack of papers sitting beside a steaming bowl of cornmeal porridge. "Chow down before it gets cold."

She scanned the headlines, shuffled through the pages, shocked at how many personal details they were able to rustle up in such a brief time. Had IW furnished each media outlet with its own press kit? Her full name, her current address, the fact she'd gone to NYU, her position at *Trend*—what, no mention of height and weight? Shocking. Thank goodness her mother and aunt's phone numbers were unlisted, making them more difficult to locate.

Particularly damning were the reports by several revival attendees recounting her speech from a week ago. No one managed to repeat much of the actual content other than one line: *I don't deserve one iota of the support you're sending my way. I am everything you despise.* Then they proceeded to equate her confession of betrayal to one of premeditated murder. Perfect.

She pulled out her burner from her robe pocket and called DeAndre.

"You saw?" she asked.

"Yeah, they even mentioned *Drift*. I'm now 'an acquaintance of the accused.' I knew I'd make it to the top someday."

"I didn't know I'd even been accused. Must have blinked and missed it."

"You're all over the TV too. Looks like Mangel's team is preparing to make a statement. Turn on channel seven."

She looked across the table at Harvey. "Malcolm, do you mind if I turn on the news?"

He walked into the living room and picked up the remote from the coffee table. She joined him, phone in hand, and they both settled in to watch the destruction of her reputation, better known as 'breaking news.'

"And reporting from Charlotte, North Carolina, April Lowery, personal assistant and public relations director for Terry Mangel, is now entering the room. She is about to address the crowd. Let's listen in."

Yes, by all means, let's.

"Ladies and gentlemen, thank you for all your calls of concern. As you know, we've been dealing with this crisis for the past six days, ever since we found Mr. Mangel assaulted in his trailer on Sunday morning. Up to now we've handled the situation privately, to spare Terry's followers any unnecessary grief."

"What's his condition? Is he still alive?" called out a reporter.

Camarin's ears perked up. It would be convenient to know if she was going to be charged with first-degree murder or just attempted murder.

"We still cannot comment on his condition at this time. I can assure you that we are doing everything possible to make sure the Feel Good About Yourself revival opens as planned next Friday night."

Ah yes, no matter what, the show must go on.

"Why haven't the police commented on any of this?" asked another reporter.

"As I said, Terry's organization is very close-knit, and we prefer to handle issues like this on our own. We would have continued to do so if those awful photos hadn't been anonymously released to the press," answered April, a bit sharply.

"If Terry Mangel isn't well enough, who will run the revival?"

"Many of Terry's followers and administrative staff, myself included, have been trained for just such an occasion. What's foremost in our minds right now is preparing for the enormous responsibility of saving thousands of fat-shamed sufferers from the limitations they've constructed in their own minds."

"Hey, is this a press conference or an ad for Mangelmania?" asked DeAndre, watching with them from four miles away.

"Apparently both."

"While I can't assure you that Terry Mangel will lead the charge against the shamers, I know he will be there in spirit," April continued onscreen.

"Yup," Camarin said to the television. "Your money is still as valuable whether he's alive or dead. Though probably more valuable if he's dead, which is why we aren't offering anything but ambiguities at this time."

Harvey threw a look her way. "Spot on. You should do impressions."

"Thanks. Something to entertain my fellow prisoners at the Sing Sing talent night." She turned her attention back to the screen.

"Ms. Lowery, do you believe what the photos suggest, that Camarin Torres is the assailant?"

"I can only tell you what I know. She was supposed to show up for an eleven o'clock interview with Mr. Mangel. I came to his trailer at ten-fifteen to prep him, and I found him just the way he looked in the photos. She never showed, which seems…odd, at best."

"Who took the photos?" screamed another reporter over the din.

"We have hidden cameras in all of the trailers, mostly to protect against theft. They take photos every five minutes or so. We couldn't find the camera from Terry's trailer after the incident, so whoever released these photos obviously procured it without our knowledge or our consent."

April pasted on her patented public relations smile.

"There is one last thing I need to share with all the loyal current and future followers of the Feel Good About

Yourself movement. Just as Terry would have wanted it, we forgive his assailant. Mr. Mangel has taught us that when we come face-to-face with those who would destroy us, we respond with love. Whoever perpetrated this appalling act, please know that God loves you and salvation is waiting." April dropped the dreamy-eyed diatribe and faced the reporters again. "Thank you for your concern. We'll release more information when it becomes available." She waved to the crowd and stepped down from the podium. The cameras switched back to the anchorman.

"Well, that was fun. And only the tiniest bit self-serving," Camarin said into the phone.

Harvey returned to the kitchen, mumbling about reporters leaping to conclusions and having to get the dishes done.

"There's more," said DeAndre. She lowered the volume so she could hear him more clearly. "You must have given your company our home number. Your boss has been calling here since dawn, trying to track you down."

"He has?" Her heart leaped.

"He said the reporters have been hounding him since the story broke, around three AM. He sounded frantic with worry. He said that if I spoke to you I should tell you he believes in your innocence one hundred percent."

"Wow. At least there's someone out there who isn't gunning for me."

"It's not surprising. Rachel said he was just as concerned when she told him you were heading to Philadelphia last weekend. You'd think he'd tell the press you were innocent, clear your name."

"Wait, what? He knew I went to Philly?"

"Yeah. Rachel got drunk last Friday, as per usual, and couldn't stop blathering on about how worried she was about you. How you were getting in over your *loaf.* She called Fletcher. I guess she figured he'd charge down on his white stallion and rescue you."

Camarin threw her head back against the couch cushions. He knew. He frigging knew all along, and he never said anything. Why not? That face in the crowd, that person staring at her as she jumped into the cab—it was him. And he'd slept with her without saying anything. Knowing what she had gone through. What the fucking fuck?

"Camarin, you still there?"

"Um, yeah, sorry," she said, trying to hide her agitation. "I'm here. I'm just a little dazed is all. Your parents, are they okay? The kids?"

"I checked in with everyone this morning. Everything is fine. We did good. Annalise is worried to death though, and I haven't said anything. Do you want to talk to her, let her know you're okay?"

She watched in horror as Perri Evans's concerned face filled the television screen. What now?

"Not now. Please tell her I'm fine, and I'll make it up to her some other time."

She disconnected the call and turned up the volume. The makeup people must have been magicians, because on camera Evans looked a far cry from the gaunt, little waif she'd met a week earlier.

"... and the hack job she did on me in her article? None of it true, none of it. Guess she hates anyone who's as thin as she is. Anyway, she told me she was going back to see Mangel. Called him...what were her exact words...a greedy manipulator...wanted me to go too. Maybe she wanted a bigger audience when she let him have it."

A dollop of bile-laced porridge worked its way up her esophagus and burned the back of her throat. She ran to the refrigerator, took a big swill of ice water, rolled it around in her mouth, and spit it into the now-empty sink.

"I've got some Rolaids in the bathroom if you need them," said Harvey. "I'll go get them."

She nodded gratefully. From the living room, she heard the television's focus switch from Perri Evans back to the news anchor.

"Thank you, Todd, for that eye-opening interview. After these announcements, we'll welcome Atticus and Levi Lehming into the studio, co-chairmen of the board at Lehming Brothers. They will discuss the impact of Terry Mangel's possible death on the company's profits."

Lehming Brothers? Where had she just heard that name? She walked back into Harvey's bedroom and typed the conglomerate's name into the search bar. Then she clicked on *News* and then *Holdings*. Pulse racing, she read and reread the results, just to be certain. They were all there—Mangel Enterprises, Blubber Be Gone, the overweight teen camp where James Masterson had lost his head. Also owned by Lehming Brothers: the store in Phoenix that specialized in weight-loss supplements, the low-calorie food line based outside Dallas, and Rez-de-Chaussée, the restaurant outside St. Louis that had fired its overweight serving staff. Even *Drift*, the Robinsons' pride and joy, was now a subsidiary. It wasn't a plot against Mangel. The Collective was targeting the conglomerate itself!

Eager for more dirt, she strayed from the main site and clicked on various Lehming–related news links. The usual issues—union problems, salary cuts, layoffs. Exactly what you'd expect from any multinational corporation with thousands of employees. Jazzed, she reached for her phone, desperate to share her possible theory with Dee, when a separate set of headlines caught her eye. And in an instant, her entire world came toppling down.

Lehming Brothers Wins Lawsuit Waged by Former Anchorwoman and Reporter, Margaret Waldman followed six months later by *Lehming Brothers' Oldie but Fattie Falls into Deep Depression*. After another year, the tone became much more respectful. *Lehming Brothers Mourns Death of Former Colleague, Esteemed Journalist Margaret Waldman*.

Camarin squeezed her eyes closed, as if the action could force the realization from her brain. Her lover, the one happy outcome of this horrific debacle, was tied up in all of this somehow. She forced herself to focus, parse out all the facts. But when her imagination pitted her worst fears against solid logic, paranoia—accompanied by cold sweats, headaches, and tremors—always emerged victorious.

Everything made sense now: Margaret's suicide was caused by Lehming Brothers' greed and insensitivity. A few years later, the corporation's holdings came under siege. Fletcher, the ex-lawyer, unable to win the case for his wife, started wreaking his own brand of revenge to make the company pay for her mistreatment. Why else would the Invisible Woman ask her to destroy *Drift* and not *Trend*, where she already worked? Why else had Lyle told her, in a drunken stupor, that perhaps he was not the man she thought him to be?

Camarin felt the wooziness set in, the disconnection, the separation from her physical self. As her consciousness begin to float up and above her body as it had during the revival, her perspective grew clearer, no longer influenced by attraction or affection. Monaeka's point of view. And from that vantage point, it was all so obvious.

Fletcher had unlimited access to her computer, her voice mails, her whereabouts. He'd handpicked her off that train platform, someone who might be willing to confront the shamers, perhaps kill on his behalf. And what else did she know about him? One last damning fact: years ago, in boarding school, when his newfound friend, Wynan, was beaten to a pulp, in one fell swoop he managed to make all those bullies magically disappear.

Where had he been all this time when the Invisible Woman started contacting her? Hidden away in his office, perhaps calling from a burner phone of his own? Or out of town, 'raising funds.' Using his new magazine as a front to get close to his targets, no doubt. Getting to know the main players. Taking their advertising money. Uncovering their vulnerabilities and destroying them. And then Philadelphia. Rachel might have called him, but he'd probably been there all along, planning the attack on Mangel. Cam saw him in the audience during her confession. And as she hailed the cab to take her to the train station. He'd killed Mangel himself after she ran from the trailer and was letting her take the fall.

Fuck the Invisible Woman rubbish. It had been Fletcher behind this from the beginning, disguising his voice over the phone with that distortion contraption. What other explanation could there be, with all the damning evidence pointing his way? The question was how could she alert the police about everything she had discovered without them taking her into custody?

It was suddenly all too much to bear. Forced into hiding, her life out of her control, all orchestrated by the man she thought she loved. But how could she be certain she was seeing any of this clearly? Or was this like back in her youth when she believed one thing and her mother told her another, leaving her unsure of her own conclusions?

Overwhelmed, trapped like a young girl tied to a bed, having her demons exorcised from her, she felt the tremors starting again. The oncoming seizure caused her to bang her head against the keyboard, as if she was attempting to force the confusion from her brain.

She heard Monaeka's laughing voice return for the first time since the revival. *That'll teach you. You left me. You betrayed me. And now I will take everything you love away from you. Now I will make you pay.*

CHAPTER
37 38 39

WHEN MONDAY MORNING arrived, Fletcher had said "No Comment" to more reporters than he'd ever dreamt existed. Between the non-stop calls for interviews and the police visits, he had no voice left for anyone but the army of private detectives he'd hired to find Camarin. Money was beside the point. Right now, there was only one thing standing between him and his deepest desire, and that was the absence of his cherished Chamorro reporter.

Since returning from San Francisco, he'd spent the last two nights at Benji's, unable to think of anywhere else to go. Neither DeAndre nor Annalise, who'd introduced herself as Cam's other roommate, claimed to have any idea of her whereabouts. Annalise seemed far more worried and panicky, leaving Fletcher to wonder if DeAndre, who he now recognized as heir apparent to his rival, *Drift*, might be holding back.

At one point, he tried to corner the pianist backstage, but two large, burly thugs pulled him away and threw him into the hotel lobby. He couldn't remember feeling more defiled and enraged, but he swallowed his indignation and hobbled home. DeAndre Robinson would get his comeuppance when his family's magazine folded, and the sooner the better.

He'd canceled all investor meetings and spent the morning watching nonstop coverage of the Mangel Affair, as his favorite channel had dubbed it, but all they reported was regurgitated information from the day before. Reporters must not have been able to locate her family but attempted to interview each of Cam's coworkers. Luckily for their future employment, no one said anything beyond "No comment." Some former classmates from NYU claimed she was headstrong but determined, and very pro-body acceptance. The reporters were relentless, interviewing her landlord, her dry cleaner, anyone who had ever met her and had something to share.

Perri Evans received the most press coverage because she had the biggest ax to grind, incensed over the cover story *Trend* had dared to run. But social media ignored most of her comments, instead commenting on her spectacular weight loss and debating whether 'lite' heroin use might be the next big fat reduction fad.

"That is our biggest problem, her and her big mouth," Fletcher told Wynan as the two stared at the television in the publisher's office. Evans was wailing out her newest single, *Make Me*, which in two days had shot up to number one on the country charts. Her interview with Camarin had revived her career more robustly than any publicity stunt her team could have concocted.

"Thanks to her, this week's issue is turning out to be our biggest seller ever," Wynan countered. "Don't worry about anyone listening to her words or her music. They're just staring at her ass. This is exactly the kind of sensationalism that should surround all *Trend* cover stories. When Camarin turns up, we must encourage her to recreate this vibe again and again. Then no one can beat us."

"The question is less *when* and more *if*. What if she saw the actual killer? What if whoever sliced into Mangel went after her as well?" He remembered watching her run from the trailer that Sunday morning. He wondered how many others had also witnessed her exit and could be convinced to testify.

Wynan sat up straight. "Are you sure that it wasn't her? We sent her to DC. What the hell was she doing in Philadelphia—attending a Terry Mangel revival, no less? She's a size two at most. What body issues does she have to be concerned with?"

Fletcher crossed his forearms on his desk and laid his forehead on top. "I think it had to do with the story she wanted to pursue that first day," he said, talking down into his lap. "Maybe she thought Mangel had some connection to the Blubber Be Gone death. It's all my fault. I should have put my foot down on day one. No big investigations until you get your feet wet. Instead, I filled her full of fanciful ideas, told her she could do anything she wanted, and I'd support her. I did try to distract her with the Evans story, but in the end, this is all on me."

"You saying fanciful ideas were all you filled her with?"

He looked back up at his executive editor and childhood friend. "Are you insinuating something?"

"Nah, I'm flat-out asking you if you banged her silly. You've had a hard-on for Cam since the day you came back from White Plains. She was all you could talk about. If you're tied to her romantically and she's involved with any of this Mangel nonsense, you might have put the entire future of *Trend* in jeopardy. I didn't leave a perfectly decent job at a top magazine to flush my entire career down the toilet, all thanks to your libidinal renaissance."

Fletcher lifted an eyebrow. "You done?"

"Pretty much, yeah."

"Good, because one more word and my fist, which is also enjoying its rebirth, is going to knock you into the next century. I happen to love that girl. I won't rest until I have her back and know she's safe."

The intercom buzzed, startling both men. "Yes, Ms. Thorsen?"

"I think you'll want to come out here, Mr. Fletcher. There's someone who claims she must see you."

"No more reporters, Rachel. I've said all I'm going to say."

"It's not a reporter, sir. It's someone whose face is covered in scarves, claiming to be Camarin's mum."

He looked up at Wynan. Maybe this would give them a clue as to her whereabouts.

"Show her into the war room, Ms. Thorsen. We'll be right out."

The woman waiting for them had removed her scarves, revealing an older, even more elegant version of Camarin. The only differences were a pair of gold-rimmed glasses and a widow's peak of silver splitting her short, jet-black hair in two. Fletcher estimated that she was only five or six years older than he, with a figure still as shapely as her daughter's. If Camarin looked this good in twenty-five years, he could count himself a very, very lucky man.

"Excuse me, which one of you gentlemen is the magazine's owner?" she asked.

Fletcher walked over and shook her hand. "Mrs. Torres? I'm Lyle Fletcher, the owner of *Trend*. I hope you had a pleasant flight from Los Angeles."

"Please, call me Ana. Yes, it was okay. A little bumpy, but then again, I don't fly much. I don't know good flights from bad." She managed a weak smile.

"I'm Hans Wynan," said the executive editor, reaching out to shake hands after Fletcher had stepped to the side. "Please sit down, let's all have a chat." He pulled out a chair for their visitor, then he and Fletcher sat across from her at the boardroom table.

"Mr. Fletcher, Mr. Wynan, I am beside myself about my Camarita. She is in all the papers. I have been calling all the numbers I have, but she doesn't pick up. I have no idea how to reach her. And all these terrible things the papers are saying. My beautiful girl. I had to hide my face to come here today so the reporters wouldn't figure out who I was and drown me in questions. I don't know what to do."

"I'm afraid we haven't heard from her either, Ana," Fletcher said, reaching out and gently placing his hand over hers. "Nothing since Thursday last week. But I can tell you that I saw her in Philadelphia, and I know she couldn't be responsible for any of this."

Wynan looked at him, askance. "You were there? Why didn't you mention that before?"

He waved off the editor's concern. "There was nothing to tell. Rachel told me she was heading down. I went to keep an eye on her, make sure she didn't get into any trouble." He turned back to Ana. "I want to say how very sorry I am for your loss."

"Excuse me? My what?"

"The loss of your other daughter, Monaeka. Camarin spoke about her at the revival. You could see how the memory tore her to pieces."

Ana turned pale. "This is very bad news, Mr. Fletcher. Very bad."

"What is it, Ana?" asked Wynan.

"I'm sorry, I thought we were past this. I normally don't share family secrets, but in this case, it's probably best." Her eyes pleaded for forgiveness, acceptance. "*Hagå-hu*, my beautiful daughter, she isn't right in the head sometimes. When she was younger, there was an incident. I was working nights when, behind my back, my sister, Sirena, brought in a *suruhånu*, a traditional healer, and a priest. Camarin was overweight, you see, the pills for the epilepsy affecting her metabolism. I tried to put her on diets, but Sirena claimed it was the devil making her fat. She believed that if they could only exorcise his possession from her soul, she could be normal, fit in. Anyway, after that she was never the same. It's like the stress of the ceremony broke her in two."

Fletcher was shaking with anger at the thought of his darling being traumatized. An exorcism? What were they thinking? What does that do to a young girl, probably already stressed with body issues? "Go on," he said, trying to keep his voice steady.

"What I'm trying to say is that there is no Monaeka. There never was. After the exorcism, my daughter took her middle name and somehow turned it into the person she didn't want to be anymore. Dissociative Identity Disorder, that's how the psychiatrist explained it. Camarin became the dominant one, constantly trying to take control, keep Monaeka down. Her weight still yo-yoed, and when she was skinny, Camarin became herself again. Hopeful. Self-confident. But when she got depressed and ate herself into a stupor, that was Monaeka, taking over. It was a constant struggle between them. The doctor says it's not all that uncommon, people taking on one personality when they're fat and another when they're thin. This is just that phenomenon taken to an extreme."

"She seemed completely normal until a few days ago," Wynan said, wincing. "But once the Mangel story hit, she started seizing, acting oddly…we should have suspected something. And yet she never seemed to deviate between two personalities, at least not around the office."

"That's true," added Fletcher. "At times, she seemed more impulsive or agitated than others, but nothing so atypical that it made me think twice."

"When she went to college, Camarin came more into her own," Ana explained. "I think she drove Monaeka further and further away. The longer she kept thin, the more 'Camarin' she stayed. I call every week or so, trying to gauge her mental state. Lately, she's sounded stable, and I had hoped Monaeka had died off completely, but now, based what you're telling me, it was all just wishful thinking."

Fletcher thought back to the bulimia Cam described at the revival. Fighting off Monaeka must be why she never ate, or when she did, she ensured the calories never stayed around very long.

"What about the college essay?" he asked.

Ana shrugged. "What about it? She took one picture when she was at her heaviest and another at her thinnest, and wrote a story about it. They liked it. They accepted her application."

"But...she tells this story of how she was responsible for Monaeka's suicide. A diet pill overdose. She's consumed with guilt over it," said Fletcher.

"She told me her sister died from an epileptic seizure," said Wynan.

Ana hung her head. "Yes, this is what I was most worried about. It's all part of the psychosis, this hallucination of hers. It's always fuzzy, changing. The psychiatrist told us that the 'Monaeka' part of her brain was very fragile, very unstable. Paranoid that the stronger twin is out to get her, starve her to death. There's no telling what could happen if Camarin lets down her guard and Monaeka takes over. She could rebel, lash out. When the newscasters reported that she spoke in front of all those people and got booed…and then that poor man was hurt in his trailer, maybe killed…"

"You think that Camarin might actually be responsible for Mangel's attack?" Fletcher sat back in disbelief, as if never having considered such a possibility before.

"Anything is possible. That's why I must see her, get her to the doctor. I need you to help me. Otherwise, who knows…" Her eyes glistened. Wynan reached over and pulled a tissue from a box to his left and handed it to the grieving mother. She thanked him, lifted her glasses, and gingerly patted her tears dry.

"Mrs. Torres, please promise us you won't share this information with anyone else. Camarin needs our help, not a cadre of police officers questioning her and driving her into some kind of frenzy," Fletcher said.

"You have my word, but first we have to find her."

"Don't worry. I have six men already on it, and I'll hire another six if I have to. Where are you staying? How can we get back in touch with you?"

"I have a room at the hotel above where Camarita works at the piano bar."

"The Laidlaw?"

"Yes, it's the only hotel in town I'd heard of. It's expensive though. I was thinking of moving to the Holiday Inn if I have to stay much longer."

"Please don't bother. The Laidlaw is a decent hotel and well-situated. You should stay wherever you feel most comfortable. I'll call the manager and have him bill the magazine directly for your visit. Help yourself to room service, whatever you need to feel at ease."

"Oh, Mr. Fletcher, that isn't necessary."

"Ana, it truly is. I hope that one day I will be more than just your daughter's employer. I hope to be more to you than just an acquaintance."

Both Wynan and Ana opened their eyes wide at Fletcher's proclamation.

"Can I have a piece of paper?" asked Ana. "I'll write down my cell number and my room number. If you find out anything about my Camarita, you'll know where to find me."

Wynan grabbed a sheet of stationery and a pen from atop the lateral file behind him. Ana scribbled down the necessary information. She traded it with Fletcher, who in turn handed her one of his business cards, which she placed in her purse.

"Please, Mr. Lyle Fletcher, please find our girl. Bring her back to us safe."

"I will, Ana, even if it's the last thing I ever do. But if she contacts you, you must let us know so we can help her, without the press and the police getting involved. The last thing we need is for her to show herself, get spooked, and then run away again. Do you promise as well?"

"Of course. When I hear, you will hear from me."

CHAPTER
38 39 40

*I*T WAS ONE *of the last warm days of October and Camarin was enjoying herself on the swings, sharing some gossip with one of the more popular girls in school. Could this be her chance to fit in with the cool kids? Apparently not. Through the sun's glare, she spied her sister across the playground, surrounded by a gang of fourth-grade bullies.*

She leapt off the swing and raced over in time to witness Alex, their leader, push Monaeka to the ground, calling her Fatso. Threaten to pellet her with stones. Which was unfortunate since Alex was the cutest guy in the class, the one Camarin had been secretly crushing on for months. Despite the attraction, she positioned herself between the boys and her dazed sister, impervious to the five-against-one threat, her expression a silent dare to just try and toss even one rock in their direction and risk her legendary wrath. Channeling the strength of her strong Chamorro ancestors, even if it meant remaining an outcast from the 'in' crowd for yet another semester. She'd made a vow to protect her sister, and no matter what the cost, she had to see it through.

She noticed, with regret, how her insurrection resonated in Alex's eyes, his fury at having his playground preeminence challenged. He drew back his stone, aiming to both wound Monaeka and reassert his authority…

Camarin felt a tug on her shoulder and forced her eyes open. The light streaming in from the window hurt her retinas, and she put a hand out to block the beams. "Please," she said in a hoarse voice, "please close the shades."

Harvey walked over and shut the blinds and then picked up a glass of water from the end table and held it out to her.

"Do you want help sitting up? You need to drink something."

She boosted herself up on her elbows, and he pressed the glass to her mouth. She managed a few sips through parched lips. They hurt going down.

"What happened?"

"You did quite a number on yourself. Knocked yourself unconscious. You've been out for two days. I had a friend of mine come to check on you—"

"You what? You know everyone is looking for me."

"Calm yourself. This man is also a friend of Xavier's father. No way he is talking to anyone. Anyway, he assured me that you were fine, that maybe it was better that you were missing out on all the excitement."

"Excitement?"

"The press coverage. You know. But there is one thing you need to be aware of."

"What's that? Have they already convicted and sentenced me?"

"No, nothing as dire as all that."

"Did they report Mangel's dead?"

"No, not that either. DeAndre called your phone, and when he couldn't get you, he tried me. Turns out his girlfriend told him your mother is in town and went looking for you at your office."

Camarin's arms began to judder, and she fought to regain her composure.

"My mother. Just when I thought things couldn't get any worse…"

"She told Dee your mom seemed pretty distraught. Maybe you want to call her?"

"Not yet. I need my strength for that call. Do you have any protein? Maybe some chicken or fish?

"Ah, my girl, I was hoping your appetite would come back. While you were asleep, I've been cooking, trying my hand at some of your native recipes. How does a little chicken *kelaguen* sound? Or maybe a little *eskabeche*?"

Her mouth watered at the mention of cold chicken salad and fresh fish cooked in vinegar sauce. Certainly, the best parts of growing up in a family from Guam. "Bring it on, Malcolm. You'll soon have me eating out of the palm of your hand."

"Just as long as you eat, I don't much care how you do it."

He slowly helped her get out of bed and into the living room, where he sat her in front of the television before heading into the kitchen. The news stations were covering an earthquake in Greece and another controversial presidential twitter storm. The Mangel affair was apparently yesterday's news. None of the reporters had stumbled onto the connection between Mangel's attack and the other diet-related murders. And without any verification that Mangel had actually died, it seemed that the attention span of the average American news consumer was mercifully short.

"Maybe you want to turn off the news, skip all that stress," said Harvey as he walked in with a plate piled high with Chamorro delicacies.

"For you, anything," she said, sitting up as he set the dish on the coffee table.

She dipped her fork into her favorite foods and mindlessly surfed through the channels, eventually settling on *Say Yes to the Dress*. She admired the sweetheart neckline on the bride-to-be's fit-and-flare gown, musing on how it might look on her, when it all came flooding back. How the man she'd loved and might have married had manipulated and betrayed her. How she was in hiding specifically because of him.

The anger caused her to gag on her mouthful of fish. Harvey pulled away her fork and started patting her forcefully on the back until she spat the food onto the carpet. She stared at the spew, mortified.

"Don't worry about it," he said, taking a napkin and wiping up the vomit. "Just have to chew more carefully next time, girl."

"It's not that, Malcolm. I think I've figured out the identity of the Invisible Woman. The person who hurt Terry Mangel. I need to tell DeAndre. Do you know where my phone is?"

"Yes, yes, but calm down. You don't want to lose any more nutrition." He walked into the kitchen and came back with her burner. "Sorry, I left it there when I was speaking to young Mr. Robinson. Now, about your suspicions, before you start throwing anyone under the bus, are you positive?"

"No way to be certain," she said, shaking her head. "But it's a very strong theory, and I have reasons that support it."

"Well, be sure you phrase it that way when you repeat it to anyone else. There's an old Jamaican saying… talk and taste your tongue. It means think before you speak."

"It's good advice. I'll be sure to keep it in mind."

She mulled over Harvey's admonition as she clutched the phone in her palm. It was true—she wasn't a hundred percent sure. It could be Monaeka again, filling her mind with crazy thoughts, unwilling to let her find happiness with her Prince Charming.

Maybe the smarter call to make would be to her mother, so she could stop her worrying. After all, what were the chances that the Invisible Woman was still watching her, monitoring her calls or those of her loved ones and friends? The damage was already done. Her photo was out, her reputation annihilated. She dialed the familiar number. Her mother picked up on the second ring.

"Nana, it's me, Camarin."

"*Gråsias adios!* Camarita, I was so worried. Are you all right? Are you *såfo*?"

"Yes, Nana, I am fine. I'm hidden away where no one can find me until the real killer is found."

"I need to see you, Camarita. You can come to me, or I will come to you. I won't sleep tonight until I see you, until I know that someone didn't force you to say you're okay just to stop me from looking for you."

She willed herself to be patient, to put herself in her mother's shoes. She could understand how scary it could be with someone you love missing, disgraced on national television, accused of terrible things. If she could spend an hour with Ana, put her mind at ease, make her promise not to tell anyone that she'd seen her, at least that would be one less thing to worry about.

"Camarita, are you still there?"

"Yes, Nana. Where are you? I will come by as long as you promise on grandmother's grave that you will not tell anyone that you've spoken to me or that I'm coming. My life and my freedom could hang in the balance. Do you swear, Nana?"

"Camarita, you know I would never do anything that would hurt you or put you in peril. You have my word. I am at the Laidlaw Hotel, Room 1402. When do you think you'll be here?"

She glanced at the clock across the room. It was 11:03. "I'll be there later today. Just for a brief time, to show you I am okay. By the way, Nana, I heard you were at my office. Do not go back there. Stay away from those men. It could be very dangerous for us both."

"Yes, Camarita, of course, whatever you say. I will see you later this afternoon. I love you, my *bonita*."

CHAPTER

39 40 41

FLETCHER AND WYNAN knocked on Ana's door about an hour after she'd phoned them. Fletcher had originally planned on coming alone, no need to involve Wynan in all of this. Hans couldn't possibly understand what Camarin meant to him, how important it was for him to deal with her alone, in private. But his friend caught him trying to sneak out, confronted him, made him admit to his destination.

"We started this together, and we're finishing this together," Wynan proclaimed and took the lead in hailing down a cab.

"Any plan on how you're going to handle this, Superman?" Wynan asked after they'd given the driver the address. "You going to swoop in, grab her, and fly off, or just reason with her, like the cool-headed Clark Kent you are?"

Fletcher frowned. "I think you'd be Clark Kent, and I'd be tough but fair-minded editor-in-chief Perry White. If you're going to throw out sarcastic analogies, at least be accurate, okay?"

"You always were a stickler over details."

He patted his friend on the back. "Years of training, my friend. To answer the question, I'm not exactly sure what I'm going to do. Play it by ear, I guess. I'm hoping that between her mother and I reasoning with her, we can convince her that the safest, most prudent thing to do is come out of hiding, get a lawyer, face these charges head-on. They have nothing but a picture, from what I can tell. No weapon, no evidence. Pictures can be photoshopped, after all."

"Well, according to your own admission, you were there. What did you see?"

"I saw a girl in pain go up on stage and rip her heart out, all so Terry Mangel could sell a few extra trinkets. You know, the guy's premise is worthy, but his methods are a joke. If his concern was truly body acceptance for all, he wouldn't ask the oppressed to pay hundreds of dollars to feel good about themselves. He's out there, condemning weight-loss clinics, fashion magazines, and the rest of the self-improvement industry for bilking millions from those who don't fit into an unrealistic vision of what's acceptable. But Mangel, with his high-priced revival tickets, retreats, books, DVDs—it's just the flip side of the same coin."

Wynan shrugged. "You know firsthand that people will pay their last dime for just one glimmer of hope. It's so terribly sad. All anyone in this world wants is love, acceptance, and based on the number of resumes I keep getting, a chance to be published, have their ideas heard. And when they finally get those things, they discover the sad truth—people are fickle, their opinions capricious. If you're waiting for their approval, you've got a long wait. Acceptance has to come from within."

"And preferably without breaking the bank." Fletcher leaned forward. "Driver, it's over there on the right."

The cab pulled up in front of the functional facade, indistinguishable from every other convention hotel in

Manhattan had it not been for the large, blinking neon sign screaming *The Laidlaw Hotel*, and then, in smaller letters underneath, *Home to Benji's Dueling Piano Bar*. They bypassed the throngs in the lobby and headed right to the elevators and the fourteenth floor.

The higher room numbers were closest to the elevator, so they needed to trek down a long corridor before arriving at Room 1402. Fletcher gave the door three loud raps. No response. He tried again, this time half-knocking and half-pounding. Then he waited, shifting his weight from leg to leg.

"Easy there, big fellow. I'm sure she heard you the first time." Wynan put a hand on Fletcher's shoulder.

"You're my best friend, but right now, please shut up. I'm nervous, and I just want to get this over with."

"I'll be there in just a minute," a voice from inside the room called out.

Fletcher looked back at his companion, chin lifted, vindicated. "See? It helped."

The door slowly opened, just enough for Ana's face to show. She wore an uneasy, almost frightened expression.

"No need to worry, Mrs. Torres. It's just Hans and I."

She looked Fletcher in the eye, as if trying to signal. Her lips mouthed the words *go away*.

"I don't underst—"

The door opened farther, wide enough for him to see the gun pointing at her head.

"Gentlemen, we've been waiting for you. Please come in. Without any sudden moves or heroic efforts, please. Picking brain fragments out of hotel carpets can take forever."

"THAT'S CRAZY. HAVE you thought this all the way through?" DeAndre asked after Camarin called and revealed her plans for the afternoon.

"Yes, Mom."

"I'm not your mom. I'm your roommate. And right now, I'm your worried-out-of-his-mind roommate. You went to all this trouble to go into hiding, and now you're going to traipse right back to where we started?"

"Traipse?"

"Yeah, thanks to *Drift*, I'm learning new, big words. It's what we future magazine publishers do in our spare time when our friends aren't mocking our vocabulary or ruining our carefully laid-out plans."

"Ah, well, if it sets your psyche at ease any, I promise not to traipse. I'm more of a skedaddler anyway."

"For someone who's about to risk her life, you're sounding awfully cavalier about all of this."

"I don't think it's as big of a deal as you're making out. First, the Invisible Woman's already published the pictures. I'm toast, and she's off laughing her head off somewhere. I'm no longer a person of interest."

"Until she thinks you might open your mouth and tell them about The Collective's recruiting Facebook post, the string of murders, the death threat against Mangel, all those trivial things that you might mention once you're in custody. Which, I must repeat, is something you're safe from now, as long as you stay hidden."

She looked over at Harvey, who had pulled her newly washed burqa from the dryer and was holding it out for her to admire. She smiled and gave him a thumbs-up.

"I understand. I appreciate your concern. But right now, my mother is waiting in Room 1402 to see for herself that I'm safe, so she doesn't have a heart attack. She's already gone to Fletcher and Wynan, and they know she's in town. If my suspicions are right and Lyle is the Invisible Woman, my mother's not safe as long as he can get at her, use her to get to me."

"Unless that's what they're already doing. Ever think of that? Maybe you're walking into one enormous trap."

"I very much doubt that's the case. They'd have no way of knowing I'd find out she was in town, or that I'd try to contact her."

"Why not? Your mom came to *Trend*, where Fletcher and Rachel work. Fletcher has seen her and me together. He knows we're a couple. Doesn't take a genius to figure out word could get back to you."

She considered his argument.

"Maybe you're right, Dee. I hadn't thought of that. I'll figure out some other way to get a message to her, maybe through Malcolm. Don't worry about me. I'll stay here and keep digging."

"That's my girl. Maybe your mom will come down to Benji's tonight and I'll get to speak to her myself."

"Okay, that would be great. Just be careful. If I'm still a target, you're still one too."

"Don't I know it. Tweedledee and Tweedledum are in the next room, no doubt still fending off Annalise's advances."

She laughed. "Well, then good luck all around. Bye for now."

She hung up the phone and looked up at Harvey, who was pulling out a hanger from the hall closet.

"Wait, what are you doing?" she asked.

"I'm putting this away. I thought I heard you say you're not going after all."

She strode over and gently took the garment from Harvey's hand.

"Oh, I'm going all right. My mom needs to get back to LA, where she'll be safe, and the only way that's going to happen is if she gets it through her stubborn Chamorro skull that I'm able to fend for myself."

The cab ride downtown was far more pleasant than the ride up had been four days earlier. Having only one layer of clothing on underneath the burqa helped, as did the lack of the nauseatingly sweet scent of molasses. Camarin patted the fanny pack that Malcolm had run out and purchased for her at the local sporting goods store. She had money, her burner phone, everything she needed to buy her mother an early dinner via room service and then call her an Uber to take her to JFK.

DeAndre was too overprotective. She was going to be just fine.

CHAPTER

CAMARIN STEPPED INSIDE the Laidlaw and smack into the suspicious stares of guests in the lobby. Typical New Yorkers wouldn't have given her burqa a second look, but unenlightened tourists from God knows what hick town? Especially with so many suicide bombings in the news of late? She hadn't considered that without the Muslims for Peace convention in town, she stood out like a sore thumb, especially unescorted by a man. She made a beeline for the elevator.

She pushed the button for the fourteenth floor, noting with shock that her hands were trembling. *Pussy.* Annoyed at her own weakness, she pressed her arms tight against her body for the remainder of the ride. Then she sought out Room 1402. *Figures she'd make me walk as far down the hall as possible.*

As she stood in front of her mother's hotel room, she took a deep breath, willing God to grant her the strength to deal with the crazed lunatic inside. She'd already played out the scenario in her head. First her mother would criticize her outfit, asking if the burqa was to hide a few extra pounds instead of allowing her to walk the streets of New York incognito. Then the meat—is that how she intended to keep her hair, so long and unruly? Was that a pimple on her chin? Was she really living up to her full potential, working as a bartender and a junior reporter? Surely, she could do better. And then, of course, the pièce de résistance: *Camarita, you're such a smart girl. How could you have gotten yourself all tied up in this Mangel horror show?* Like it was entirely her fault. Maybe Monaeka had been the smart one, checking out early. Not having to deal with all this garbage.

She knocked at the door and heard a female voice yell out, "Come in. It's open."

That's odd, she thought. Her mother was as cautious as they come. She pressed the handle, and sure enough, the door was unlocked. She ventured inside.

"Nana, what are you thinking leaving the door unbolted? Maybe I'm not the only one who should—"

She stopped dead in her tracks. Directly in front of her on the bed sat Fletcher, Wynan, and her mother, gagged, with wrists and ankles bound, their eyes imploring her to save herself. Two heavyset women stood between her and the captives, one positioned at an angle, pointing a gun with a silencer at the three captives. Camarin recognized her as Maria Whalen, one of the speakers from the revival and Mangel fiancée number one, the computer programmer who'd been fired from the cosmetics firm. Guess someone else was handling Mom's dialysis today. The other woman was Grace, the woman who'd been working the customer service booth at the revival. She looked to be unarmed and, judging by her confused expression, was apparently out of her element.

Cam felt herself paralyzed, starting to once again float outside of her body, unprepared, unarmed, and unable to deal with the fact that everyone she loved was about to die, and she could do nothing to help.

"So glad you could join us, Camarin," Terry Mangel made his grand entrance, emerging from behind the bathroom door. "Grace, help Ms. Torres off with her cloak so we can see her hands."

Grace, looking almost apologetic, pulled the burqa off Cam's body, and threw it in the corner. Camarin remained unable to move or resist.

"Search her. Make sure she isn't armed."

She patted Camarin down, checked her fanny pack, and then nodded to Mangel. "She's clean."

Satisfied, Mangel waved Grace to return to her original position beside Maria.

A rush of outrage flooded over Camarin, feeling violated by Grace's inspection but unable to swat her off. Just as she couldn't fend off her aunt tying her to the bed, or the priest wresting the demon of gluttony from her soul.

Camarin shifted her glance to her mother and recalled the day after the exorcism, when her mother had learned of the ceremony and had assured her that such an atrocity would never happen again. *"In times of great need, the* Taotaomo'na *will protect you,"* she said, trying to assuage her daughter's fears. *"They are the collective spirits of our Chamorro ancestors, our guiding spirits. When you are in grave danger, they will always be there for you. This is all you have to say…"*

Mananiti, *if you have ever truly loved your family, then help us right now!* Camarin's silent war cry reverberated in her head, the power of the words bringing the feeling back to her arms and legs.

"You're really a very difficult lady to pin down, even with my top-notch hacking and tracking team here," said Mangel, holding his hand out as if encouraging her to applaud his team of criminals. "They've been following you since the moment you ran out of my trailer. Nice staging, eh? Giving you an excuse to fight me off? And grabbing that letter opener was an unexpected bonus. Fingerprints galore, they made the photos even more incriminating. Thank you for that. It's amazing what you can do with Photoshop, a little corn syrup, and some red dye. Even fooled Ms. Lowery. She still thinks I'm recovering in some secluded hospital. Only way to make the press conferences sound convincing, you know."

Camarin knew she should be angry or terrified, but she stood solidly in place, blessedly overtaken by a calm she attributed to her ancestors looking down over her, protecting her from harm.

"You're the Invisible Woman?" she said, half-sneeringly at Mangel. "You faked that Facebook post, the death threat, just to throw me off?"

"I prefer to think of every forgotten female as an Invisible Woman," he said smugly. "Maria here, Grace, all my followers. They each know what it's like to be forgotten, overlooked. That's why they do as I direct them. They perform little tasks for me, helping me rid the world of those who might hold a bias against them. Isn't that right, girls?"

He walked over and ran his hand down each woman's hair, lovingly, as if they were a pair of prized Irish setters.

"More like they help you wipe out the competition, isn't that right?" she asked brazenly. If she was going to die, she might as well do it with a bang.

And if Fletcher wasn't the killer, her research had given her a new theory about why Mangel was behind it all. Something that might change his supporters' minds about cooperating in his murderous schemes.

"You don't care less about body shaming or fat bullying, do you? Those people you killed, they just stood between you and a few more dollars of profit. And you figured if you could blackmail me into killing on your behalf, you'd shut me up for good. Admit it."

A funny look came over Maria's face. *Maybe I'm getting my message across.* One ass squeeze from Mangel later, she returned to her smiling, gun-wielding self.

"Ms. Torres, you're sadly mistaken. I've never killed anyone. My hands are clean. If my two followers here have chosen to rid the world of their oppressors, and I just provided them the names, the means, and the opportunity, then so be it. My message has consistently been one of love and acceptance."

It was as if he were back on stage, preaching. She wasn't sure if he was lost without his limelight or was simply reminding his henchwomen of why they were there. Perhaps he was merely trying to clear his own conscience of responsibility.

Regardless, she was amazed by her own clear head and focus. Not one shake of her knees, not one bead of sweat on her face. She knew these ladies' mindsets, their deepest fears. Being laughed at. Being used. And then discarded. And why wouldn't she know? She and her sister had known that dread their entire lives. She gave her compadres on the bed a nod and pressed on.

"Tell it to the sheep who follow you around the country, Terry, but I'm not buying into that horseshit. All you are is a failed ad executive who realized that you could reach your overweight consumers more effectively by offering them hope and an occasional engagement ring than by selling them low-carb frozen dinners and diet pills. Your message of 'love your oppressors' is a sham. What happened? Did the layoffs and pay cuts at Lehming Brothers start eating away at your profits? Did you figure that by murdering off the competition you'd inspire some copycat killings? Put more focus on fat oppression, more reason to rebel? And maybe

Lehming Brothers would start paying better again? Especially with fewer subsidiaries left to support? Say what you may, but I know the truth, and deep down, I think these ladies here know it too. You don't care about the size of anything except your wallet."

"You shut up, you fucking bitch." It was Maria, still brandishing the gun at her hostages but obviously rattled by Camarin's tirade. "He's a good man. He loves us. You're the problem here, snooping around, wanting to hurt Terry with your article, portray him as a sham. You're going to watch while we kill these three. Then it's your turn."

Knowing time was running out, Camarin had to think quickly. "Maria, listen to me. I might be a dead woman, but you can still save yourself from a life of misery."

"You're crazy. I'm the happiest I've ever been."

"You're blind. He's been using you."

Maria turned and faced her accuser, leaving the trio unguarded for a second before turning back.

"You're lying. You're just saying that, trying to buy time. But it isn't going to work." She cocked the trigger and pointed it right at Cam's mother's head. The older woman started groaning under her gag, tears running down her cheeks. "Let's get this show on the road, shall we?"

Mangel gave Maria a kiss on the cheek and walked to the other side of the room. "Ladies, Make it quick. You know how I dislike violence."

Seeing her mother with only seconds to live, the gravity of the situation hit Camarin hard. First, she'd caused Monaeka's suicide and now she was going to be the reason her mother died as well. Then she remembered her fanny pack. "Maria, wait!" she screamed. "He's been cheating on you with April Lowery."

"Liar!"

"I can prove it."

"Really? How?" Her incredulity was palpable, but Camarin had clearly piqued her suspicions.

"Grace, go into my fanny pack. Pull out my phone."

Grace looked at Mangel, confused as to whom she should be obeying. For the first time since Camarin had entered the room, the evangelist seemed less self-satisfied, a hint of panic seeping into his eyes. Maria, too curious to endure her colleague's hesitation, reached inside the fanny pack herself and pulled out the phone, never taking her eyes or the gun off Cam's mother.

"Maria, what are you doing? Get on with it," Mangel ordered, his voice shaking.

By now Maria was clearly agitated and determined to remove any doubts as to Mangel's true affection. But she was also unwilling to take her sights off her target. She held out the phone to Grace. "Do what she says. Do it now, or I'll shoot you too."

Grace walked over and took the phone from Maria's outstretched hand.

"Go to the memos app," Camarin said, a quaver finally making its way into her voice. "Listen to the one labeled *April*. It's an interview I did with her during the revival. You have to know the truth before you make another giant mistake."

"Maria, she's trying to distract you," yelled Mangel, his voice two octaves too high to sound innocent. "Get on with what we came for."

"Quiet!" Maria, wielding her weapon, was clearly in charge now.

She motioned for Grace to continue. Her comrade clicked on the app and turned up the volume. April's recorded voice filled the hotel room.

"That's just gravy. I mean, now that I'm happy, I don't feel compelled to stuff myself all the time, but Terry didn't tell me to diet."

"Fast forward," said Camarin. "It's toward the end." Grace moved the recording ahead.

"And I've always been good with people and…wow, this is so amazing. No one ever asks about my story, and you seem so easy to talk to. Could I share something with you, off the record?"

There was sound of movement, and then the recording became more muffled but still loud and clear enough to understand. Camarin watched Maria's eyes grow wide as she listened.

"Don't tell anyone—this can't go anywhere beyond this room—but during that week? We fell in love. Terry said he never wanted to travel anywhere without me again. And look! We're engaged! We don't talk about it because, well, you know how tongues wag in confined spaces. Terry doesn't want to put people's noses out of joint or have them think I get preferential treatment."

"It's beautiful. When's the big day?"

"We haven't set an exact date yet. I just hope it's soon. Sometimes, I'm so scared the weight might come back on and…well, I have my heart set on a size-four wedding gown."

"Would it make a difference? Gaining the weight back? I mean, if you're happy and love yourself no matter what…"

"I don't think…I don't think he'd still marry me."

"Why not?"

"It's this thing he said. We were in San Francisco, shopping for dresses. I found this gorgeous Vera Wang and modeled it for him— I couldn't believe how stunning it looked on me—and I joked to the salesgirl, 'I'd better buy it now, before I gain back any weight'—and he said…"

"Don't leave me hanging. What did he say?"

"He said, 'Don't do that. It would be like slashing the *Mona Lisa*.'"

"Turn it off. Now."

Camarin could see the glistening in Maria's eyes as she fought back the sobs. As usual, Grace did as she was told.

"Maria, it's a fake. I don't know how she did it, but that recording is—"

"Silence!" Maria pointed the gun directly at Mangel, who froze in sudden terror. "I got fired once. I have no intention of it ever happening again. Not from an engagement. And certainly not by a two-faced weasel like you."

The sound of the gunshot was muffled, but the scent of sulfur filled the air, blending with the sweet, coppery smell of the blood pouring from Mangel's chest as he fell to the floor. His face bore a pained yet stunned expression as he collapsed into a pool of red. Camarin wondered which surprised him the most: that Maria had pulled the trigger, or that his charisma had finally failed him. In any case, she was satisfied that the blood was authentic this time.

Maria stumbled back from the force of the recoil, obviously unused to firearms. Camarin seized the moment and sprang for the hand holding the gun. The two struggled, Camarin, at a hundred pounds thinner, the more physically disadvantaged of the two. Their four hands clamored for the weapon, which waved wildly back and forth. Two shots fired, the bullets ricocheting off the ceiling. Maria pulled her hand down and elbowed her opponent hard in the chest and then pushed her to the floor.

"They say don't shoot the messenger," she said, aiming the gun at Camarin's head, pure hatred emanating from her eyes, "but I'm tired of taking orders."

Camarin crawled backward slowly, knowing it was a lost cause. "Nana, Lyle, I'm so sorry for everything. I love you. Goodbye," she cried, squeezing her eyes closed and waiting for the inevitable, the pain that would rip her chest apart and send her into eternal oblivion.

She heard the explosion, but the pain never came. She opened her eyes to witness Maria falling backward, hitting what was left of her skull on the television before collapsing next to her betrothed. Then Camarin swung her head around to where the shot had emanated. A brawny man in his thirties with a crew cut and a muscle shirt held a smoking pistol, which he now pointed at Grace. Beside him stood another just like him, with DeAndre, holding a keycard, standing between them.

"Tweedledee, I presume?" she asked.

"I knew it. I knew it. I knew it," said Dee, walking over and helping her to her feet. "You said you weren't coming here, but I knew you couldn't help yourself. Fantastic job, little Ms. I-Can-Take-Care-of-Myself."

She hugged her roommate tightly as she heard Tweedledum call out, "Someone call 911. Man down."

She turned toward the bed and saw Fletcher, who was lying flat on his back, still bound and gagged, a red, circular stain near the shoulder of his button-down shirt spreading quickly in diameter. "Oh my God, Lyle," she screamed, running to his side. "Someone get me a knife or scissors or something." She pulled the bandana from his mouth. "Can you hear me? Can you speak?"

"No need to shout, Ms. Torres. I'm wounded, not deaf. And, yes, I think I'll be fine. As long as you promise not to run off and start fighting crime again without me by your side."

"I promise," she said, feeling a tap on her shoulder, "but right now I do have to leave you, so these nice men can unbind you and take you to the ER."

Camarin's head started spinning as the room turned into a teeming bustle of activity. The two bruisers cut off Fletcher's bindings while several police officers filed in, cuffing Grace, untying and ungagging Wynan and Camarin's mother. Two medics wheeled in a gurney to transport Fletcher to the hospital. Others raced over to Mangel and Maria to see if there was still any life left in them to save.

A young, anemic-looking man with plastic-rimmed glasses and a cheap brown suit introduced himself as the hotel manager. He was quick to grab some credit for the rescue. "We had reports of terrorists and a wanted fugitive. Turned out both led to the same place. So glad we were able to get up here in time."

When a trio of policemen tried to arrest Camarin, it all became too much for her to bear. She fell to her knees, begging for everyone to leave her alone. Wynan knelt beside her to her left, her mother on her right.

"Don't worry, Camarin. Both Lyle and I know the city's best attorneys. Mangel clearly survived the faked attack in Philadelphia, and we have three witnesses here who can testify to that. We'll get the whole thing cleared up in no time."

She nodded gratefully, trying to control her sobbing as they helped her to her feet.

"Not me," said DeAndre, who was standing nearby. "You all go to the police station, but me, I'm going back to the office. This is one scoop that *Drift* is going to get on the stands long before *Trend* has a chance to turn on their computers."

CHAPTER
41 42 43

FLETCHER SAT OPPOSITE Camarin at One if by Land's most private corner table, noting how her dark eyes reflected the flickering of the candle flame. It had been a long week. Between assuring the police of her innocence and convincing Ana that she could return to LA, secure in the knowledge that her daughter could handle the big city on her own, things were finally starting to calm down. His girl deserved an evening out of the spotlight, one shared with only him.

The waiter brought the bottle of Gavi di Gavi he'd ordered and drizzled a smidgen for Fletcher to sample before filling their glasses with the dry, white wine. Fletcher held up his glass and clinked it against Camarin's, inviting her to join him in a toast. It hurt to lift his arm too high, with his left shoulder still bandaged and healing from the gunshot wound.

"To a lifetime of sharing everything, my darling. Here's to no more secrets."

She eyed him suspiciously and took a long sip. "Are you referring to anything in particular, or is that just a blanket statement?"

The waiter arrived at the table with their individual beef Wellingtons, a house specialty. "Let's talk about it after they serve the entrée."

Once they were enjoying their dinner, she brought the subject up again.

"It's the thing I said at the revival, right? About Monaeka. You're upset I didn't tell you about my sister?"

He knew this was a delicate conversation, and if he didn't handle it right, it could scar her for life. He'd been debating how to handle it and had consulted with two psychiatrists who specialized in split personalities and trauma recovery.

"It was a surprise, I'll admit," he said, running his finger down the hand she was using to hold her fork. "You were so expressive, but I could sense your pain. It must have been very difficult for you."

"It was. Hard to live through and even harder to talk about."

"I understand. I was thinking, I know a very good psychologist. She helped me when I was getting over Margaret's death. You see, like you, I also blamed myself. If only I'd hired better lawyers to defend her. Stood up to the Lehming Brothers on her behalf. Given her better advice. Never left her side, given her the opportunity..." His voice drifted lower. "Anyway, I know how you feel, and I know how much Dr. Joan Eisenstodt helped me. Maybe you'd like to spend some time talking to her. Take as many sessions as you need. My treat."

"I don't know if I can accept that. It's very generous. Almost too much so."

"I insist. Whatever I have, you have."

"Well, I tell you what. I'll agree to see Dr. Eisenstodt if you answer a couple of questions of mine. You know, reporter-type stuff."

"Happy to. I'm an open book."

"Are you completely over Margaret's death?"

She gave him a beseeching look, as if to ask if there was enough room in his heart for both her and the memory of his former wife. He had to be honest. There was no other way to start the type of relationship he wanted them to embark on together.

"In some ways, yes. In other ways, I'm haunted by it." He looked past her, his shame making it impossible for him to stare her in the eye. "When I said no secrets, I also meant none that I would keep from you. There's something I must confess. It's been weighing on me for a while. I just hope that once you know, you'll still feel the same way about me."

Her expression reflected great concern. "You're scaring me."

"I'm scared too, but I know we can't move forward unless I share this with you." He felt the sweat beads forming on his forehead. "When Margaret passed, I was overcome with grief. And I blamed Lehming Brothers, the people who'd fired her for totally undeserved, cosmetic reasons. I was determined to punish them for that decision, even if it took every penny I had."

Camarin nodded. "I know a little something about Lehming Brothers and their connection to the murders. At one point, I actually thought you might be involved. Crazy, I know."

"Not so crazy. During my attorney days, I worked with a lot of not-so-innocent, white-collar criminals. Corporate espionage, that sort of thing. It gave me some ideas about decimating Lehming Brothers from within. I analyzed all of their holdings and then met with each of their strongest competitors. The plan was that I would recruit competent workers at all corporate levels, from the mailroom to IT to accounting, and convince them to apply for jobs at Lehming

Brothers–owned firms. They'd ask for less-than-average salaries so they'd definitely get hired. Once inside, the workers would uncover the companies' weaknesses, so the competition could exploit those issues however they chose. It's why I was out on the road so much, supposedly fundraising. I was out making new deals, increasing my army of spies."

Camarin remained silent, merely nodding as she listened.

"I bought *Trend* mostly as a vehicle for those rival companies to buy overpriced ads. I used the excess to make up the difference in the workers' pay."

"So that's why the ad pages were increasing but the magazine's finances were still shaky?" Camarin asked.

"Exactly. I even hired Wynan to make the whole thing look legit. And it was all working beautifully. Lehming Brothers companies were having labor problems, bad publicity, all instigated by my spies. Ironically, those were probably the money issues that launched Mangel's own plot of revenge against the conglomerate, so I guess, in some way, I am partially responsible for those poor people's deaths. For that, I will be eternally remorseful."

"How could you have known, Lyle?" Her eyes were filled with sympathy, and he wondered how he could have been so lucky to find her.

"That's what happens when your actions are tainted by bad intent. In the end, it all came back to bite me. The infiltrators started getting greedy, asking for more money. I had to borrow from the magazine's meager profits, even sell my own properties to make up the difference. But with my goal so close in sight, I wasn't thinking clearly. All I could see was revenge. When the murders started, I celebrated that the companies I was targeting were experiencing even more troubles. I doubt if Lehming Brothers ever connected the dots between the deaths. I mean, with thousands of holdings, each ruled by different divisional vice presidents, a few losses here and there wouldn't have raised an eyebrow."

"If that's true, it's so terribly sad."

"That's unfortunately the essence of big business. In any case, then you came along, and everything changed. Your lofty ideals made me realize that if I transformed *Trend* into a legitimate, more serious publication, I could defeat Lehming Brothers at their own game by driving their publication *Drift* out of business. I mean, no offense to your friend DeAndre and his family, I'm sure they're very nice, but this was an opportunity for legitimate competition. How could I have known you were the roommate of the owners' son?"

Camarin fidgeted but said nothing. Despite her silence, Fletcher knew he couldn't stop until he had completely cleared his conscience.

"I am ashamed to confess this, but revenge has been a toxic, driving force in my life for the last three years. The other day, after seeing how it destroyed Maria, what it drove her to do, I realized that there's not enough room in my life for both love and hate."

"What does that mean?" she asked.

"It means I am extricating myself from the recruitment business. I'm finished with operating from a place of loathing. And if you can see your way to looking past this blemish in my character, I'd like to choose love. A lifetime of love with you." He tentatively broke into a smile.

She took a long sip of water. "Sounds to me like you never personally hurt anyone," she said. "You never shared any corporate secrets. You just helped people find jobs and then supplemented their incomes. Isn't that right?"

"That would be a generous way of looking at it, yes."

"And now you own a vehicle to make a real difference in people's lives."

"That's true. With your help, that is."

"Then I'm satisfied that all you did was give Lehming Brothers a taste of their own medicine." She smiled, her look of joy matching his own. "There's just one other question I'd like you to clear up." She pierced her last morsel of beef Wellington with her fork. "Those boys in boarding school. The ones that were bullying Hans. He said you disposed of them. Exactly what did you do to them?"

"Ah, he told you about that? Wow. Well, nothing particularly heroic, I'm afraid. My father was one of the board of trustees at Greendale Hall. One of the reasons I was even able to get into that school, to be honest. I gave him a call and mentioned those boys' names and what they'd done to poor Hans. I guess he called the headmaster, because the next thing we knew, they were gone. What can I say? Sometimes it helps to have connections."

"Especially ones who have conveniently left town for the weekend, so you could have the whole apartment to yourself." She winked.

He downed the last of his wine. "Are you hinting that you'd like to go back to my place?"

"I am."

"You know I'm injured, not myself. And turning forty next week. I can't promise you the type of jaw-dropping, fireworks-filled ecstasy you've come to expect from this herculean specimen of a body."

"Yeah, yeah," she said, playfully waving him off with a grin on her face. "Stop fishing for compliments or looking for excuses. I'm sure we'll make out just fine."

"As long as we make out," he agreed.

They grabbed a cab for the short ride to Wynan and Austin's midtown apartment. He reached for her in the back seat, but she held him off, refusing to even kiss him, teasing, "I'm saving myself for the right man."

She continued her standoffish routine, even as he tried to paw her in the elevator and at the apartment door as he fished through his pockets for the key.

"I don't say yes to just anyone, you know. I'm very selective."

By the time he got her inside, her aloof persona was driving him insane, and his cock was so stiff he could barely walk. He grabbed her with his good arm and pushed her against the back of the door.

"A little haughty tonight, aren't we, missy?"

"Maybe so," she answered, her breathing fast and shallow, her eyes dancing with his. "But I need a man who can take me in his arms and know what to do with me. A guy pushing forty, with an injured wing… I'm just not sure you can do the job."

"I'll take that as a dare."

"I don't care how you take it, as long as you can manage to take me."

"I wouldn't worry too much about that."

With his good hand, he grabbed a handful of hair and pulled it so high above her head, she had to stand on tiptoe to avoid succumbing to the pain of the tug. He watched her struggle to balance, hoping she'd note the wicked gleam in his eye.

"Ms. Torres?"

"Yes, sir?" she answered, straining to maintain the pose.

"I must warn you, I plan to assign you projects like this on a regular basis."

"Will overtime be required, sir?

"Absolutely," he said, pulling her hair just an inch higher and causing her to emit a gasp. "As long as my heart doesn't give out first."

CHAPTER

42 43 0

A YEAR LATER, on a sunny Saturday afternoon in July, Camarin and Rachel were chatting excitedly on the platform of the White Plains train station, waiting for the 4:03 back to Manhattan. Camarin was bogged down with shopping bags from Sandel's, the snazziest bridal shop outside Manhattan, and about half the price of the city boutiques. One package contained a pair of Christian Louboutin white-lace pumps and Oscar de la Renta crystal earrings. The dress she'd left behind for altering—a Sottero and Midgely classic A-line gown of Shavon organza, with a sweetheart neckline, and delicate spaghetti straps accented in Swarovski crystals—was everything she'd ever dreamed of. She wondered if Lyle would regret giving her a blank check in terms of a wedding budget.

"You're losing something there," she said to Rachel, pointing with her chin to the package that had fallen halfway from her equally stuffed bag of goodies, though hers was from an upscale lingerie boutique, not a bridal salon.

"Ah, thank you, luv. My feet are killing me. What I wouldn't give for a *Tony* right now."

"Blair, chair. You'll sit on the train. It should be here in a few minutes—I hope."

"I think Dee's really going to enjoy this one," said the receptionist, setting the bags down and pulling a leopard-print negligee from the one on the left. "He likes to play Tarzan and Jane."

Camarin winced. "Please, you promised you wouldn't make me listen to the gory details. He's my former roommate and one of my closest friends, after all."

"Yeah, well, you're living with one of my favorite bosses, so keep your naughty bits to yourself as well." She stuck her nose up in the air before breaking into giggles.

"Excuse me, isn't your name Camarin?"

Oh God. Not another autograph seeker. The Mangel thing has been over for a year now.

She looked over at the heavyset woman smiling at her. She wore a low-cut dress that hugged her ample hips, and she stood confidently, waiting for Camarin to respond. There was something so familiar about the woman, but Cam couldn't place the face.

"It's me, Lexie. You remember… you ran after the woman who stole my Kit Kat bar."

"Oh, yes, of course, Lexie. How are you, honey? This is my friend, Rachel."

"Friend, coworker, bridesmaid supreme, you pick." Rachel reached out her hand. "Nice to meet you."

"It's been like a hundred years. So much has changed. That guy who bought us the replacement chocolate? The plumber?"

Camarin nodded though the memory was vague at best. What she did remember was how Lexie had cowered in an oversized raincoat on that sunny day a year back, hiding her body from the world. Those days were clearly way behind her.

"His name is Ben. We're engaged!"

She beamed as she held up a tiny ring on her fourth finger. Camarin kept her own hand by her side, secretly maneuvering her ring so the diamond was hidden from view. She didn't want her five-carat rock to show up Lexie's.

"It's beautiful, Lexie. I'm so happy for you."

"What's new with you since we met?"

Camarin just grinned. What wasn't new? Lyle had decided that Wynan was right—you can't be something you're not. So he sold *Trend* to his childhood friend and launched *BAT*, or *Body Acceptance Today*, and named Cam as developmental editor. The content, which promoted people of all sizes accomplishing their dreams and ambitions, had struck a nerve with a burgeoning circulation of readers, liberated from worry over society's opinions of their looks or their life choices. She was engaged to the man of her dreams, living in a two-bedroom apartment he'd purchased for them in the Village. And with Dr. Eisenstodt's help, she'd managed to put the guilt over Monaeka's death aside and finally felt whole, as if she and her twin had melded into one stable, happy, well-adjusted woman. No flame tree or Two Lovers Point tragic ending for her. Nothing was going to keep her from the man or the future she deserved.

"Same old, same old," answered Camarin, refusing to say anything that might upstage Lexie's happiness.

"You like dueling-piano bars, Lexie?" asked Rachel. "My boyfriend is one of the headliners at Benji's, and it's a fine place for some *Britneys* and a *Lilley*. You should join us tonight. Bring Ben. We'll make it a triple date."

The Manhattan-bound train thundered into the station, and the three women grabbed a set of four seats, two facing two. They piled their packages onto the empty place by the window.

"It all sounds great. I'd love to, and I'm sure Ben would too. Except for one thing. What's a Britney and a Lilley?"

"Welcome to my world," Camarin said with a laugh. "Just go with it. It seems to all work out in the end."

Lexie gave her a quizzical look and then shrugged.

"Why not? The best things in life are the things that drop into your life that you never expected. Like a brave woman standing up for your honor on a train platform. One minute, life is one way. And in the next, everything's different."

Camarin nodded, impressed by Lexie's astute observation and so proud of how far they both had come. She sat back, closed her eyes, and remembered an old proverb that her mother used to recite when she was younger. She couldn't recall the actual Chamorro, but she'd memorized the translation.

There is no death without an illness. There is no brightness without darkness. There is no body without a shadow. There is no death without suffering. There is no action without a reason.

This past year God had seen fit to show her the reasons for his actions. She'd learned. She'd endured. She'd come out stronger. She'd mended her relationship with her mother, and more importantly, another with herself. She'd helped Lyle come to terms with his guilt over Margaret's suicide and its aftermath, and had led him to a different, more loving and productive path. But this was only the beginning. She grinned, picturing herself married, graduating from law school, and then devoting herself to a lifetime of delivering those lost in darkness into the light.

The End

FOR FURTHER READING

The information on fat politics and body acceptance found in this book might strike a nerve with some who would like to read more. Here are some books I'd recommend, but this is not an inclusive list by any means:

MENTIONED IN *Murder Worth the Weight*:

Poulton, Terry. No Fat Chicks: How Big Business Profits Making Women Hate Their Bodies How to Fight Back. Birch Lane Press, 1997.

Solovay, Sondra. Tipping the Scales of Justice: Fighting Weight-Based Discrimination. Prometheus Books, 2011.

OTHERS, IN ALPHABETICAL ORDER BY AUTHOR'S NAME:

Bacon, Linda. Health at Every Size: The Surprising Truth about Your Weight. BenBella Books, 2010.

Chastain, Ragen. The Politics of Size (2 Volumes): Perspectives from the Fat Acceptance Movement, Praeger, 2014.

Cooper, Charlotte. Fat and Proud: The Politics of Size. Woman's Press, 1999.

Couret, Rene. Fat or Fad: The Struggle to Choose Between Fat Acceptance and Weight Loss, 2015.

Farrell, Amy. Fat Shame: Stigma and the Fat Body in American Culture. NYU Press, 2011.

Greenhalgh, Susan. Fat-Talk Nation: The Human Costs of America's War on Fat. Cornell University Press, 2015.

Harding, Kate and Kirby, Marianne. Lessons from the Fat-o-sphere: Quit Dieting and Declare a Truce with Your Body. TarcherPerigree, 2009.

Kulick, Don and Meneley, Ann. Fat: The Anthropology of an Obsession. Tarcher, 2005.

Orbach, Susie. Fat is a Feminist Issue. Random House. Berkley, 1987, newest edition: Random House, 2016.

Rothblum, Esther and Solovay, Sondra. The Fat Studies Reader. NYU Press, 2009.

Wann, Marilyn. Fat! So? Because You Don't Have to Apologize for Your Size. Ten Speed Press, 1998.

By day, I'm a mild-mannered salesperson, wife, mother, author groupie, competitive trivia player, and rescuer of senior shelter dogs, happily living just north of New York City. By night, I'm an author of sex, suspense, and satire.

My background includes stints in travel marketing, travel journalism, meeting planning, public relations, financial services, and real estate. I was, for a long and happy time, an award-winning magazine writer and editor. Then kids happened. And I needed to actually make money. Now they're off doing whatever it is they do (of which I have no idea since they won't friend me on Facebook) and I can spend my spare time weaving tales of debauchery and whatever else tickles my fancy.

The main thing to remember about my work is that I am NOT one of my characters, though I will admit to being a yo-yo dieter with an unhealthy addiction to chocolate and cream sauce. I have felt and experienced much of what I have written herein. They say that the best books result from slicing open a vein and pouring the blood onto the page. Here's mine. Be kind.

D.M. Barr's Website:
www.dmbarr.com

Reader eMail:
authordmbarr@gmail.com

If you enjoyed *Murder Worth the Weight*, you'll love
Expired Listings!

A sexy psychological thriller that takes jabs at the real estate
industry--suspenseful with a touch of romance. Someone is
killing off the unethical Realtors in Rock Canyon (meaning
all of them!) and the clues are all pointing toward Dana
Black, a kinky, sharp-witted yet emotionally skittish Realtor
with memory lapses, who has no alibi for the crimes
because during each, she was using her empty listings for
games like Bondage Bingo with her twisted lover, Dare.
When alluring but vanilla detective Aidan Cummings
comes onto the scene, Dana has increased motivation to
investigate by his side and clear her name. What she learns
startles her on many levels and leaves her to wonder about
her romantic future and more importantly--is she the
'Realtor Retaliator' or will she be his next victim?

A buoyant, commendable mystery that piles on red herrings with ferocity and glee... the spiraling final act, culminating with the killer's staggering reveal, is an exhilarating ride.
— Kirkus Reviews

Exceptionally well written... a consistently compelling read from beginning to end... a masterfully crafted suspense thriller that will prove to be an enduring popular addition to personal reading lists and community library collections.
— Midwest Book Review

"Expired Listings *is a sumptuous and starkly original mystery in which real estate agent Dana Black finds herself chasing a killer instead of just a listing. D.M. Barr's debut effort mimes the best from Sue Grafton, Susan Isaacs and Judith Krantz with an aplomb normally reserved for a far more seasoned writer in a tale that satisfies at every level. Splendid, searing, and sensational!"*
— Jon Land, USA Today bestselling author of The Rising

Winner/Bronze Medal (Mystery)
--2017 Global E-Book Awards

Winner/Honorable Mention (Humor)
--2017 Readers Favorite Awards

Made in the USA
Columbia, SC
03 March 2023

13213407R00205